PRAISE

PRIDE AND PROTEST

"A spectacular, unputdownable debut that just rocketed its way onto my 'Forever Faves' shelf. The sharpest, sexiest, wittiest, brightest *Pride and Prejudice* retelling I've ever read, period. Nikki Payne is the writer I aspire to be, and I'm going to recommend this novel to everyone I know, every chance I get!"

—Ali Hazelwood, #1 *New York Times* bestselling author of
Love, Theoretically

"An entertaining and politically charged retelling of *Pride and Prejudice* that tackles gentrification, prejudice, and the intersections of race, class, and gender. . . . The redevelopment plot puts a fresh twist on familiar beats and the enemies-to-lovers romance sizzles. This is good fun."   —*Publishers Weekly*

"A lively, sexy, and fresh take on a beloved classic."
—*Kirkus Reviews*

"Payne has managed what I thought was no longer possible: to write a *Pride and Prejudice* retelling that feels completely fresh and yet absolutely grounded in Jane Austen's beloved romance. . . . Liza and Dorsey's romance comes with the sizzling animosity we expect from this classic enemies-to-lovers story line while deftly tackling heavy themes like generational trauma and classism with humor and heart. This debut is incandescent."
—*The Washington Post*

"This new imagining of *Pride and Prejudice* is an inventive take on a classic love story."   —BuzzFeed Books

"This modern retelling is clever, fun, and one of the best reads of the year. . . . Payne's cast of characters are wonderful takes on classic characters, breathing new life into this classic story of misunderstandings and love."   —Manhattan Book Review

"Romantic, creative, and embroiled in the spirit of *Pride and Prejudice* without feeling shoehorned into the plotline of the original novel, this is one of the best retellings of my favorite novel I've read in a long while."   —Dr. Lizzie Rogers

"A memorable retelling of Jane Austen's *Pride and Prejudice* with great dialogue, dynamic characters, relevant themes, and a fantastic romance! . . . It's funny, sexy, and smart, and it modernized the classic novel so that it feels fresh and new, yet familiar."   —One Book More

SEX, LIES AND SENSIBILITY

NIKKI PAYNE

BERKLEY ROMANCE

New York

BERKLEY ROMANCE
Published by Berkley
An imprint of Penguin Random House LLC
penguinrandomhouse.com

Library of Congress Cataloging-in-Publication Data

Names: Payne, Nikki, 1982- author.
Title: Sex, lies and sensibility / Nikki Payne.
Description: First edition. | New York : Berkley Romance, 2024.
Identifiers: LCCN 2023024292 (print) | LCCN 2023024293 (ebook) |
ISBN 9780593440964 (trade paperback) | ISBN 9780593440971 (ebook)
Subjects: LCGFT: Romance fiction. | Erotic fiction. | Novels.
Classification: LCC PS3616.A976 S49 2024 (print) |
LCC PS3616.A976 (ebook) | DDC 813/.6—dc23/eng/20230628
LC record available at https://lccn.loc.gov/2023024292
LC ebook record available at https://lccn.loc.gov/2023024293

First Edition: February 2024

Printed in the United States of America
1st Printing

Book design by Ashley Tucker
Interior art by Natalia Sanabria

To my sisters, Darcy and Tasha; we are both alike
and wildly different in the most important ways.

AUTHOR'S NOTE: THE WORK

The process of writing this book was, literally and figuratively, a journey.

While the tale I tell is not an Abenaki story (at its heart, it is still a story about two Black women who are forced to make a new way for themselves), my endeavor to write about a romantic hero from such a community was guided by a profound sense of respect, humility, and a deep ethnographic engagement. I put on my Cultural Anthropologist hat and spent months immersed in the rich cultural tapestry of the Wabanaki Confederacy in Maine, a confederation encompassing the Penobscot, Passamaquoddy, Maliseet, and Micmac tribes, as well as my hero's tribe, the Abenaki.

Careless, even harmful depictions of POC in media, like romance, have made communities close ranks around issues of representation. As such, I understand that this character's existence, while born of my imagination, is still inherently representative. It is out of antiexploitative, antiracist humility that I attempted with extreme care to tell a story that is as compelling as it is true to my character's lived experience. I respected Bear's truths and resisted homogenizing or oversimplifying his experiences to make them palatable to mainstream audiences.

The same dedication was applied in my research with the African American community in Maine and track athletes in my home state. As a Black woman in America, I could write for a century and still not scratch the surface of the vast spectrum of experiences and stories within the African American community, and yet there are some who would recite the oft-touted wisdom to "write what you know." We don't have to agree on this, but we don't actually *know* that much. Empathy is largely an endeavor of imagination.

I'm excited for you to delve into Nora and Bear's world, and I have the anxiety of any artist showing their art to the world, but I also have the peace of a creative who has done the work—and with love to boot.

With respect and sincerity,
Nikki Payne

SEX, LIES AND SENSIBILITY

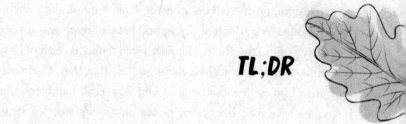

TL;DR

OCTOBER 1

WHAT DID IT SAY ABOUT THE SAD STATE OF HER LIFE that she was at her father's funeral, and all she could think about was her sex tape? Okay, it wasn't a "tape," but an infinite network of links that popped up right when potential employers were searching her profile. "Nasty Nora" still made the rounds seven years after her boyfriend posted it. But what really immortalized her was the freeze-frame shot of her grimace after her boyfriend asked if she'd *finished*.

People attached her face to all kinds of dubious truths:

- Did you remember to defrost the chicken? Nora's face.
- Do you like my new jacket? Nora's face.

Her mentions would calm down until someone rediscovered the meme's origin, and then the video would trend. Most recently, MBO did an explosive exposé on the adult film industry and highlighted her video on the rise of amateur "disruptors." It was exhausting, which is why she had to get out of this dangerous crush of people.

This was a sizable crowd for such a private man. The enormous poster of him, positioned on an easel, looked more like a shrine to seasonings. A garland of thyme and baby's breath was draped elegantly around the photo. Her father had founded Dash of Love Seasonings right here in Maryland, so it fit that they would memorialize him with mountains of Old Bay, crab hammers, and hot sauce crammed like *Tetris* pieces on a slick wooden table. Nora searched her bag and huffed in victory when she found two salt and pepper packets from a month ago. She moved through the line and solemnly added them to the teetering tower. She swore she saw her dad's eyes twinkle. In this picture, he looked a lot like her little sister Yanne, with his sandy skin, smooth hair gelled back, and myopic greenish-brown eyes that kept her younger sister in prescriptions since she was five.

Her phone buzzed in her hand. Yanne, with an excuse.

Late. *Like I knew she would be.* Yanne had an infuriating habit of never being there when Nora needed her. There was always some poetry reading, love of her life, or social injustice that took precedence over everyone and everything else.

Slipping her phone down into her purse, Nora noted all the exits and bathrooms. Did she imagine the quick glances at her? The whispers behind funeral programs? She smoothed the black pleated crepe of her Balenciaga dress. It was the most expensive thing she owned. Her father had bought it for her when she'd won the women's hundred-meter hurdles at the Penn Relays. Right before he'd stopped talking to her.

You're drawing negative attention to yourself, he'd complained. *At least a prostitute gets paid for showing her ass.* The last time Nora saw her father, he was throwing hundreds at the floor demanding that she pick them up.

Nora had applied for a job that very day and sold her Land Rover for a Nissan. She'd almost sold *this* dress on eBay, but it was too beautiful. When she heard the news about his death, her anger lost its power. She'd tried so hard to be more than the girl in the video, but standing in the middle of these murmurs and stink eyes made her feel like she would never get away from that image of herself.

There was a time, pre–sex tape, when she would have welcomed the attention. No one would know it to look at her now— working at the CVS so she wouldn't have to talk to her father, obsessed with HGTV so she wouldn't have to fix anything real in her own life—but Nora had been lively, bulletproof, and bold. Back when she was semi-famous for her athleticism and record-breaking races, every step she took was the right one. She had even graced the cover of *Track and Field* magazine. It was easy to think nothing could touch her. The arrogance of a world-class athlete who thought her youth, strength, and money would protect her from the nasty parts of the world. But it didn't protect her from her father's rejection, his disgust. Even his funeral seemed like an indictment of her. She and her sister were not even on the flickering slideshow.

She didn't frequent many funerals, but this one seemed particularly strange. Everyone looked too damned good, for one. Everyone here, the high society of the DC-Maryland-Virginia area, treated the event like Easter Sunday—decked out in their best black, exchanging cards, and speculating on the price of her father's mahogany casket.

Were these her father's friends? How well-known was he? Nora had never actually thought to google him. Was he more than a dreamer with plans to move his family to some lobster farm up north? More than a punctual deposit in her bank account every Friday?

Who are *these people?*

She even saw *the* Beverly Bennett. Her mother's gossipy over-the-top girlfriend, who regularly screamed her daughters' net worth to the rooftops. Beverly Bennett patted her mother's back, and a ring the size of a traffic cone glinted on her finger. To think the relatively well-off Dash women used to buy handsewn dresses from those "poor Bennetts" out of pity. The world had turned upside down.

It was like someone flipped her dad over and shook him, and out tumbled all of these people she'd never even met. Somebody's nephew was playing an up-tempo high school marching band rendition of "When the Saints Go Marching In." Nora decided right then that there would be no upbeat numbers at her funeral. *I want that shit sad.* Not jazzy and vaguely sexy like this one. Even stranger, she and her mother, the chief mourners, were being aggressively ignored. No bereaved aunties and uncles coming up to her. No one gave them their thoughts and prayers or handed them lukewarm potato salad. Just Bev holding Mom's hand between flashing pictures of her granddaughter and speaking loudly over the band music. She knew her mother was not on good terms with her father's family, but this was downright cruel.

Nora felt a light tap on her shoulder and jumped a bit too high. She was terrified of that tap. That someone in a crowded room was going to squint their eyes and walk toward her. A man sucking his teeth, saying, *You look so familiar. Have I seen you somewhere before?* And, of course, the question was rhetorical.

Of course they had seen her. All of her. She used to blow kisses after every victory, soaking up the limelight draped in the University of Maryland flag. She couldn't take a wrong step.

Now, every tiny little action Nora engaged in always, *always* had outsize consequences. Which is why she liked to minimize her mistake footprint altogether. It was simple. No risky decisions equaled no traumatic mistakes. She was the poor kid in that *If You Give a Mouse a Cookie* book.

Here's what happens when you make a hot sex tape with your college boyfriend:

1. First, do *not* make a hot sex tape with your college boyfriend. He will be your boyfriend for three more months. Tops.
   - And if you are incredibly ridiculous and say yes, don't be the supercool girlfriend when he suggests you put it online.
   - Don't say, "Yeah, it's cool." It's a little sexy to be watched, right?
   - It *won't* be sexy. It will only make you infamous in the DMV area for an excruciatingly long time. You'll learn fast that you're not bulletproof.
2. Because of the morality clause, you'll lose your track scholarship. (You loved track *more than you loved your boyfriend.*)
3. You'll get a nickname like Nasty Nora.
4. You'll drop out of college nine credits shy of your degree.
5. Instead of being a hot PE teacher at a progressive artsy elementary school, you'll be lucky to get a job as a pharmacy tech at a big chain drugstore.

TL;DR: boldness doesn't pay. Stay in your lane.

Another tap on the shoulder, this time more insistent.

"Are you Shenora and Maryanne Dash?" A twitchy, round-faced white man gave her a thick cream card.

An estate lawyer. This should be interesting.

"I'm Nora, and this is my mother, Diane. My sister hasn't arrived yet."

"Mrs. Dash would like to speak to you in the offices upstairs."

THE PLUMP, BROWN-SKINNED WOMAN'S UPTURNED MOUTH dropped like a stone when she saw Nora enter the office. She sat at the head of the table like a Mafia don. Fur coat, thick gold rings, a soft cotton halo of shoe-polish-black hair. Nora saw that she had white teeth like piano keys when she spoke.

"You have a lot of nerve showing up here, Diane," the woman hissed at Nora's mother.

"Excuse me?" Nora asked. Sure, her parents weren't married, but what was this, the 1950s?

Mom rolled her shoulders. "It's not about me. It's about my girls. They have the right to pay their respects."

Nora couldn't seem to stop blinking. "Mother, don't respond to that. Of course we do."

Mom didn't meet her eyes. "Nora, please."

Nora, please? Why was she allowing this woman to talk to her like this?

Mom looked behind her at the door. "Nora, this is Mrs. Dash."

So? Why was some auntie allowed to talk to her mother this way? Nora locked arms with her mother and moved to push past the threshold when her mother froze.

"Mrs. Dash is your father's wife of thirty-five years."

Your father's wife.

Nora couldn't push enough air out of her lungs to speak. Everything rolled over her in slow motion. She gasped and stumbled like she had missed a step on an invisible stairwell. She felt streaks of hot and cold panic roll around inside of her. Her stomach threatened to spill the ham sandwich she had for lunch. Her hands shook with impossible tremors.

My mother was a mistress? Don't you have to be sexy and mysterious to be a mistress? Do mistresses bake pies?

Her panic attacks had gotten worse in the past year. She could feel them coming but was powerless to stop the crippling panic from washing over her. Everyone in the room was looking at her. So many eyes.

Her father, already a hazy, distant man, was coloring himself even further out of the picture. He had always been obscure, mercurial, chronically late, and impossibly charming. He had winked after telling a bawdy joke and never made it to a single sporting event she was in. *Her* father, on top of being all of those things, wasn't even only her own and Yanne's.

The constriction of Nora's throat intensified. Maybe she would suffocate to death right here at her sexy mistress mother's feet.

"Nora! Have some water! Nora!" She heard their distant alarm but couldn't reach out to them. She just stood there, compulsively swallowing and sweating through her lovely dress.

Oh, another reason not to make a sex tape with your college boyfriend:

6. You'll develop an inconvenient panic disorder that makes even the smallest tasks seem impossible.

"Oh, get ahold of yourself, Shenora." The *real* Mrs. Dash flicked her wrist dismissively. "If that little bit of thirty-plus-year-old news has shocked you, you're going to need a stretcher for this next part."

BALENCIAGA

HALF AN HOUR LATER, NORA'S SISTER YANNE TUM-
bled into the room in a cloud of weed and floral perfume.

"Someone said you guys were up here?" Yanne pulled off her
long, puffy jacket, leaving the thick scarf wrapped up to her chin.
Her sister was wearing black, and her sandy locs were bound up
in a regal-looking bun. She had opted for enormous glasses instead of her contacts. The resulting look was a plump Lisa Bonet
as a goth substitute teacher.

Nora pulled her sister aside. "Mom has been lying to us. Dad
has a whole other family." She gestured to the people in the room.

Nora knew how she *should* feel. She should clutch at her chest,
reeling and breathing into a paper bag. Even righteous fury at
her mother's lifetime of lies failed to breach the protective film of
Lexapro. Instead, all she could feel was the slow, heavy dullness
of an exhausted fight-or-flight system.

Yanne, traditionally more excitable than her older sister,
would have to be the fireworks show today.

"Well . . ." Yanne crinkled her face in a half apology.

Nora gasped. Yanne *knew? How long? When did she find out?
Who told her?*

"Can we get to business, please?" A petite woman with a short haircut and a pert air of authority shook her head. In the right light, she could be Halle Berry's younger sister.

Yanne waved a benevolent hand. Her bangles tinkled noisily, and the petite woman who just spoke looked mesmerized by the tiny tattoos of the phases of the moon spread out on the base of her sister's palm.

"It's important to honor your emotions, my sister." Yanne bowed dramatically. "But I can't really be a part of your low vibrational energy right now. Your mother invited my sister and me." The woman's lips tightened, and for a second, Nora thought she would make a scene, but she only shot a frustrated look at the real Mrs. Dash.

Fake Halle Berry reached out and squeezed her mother's hands. "You humiliated my mother at her husband's funeral, and you have the nerve to show up in a seven-thousand-dollar dress?"

All the stares suddenly made sense. It wasn't because of the video; they all knew who she was to her father.

The room suddenly had the mysterious vibes of an Agatha Christie novel. Everyone gathered in a small space, each one with a simmering dislike of the other. There was even a twitchy lawyer. Nora expected someone to accuse her of murder at any moment. Yanne, sensitive as she was to "energies," must have picked up on the change in mood.

"If I may?" Yanne's voice was soft and honeyed. "Mrs. Dash, this is a time for uterine unity, not phallic falsehoods. He was dishonest with *us* too. But it doesn't make any of us, including our mother, bad people."

Mrs. Dash's eyes lifted from Nora for a merciful minute. It was her first time seeing Yanne, and Nora watched the recognition wash over the woman. Yanne looked the most like Daddy, with her beachy skin, briny seawater-green eyes, and soft curls. Mrs. Dash had to see that. Nora could see her veneer cracking. A slow tear slipped down her cheek.

"Are you the sick one?" Mrs. Dash asked.

Yanne recoiled and pushed out her soft belly. "I can assure you, I'm the picture of health."

"He said one of you girls had it like him. Sickle cell. Is it you?"

Yanne flinched. "Oh, I—I do suffer an occasional bout of that most painful affliction. Why do you ask?"

"Your medical bills. He"—she breathed—"mentioned it. I will always cover them."

Yanne, blissfully unaware or uncaring that her medical bills were suddenly negotiable, nodded and draped herself over the adjacent chair.

"Most obliged, ma'am."

Yanne didn't like to be reminded of her illness. She hated the tone in people's voices when they called her story *an inspiration*. Through her dogged avoidance of any personal or professional distinctions, it was almost like she was dedicating her life to being a non-inspiration, just to spite everyone.

"I swear to god, I only found out a week ago," Yanne whispered, reaching for Nora's hand. "I heard Mom arguing about putting our names in the program. Broke Catwoman over there is Mrs. Dash's kid from an earlier marriage, and they wouldn't let her do it. If *Monster's Ball* or *B.A.P.S.* is too much to remember, her real name is Felicia, as in 'Bye, Felicia.' She is an absolute cartoon villain."

The lawyer pulled at his tie. "There is a small matter of the rental property in the Norland Park Community in Montgomery County, Maryland."

Yanne's fingers froze over Nora's hand. Mom's house. *Our*

house. Working her spite job as a pharmacy technician at the CVS wasn't enough for Nora to live independently, and Yanne, an actress at a Black Shakespeare theater company, worked at least three additional gig jobs. Nora thought they owned the house.

But Dad owned it.

I'm not mad at my mother. I'm not mad at my mother. I'm— It was no use. Nora was pissed. *How could she not protect herself? Or her children?*

"Yes. We have plans for the rental property. It's a prime location for an Airbnb." Felicia was covering her excitement poorly.

"You know we've lived there for twenty years," Yanne said. "Why are you calling it 'the property'? It's our home."

"Um, I'm sorry. I know this is difficult to hear. Did you, by any chance, sign a lease?" She knew they hadn't. Hence the lawyer. Nora shook her head. Her vision blurred around the edges. The heat of her anger could burn through the room.

Felicia continued her false concern. "Are you and your mother's names on any paperwork? Have you paid any tax to Montgomery County? There has to be something."

Nora didn't respond because she and Felicia knew there was nothing. Yanne kept looking at her to say something or even do something.

"I'm really sorry that my stepfather put you all in this situation. He was a weak man."

Mrs. Dash's back straightened. "Felicia, you will respect my husband. I expected him to look out for me and mine"—she shook the will defiantly—"and he did it until he died." She looked at Yanne. Mrs. Dash's eyes were shimmering, and Nora knew what Yanne's face was doing to the woman—forcing the truth out of an ugly situation.

We are a part of him too.

"I know this is difficult, so we're giving you thirty days to vacate." Felicia said it as if she were doing them a favor.

Nora stood, nearly flipping the chair. "Thirty days! We've lived there for twenty years."

Yanne looked up at Nora in surprise. "Y'all done messed up now." She looked like she was watching Wimbledon as her eyes volleyed between Felicia and Nora. Yanne knew what Felicia didn't, that Nora had not many—but just enough—*fuck its* left to be dangerous.

Nora turned her whole body toward the lawyer. "Can they do this?"

"I'm afraid they are within their rights. You never established a landlord-tenant relationship, so you don't have renters' rights."

"The Montgomery County sheriff will be there in exactly twenty-nine days to help you pack," Felicia said.

Nora looked up to find the kind eyes of one of many Black Jesuses looking down at her. *Off-the-wall behavior got you on the internet, Nora,* He said. She sat down and fiddled with the collar of the dress. The one that looked like LeVar Burton whispered, *Blessed are the meek.* Nora found Mrs. Dash's eyes. "You said there were two things."

"Yes, well, there is a—" She faltered. "There is a property that he owned. He mentioned you two. In a last-minute change. There is . . ."

"Please say something before I have to pay for the extra half hour at the parking garage," Nora said. "You know we can't afford it now."

Mrs. Dash spat it out. "He left you Barton Cove."

Felicia tittered behind her hands. Even Mrs. Dash looked down at the carpet.

"What is Barton Cove?"

"It's a lovely—"

Felicia sighed. "Mom, tell them the truth. Please. There have been enough lies to last a lifetime." She reached out to touch Yanne's hand. "It's a dump. Most of the year, it's freezing. It's in the worst part of the woods and the deadest part of the beach. It's on the quiet side of Mount Desert Island in Maine."

The lawyer spoke over Felicia. "The decedent has provided Barton Cove and a substantial inheritance for you and your sister."

Nora's face tightened. "Define 'substantial'."

"He has set aside two hundred fifty thousand dollars each, but—" He paused, and his voice cracked like a teenager. "Barton Cove is currently in foreclosure."

"So he stopped paying for our inheritance?"

"It seems that way. The bank requires full repayment of the outstanding loan amount in a single payment before Labor Day of the following year."

"How much is owed?" Yanne asked.

"Five hundred seventeen thousand dollars."

"Our inheritance can't cover it?"

Felicia snorted. "Your inheritance won't even cover the renovations."

The lawyer pulled off his glasses. "However, if Barton Cove meets the foreclosure agreement, you and your sister will be entitled to the entirety of your father's Estate Improvement Fund or EIF for the estate."

Nora nodded. "How much is the EIF?"

"Three million dollars," the lawyer and Felicia answered in unison.

"So we get three million for paying off the foreclosure? How would we even do that?" Nora worried her bottom lip.

"You can't. Which is why we've drawn up an alternate

agreement." Felicia pushed a manila folder full of documents under Nora's hands. But Nora held her hand up.

"What exactly happens if we can't pay off the foreclosure amount?" Nora asked.

"Then the money goes to the new owners of Barton Cove," the lawyer repeated.

Within her, something flickered—then caught. Something she hadn't felt for a long time—maybe purpose. She'd watched more hours of HGTV than anyone she knew. Yanne could bake her ass off. They could renovate the space and turn it into a cool bakery or an inn.

Felicia must have noticed the spark of hope in Nora's eyes. "Nora, I know you have some pretty impressive and"—she raised her eyebrows—"*lucrative* skill sets, but you'd have to open a brothel full of Noras to make *that* kind of money."

Nora's cheeks flared. She couldn't tell if it was anger or embarrassment. But something cracked and groaned inside of her like ice giving way under the weight of a heavy boot. Once again, Yanne's wide eyes bounced from Nora to Felicia. She could always perfectly calibrate when her older sister was about to blow. Sure, it took three times as long as most people. But it was worth the wait.

She might have to slide off her earrings at her own father's funeral.

"We've drawn something up that we think you'll like." Felicia finally pulled open the manila folder and passed out a thick stack of papers to Nora and Yanne. "This is all silly lawyer-speak, so let me make it plain. We'll give you both something for financial stabilization, say, 200K." She paused here for effect. And suddenly Nora could read her whole play. Snatch their home from underneath them so they would be desperate to sign over the other property. "We pay the foreclosure and take this ridiculous Barton Cove project off your hands."

"If we sign this, what happens to the three million?" Yanne asked. "The EIF?"

Good question, sis.

"It's a hypothetical three million, in the miraculous event that we ourselves could scrape up enough money to pay off the foreclosure." It was a wicked lie.

"What happens to the three million?" Nora asked again. Yanne's fingers were tapping the table. Her nervous energy rippled around the room.

"That is, of course, transferred to the new owner to make improvements." The lawyer clarified, "To Ms. Felicia."

Yanne and Nora didn't even have to glance at each other. "No." It might have been the first thing they'd agreed on in years. Maybe they would fail. But they could at least deny these assholes an easy lap.

Felicia's cool face snapped with a flash of anger. "Fine. In that case, here is an itemized list of all goods of value purchased under the Dash of Love name that we will have to collect in one month." Felicia slapped the paper on the table. "The highlighted items need to be collected ASAP." She took out a highlighter and circled the seven-thousand-dollar black Balenciaga.

Nora stood up and walked to Felicia's chair.

She flinched when Nora stood, perhaps expecting the slap across the face she richly deserved. It was the only language bullies understood—their own violence thrown back at them. Felicia had miscalculated. Though Nora's hands itched to make contact with her face, instead, she clenched her teeth and, hands shaking, reached back behind herself to grab her zipper. Nora held Felicia's gaze, pulling the thin zipper down to her low back.

To wide eyes, she shrugged the dress off. The soft crepe pooled at her ankles. She'd be damned if these people thought they owned her choices because they had the money or power. If the dress was a shackle, she would release it.

She stepped out of the dress, only slightly chilly in her black bra, panties, and six-inch heels. She sat back down and crossed her legs like she was in a power suit. Yanne whooped and threw her long puffer coat over her sister's shoulders like one of Elvis's crewmen. The LeVar Burton Black Jesus painting shimmied its approval as the heat powered on in the room.

Nora was shaking with anger, adrenaline, and indignation. One of the worst things that the video had robbed her of was something to care about. After track, she struggled mightily to feel deeply about anything, too afraid someone might snatch it away. But this simmering in her belly felt like home.

She cared.

Her hands still shook, adjusting the coat, and her skin burned hot. She had that elated queasy feeling you get unbuckling from a wild roller-coaster ride. She had touched the bright corona of something in herself, and she . . . well, she liked it.

Yanne raised her glass of water, practically vibrating with open admiration. She blew an exaggerated kiss, Nora's old move after she'd won a race. "To unpathed waters, undreamed shores," she toasted when Felicia sputtered derisively.

Yanne clapped Felicia on the back. "That means we're taking our asses to Barton Cove."

ONE OF THE GOOD ONES

OCTOBER 31
SOUTHWEST BAR HARBOR, MAINE
43 WEEKS UNTIL FORECLOSURE

ENNIS BEAR FREEMAN ALWAYS DID WHAT HE SAID HE would do, and right now that was a pain in his ass. This last trail walk of the day was special. All the patrons paid through the nose for a Halloween experience, and Bear had paid some teenagers to run out of the woods with fake blood at the clearing ahead. But one of his customers dove into the water reaching for tree moss, and now Business Bob's little scuba dive would put them off time.

Bear strained against the tree for leverage, trying to pull a 315-pound man out of a freezing muddy creek. Business Bob flailed and gasped in what was—at most—waist-height water. The man's wet limbs slipped through Bear's hands again.

"Sir, just stand up." The soles of his boots dug into the soggy creek bed when Bear sprang and lurched for the man's hand. Freezing water sprayed on his face and dampened his shirt. When he finally clamped on to a chilled forearm, Bear counted down with the other men and gave one last pull. He was rewarded by the sound of Business Bob's soaked clothes squelching as they met the brown earth. Bear leaned against the tree and caught his breath. Two other brawny men heaved and rested their hands on their knees.

There was always one of these on the trail—a Business Bob, an Earnest Elaine, or a Sulky Son. Tourist types who disregarded the rules because they thought they knew better than the guide.

People of the Dawn Sunshine Trails was number one in "Authentic Native American Experiences" on Trip Tips. *Still*, a couple of critical reviews would have wealthy tourists looking elsewhere to spend their vacation money. Bear stood, still relatively dry, and held his hand out to the man. Bob pulled himself up, reddened and freezing. If he stayed out here any longer, he'd get hypothermia. Shifting his backpack, Bear pulled out the emergency Mylar thermal blanket and carefully wrapped the shivering man in the foil sheet.

Bob shuddered. "I know you're going for a wild experience, but it wouldn't hurt to make the trail a little accessible. I could have died." He took a wobbly step.

"*W-wild* is nowhere in the literature, b-big man." Bear heard his stutter and clamped his mouth closed. *Maybe no one heard?*

Bear was overstimulated. He had to remember his breathing exercises, no matter how ridiculous they made him look. Placing one hand on his chest and the other on his belly, he inhaled through his nose slowly and calmly. The bite of the cool air in his lungs and the feel of his hand rising and falling recentered him.

He caught the quizzical looks.

A woman wearing her weight in turquoise jewelry mimicked his breathing and posture. "Is this to call on your spirit animal for strength?"

Bear smiled broadly, dazzling the woman out of her ridiculous question. "You all should note the need to stay on the prescribed path as per the waiver form." Good to remind them they signed a waiver. But he took Bob's point. He didn't have the right infrastructure to support the trails. These lands had once been free to roam. Now Bear did everything to avoid paying fines for trespassing or new fencing or expanded hunting grounds.

He would have to cut the walk short and get Bob to a warm location for his safety. "Folks, I think we'll have to pack up the tour."

"Good call," Bob said through chattering teeth. "I've never feared for my life at the Willow . . ." Here we go. His fourth reference to the Willow Bee, a sprawling, cutesy resort in nearby Mount Desert that sold fussy, overly produced outdoor packages. Zip lines that marred the horizon and bald, sterile clearings set aside for glamping yurts in the summer. The Willow Bee's security had been expanding and patrolling the woods, forcing his medicine walks farther and farther east.

He'd planned to drop this collection of folks off at the clearing, where they could buy drums and trinkets and booklets from Moxcy. In the busy summer season, they could run about ten of these walks per day from dawn to sunset. Some of the cash cows would pay through the nose for the wigwam experience, but less so in the fall and winter. These were lean times for his operation.

He saw the long black sheet of his cousin's hair through the trees in the clearing. She rounded her eyes, gesticulating wildly about something Bear couldn't make out.

As he walked farther, he could see what Moxcy was warning him about: the figures of two men standing between two arching trees. As Bear got closer, he could see that the men's eyes were darting from him to his jacket. This was happening more and more often. Paths closed off, fences being erected, his world getting smaller and smaller.

"Sir, I need to see some identification," the first officer said.

"Sure." Bear paused. "I'm reaching for my wallet." He tried to sound as nonthreatening as possible. Native Americans were harmed by police violence at a higher rate than any other ethnic group in the United States. The second, smaller officer appeared to be still in training, and the older officer narrated the events as if he were on an episode of *Cops*.

"Lot of meth heads come up and down this path. Lot of drug deals going down," he explained. Moxcy waved at the crowd and ushered them backward away from Bear and the officers.

The cops didn't move, their eyes locked on his jacket. "I don't have any ID on me," Bear said, his voice low and steady. When the wind shifted his jacket, the shiny glint of his hunting knife shone in the light. Both officers startled at the sight.

"I hunt," Bear said quickly.

"Can I ask what you're doing on this land?" the older officer asked, his hand hovering near his holster.

My ancestors could ask you the same thing, Bear thought.

Bear measured his words carefully, then spoke in a voice that was barely above a whisper. "I'm just running a business. My name is Ennis Freeman."

"Wait. Bear?" One officer tapped the other one, and his shoulders visibly loosened. The officer pulled off his cap, showing him the lines of his face. "Bear!"

Bear was bussed to a private high school on a track scholarship but didn't keep in much contact with the alumni group. But he recognized the face. Joshua Stubbs.

Bear looked back to the milling crowd. How the hell was he going to get them out of here?

"I thought I'd see you on the cover of *Sports Illustrated* or something." He laughed. "You really never left this town?" He pulled his cap back on and scrolled though a handheld device.

"Surprised to see so many trespassing citations here, Bear. You seemed like one of the good ones. Weren't you in the news a few years back for saving some preschoolers?"

Ah . . . the legend extends beyond the rez now. The truth is unrecognizable.

"Nope. Not me." Bear glanced backward at his tour.

If he had one wish, it would be never to hear that story parroted back to him again.

"I'm sorry, Josh, but we have a situation on our hands . . . so we'll just get out of your way—"

He chuckled nervously. "Can't let you go there, Bear."

"But our trail ends a half a mile this way," Bear said.

"Come on, schoolmate or no, you know what you're doing is illegal." He dragged the flashlight out and flicked it in the crowd's direction.

"We try to manage tribal relations," Stubbs explained to the younger cop, "like sometimes looking the other way for expired vendor licenses, that type of thing. But we have to put our foot down somewhere."

Moxcy came jogging up. "Bear, we need to get to shelter. Bob's shivering. Is there a problem, Officer?" She folded her arms. His younger cousin and second-in-command loved to play first-year lawyer when her ass wasn't on the line.

Bear turned toward Moxcy and whispered, "We can't meet at the rendezvous point. Tell the folks that there are some downed trees up ahead. We may have to make a turn."

"We'll be getting out of your hair, Officers." Moxcy urged Bear along. The relationship between natives on the rez and the police was tentative at best, and everyone knew how to comport themselves in front of cops: slow and loud.

The officer replaced the flashlight and nodded. "If you don't mind, we'll hang out here and make sure you all get on home."

"Mostly harmless," he heard Stubbs tell the other officer. "Living off gullible wealthy tourists, selling overpriced crafts."

"Bear," Moxcy warned, pushing his shoulders. "Let's get the hell out of here. Let's just go."

Bear nodded tightly and walked away with Moxcy. "You know what this is about, right? Everyone tied to the power plant in town is on my ass. Stubbs is no different. They want to build a dam and think the tribal council is holding it up."

Bear's chair on the council was mostly symbolic until recently. He and a cohort of the tribal council had been standing firm against Maine Power's brazen attempts to sway the community with their dam project.

Moxcy pulled at his wet shirt. "We can't go on like this, you know. As your second-in-command and lawyer, I need to tell you we'll have to change the language of our brochure if we can no longer offer folks the same length and extent of experience."

"Are you trying to get me to vote yes too?"

"Honestly, Bear, I think you're paranoid. Stubbs doesn't know anything about the dam project. He's just too damned serious about his job." Her voice had lost some of its mirth.

"Barton Cove is less than a mile south. Should still be easy to break into."

Southwest Harbor, the major town on the west side of Mount Desert Island, had all the charm of the more famous Bar Harbor and fewer crowds. The "quiet side" was great for trails but terrible for selling their beadwork and baskets. Not to mention private companies were making it impossible to run his business.

Bear held his hand up to get the tourists' attention and gather them around him.

Moxcy stepped in front of him, voice booming and direct. "Change of plan, folks. We're gonna head to an old, er . . . haunted inn. We'll warm up a bit, and you all can catch the ferry from the eastern side."

The crowd murmured in excitement, and Bear kicked the hard ground with his boots.

Moxcy raised an eyebrow. "You okay, boss?"

"I will be. Let's get these folks to safety."

Moxcy shouted for Jennings, Bear's youngest and most ubiquitous cousin. He came ambling up the pass, red-cheeked and gripping his gaming system.

"J, run ahead and get the golf cart. Sweep out all the beer bottles, bongs, and condoms from Barton Cove."

Moxcy patted his shoulder. "The Lord's work."

If they cleaned it up enough, they could have trail walkers stop there every day. No one had to know they didn't own it. No one owned it.

Victimless crime.

BEAR STUMBLED UPON THE WINDING ENTRANCE TO BAR-ton Cove faster than expected. The rotting wood nameplate, faded blue and weather-beaten, rocked back and forth in the wind. There was a picture of a lobster tail with little red dots of seasoning all over it.

Whose big dream had failed here?

The house sat at the end of the road, down a long, private lane. He could imagine dogs running around without getting into much trouble here. The only good thing he could say about the sprawling bungalow was that it had an enviable setting on the beach. He took a tentative step up to the house, and the rotting wood porch step almost collapsed under his weight.

Moxcy hissed, "What am I supposed to do with these people in this scuzzy place?"

"Moxcy, it's Halloween." Bear rolled his eyes. "Tell them a ghost story. They'll think it's part of the deal."

Moxcy was right, though. This place was a lawsuit waiting to happen. He looked back at Bob, whose thin lips had taken on a bluish color. The sun was dipping below the horizon, and it was fifty-five degrees with the sun *out*.

Bear reached for the door handle, but his cousin jerked it open, smiling broadly and a little winded, like a nervous host of *MTV Cribs*. Jennings opened his arms in a majestic flourish a bit too out of step with the drab interior.

It was Halloween perfect at least. No one would sue them for wild negligence today.

The space was dark but illuminated by beams of the sunset from windows and poorly patched holes in the roof and walls. Imposing wood paneling made the extensive area look claustrophobic.

He had to build a fire. This crew was going to get an authentic experience, all right. Volunteers rounded up dry wood and placed it in the massive fireplace. Business Bob was still shivering, and his wet clothes would only make him colder.

"You're going to have to remove your clothes," Bear said. "We'll put them here by the fire to dry."

"But what will I wear?" he screeched, half pleading, half scandalized.

Bear rummaged through his backpack. "I have three more of these blankets. We can wrap you up." *Like a burrito*, he started to say. "L-like a Roman."

Bob's shoulders straightened, and he grabbed the foil blankets like a senator taking an oath. He returned from the bathroom looking like a ten-day-old potluck casserole. All he was missing was a staff, and he would be the Foil Lord. But he was dry and getting warm. The pink was coming back into his cheeks. Bob settled in by the fire, and Bear finally relaxed.

Bear stripped off his own soaking wet shirt and draped it over the fireplace. Ignoring the stares and uncomfortable throat clearing from the tourists, he bundled his grandfather's knife in the holster and placed it deep in the bag. He threw on a vest with traditional beading down the front and proceeded to tell the crowd about Abenaki beadwork.

After he'd finished his talk, he allowed Moxcy to answer questions. He looked around. This place actually had a bit of potential.

Maybe we could buy this old place. He *did* actually have a bit of money to throw toward a down payment.

But what do you have to do to get that money, Bear?

It was more than he was willing to pay.

The purplish hues of dusk limped into the house, and the group passed a flask of bourbon between them. They would never forget this outing. As the night darkened, firelight danced across their taut faces as Moxcy finished the chilling story of the Abenaki swamp woman—a siren/ghost living in shallow waterways.

". . . And anyone who tries to follow the sound of her crying is lost forever."

Just then, the door burst open with a thunderous boom. Fog rolled in in thick clouds, and a dark silhouette stood in the threshold. A female shriek cut across the foyer.

TWO OF CUPS

SAME DAY

THE FIRST THING NORA SAW WAS PINK, FUZZY TESticles.

A beefy man wrapped in foil stood up on quaking knees and ran behind a young woman. At least seven other people screamed and ran in scattered directions. An older woman fainted against a shaky banister, and a pimply-faced teenager stood in the center of the room, knees shaking and clacking together noisily.

"We won't follow you!" someone shouted.

This is why there are no Black people in Maine. Did I just walk into some culty human sacrifice séance shit?

"If you're looking for a place to get drunk or high, you need to leave." A man stepped out of the shadows, bathed in the firelight. The first thing she noticed was the sheen and length of his hair, then his ridiculous costume.

He looked like the cover of those racially problematic romance novels her auntie used to read called *Frontier Lover* or something like that. And *this* man, dressed like racism, had the nerve to ask *her* if she was trying to get drunk or high?

"*I* am the owner and proprietor of this establishment. Who are you?"

His eyes widened, and he looked like he was about to say something.

Oh yeah, he is high as a kite. All he could get out was a soft *G* sound.

A woman, stunning and sharp jawed, ran her hand down the man's arms. "It's okay, Bear, the ferry's here. Let's get these folks out of here."

The woman handed Testicle Tom, still wrapped in foil, a bundle of clothes and painted on a smile. Her arms flew up in a flourish.

"And scene," she said, bending at the waist. "That, folks, is an authentic experience! Happy Halloween! Hope we didn't scare you too much. Tips are welcome. Please watch your step on the way out." Some confused applause rang out, and at least thirteen people shuffled out of the door.

People shoved five- and ten-dollar bills into Nora's hands.

"You really got us."

The teenager finally cracked a smile. "Raddest tour ever!"

Nora couldn't seem to form the right questions.

Who are these people?

Why are you naked?

Why are you in costume?

They all seemed insufficient. As soon as she dropped her luggage, Testicle Tom came running out of the bathroom, foil Mylar blanket still tucked into his underpants and billowing behind him.

The man in costume only stood there, breathing with his hands on his chest and stomach. Something about the bicep flexing as he breathed made him look more dangerous than peaceful. Probably some tantric yoga cosplay sex cult meditation. Why was he dressed in a flimsy beaded vest in the fall, anyway? Probably so high on bath salts he couldn't feel the cold. Nora folded the money and pulled up her jacket, ready to slide the bills into the hip pocket of her athleisure pants.

She saw his neck turn, fast as a cat, at the flick of her hand on her thigh. *Eyes on the money, huh?*

"I'm keeping this money, if you're wondering," Nora said.

His lips quirked in a half smile. "Not what I'm wondering, ma'am. I'm Ennis, by the way." He held his big hand out to her, and Nora folded her arms and leaned back.

Doubt that's your real name, but whatever. "'Ennis.'" She air quoted. "You need to talk or walk."

Yanne burst through the door, pushing Nora with the force of her enthusiasm. Nora stumbled for a minute but gained her footing. The benefit of running track for ten years was being sure-footed.

Bear's eyes sharpened at the movement.

It was the face people made when they were trying to place her.

Hell no.

Yanne dropped her luggage in the middle of the floor, arms gesticulating wildly. "Nora, I think I'm in love . . . like, actual love. So, I'm struggling to bring my luggage all the way down that plantation road. I asked you to help me, but did you? No. But that doesn't matter now, because *who* passes by me but a vision? A woman unlike *any* other." Yanne paused for dramatic affect. "Her name is Moxcy. And I think we're dating?"

Ennis ran his fingers through his hair, and it came down in shampoo-commercial waves. "Careful, she makes everyone think that."

You look a little practiced at it yourself, buddy, Nora thought. Scammers, the both of them.

His entire left arm was a swirling, intricate tattoo of what looked like a zombie bear: hairless, sinewy, red eyed. Was he one of those guys who pretended to never feel cold? This was DC January weather, and it was only October.

The woman, apparently named Moxcy, walked in. "Boss, we got everyone in. Tips tripled, at least. I'm convinced this has to be a pit stop."

Nora took her sister's shoulders. "Yanne, these people are trespassing on our property. They're profiting from some sex cult—"

"Whoa, whoa," the two cultists protested.

"Oh, Nora." Yanne brushed her sister's arms away and stepped farther into the light. "Look at this man! Does he look like he could be in a . . ." Yanne's voice faded away, and she stage-whispered, "Okay, *maybe* him, but *not* my Moxcy. She was helping old ladies onto a boat! She has a kitty named Snowdrift with only three legs."

Ennis cleared his throat. "T-there's been a misunderstanding." His voice was so soft and low that Nora and her sister leaned into it. Even in the firelight, his eyes shone black and vivid.

Does he look at everyone this way? Like he knows why she's out of D batteries?

"This place has been abandoned for as long as I can re-member," he said.

"Well, it's *un*abandoned as of today." Nora stomped her foot for punctuation. He watched her movements *so* closely, as if he thought she carried a concealed weapon.

He tilted his head and squinted again.

"That face."

Shit. The blood rushed to her cheeks. She felt hot and sud-denly nauseated.

Moxcy elbowed him in the ribs. "I thought the same thing, Bear."

He took another step closer. "I've seen you somewhere, I know it."

"No, you haven't." It came out sounding like a wish. Something tightened around her lungs. Like sudden-onset asthma.

"Yes, something to do with sports? You were sweating . . . and moving."

Yanne frowned. "Was there moaning?"

Nora kicked her sister in the shin and raised her voice. "You don't know me. You can't have—"

"Did you run track for UMaine?"

"No. Now if we could just focus—"

But he was bouncing his knuckles on his lips and easing around her with the slow thoughtfulness of a person in the market for a used car. The faint whisper of roses, leather, and cinnamon trailed behind him.

"I've seen you." He paused. "I've seen you move." Why was his voice doing that? Slowing down and dragging out the word *move*, making it sound obscene?

Nora shifted her weight to the other foot. He really would not let it go. "I ran track for the University of Maryland."

"That's it." He snapped his fingers at his ears. "God, that body. The way you move. I should have known." Relieved, he reached out as if to high-five her, let it hang in the air, and then dropped it.

He looked slightly embarrassed and turned away to face the fireplace, bringing his sharp nose and soft eyes into the light. "A-a-also, the GPS watch and water bottle hooked to your backpack are dead giveaways. I ran for Maine. We must be around the same class . . ."

His words were rushing together. There was no way in hell

she was telling this man anything about UM. He'd get around to asking her questions about why she'd quit.

But there *was* a flicker of a memory. A ribbon of hair floating behind him, a podium. At the D1 level, the track world was small. You would meet the same handful of folks pretty regularly. Still, she didn't think the men paid much attention to the female athletes. Perhaps he really did remember her, even after seven years? A flush of pride washed over her. She *had* been pretty good.

Maybe not everyone in the US has seen me naked.

Nora rubbed the back of her neck. "That was so long ago."

Moxcy huffed. "Long ago? Do you know how long it takes to break collegiate records? Bear here is a coach. He gets paid to watch tape and memorize stats."

Ennis put his hand up as if to bat away praise. "Only at the high school level for now. Your name is Dash, right?"

Nora was full on blushing now. "Yeah, I'm Nora Dash. I . . ."

"You were amazing," he finished.

Nora's belly flopped. But *just* a little. Not enough to tell anyone about.

Here's what was bound to happen when she told girlfriends/Yanne about a guy she just met:

1. She'd mention he'd said something to make her insides squishy.
2. They would hype her up and pick out wedding colors.
3. She'd feed on their excitement and get excited about the guy as well.
4. She'd go on a few dates. Things would look promising!
5. And then he'd google her. He'd see her giving head to another man in shitty lighting.

6. And then she'd get the *I like you. You're just not the type of girl I can take home to Mom* spiel.

TL;DR: keep your lips zipped when a man says something that gives you butterflies.

Yanne, unused to attention not on her, coughed and leaned seductively against the back wall. "I, too, am sports." She pantomimed a tennis swing and winked at Moxcy. "Most of it was too aggressive for my taste, but I played tennis for a month in the fourth grade."

Moxcy's nose wrinkled. "I never liked balls flying in my face."

Nora reined in the conversation. "Okay, college sports aside, this"—she waved her hand around—"isn't something we can repeat in our future respectable establishment."

Ennis and Moxcy look at each other. Unspoken communication snapped back and forth between them.

Ennis spoke first. "*Our* business *is* respectable."

Nora was unconvinced. "We are trying to create an exclusive, family-friendly inn, and I saw a man's balls tonight. I'm sure you're nice, but you have to go."

Ennis flinched at the words. "You're Christopher Columbasing."

Nora folded her arms. "Don't you dare."

"I do dare. You walked in here and *discovered* a place already occupied. Now you're trying to tell us to leave."

"My deed and my keys say I can."

Ennis shimmied the door handle, and Nora could see that the metal sat too loosely in its frame. "We haven't needed keys for this place in ten years." Something about the way he handled the door felt obscene. He knew this place like an old lover, and he made sure she knew it.

Moxcy lit another candle on the mantel. "And, colonizer, your deed may not be worth the paper it's written on." Her chin tilted up. "I'm kind of a lawyer, and we adversely possessed this land."

Nora and Yanne nearly choked at the word. A series of dry squawks escaped their throats.

"*I* can't be a colonizer," Nora finally sputtered out.

"You fit the description right now," Ennis said. Yanne looked like she was about to faint.

"And what do you mean you're 'kind of' a lawyer?" Nora continued.

This woman had the nerve to be looking at her phone. She was actively googling law terms and threatening them with the search engine results.

Moxcy's hands made a tenting gesture. "Yes, um." She licked her lips. "It's squatter's rights. We, People of the Dawn Sunshine Trails, take possession of the land based on continuous occupation."

Ennis kicked a bag of beer bottles. "The previous owners abandoned this place for twenty years. And we don't have to leave suddenly because you *say* you own it."

Nora looked at Moxcy. "I'll call the police."

"Sis!" exclaimed Yanne, who suddenly had a grave look on her face.

Moxcy and Ennis shared a quick glance.

"Excuse us." Yanne yanked her sister away.

"Yes, ma'am," he answered, looking at Nora with something tricky in his eye. She didn't like his tone either. That *yes, ma'am* had a *you'll see* quality to it that didn't sit well with her. Not to be trusted, that one. Yanne led Nora to a dark room around the corner, stumbling as she went over raised floorboards and old beer bottles. The house was dark as pitch on this side. "Are you insane right now?"

"What do you mean?"

"People of the Dawn?" She flashed her sister the Google search page. "The Abenaki Native American Tribe of Maine."

"So what?"

"So, colonizer, are you really going to stand here breathing Harriet Tubman, Cesar Chavez, and Audra Simpson's air and tell a Native American to get off your land?"

"It's not like that." Nora tapped her foot. She didn't have *Expel the natives* on her Maine checklist. It wasn't fair that they put her in a position to do this. She was making due with what she had, just like they were. And now she had to claim a space for her and her sister.

"While you all were jerking each other off with sportsball memories, I pulled a one-card reading on them."

Yanne wanted tarot to be law, and it just wasn't. Whatever fuzzy truth she saw in the cards, she would try to force on everyone.

"I got a Two of Cups, Nora." She paused for Nora's reaction but got back a blank stare. "Divine partnerships! Mutual attraction."

"Look, Yanne, you didn't see what I saw when I came in here. I'm not blowing our shot because you're hot for Moxcy. They have to go."

"I won't be a part of it." Yanne held up her hands. "The ancestors are *not* happy. Bob Marley is rolling in his grave right now. How can you ever sing 'Buffalo Soldiers' again?"

"Yanne, I hate to offend Bob Marley and the ancestors and the tarot, I *really* do."

She didn't.

Nora pulled at her sister's slouchy turtleneck until their noses were touching. "But do you understand that we have three million dollars on the line? We have a year to turn this dump into a profitable establishment. And it will not happen letting vagrants throw sex parties here."

"These are *Native American* vagrants, Nora."

"Do we even know that? Do Native Americans *really* dress like this, like, three sixty-five? I doubt it."

"Ask them. I dare you. Ask 'em. *ArE yOu ReAl NAtiVe AmErIcAnS?*"

"Okay." Nora released a breath. "Let's not." Nora was not in the habit of asking *anyone* about their racial background. It reeked of the curiosity obsessed with order. "But they have to go, Yanne."

"You *are* a colonizer, do you know that, Nora?"

Nora smiled and clasped her hands together. When they made their way back into the foyer, the trespassers were gone.

So was *all* the light in the house.

The cultists took their flashlights and candles and had doused the fireplace, and now the room was insufficiently lit by the moon. Yanne turned on her phone flashlight just in time to see the iridescent eyes of an animal glare back. She dropped the phone and clung to Nora.

"I'm on seven percent battery," Yanne whimpered.

Nora heard the skittering of rodent feet, and dread knocked around in her belly. Their Lyft driver was long gone. They had no supplies, no knowledge of the area.

Yanne groped for her hand in the dark. "Nora, please find the vagrants."

Nora's heart plummeted at the sad reality that they were so helpless out here. The doubt gnawed at the inside of her ribcage. Had they made the right choice? Should they have just taken the money from Felicia? Did she drag her sister into her failure?

Right now, the sex cultists were all they had. "I can try."

Nora tiptoed carefully to the door. She clamped her mouth to keep from screaming as she stepped on something plush and still moving under her boot. The sickening squish made her stomach twist.

Nora, don't you dare cry. If she found Ennis, she would beg him to . . . what, exterminate? She didn't know yet. On foot, they couldn't have gotten far.

She pulled open the front door and prepared to race out head-first into the night.

Instead, she ran into a warm wall of cinnamon, leather, and roses.

Him.

Bracing himself, Ennis wrapped his arms around her, slipping inside her coat instead of over it. In the same instant, he stepped toward the door, and she moved away from it. His thighs slipped between hers as they pushed together instead of apart.

Was it a gasp she heard, or the ocean? Did his eyes flicker over her? In the thin sliver of moonlight, all she could see clearly was the slope of his cheekbones.

Nora arched her back. "I think you're stable now."

Ennis held her tighter. "You don't know which planks are rotten." His thumbs pressed gently into her ribs just under the swell of her breast. It was the type of detail you leave out of a story. In retelling this to Yanne, she would be sure to leave thumbs out of it.

He finally released her waist and settled her on a solid board.

He had been waiting there on the porch the whole time, the cinnamon bastard.

His voice rose in petty glee. "Are you ready to talk now?"

BEAR PROTECTION PROTOCOL

SAME DAY, LATER THAT EVENING

SITTING ON THE PORCH WITH HIS HANDS BURNING, Bear knew he couldn't ruin their chance here. If People of the Dawn Sunshine Trails could operate in a more official capacity on this side of the island, next summer could be all about profit. All he needed was a few months with this cabin as headquarters, with no rent.

It could give him a way to keep his seat on the council and try to fight for his own neglected dreams. Being a collegiate coach was a choice Bear had dreamed for himself, without weighing other people's needs against his own. He almost felt guilty for even wanting it.

This woman, Nora, was going to be the key. It wasn't nice what he and Moxcy had done, but it was effective. The Wabanaki Confederacy was composed of the few Native American tribes *still* living on their ancestral lands, and they didn't stay here by playing nice with settlers.

Nora looked up at him, her skin soaking up all the moonlight. He couldn't read her face. "That was unfair. We need the light."

"My cousin and I built that fire. You said you wanted us to go."

"We—"

"Even if you had the fire, what then? Where would you sleep?"

She buried her face in her hands. "Fuck. I don't know."

She wore her shoulders like earrings, and Bear had to fight the irrational need to push them down.

Nora looked up. "But I can't walk back in there and tell my little sister I don't have a plan. I won't." Nora quieted at the sound of her sister shuffling toward the door.

He knew that frustration deeply. When everyone was looking at you for answers, but there were none.

"You can't sleep here tonight. It's not safe. My number two, Moxcy, grabbed the golf cart from around back. Allow us to take you to a hotel? And we can talk about how we might work together."

"This is blackmail."

"You should thank us. The natives are sharing their bounty with you so you can survive the winter. That story should sound familiar?"

"I didn't come over on the *Mayflower*, and I'm not thanking you for forcing our hand. But I would appreciate any leads you have on a hotel."

"There's a motel near here. Seventy-nine dollars a night." Though Bear didn't think the motel was that big a step up from Barton Cove, it was the closest option.

"Is it close?"

"About two miles away."

Moxcy gestured carefully. "Got the golf cart. It might be easier to leave your luggage here."

"Not a chance."

They piled into the golf cart, and the ridiculous suitcase Nora insisted on bringing was the largest passenger in the vehicle.

They pulled up to the motel, and Michael, who had worked there for thirty years, sat watching an ancient lacrosse game on VHS.

Bear slapped the counter. "Michael, we have customers."

The old man pulled at his cap, nodded, and powered up the old desktop.

Yanne's voice was hopeful. "Do you have an indoor pool, by any chance?"

Michael only looked at Bear, then continued to tap on the keyboard. "These women occupy Barton now," Bear told him.

Michael looked up from the monitor. "Got swindled. Place is a dump."

Nora cleared her throat. "Um, we don't *occupy* Barton, we own it."

"Even worse." Michael clicked enter with a hard finality. "You're number nine. No parties, no reefer, no overnight prostitutes."

Yanne grabbed the keys. "We can do two out of three."

Bear leaned against the lobby exit and folded his arms. "So, let's meet in the lobby here at nine a.m. and discuss a partnership. We'll take you to Barton and then to the store afterward."

Nora reached around his vest and pushed the door so Bear would lose his balance. "Me accepting this motel was not me agreeing to a partnership."

Bear kept his footing and resisted the urge to shout, *You're not the only one with fast feet.* Instead, he let her pass in front of him. "Can you agree to talk?"

Yanne stepped in front of Nora. "She can. We believe in divine partnerships and would be pleased to speak with you. Thank you, beautiful children of the First Nations, for your help. I'd like to draw your tarot one day to say thanks." She blinked up at Moxcy, who winked back. This was getting unprofessional fast.

Walking toward the last room on the ground floor, Bear heard the words coming out of his mouth. "No problem. I should probably check your room out for anything sketchy." He couldn't say why he offered to check this room even if he had been attached to a lie detector.

Yanne came up and squeezed his middle in a surprise hug and handed him the keys. She was a cozy, plump woman, lighter skinned, lighter eyed than Nora. *She* seemed to trust him fully. He hoped she would work on her sister.

"Thank you so much!" She detached from him as color rose up her neck. "You'll have to excuse me. There are times when masculine energy is a comfort to me." Her voice cracked like she might cry, and Bear didn't know what he should do. She was scared, and he felt a little rotten for playing that nasty trick on them. Nora pulled her sister back to her side with a flash of pain in her eyes.

They had lost something, or someone.

"We weren't expecting it to be quite so rough in there," Nora said by way of explanation.

Bear turned the key and pushed open the motel room door. Standard room. He switched on the heat. Turned on the light fixtures. Looked under the bed. Nora, the oldest one, pulled off her puffy jacket. Bear wanted to laugh out loud as she searched for a coatrack or even a hanger. The younger one kept asking for a room service menu and kept requesting something called *amuz boosh*. These women were doomed.

He turned to see Moxcy walk her fingers up Yanne's shoulder. "Okay," Bear snapped. "Looks like everything checks out here." He shoved on his jacket and pulled Moxcy toward the door. "See you ladies tomorrow."

As soon as they were far enough away from the door, Moxcy laughed out loud. "Bear. Holy smokes, that woman Yanne is . . . whew."

"You need to manage yourself. That was wildly inappropriate."

"Okay, Saint Ennis. *I'm going to check your room for anything sketchy?* I mean, yeah, right? You were definitely waiting on the uptight one to thank you with a hand job."

"That was basic human decency, Moxcy." He would never admit it, but something about her accusation rang true in his head. Not about the hand job, but Nora had turned on some old rusty pipework in the back of his head. She had him thinking about gold medals, cheering crowds, and breaking red ribbons.

Possibility.

"She seemed tired and scared," he added.

Moxcy laughed. "Oh, Lord help her if she's activated the Bear Protection Protocol. Another legend in the making? It's getting crowded in there, huh?"

"Grow up, Moxcy. Don't joke about that."

"If you want to break the *Perfect Bear* curse, you should do something unforgivable." She swirled her hands over his head and chest like she was holding a smudge. "Maybe start with cheering up that sad cheerleader. And I'll take her sister."

"We are adults, and we are going to behave like it. So, no, don't you even look at that woman."

"This week?"

"For as long as we need them to cooperate." Bear started the car.

·   ·   ·

THE NEXT MORNING BEAR AND MOXCY WERE UP BEFORE
dawn cleaning Francis Freeman's computer of the spyware and
Trojan horses he accumulated every few months. The man
clicked on every pop-up promising him easy money.

His father's home differed from his gma's humble single-
wide. The McMansion sat smack-dab in the middle of modest
homes and sprouted up like a jagged adult incisor in a mouthful
of baby teeth. The brick edifice combined with helicopter-bright
Christmas decorations made everyone wince. His father's cir-
cumstances had changed recently, the result of a tiny portion of
a Powerball win, and he'd needed everyone to know about it.

"Have you spoken to your mother?"

Bear rolled his eyes. "Yes, Dad, she's three blocks over at
Auntie's house."

"Is she well?"

Bear swirled his coffee. "She's got about two hundred dollars
left, so you'll see her by Wednesday."

Dad snorted. "It has nothing to do with money. The soul con-
nects your mom and me. I said I would love and protect her forever. For Penobscot, our word is everything. "Your mother's
Abenaki so . . ." He said this as if it explained everything about
their separation. "She's talking about going back home to Vermont." He scoffs. "Marriage is a commitment, one that *I* take
seriously."

*Having children is a commitment, too, but you were just fine walk-
ing out on that.*

"Dad, you have to be joking. You left me covering for you because you *said* you were going to be there and weren't. Don't give
me that word-is-bond shit."

"No. I never said I would *be* there, I said I would *try* to make it. Any person who has ever accused me of backing out of my word wasn't listening hard enough."

"So the whole rez had corn for ears?"

Francis was quiet for a long time. Maybe he didn't always need a reminder of the promises he'd broken, before his first cup of coffee.

When Francis finally spoke, his tone had shifted slightly. He sounded sad, even distant. "You think good little boys make the world go round?" Francis shook the last of the powdered creamer out of the container. "You think if you do everything *the right way* that your life will work out? How is that going for you? How did that work out for your grandfather?"

Bear's grandfather had been an eccentric old cuss. Instead of burying his money underground or forcing his grandchildren on a scavenger hunt like regular grandfathers, he left them a trust to be released upon marriage. Every single grandchild had proposed marriage to their first boyfriend or girlfriend to release their funds. One cousin caused the biggest scandal on the rez when he married an eighty-year-old widow at eighteen. The only two holdouts left were him and his cousin Basil. As if they were locked in some unspoken competition to not rely on Thunderbear's money. Bear didn't know why he attached some sense of pride to not using it yet. He didn't like the idea of using the money to prop up someone else's dream. He wanted to save it for his own.

"You're forgetting the old ways or only paying lip service to it, but want to nail me to the wall when I live a real life." He pushed Bear's heavy unbound hair over the opposite shoulder, letting it cascade as proof of the truth of his statement.

His hair? When an Abenaki man found a woman he wanted to marry, he would braid his hair into a single plait. It symbolized bonds and interconnected lives, a sweet old tradition, but not everyone followed it. Francis Freeman didn't get to pick and choose when he wanted to be a guardian of culture. He had left, Basil had left, but it was *Bear* who wasn't keeping the old ways? No way would Bear get sucked in playing the *who's-the-most-traditional* game.

"You know Barnard flipped to a yes on the tribal council?" Francis asked.

Moxcy slapped the dining room table. "Yeah, they got his son on some trumped-up charges. And by the time they let him go, Barnard was a yes for the dam project."

"They're playing dirty," Bear said.

Moxcy and Francis looked at him like he had sprouted another head.

"Of course they are," Francis scoffed.

Last month at the council meeting, his own dad had been trying to get him to vote yes. But damming up the river would be an environmental disaster. People always thought of the benefits of a dam like renewable energy or flood prevention, but the people who got those benefits were upriver. Downriver got destroyed habitats and a slow, sluggish river that barely supported salmon, much less other fish, birds, and bears. And guess what was downriver of the plant and proposed dam? The Wabanaki Confederacy Reservation. As long as he owned the island's most influential business, he had a powerful seat on the council.

His answer would always be no.

His father's persistent pitch to let his successful cousin Basil buy Sunshine Trails had been ramping up in intensity lately. And Bear knew it had everything to do with the money Maine Power was dangling over their heads.

"That's why we have to strengthen Sunshine Trails' influence *outside* of the rez," Bear said, then looked his father in the eye. "We're building a new business partnership."

"Partnership." He made it sound placating, the way a parent would humor a precocious child.

"Yep, the beach house has owners now," Moxcy said.

Francis's eyes went round as saucers. "Some fools bought Barton Cove, eh?" He shook his head. "White men with more money than sense."

Bear smiled. "No, Black women."

Moxcy finished, "With more money than sense."

"Terrible investment. No foot traffic out there."

"We have to go meet them soon—"

"You're working with them?" Francis shook his head. "That's your big partnership? You and I both know they'll be bankrupt before the year's up. Why waste your energy? Why not go with that big-time Willow Bee asshole?"

"I think the answer to that is in the question. Besides, we don't need them to be a success. We need them for next summer." Bear rinsed out his coffee cup.

"And when you're done with them next summer?"

"I want to press into being a collegiate coach and then maybe the Olympics." Bear shot a look at Moxcy. It was the first time he'd said this out loud to his father. Something in him was waiting for the laughter.

When it came, it still stung.

After laughing behind his hand, Francis sighed. "Bear, where in the hell is this coming from again? You sound like you did when you were thirteen. Coaching an Olympic team?" He smirked. "You've been coddled by these people who think you shit rainbows.

You're fat on the teat, son. Besides, you'd have to give up your muckety-muck chair on the council."

"I won't have to give up my chair."

Pursuing a collegiate coaching career had always felt just out of reach, but this track superstar dropping into his lap *had* to be a sign from the Creator.

But last night, he felt like he was in a fever dream. He put a portfolio together and mapped out universities up and down the northeast corridor. He hadn't felt this energized in a while.

The door creaked open, and a broad-faced Jennings bumbled through the hall. Flecks of apple shot across the room as he shouted, "Are these the same ladies that crashed the tour yesterday?"

"How many people did you tell already?" Moxcy asked. Jennings shrugged. To call his baby cousin Jennings nosy was perhaps a nice way to call him the biggest busybody on the reservation. Since he was a child, he slipped in and out of homes spreading every family's joy and pain.

"Can I come? I want to see how fast they decide they can't do it."

"Get in the car, and don't say a word," Bear said.

"Are those fresh Jordans?" Jennings pointed to his shoes, and Bear flushed purple. "What airtight vault did you pull those out of?"

"We're making a good impression." Bear pretended to give chase to his cousin, and the boy made a fast break to the door. If Jennings could break that fast at track meets, the team would be swimming in gold medals.

They left the house with Francis Freeman screaming after them, "Give my regards to the newest fools at Barton Cove!"

In the car, Moxcy rolled down the window. "Is there a reason you doused yourself in the entire bottle of cologne this morning?"

"I don't smell a thing." The lie came out with a straight face.

"Gah, this guy. You're nose blind. It's a thing—" Jennings said.

Moxcy snorted, ignoring Jennings. "You're such a hypocrite."

"Cologne makes me a hypocrite?" Bear asked. Moxcy had been sour since last night when he rightfully told her to stand down on these women.

"This much cologne and those uncreased Js make me think you're trying to snag that cheerleader." Moxcy took a deep breath. "Bear, hear me out, though. This is actually a good sign. The accident was three years ago. You, or some part of you, is ready for a change."

Bear tried to laugh it off, but his hands held the steering wheel tight enough to snap it. *The accident.*

"You need to think about your next steps, an exit plan." She lobbed the words so gently, and they *still* pissed him off.

"Moxcy . . ." Bear warned. "We're trying to start a new partnership. For Sunshine Trails. I want to make a good impression. That is all. Please stop." His voice was shaking with the effort of keeping it calm.

The accident.

The legend.

The lie.

"I'm not saying that Uncle is right, *but* have you thought about exactly why you're still—"

"Moxcy. Fucking. Stop." The words came out deep and hard, cutting across the atmosphere like a blade. It was too much. But he didn't apologize. Why couldn't everyone just shut up about *his* choices?

"I know I put myself in this position. I think about it every day of my life. I don't need you to think about it for me. It's just cologne."

Moxcy looked out the window. They rode the rest of the way in tense silence until the light of the motel came into view.

Moxcy stalked into the motel and blew the door open with the force of her anger.

Let her be pissed. He'd done nothing wrong. She was wrong for pretending like that part of his life was under his own control.

WRONG FOOT

YANNE, REMEMBER, WE DON'T KNOW THESE PEOPLE from Adam. Don't overattach." Nora pushed her cashmere robin's-egg-blue cardigan across her chest. The tiny little orange high-tops embroidered into the pockets made her feel a bit like the fun elementary school teacher she had always wanted to be.

"Me?" Yanne looked perplexed.

"Yes, you. Or did you forget you held Ennis in a hug for three minutes yesterday?"

"Yesterday was next-level traumatizing. Look around! This is the setting of a Stephen King novel. I don't even think this place has turndown service," Yanne said. "Honestly, I didn't want them to leave. I would have slept on his lap."

Nora took a deep breath, grateful to see Ennis and Moxcy and a young boy approaching. "Well, lucky us, they're already here."

The lobby of the motel was like the rest of the place, largely neglected. Ceiling tiles were stained with watermarks and sagged in places, threatening to fall at any moment. Dim fluorescent lights flickered and hummed, casting an eerie glow over the shabby furnishings.

Bear leaned against the small, cluttered desk in the center of the room, the same dusty cash register and battered phone from last night. The same sleepy clerk slumped in a chair behind the desk, staring blankly at a lacrosse game that looked like it was taking place twenty years ago. Nora wondered, perhaps unkindly, how anyone could make a life here.

"Two blueberry bagels with a blueberry napoleon." Moxcy shoved the bags into her hands like a football.

Peeking inside the bag, Nora winced. "Is that blueberry cream cheese?"

"We figured you should learn to love it now," Moxcy said. "You look nice. You, uh, wanted to make a good impression?"

Nora rolled the collar of her blush-pink silk blouse and checked for the third time to make sure it was tucked artfully *and fake effortlessly* into her fitted jeans.

"No, just casual." She shrugged. In fact, she was overdressed.

Bear wore slim gray sweatpants. The same gray sweatpants that *every* athlete she knew wore. Where *was* this outlet store? There had to be a secret Amazon link for indecent joggers.

"Do you like Bear's shoes?" A teenager peeled himself off the wall and threw his arms down toward the floor, where Nora saw a modest pair of Jordans.

"I hadn't noticed." Nora nodded thanks to Moxcy. "Good morning, Bear, Moxcy . . ." She paused, waiting for an introduction.

The teenager stepped up and pumped Nora's hand. "Yes, it's a pleasure to meet you. I'm Jennings, available for odd jobs, errands, and ad hoc services."

"Nice to meet you, Jennings." Nora pulled her hand out of the boy's grasp.

"What does *S* stand for?" Ennis blurted out. He pointed to her collarbone, where a tiny *S* sat crooked and glinting.

"Oh, um, it's me. Shenora."

"Which do you prefer?"

She fingered the *S*. "Nora is fine."

Yanne swirled around them, kissing cheeks like a Parisian socialite. She bowed slightly and pressed her hands together.

"The light in me recognizes the light in you, Indigenous family." She paused dramatically and waved her hands. Ennis and Moxcy glanced at each other and did not return her bow.

Yanne rummaged through her macramé bag that reached down to her knees. "I'd like to draw your tarot."

Ennis made a confused face, and Yanne dropped her hands. "My readings usually go for like eighty bucks a pop so—"

He pushed the deck away. "That *really* won't be necessary."

Nora reached for the cards, somehow defensive of her sister and embarrassed at the same time. "Yanne, we have actual things to talk about—"

Yanne slapped her sister's hands away. "This is an *actual* thing, Nora. I want to say thank you to our First Nations saviors."

Yanne cleared a table in the corner strewn with outdated brochures and discarded newspapers. She pushed a few mismatched and worn chairs together and clapped with accomplishment. "Now the first thing I want to do is acknowledge the land." Yanne pulled out a miniature djembe drum from her massive bag, and lord did Nora want to just float away.

"The old name was Pesamkuk, and Bar Harbor was called Moneskatik—the 'clam-digging place.'" She slapped the drum. "Our ancestors honor yours. *First* here and *forced* here—"

"You don't have to do that." Moxcy flicked her fingers under her chin, signaling for Yanne to expeditiously cut the bullshit. "Thank you for your *performance*, but save it for your slam poetry readings at the college."

"It's not a *performance*. You know Nora and I actually have—"

Oh hell no. Yanne was *not* about to bring up their made-up Cherokee great-grandmother to these people. Every Black person she knew had a mythical Cherokee—always Cherokee—distant matriarch to explain a straight nose or a wave in the hair. But that DNA ancestry kit her mother had paid three hundred dollars for proved (*in her Maury Povich voice*) that was a lie.

"Yanne!" Nora grabbed the djembe drum. "Let's . . . um, let's move on, shall we?"

Yanne's face crumbled. It was maybe because she looked like she was about to cry that Bear grabbed the deck. "It's fine. Let's do it."

After pulling four crystals out of that damned bag, Yanne took Ennis's hand.

"Oh, warm hands. You have a big heart, Ennis."

He cut the deck absently while checking his phone. Nora heard the distinct sound of a starting pistol. *What race is on?* She checked the date.

"Are those the qualifiers?" Nora peeked at the image on his phone. Olympic qualifiers for track and field were her absolute favorite to watch. Hopeful kids trying to go for gold always absorbed her attention. Ennis sat up straighter in his chair and turned his phone to face Nora. They were both leaning over the shaky brown table, foreheads nearly touching.

"When is your birthday?" Yanne waved a quartz over the screen to get Ennis's attention.

"January eleventh," Bear told her, then snapped his eyes back the screen. "Semi-qualifiers. This kid is lightning fast. No one's going anywhere near that time. Can you imagine coaching that kind of raw talent?"

Nora squinted. "Wait, is that—"

"The coach? Yes, it's Jason Mail. Ran for Virginia."

"He was a terrible runner." Nora couldn't hide her shock to see a runner they had nicknamed *Snailmail* coaching in the Olympics.

"Wild, right? Losing taught him more than winning did." Bear's face looked like someone had plugged him in all of a sudden. It was a face she couldn't imagine leering in malignant curiosity.

I saw that video. I know what you like.

Then his eyes popped up—too quick for her to dart her eyes back to the screen.

She was caught looking at him.

For a fraction of a moment she froze, and then she rushed for something to say.

"Moxcy said you coach high school. Do you want to coach D1, eventually?"

"Oh my god." Ennis nearly slid down off the chair. "It would b-b-b—" He seemed to get stuck. "I would love to," he recovered. "That's why we're pushing so hard this year for Sunshine Trails. This will be our last year-round cycle. We're going seasonal s-s-so I can give it a shot." He held his chest, and Nora saw what looked like embarrassment flash across his face. "I'm so sorry, I—"

"No, you're fine. Go as slow as you need to." She'd worked as a teacher's aide in college, and she recognized his slight stutter. "Coaching. I love that. I'd like to work with younger—"

Yanne slapped her sister's hip. "Sit down, Nora. Ennis, I need your energy in *this* space. Eyes on the ball." She waved the deck in front of him for him to choose a card.

Yanne pulled out the card he chose, and gasped. She pulled her enormous glasses up on her nose.

"Aww, poor baby." Yanne shook her head. "Eight of Swords." She took his hand again and pulled it to the center of her bountiful chest. "You're bound up, baby boy. You feel restricted. By forces outside of your control. This could represent a controlling partner or all-around terrible partnership. Oh, Ennis." Yanne shoved a crystal in his hand. "And you're a Capricorn too."

"What's so terrible about being a Capricorn?" he asked.

"Nothing by itself, but with the Eight of Swords and your stubborn vibe, you're going to be in this energy for a looong-ass time. You're too inflexible to get yourself out of it."

Moxcy laughed so loudly that Ennis winced. She slapped the table and cut her eyes to her cousin. "You've made me a believer, Yanne."

ON THE TRAIL LATER THAT MORNING, NORA WAS SURE every rock in the state of Maine was on this path forcing her to stumble. Bear kept eyeing Nora's boots skeptically. Her sister had no interest in coming back to Barton Cove and jumped at the chance to flirt with Moxcy on a trip to Costco. She knew what he must be thinking, because it was coming off him in waves. She made that same face when she was watching orcas circle a seal in a nature documentary.

He seemed to grow even less confident when she startled at a darting chipmunk.

"You have *got* to relax," Ennis said.

"Oh, oh, I didn't know it was that simple. I'll just relax then." She shook her head as if to say, *Do you not see how out of place we freaking are?* He might think that they were doomed city girls, but Nora had months of DIY Pinterest boards saved for *something*. YouTube tutorials had taught her how to flat twist her *own* hair in a mirror. Surely she could scrub a few walls and decorate her daddy's inn?

After stopping to uproot a partially hidden seashell with her foot, Nora sighed. She should just get this out of the way. "I realize we got off on the wrong foot last night."

Ennis folded his arms. "Yeah, you accused us of being in a sex cult."

"As I said, wrong foot," Nora repeated.

His footfalls were loud and heavy beside her. Crisp leaves crunched like potato chips under his Jordans. The November light was crisp and buttery, warming what would be a frigid morning. This place was so isolated, and suddenly so quiet.

The thought crossed her mind that she was alone with a man she met in the dark only twelve hours ago.

"Do you want a knife?" he asked.

"What?"

"Do you want a knife? You keep glancing back at me like I'm going to murder you. I can walk in front of you, and I can give you my hunting knife."

She nodded. It's not like she knew how to use a knife. She would just like a teensy bit of power back in this situation. Bear unbuckled the holster, then wrapped his arms around her waist to strap the band in place. Nora's breath parted the hair above his bent head, and that whiff of roses and cinnamon fluttered around her.

"Better?" he asked.

Her eyebrow rose. "Um, yeah, actually." And she meant it.

Her hand smoothed over the hilt that felt a hell of a lot like bone, and she blew out a relaxed breath. Having the knife on her hip made her feel like the sheriff of a lawless town.

"In the light of day, Ennis, Yanne and I believe we could benefit from your local knowledge." She watched his strong stroll in front of her. He walked around the obstructions in the path like he was playing no-look hopscotch. The fluidity in his motions told the story of an agile body that moved with grace and effortless speed.

Oh, he is fast.

She understood how he had clocked her as an athlete yesterday. "Ennis," Nora continued, "you're from Maine, and we'll need—"

"I'm not from Maine," Ennis corrected. "Maine is from me. The Wabanaki Confederacy predates Columbus and the United States of America. Barton Cove has your name on the deed, but I know the surrounding area better than anyone who's ever owned it."

"Don't you live two hours away? On the river? How do you know this place so well?" Nora nodded and stumbled on another branch in the path. She wanted to throw these boots into the ocean.

"Not the travel-for-work type, I see," Bear said. It didn't *sound* like an insult, but it definitely wasn't a compliment. "Yeah, the *reservation* is near Old Town a few hours away, but we've always used this island as a central meeting place for trading, hunting, and fishing with one another during the summers, and now Mount Desert is a lifeline for work for this whole region. It's literally my job to know this place." He was giving her this tour guide voice, and she had to stop herself from raising her hand.

"So it's like how Yanne and I know all of the good places to eat in Rehoboth because we summer there."

"Probably not like that at all." Bear glanced out toward the water.

"Even so, I think you could benefit from making Barton Cove a more official rest stop on your tour."

"Not a rest stop. Headquarters." His lips turned up in a half smile. He eyed her boots, then her hair, which she kept in a high ponytail with flat-ironed curls. "Tours begin and end there, with dedicated space for selling merchandise and building crafts. We get unrestricted use of the land and private beach."

Nora's hands hopped to her hips. "Wow, Ennis, let me know when we get to the mutually beneficial part."

"I'm not done. We would need your resources to identify any healthy seed-producing Black Ash trees on your land. We also need you to promise to donate any Black Ash that needs to be cut or harvested to the tribe."

Nora met his gaze. "That seems like a lot for just pointing us toward the nearest motel."

"But I—*we* can do more than that." Nora's eyebrow raised only slightly. "We can connect you with the best contractors at the local rate. We can bring foot traffic to this part of the island. We can expedite your licensing. We can also facilitate multiple family-friendly activities—beading, the wigwam experience—"

"Wigwam what?" Nora screwed up her face.

"It's our biggest seller. People spend five hundred dollars to sleep overnight in a wigwam and eat traditional food. I'm saying you'll be up and on your way much faster."

"Faster's what we need."

Bear ambled to a stop, and suddenly they were back in front

of Barton Cove. The windows were boarded up. Someone had spray-painted *Barton Hole* across the peeling gray siding. The roof sagged like a wet mattress, and Nora could swear she saw an old Victorian white lady shimmering in an upstairs window.

This house was so bad. How could this have been her father's dream for their family? Perhaps that was the message. That he had neglected his dreams for them and done the right thing by his "real family."

What would it mean for her to make this place whole again? To complete her father's dream? Maybe after his death, she could regain what he refused to give her after the links came out—his blessing, his acceptance. All of this had to mean something. She swiped a tear away and looked up to catch Ennis eyeing her.

"Everything okay?" He shoved his hands in his pockets.

"Yeah, just great," she lied. Nothing was great. Wasn't the ocean supposed to be majestic? Even the beach here was lackluster. The low tide exposed muddy rock, gasping fish, and a wood-rotted staircase overrun with barnacles. Their tiny strip of beach curled like a letter *C* and was littered with beer bottles, firepits, condoms, six-pack rings, and Hot Fries bags baked in the sun and salt. The white fence was bent low like an elephant had taken a seat on it. Sand and rocks spilled through the slats.

Turning back to the house itself, she saw that the porch was an even worse disaster. A sun-bleached couch with stuffing pouring out of the right side sat on the far end of it. The other side was cluttered with broken chairs, rusty cans, and discarded fishing nets. The porch was a land mine of rotted wood and a rattling railing that shook as the wind blew.

Pinterest boards couldn't save her now.

She needed Ennis.

She thought of how he had righted her on the porch last

night. His hands bracing her. Thumbs kissing the soft underside of her breasts. She had been here for a night, and this house already had memories attached.

Any hope for a fast renovation was destroyed when she stepped inside and saw it in the cold light of day. The air was damp and salty, and the walls had circular blossoms of mildew. The huge stone mantel had what looked like decades of multicolored wax falling like stalactites in front of the fireplace. A stiff shirt hung over the mantel.

Her mother would call this place *tore up from the floor up*.

They were in way over their heads.

SPEAKERBOXXX/
THE LOVE BELOW

SAME DAY

BEAR WATCHED NORA STEP CAREFULLY AROUND THE house, less to not break anything and more to protect her three-hundred-dollar boots.

This was going to be wildly expensive to fix. He hoped this woman had a bucketful of Benjamins, because this was looking like a complete wash. He hoped she wouldn't pack up and leave at the sight of this dump.

"Good bones," he heard himself say. Nora turned in to an absolutely disgusting bathroom and immediately reversed course, holding her hands over her mouth. Ennis stepped aside quickly to allow her to pass. Her shoulders sank farther and farther with every room.

"Well, the upstairs rooms are in great shape," he said, trying to find some silver lining. She fingered the stag antler knife hanging off her waist. His grandfather's knife. It was due for a good sharpening, but he never carried it around to gut anything anymore. It was just good medicine. Thunderbear's knife made him feel confident and in control even when everything spun around him. He sensed she needed to feel a little bit in control. Seeing her palm it so lovingly rattled his insides a bit, though.

"That mold." She shook her head. "It's the kiss of death."

Kiss.

An image flashed in Bear's head of Nora jumping—tiny nylon shorts crawling up her thighs—blowing a kiss. "You used to blow kisses, right?" Bear blurted out. His eyes bounced away from her mouth.

Don't make it weird. Reel it in. "When you won a race?"

"Wow, I can't believe you remember that. Yeah, it was my little thing." Her high ponytail bobbed, and Bear understood—*but did not condone*—Moxcy's cheerleader reference.

"You underestimate how good you were. Everyone remembers that." *Could anyone forget you blazing past them, breasts pushing out of your compression top, blowing them a kiss?*

The sound of an unfamiliar voice jolted him, and Nora reached for the knife like it had always been there.

"Who's there?" The voice boomed with authority.

Nora and Bear rushed to the front of the house to see Stubbs again, this time with an older partner. They must have taken him off police academy babysitting.

"Bear, what the fuck? You know the law good and well. No more slack. Get the hell out of here and take your lady friend with you."

"Excuse me?" Nora stupidly stood in front of him. He pulled her back behind him. If he didn't know she was rich, he would have guessed it now.

"You heard me. This is occupied property. The owners are due out any day. I don't care what you two were up to, but—"

"I am the owner," Nora said, looking from Bear to the cop.

Stubbs smiled and wiggled his eyebrow at his partner. "You're the owner, huh?" He sauntered over to her, looking at the grip of Bear's hand on Nora's upper arm. The diamond tennis bracelet on her wrist must have convinced him, because he backed up.

"Well, welcome to quiet side, ma'am, and we'd like it to stay quiet." Stubbs chuckled. "I hope this man isn't bothering you or trying to sell you something."

"He isn't. He offered to show me around the property."

"Sure, sure." Stubbs eyed Nora's wrist again, and Bear let her go. "Just be careful of smooth talkers. Talk to the authorities before any money changes hands."

"We will," Bear said, thinking of the dam project.

Stubbs turned to Nora. "We'll be checking the records and the information, ma'am. Bear's already in the system, so to speak. If your story doesn't check out"—he turned around to Bear, poking his thick finger into his broad chest—"I'm slapping Bear with a fine hefty enough that his grandkids will be paying it off."

He walked away and stopped again on the threshold. "Welcome to the neighborhood." He nodded in Nora's direction. "I'll be seeing you."

Nora and Bear didn't exhale until the cop car disappeared down the long driveway.

"So . . . *that* relationship doesn't seem cozy. Should I be worried?"

"In this town, I think you should be worried if it was."

BACK IN THEIR HOTEL THAT EVENING, YANNE FLIPPED through the television channels while Nora stress cleaned.

"Nora, I can't believe we missed the police!"

"You didn't *miss* the police. It wasn't a concert."

"And Bear pulled you behind him?" Yanne asked. "He might be a real one."

"I was shocked, really." *Shocked* wasn't the best word. "I don't know what I felt. It wasn't terrible." When he touched her, moved her—she fought to keep a stupid blush from burning up her face. It was a weird and wrong reaction to what was actually happening, but there it was all the same.

"The human emotion you are looking for, *Sisborg*, is safe. Bear made you feel really protected and safe today. Good on him."

Nora tipped her chin to give in to her sister's point. The way he angled his body and stood in front of her. Like he was willing to go to the mat.

You used to blow kisses, right? he'd asked.

Yanne riffled through a bag of nail polish before deciding on a pale yellow. "So he's not friendly with the cops. But what do your instincts say?"

"I don't need instincts about people, Yanne. They show you who they are by their actions. Look at Mom and Dad. Where were our instincts when they were lying to us our whole lives?"

"What Mom did, she did out of love. She didn't want us to feel *less than* for any reason."

"Well, here the fuck we are, Yanne." She gestured to the dingy motel room. "Less than anyway."

"Still, you were harsh with her," Yanne said.

Here we go. It was somehow Nora's fault their mother wouldn't come with them to Maine. After Nora confronted her about the lifetime of lies, her mother had moved in with Auntie Charlene, and that was the end of it. She had never seen her more resolute. What was Nora supposed to do? Take it back?

"Mom made her decision." Nora lifted her foot, and Yanne painted Nora's big toe.

"Your holier-than-thou routine didn't help. She felt terrible."

"I mean, I'm *not* wrong." Nora flexed her feet.

"You make being right the prize when, really, getting her on the plane was. It's bad instincts. You think you know how everything will work out."

"I do." Nora stretched her foot back on the floor. She didn't even feel bad saying it. She had an uncanny ability to suss out bullshit and see exactly how everything was going to crash and burn. Call it a gift. Yanne rolled her eyes and clicked away from the basketball game that she knew Nora was partially watching.

After half-hearted channel surfing, Yanne handed her sister a Red Vine. A silent peace offering. Nora took it without looking at her.

"Did you hear Ennis is a Capricorn?" Yanne said.

Nora pulled the corners of her bed tight. "So what?"

"So, you're a Cancer." She said this like it explained something.

"You're losing me, Yanne."

"He's basically the zaddy of the zodiac. The sex alone would be worth it."

"Yanne." Nora's tone was resolute. "No."

"Oh, come on. Ennis is the unenlightened PE coach of your dreams. Big hot hands too? I'm calling it."

"Yanne, you're being . . ."

"No, not being anything. Shall I make a list? One." She held out a still-wet fingernail. "Today he wore enough cologne to choke a horse."

"It was a business meeting. I sprayed some perfume, and so did you."

"Yes, and I did because Moxcy is ghost-pepper hot. That only proves my point. Two. If it was a business meeting, why did he wear those damned gray sweats? In the right light, I saw the outline of that *whole* plantain."

"Yanne!" Nora bit the inside of her cheek, but she'd seen it too. There was an absolute hammer in those sweats.

"Three. He looks at you differently. It's not hot or leering. He just looks at you like he's scrolling though old photos, you know? Or like he's already reproducing genetically superior children with you in his head."

Nora remembered his heavy-lidded gaze, dark and full of questions, following her around the empty rooms at Barton Cove. He'd trailed behind her like he was tied to a string.

"And three," Yanne concluded, "he even stutters when he speaks to you."

"You already said three."

"No, I didn't."

"You totally did."

"Fine. Three and a half. He just clams up when you look at him."

"I think he just stutters." Nora fluffed her pillow. "With everyone."

"Oh." She considered that. "Now that you mention it. But it doesn't take away from anything else I said."

"Yanne." Nora hopped on the bed, her half-painted toenails winking in the lamplight. "You understand we didn't take the 200K they offered us, right?"

"Right."

"There is no life raft. No one is coming to save us. It's just us."

"I get that but—"

"No. You promised me we're going to really throw ourselves

into this. I really need your commitment. *I'm* committed. No men, no women. No jobs. No social media."

"I never agreed to a dry year."

"Please, Yanne." Nora pressed her hands together. "No tangents. No detours. It's this, or we go back to Maryland homeless and broke."

"Okay, okay. But now that you've seen Ennis's mushroom cap, can you just admit here and now that *Backshots from Bear* is a KU book you'd absolutely read?"

"I'll peacefully read and use these." Nora patted her glitter box with all manner of sex toys inside. She had nicknamed the box Speakerboxxx/The Love Below. She shook it, and something buzzed inside.

"Ten months, Yanne. No fuckups."

A REASON TO SWEAT

BEAR OPENED THE FERRY BILL IN THE SWELTERING parlor room at Barton Cove. Nora and Yanne were there this past week making whatever improvements they could. To the untrained eye, the rooms looked chaotic and disorganized. Walls, ceilings, and floors had been partially removed, exposing electrical wires, pipes, and ductwork. Nora was so concerned about mold, she spent a sizable amount of money gutting most of the house. They were burning through money, and they were less than two weeks in.

Maybe they wouldn't be here long at all. But Bear could already tell Sunshine Trails was benefiting from the half month of low overhead. Moxcy had run six tours this week already. The venture was showing signs of stabilization, but payments were lagging. If he paid one thing in full, there would be negative ninety-five dollars in the company bank account until last week's tours paid by credit card finally posted.

Everything about this business was bowing and scraping. Borrowing from one account to pay another.

But Barton Cove freed up so much money, it was ludicrous

that they hadn't thought of it before. His phone buzzed with an email alert.

The University of Virginia. His first official application sent in an excited rush the night Nora and her sister had crashed into Barton Cove.

Here goes.

His fingers tapped on the open button. This could make all this worrying a null point. Coaching at the collegiate level would change everything for him. He could hire a lawyer (real one, not his cousin) to make sure those fat cats didn't take the river, after everything else they had taken from their community. The business debts ticked down in his head.

We thank you for your application, but . . . He immediately looked away from the page.

Shit.

He threw down his phone with enough force to turn the room's focus in his direction.

"UVA is a no," he said.

Moxcy shook her head. "Isn't their mascot like a Confederate soldier?"

With a phone pressed to her ear against her shoulder, Nora plopped a hot blueberry-infused coffee next to him with a sugar cookie. Then she rummaged for a Post-it and scribbled a note on the pad. The swell of her hip hit his makeshift desk—a set of crates topped with a wood plank—and Bear held it to keep it from toppling.

You'd hate their facilities, she'd scribbled.

Bear took his Sharpie and notepads and forced his eyes away from the frayed hem of her shorts.

Still sucks ;-I, he wrote.

Nora was desperate to fix the furnace. While Yanne walked

around in a geometric-patterned bikini and a fan mister, Nora had been on the phone for most of the morning and paced with a deep V of sweat down her back.

"Nora, it is hotter than a priest's balls on the equator in here. Why don't you open a window?" Moxcy asked, holding blueberry jam and a handful of baskets the aunties made. They usually sold them to tourists and split the profits with the elders.

"Oh, thank you, Moxcy, we never thought of that." Nora flicked through her phone and gestured toward the windows. "Most of these windows are sealed shut." Nora passed the plate of store-bought sugar cookies to Moxcy, who took three.

"We tried to open the doors last night, and when we got here this morning, it was like Noah's ark," Yanne said.

Bear shook one of Nora's shoulders. "You should *definitely* never do that again. Bears are looking for a lot of calories right now to prepare for hibernation. You're going to wake up one morning with a big one in your bed."

Bear heard it as soon as he said it. He locked eyes with Nora's sister, and a knowing half smile crept across Yanne's face.

"I can't bring a group full of folk in here. They'll pass out." Moxcy pointed toward the door.

"We're working on it," Nora said.

"Don't you have a cute little Pinterest board for this?" Bear asked.

He was rewarded with a hard stare from all three women. "Or . . ." he recovered, "have you tried YouTube University?" Bear shook his phone.

Nora lit up. "You are exactly right!"

Bear was just starting to get concerned with the crazed look of determination in Nora's eye. "But you shouldn't recklessly try to fix it—"

She grabbed a wrench that looked like a dinosaur bone in her hands and headed downstairs. Bear rolled his eyes and followed her down the dark stairwell. *She's going to kill us all.*

The basement was unfinished and dark enough to necessitate a flashlight. "These old furnaces are really temperamental, Nora. You shouldn't just—"

He froze as she knocked the wrench against the furnace.

"What happened to YouTube University?" Bear yelped.

"Too many commercials."

"Nora! Wait." He grabbed at the wrench and yanked it over her head, but she didn't let go, and instead the force pulled her toward him.

"Let go."

"No."

"I'm fixing it."

They tussled, but she was on him like an elite defender. If he'd had a basketball in his hand, they would look like they were at an AND1 tournament. God, she moved like her joints were on a swivel. He had to get her in front of his kids. When would they get the chance to see an elite athlete in her prime? Her soft, dewy skin was slick to the touch and radiating heat.

In a hot basement with her warm curves pressed against him—

No.

He couldn't continue like this. He knew how to end this. Wrapping his arm around her, he pulled her into his hot, over-heated body—an old big-brother move that always worked with his cousins. *You can't move when you're pressed into my armpit*, he would yell to Basil. And with the heat, his armpits weren't the most pleasant place to be for any nose.

Nora pushed herself off Bear's hot body. "Gross." But she laughed saying it.

They both heaved, and Bear wondered how well Nora still ran. And if he could outrun her—exhaust her—give her a proper reason to sweat.

Images from that horrible night came tumbling into his head unbidden.

Laughing at a bar with a pretty woman with dark eyes, laughing while disaster crashed around me.

"Nora, look here. The temperature sensor inside your thermostat is detecting the wrong heat levels. It thinks it's only fifty degrees."

She had to jump to see the temp sensor, and her powerful thighs flexed and her ass bounced. Bear turned his face to the light of the stairwell. She must be punishment for all his lies of omission.

"Sorry for taking the wrench, but I had to get you to listen. If you had gotten to the end of the video—"

"It was fifteen minutes, plus all of those ads!"

"If you would have gotten to the end," he repeated, "it says you have to manually shut your furnace down and reboot the sensor. That works eighty-five percent of the time." He still held the wrench high above his head.

"Okay, that seems doable." Nora got down on her knees to look under the furnace. Bear jammed his fingers into his pockets and turned away.

Punishment.

"Ennis, where are you going? I need you to hold your phone for a flashlight."

Bear tiptoed to Nora and reached over, stretching himself to flip the switch. If he had a ten-foot pole, he would have used that instead. If he stood any closer to this woman, wet shirt plastered to her body, sweat beading and falling down her neck, and on all fours, he would detonate. "I can just shut it off."

She stood up and dusted off her knees. "Nice! I didn't even see that switch. I was looking for a pilot light or something."

His smile was tight and didn't reach his eyes.

"Are you sad about UVA?" she asked with her hands on her hips, misreading his discomfort.

"Nah, I kind of rushed it. I'm not surprised."

"I could look over your application materials," Nora offered.

"You don't have to do that."

"I know."

When they returned up the stairs, Moxcy and Yanne quieted down and looked away. Bear got the distinct impression they were being discussed.

"What was all of that scuffling?" Yanne asked between glances at Nora and Bear.

"We were fixing the furnace." Nora pulled her hair up in a ponytail, and Moxcy wrinkled her nose.

"You smell like Bear," Moxcy said. She couldn't wait to scream, *I told you so.*

"Then he must smell like *work*." She pulled the wrench out of Ennis's hands and slapped it on the countertop. He looked up to find Yanne and Moxcy watching him watching Nora move.

When Nora turned around, all three heads snapped up. She pointed to Yanne and Moxcy. "What are you two debutantes doing?"

"The writer of the family is drafting a presentation for Ennis to complete during check-in." Yanne slipped across the room in her ridiculous bikini. She flitted to him and fanned herself with three single-spaced typed pages of text like she was in a bur-lesque show.

"These are the key features and procedures we want to make sure you say during your presentation. Nora made a bulleted list, but I made it beautiful." She bowed.

Bear took two glances at the wall of text and knew he wouldn't be able to say all of these words, not without three months of practice.

He shook his head. "Nope."

Yanne shoved the papers under his nose. "What do you mean 'nope'? We added all of your stuff to the website."

"*That* was all necessary. *This* is too much." He would stutter over it for a year before he could memorize all of this. Every aspect of his presentation was memorized. Even the parts that felt spontaneous.

"Yanne, look, I appreciate all the work you put into this but—"

"But *what*? This is art on the page. We've got puns, we've got Vegas-style banter. I could submit this to the Tonys."

"No." He didn't say no a lot. And he was surprised to hear himself so firm now. His embarrassment over his stutter was stronger than his need for acceptance. People didn't realize the invisible work, all the mental preparation it took him to speak.

Yanne slapped her essay down. "It doesn't look good for you to be backing out."

"No one is backing out of what I-I said I would do." He spat it out with too much venom and felt immediately contrite when her neck snapped back in surprise, and Nora's eyebrows rose in concern.

"Shit, I'm sorry. I-I . . ." *Fuck, just finish.* Frustration and em-barrassment crept up his arms and streaked across his chest. His emotions were rarely this close to the surface. He was known, in fact, for being a pretty timid guy. *Easy E* was his nickname in high school. He didn't want Nora to hear him tripping over words.

Bear took a deep breath. *No one here is laughing at you. Just do your breathing.*

"I'm calling every one of my contacts, and Barton Cove is already under way cheaper and faster than you could have done on your o-own."

Nora nodded wide-eyed and slow like a hostage. She took the sheets from Yanne and folded them in half. "You have done all of those things. Yanne, let me look at those notes, and we'll get back to y'all with our next steps."

Bear caught Nora's eye, and they shared a tiny look. His chest popped with little flutters. He looked away. Why couldn't they have met any other time but now? Now, when they were impossible.

But he wouldn't be his dad. He wouldn't abandon all of his responsibilities for a pair of sleek brown thighs.

He said his goodbyes and left the stifling house, Moxcy trailing after him.

"You like them," he accused her as soon as they were far enough down the pebbled driveway.

"They *are* kind of cute and helpless." Moxcy wrapped her hair away from her face.

"We shouldn't overinvest, yeah?" Bear warned.

"Says the man who just fixed the furnace for free."

"You don't wanna know what she was doing down there. I saved our lives."

"You and Nora work well together." The wind whipped her sable hair around her head. The clouds were low and gray, and the ocean in front of them looked cold and unforgiving.

"Stop."

"What? It's a fine partnership. I can't say that?" Moxcy looked up at him.

He walked a few more steps. The caution in her tone made him realize how much he'd been overreacting to their conversation.

"You can say that." His breath came out in misty puffs. "How are you and Yanne?" he asked.

"We're nothing. I mean, we got physical, of course."

"Moxcy!" Bear's voice rose. *When had they had time to do anything?*

"What? On the way to Costco, things got a little hot, okay? But she started telling me about her Cherokee ancestors—"

Bear rolled his eyes. "Say no more."

"Yeah, you know that Generikee shit dries me up. Plus, I agree with you."

"Whoa. You agree with me?"

"Crazy, huh? No, you were right, it's just too messy. This is our livelihood, and the livelihood of fifteen other people. And, after you told me that Stubbs walked in on you and Nora at Barton Cove, I realized that maybe you're not paranoid about that dam proposal, like probably they're gunning for you to fuck up in any way."

"Agreed, and I was thinking of setting Brandon up with them. He's a hell of an accountant, and they need some financial guardrails."

"No kidding. At the Costco, Yanne was checking the thread count of sheets. Like, excuse me, ma'am, this is a Wendy's."

"Nora bought a four-hundred-dollar duvet without even blinking. What even *is* a duvet?"

"It's a blanket for white people," Moxcy told him, "but you

sure you want to bring Brandon into this? I wouldn't. He's gonna go for Nora. I know you want to avoid messiness."

Bear stopped mid-stride. "What?"

"Nora's a certain type of man's fantasy, yeah? All that sweet shit she does? I told her I like sugar cookies once and she's had them at the house for two weeks. It's weird. She'll probably lie down and let you do whatever you want to her in bed while she thinks of England."

Bear said nothing and opened the passenger-side door, jerking the ice from the handle.

"I don't want to guess Brandon's sexual preferences." Bear pulled out of the drive. "Especially when it has nothing to do with being their accountant."

He was getting annoyed. He could sense it, but he couldn't stop it.

"It has *everything* to do with being their accountant. Mark my word, cousin. Nora's going to knock him on his ass. All that grannycore shit she does, body tight as a drum, *and* she's Black? Brandon's going to think she fell from heaven."

"Moxcy, Brandon's not . . . Brandon's not looking for—"

"What if he is?" Moxcy's eyebrow rose.

"He's not," Bear said in a clipped tone.

Now he was riled up, and Bear was entirely sure that Moxcy had intended it that way.

CHANTERELLE

NORA SPENT THE NEXT TWO WEEKS PLOWING THROUGH the list of contractors Ennis gave them—exterminators and plumbers and electricians and cleaners. At this rate, they could be living there in a week and a half. Maine still felt like a terrifyingly different place. In her many rides to Lowe's and Hannaford, Nora noticed everyone inexplicably had walking sticks, backpacks, and river shoes. *Where are they all coming from?* Even infants looked like L.L.Bean models. So far, being the only Black people for a hundred miles was . . . new, but not sinister. She and Yanne got curious stares at the store and even got their pictures taken in Orono for the local newspaper, but nothing felt unsafe.

Yanne yawned. "I'm starving and bored. I'm gonna grab a snack and wander around."

"No more Pat's Pizza." Yanne had become obsessed with Pat's because of their vintage booth jukeboxes and oversharing staff.

"It's so good, though." Yanne zipped up her jacket. It *was* dangerously good.

"Don't get lost," Nora said.

Yanne grabbed her purse. "There is *one* road."

Nora continued down her list of contractors. After two hours she had only one left.

She stopped on the small notation. She already recognized the strong, sure handwriting.

The best Kind of asshole. Mention my name ;-)

"Hello, is this Brandon Kern, CPA?"

"Who's asking?"

Okay, not starting off well.

"I'm, um, Nora, Shenora Dash. I wonder if you're taking on new clients."

"No." Nora heard the phone go dead. She laughed in surprise and dialed the number again.

"Yes?"

"I was told to mention Ennis Freeman?"

A deep sigh from the other end of the line.

"What do you need?"

How was this cactus man the best accountant Ennis knew? "Um, an accountant. We own Barton Cove."

"You sound Black."

Nora recoiled. "I am. Are you going to refuse me service?"

"No, sorry, I'm Black too. I was just . . . surprised."

"That a Black person could own property?"

"And be living in Maine in the woods," he said.

"So, can we set up an appointment?" Nora asked.

He was quiet for a long while. "Bear certainly has a sense of humor."

What in the hell? "If you don't want to come—"

"I didn't say that. Saturday, nine a.m."

Then the phone went silent.

Damn. He'd better be good; she didn't think she could put up with his personality even at the discount. The phone rang again, and Nora was sure he was calling back to cancel.

It was Yanne.

"Yes, Yanne?"

But it wasn't her sister's but a man's voice sounding frantic. "Are you 'Big Sissy Nora Bora'?"

Yanne saved the most ridiculous names in her phone. "Yes? Is there a problem? Why do you have my sister's phone?" Her throat tightened.

"Your sister's in the hospital."

TWENTY MINUTES LATER, NORA SLAMMED THE DOOR TO the Lyft and ran into the Penobscot Valley Hospital.

The nurse at the front desk was already waiting for her.

"I'm here for Maryanne Dash."

"Yes, she's in room 4C."

Nora burst through the double doors with her stomach in knots. This was all a terrible mistake. If Yanne was okay, they would take the next plane out of here and beg Felicia for the $200K deal back.

She opened the door to 4C and was surprised to see a man that looked like a live-action Gaston from *Beauty and the Beast*. He had thick, curly jet-black hair, cobalt eyes, and shoulders that looked like curtain rods. No, not Gaston. Superman. He looked like Superman.

"Excuse me, who are you?"

"Hi, Nora Bora." That smile was a killer. Maybe he was too. What had he done to her sister?

"Just Nora," she snapped. "What happened to her?"

"I'm Jon. I manage the Willow Bee, the resort in Bar Harbor."

She brushed his hand away. "Jon. What. Happened?"

"I stumbled upon Mary here—"

"Yanne, she goes by Yanne," Nora corrected. At seventeen, her sister decided she didn't want to be trapped in the "Madonna-whore cycle" that a name like Mary evoked, and had gone by Yanne ever since.

Jon continued, "I happened upon Yanne picking what she probably thought was a harmless chanterelle."

"Chanterelle?"

"Mushroom. But it was a highly poisonous jack-o'-lantern. It was only when she offered me some that I recognized her mistake. I tried to make her vomit. But she only bragged about not having a gag reflex."

"Oh, Yanne." Nora's shoulders shook as she threw herself at her sister's feet.

"They are going to keep her for a few days. They just needed to get fluid in her so she doesn't dehydrate. They pumped her stomach."

"They need to know she has sickle cell. Thank you for staying here for all of it."

"Of course. I wouldn't leave her alone. I—we—kind of bonded."

Oh lord. Nora could read the trouble in his eyes. He was halfway in love. She hadn't known Yanne to go for his type. Yanne was in a real spiritual cycle lately. She even cooled it with Moxcy. Which Nora was quietly grateful for.

After a few minutes, Yanne's eyes fluttered open. "Nora!"

"Yanne. What are you doing eating wild mushrooms?"

"I did a micro gig in an urban garden, and I thought I could spot the differences in mushrooms." Her voice was hoarse, and her lips were cracked and dry. "Where's—"

"I'm right here." Jon rushed to her side.

Why would Yanne be talking about you? She was probably about to ask for their mother.

"Yanne, do you remember Jon?" Nora asked.

Yanne's red eyes shimmered with tears. "Nora, yes, he was amazing." Her chin wobbled. "I think he saved my life." She reached for him. "I'm so thankful you were there."

He swooped over her like a soap opera husband. This all looked like a stage play to Nora. How could he look so devoted so quickly?

"So am I," Nora said. She felt out of place in her own sister's hospital room.

Jon and Yanne were looking at each other in the deep, unflinching way young lovers do. Nora suddenly felt like she was intruding on a moment. She took a seat at the corner and pulled out her library book as they chattered. She wanted to learn a little about stuttering, or what the book called fluency disorders, so she didn't feel like she was bombarding Ennis with a wall of words. He was clearly not having it.

"So, you two are the new owners of Barton Cove?" Jon asked. "Hell of a project." He was one of the first people not to laugh in their faces about it. "The place has a ton of potential, if you clean up the beach, clear a lot of land for activities." He leaned near Nora. He smelled like Philly cheesesteaks and something old and vaguely expensive. "I don't know if you know this, but it's become kind of a lovers' cove. The place has a lot of raw sexual energy. I suggested to Yanne that you all get a spiritual cleanser."

A flash of that man's testicles flipped through her mind. *Deep cleanser.* "I can see that."

"I think Barton Cove will never get over the local stigma, but you don't actually need locals to be successful. Not the best clientele, if you catch my drift."

Nora twisted her mouth. She didn't know the demographics of the area, but his statements held a vague classism wrapped in business sense that she'd heard in college when they were campaigning for a Whole Foods in College Park. This Jon sure didn't hold back. Yanne would like that.

"I want to help you all out in any way I can." He looked at Yanne longingly. *Wow, this man is a goner.* "We have more lodgers than we can manage at the Willow Bee and a wait list a mile long, so we'd love to set up a referral system if the standards are up to par."

Nora sat up. "Really?" With a wait list a mile long, they could be full this summer on Willow Bee referrals alone.

"Really. We would have to share some resources, like that amazing creek. The beachfront. But you'd never worry about having extra beds. You could divert your advertising budget to cozy little finishing touches."

Nora nodded but didn't accept right then. There was no such thing as a free lunch, and Jon was a little too keen on helping them. Didn't he own a much bigger inn?

When Nora got up to stretch her legs, Jon eased into the seat near the bed. Nora wanted to poke him with the IV pole.

This is my sister! Why are you still here?

Instead she took the other seat near the window and tried to doze off.

NORA WOKE TO THE SOUND OF CARDS FLIPPING.

"So what do the cards have in store, Yanne?" Jon leaned over the bed, his eyes suggestive. Nora never understood how people could go from zero to a hundred in a matter of hours.

"Maybe this is you. My Knight of Coins. Stable, good with money. Persistent, hardworking."

Jon laughed. "This guy sounds like my dad. Who else comes up?"

Yanne laughed and shuffled the deck again.

"Who is the man of my dreams?"

She pulled out a card, and the Knight of Coins flipped out again.

Yanne smiled. "I guess you're more like your dad than you thought."

Jon cut the deck and pulled out a card. The Moon. "Should someone be careful of lies and deceit?" Jon asked. "You know everyone is talking about you all working with Bear and his cousin." Nora's ears perked up. "Are you sure they are the best partners you could choose on Mount Desert Island? He's blocking a lot of progress in the area. They operate at a loss nearly every year. I know because they're always late paying me."

"Late payments are payments," Nora shot back, startling both Jon and Yanne. Her streak of protection felt strong and immediate, and it seemed to spring up from absolutely nowhere. If Ennis and Moxcy were lying to her, she would need more than a piece of cardstock to tell her what to do. And what did *blocking a lot of progress* mean?

Nora smiled weakly at Jon as he tucked the card back into the deck and sat back down near the corner of the room. Somehow, she was the third wheel, and she had no idea how it had happened. Yanne was great at beginnings, but Nora had a superpower too.

She could see the end of things.

ACCOUNTING AND
SHAKESPEARE

T WAS EIGHT FIFTY-EIGHT IN THE MORNING WHEN THE
door to Barton Cove shook with a police knock. Her sister was
being released from the hospital today after an extra day of observation, since her sickle cell complicated her treatment. The
small hospital made it a point to tell them that they had limited
expertise with Yanne's condition.

TL;DR: get sick someplace else next time.

Nora walked slowly to the door because there was a special
circle of hell for people who showed up early to someone's home.
And an even hotter circle for those who knocked loud enough
to make her stash her egg salad sandwich in a drawer. She
pulled her hair up in a quick ponytail and pushed open the heavy
door.

In an interesting turn of events, Brandon was damned handsome. Brown skin like rain on a clay track with a more than respectable fade. Shorter and broader than Ennis, not that she was comparing. But his face was open and expressive where Ennis's was cloudy and unreadable.

Not. That. She. Was. Comparing.

He had two books in one hand and a coffee in the other. There was even a roguish dimple in his cheek.

Cute.

If this coffee was any good, she was going to have to propose. He looked like the kind of man Nora would hurry up and like if she didn't already know that it would all come crashing to a halt.

He handed her the cup, and Nora noticed the tiny tremor in his hand. The way he looked at her with such clear unmuddied attraction—Nora had to bite back a thank-you.

Oh, honey, nothing is happening over here. Put those puppy dog eyes away.

She put the cup to her lips and took a long drag of the coffee, arching her back in a way she hoped he thought was cool and unbothered.

"Shit!" The boiling liquid burned her tongue, and Nora spit it out of her mouth. The volcanic stream dribbled down her shirt, and Brandon ripped out a napkin from his pocket and dragged it haphazardly across her face.

She had to slap his hand away to stop him from wiping.

"Sorry. It's hot." He fumbled with the books, and then they tumbled out of his hands.

Brandon folded the napkin back into his pocket and reached down for the books. "I like to get it extra hot because it takes me a while to get to it."

Whew, his body bent over getting books was a sight she could get used to. Were accountants supposed to have muscles?

Here's what you can expect when an unusually hot man with a boring job comes to your home:

1. He will offer to get between your spreadsheets.
2. He will pull out a tiny boom box from nowhere.
3. He will yank off his tear-away suit to reveal a stuffed Speedo and a thigh tattoo.

When none of that happened, Nora gestured toward the only two foldout chairs in the sitting room.

"Please thit down." Nora's scalded tongue was thick and clumsy.

Brandon crossed his legs in the chair. "Next time I bring coffee, I'll be sure to check the temperature." He raised his eyebrows.

So this is flirting? How did I get here? Did she even still remember the moves?

"Thir. I think I need an ambulanth."

Brandon straightened his tie. "Nah. You need ice."

Nora padded to the kitchen and let cool water run over her mouth and lips. She caught his embarrassed glances in her direction. He was younger than she thought he'd be. Much younger. A Black man in Maine was already more than she'd hoped to find, but to find one so damned eligible was a miracle.

Maybe she was being too hasty shutting him down.

He sifted through her books on the table and stopped at the stack on speech impediments. "Do you stutter?" he asked.

"Me? Um, no. I just checked out a few books about it. I wanted to understand it better."

"For Bear?" he asked.

Nora blinked and met his eyes, keeping her face inscrutable as stone. She was a master at giving away absolutely nothing.

After the video, she had to learn to never show her hand. Showing vulnerability was how they knew right where to stick you.

After too long a minute, Brandon let out a breath. His eyes lingered on the half-spilled coffee. He let the question and its implications deflate.

"Bear told me you're a runner. I actually remember your collegiate run. What happened to you? You just dropped off—"

"That was all such a long time ago," Nora interrupted. It was soft but final. Why did the conversation always make its way to track? Didn't people have better things to think about than sports nearly a decade ago? Nora thought of one of her dad's stories: how he, fifty years later, could remember the first and last names of kids from high school that tackled him and outran him on the football field. Memories were strange like that.

Brandon tsked. She could see him ticking away mentally for things to talk about. "So, I saw a Shakespeare book. I actually love the Bard. I played Othello in college—"

"I'm, um, not really into him." She laughed nervously. *Let's just get to accounting, champ.*

He made the tiniest little tick of distaste. Okay. He already found her too basic for Shakespeare. Maybe she should try to sound smart so he would want to work with her? This *was* a two-way interview. Ugh, but how would she keep that up? What if he wanted to talk accounting and Shakespeare every day?

"I watch a lot of reality TV. *Spinster Island.* Have you heard of it?"

"Oh, I don't own a TV."

That's it. He was definitely running back to Ennis to tell him she was dumb as a box of rocks. Nora saw she was losing him, so she grasped for something, anything else interesting. "I've practically memorized Michael Jordan's *Last Dance* documentary."

"You like MJ?"

"Oh, as an athlete, for sure. But he's just such a terrible *person*. The documentary is proof of that. How do you get so bad that Scottie Pippen doesn't like you? *Scottie. Pippen.*" Nora was about to dig into her ten-point anti–Michael Jordan treatise, when Brandon cut her off.

"To business then."

The lack of chemistry between them was surprising and made their conversation fizzle with the wet gurgles of a doused flame.

Nora flipped through the books he brought her: *So You Bought an Inn* and *Maine Parks and Recreation Summer Lodging List*.

Brandon pointed to the second book. "You have to get on this summer lodging list. People take it seriously, and if you're not in there, you're dead in the water."

"I want to be there then. How do we get on this list?"

"This late in the game? You're going to have to go right to the source. They have two expos a year, but they're practically impossible to get into."

"Practically?"

"Actually, very impossible. So let's focus on what's going well, shall we? You all have electricity, running water, and trapped racoons. That's a great first month."

"Nothing has been exactly cheap. We are watching our funds carefully, Brandon, but we have so much to do. We have people to hire, a payroll system to set up, advertising, and renovations, and we have to run a profit by Labor Day."

Brandon's face turned up in a frown. "Why? You'd be extremely lucky to break even in five years."

"We have to make a profit, or we lose it all."

"Someone has set you up on a fool's errand, Nora." His eyes kept traveling to the coffee stain at her collar. "I can set you up on a financial plan and monitor every penny. It might even be helpful to save a buck or two, but no CPA is going to make this place profitable in ten months."

"That'll be our job then."

VICTORY LAPS

SAME DAY

BRANDON DROPPED NORA OFF AT THE HOSPITAL, saving her a whopping fifty dollars during the surge pricing, but his words kept swimming around her head.

No CPA is going to make this place profitable in ten months.

She was exhausted, yet there was so much work to be done. She couldn't allow herself to think about what would happen if they couldn't follow through. Homelessness? Returning to DC to couch surf from friend to friend? She had to stay focused on her true north. Profit.

Brandon walked her to the door, and when he didn't leave, she walked in the cozy hospital room with him trailing behind her. Jon was *still* there. Didn't he have a successful resort to run?

But Yanne stood dragging an IV pole back and forth while he read from a tattered collection of Audre Lorde's poetry. The backlit hospital gown looked like an X-ray of Yanne's luscious figure.

"What the hell? I'm . . . who the hell is this?" Brandon looked like someone had knocked him upside the head with a rock.

"Are you having a stroke?" Nora waved her hand in front of his face.

Brandon turned around in deference to a modesty Yanne did not possess.

"Oh." Nora clucked. "Yanne, we can see through your hospital gown. Step away from the sun."

"'And I knew when I entered her I was / high wind in her forests hollow.'"

Jon's northern accent made the words seem strange and foreign, like when a teacher tries out the latest slang. It made Nora wince. But Yanne rubbed her chest with her Tarot deck and gave Nora a hopeless look. She ignored Brandon but stepped out of the sunlight.

"Yanne, this is our accountant, Brandon. Brandon, my sister, Maryanne Dash."

"Wait." Brandon turned around, still with ridiculously squeezed-shut eyes. "I didn't account for this little hospital stay. Do you have insurance?"

"Brandon, you can open your eyes," Yanne said. "I'm decent. First, nice to meet you."

Brandon turned around and looked at her then, as if still looking at the sun, quickly down at his feet. "It was nicer for me, I'm sure. Do you have insurance?"

"Dude. I have an IV in my wrist. Do we have to talk about this now?" Yanne looked appalled.

"That sounds like no. When the bill comes, I'll add it."

"How about we start with hello?" Yanne offered. She raised her wrist, and the tarot deck spilled to the floor. That persistent Knight of Coins card slid across the floor.

"Nora already introduced me." Brandon dropped down to collect the card.

"Whoa, whoa, I don't like people touching those. It changes the energy." Yanne snatched the card from his hand. Nora noticed him freeze a little at the contact.

"There is no *energy.*" He pushed his glasses up. "The tarot is like any other mathematical game of probability. I see they gave you a hot pack. Blood disorder? Is this a chronic condition? This will be important for accounting."

"Nora, who *is* this?" Yanne said.

How many times do they need to be introduced? Nora wondered.

"Yanne, this is Brandon." But Yanne was really asking, *Who the hell does he think he is*, a question Nora couldn't yet answer.

"Brandon Kern, bean counter." Jon slapped his back.

"Hello, Jon." Brandon looked from Nora to Yanne, then back to Jon. "I've got to get going."

"Nora, Maryanne, a pleasure." She noticed he'd left Jon out. His eyes lingered on Yanne's IV pole, then back to Nora. "I'll get us started." He closed the door behind himself.

"Ugh." Yanne and Jon's musical laughter filled the small room.

"Awkward as hell," Jon said. "He's always been like that. A Steve Urkel who hits the gym every once in a while. I went to high school with that guy, believe it or not."

Nora couldn't imagine this overgrown man-child in high school. But she needed him to leave his sentry post long enough for her and her sister to talk.

"Uh, Jon—"

"Oh, no problem if you like him, though," he said, quickly defending himself. "You two seem like a safe match."

"No, I wasn't going to say that." She paused for a moment. *What the hell was that supposed to mean?* "No, I'd like a moment to chat with my sister." When he didn't move, she raised her eyebrows. "Alone."

"Say no more, sister! I'll get us some lunch, and you two can gossip about the new men in your lives." He left with a wink.

Yanne looked at Nora. "How could you hire someone like that without me?"

"Ennis recommended him."

"Oh, *Ennis* recommended," Yanne chided Nora. "You're taking notes when Ennis speaks like he knows everything. Now you're hiring all of his cronies. Do you think he could be getting a kickback? Robbing us blind?"

"Wow, this is rich, coming from Ms. Divine Partnership Hot Hands, First Nations—"

"That was before I spoke with Jon, who's been around the block around here. He said we have to be careful of people trying to take advantage of us. You mentioned the police coming to our door and calling Bear by name. He has a history with the Five-O. Jon said—"

Nora cut her off. "You've known Jon for hours, and now he's making you question the only people who have offered us real help?"

"The help ain't for free."

"Why should it be for free? Yanne, we just talked about avoiding relationships last week."

"Nora, I wasn't the same person last week. I'm looking you in the eye and telling you I am transformed. I vomited and shit every old thing out of me, and all I have in me is Jon."

"It has been forty-eight hours. You can't be filled up with Jon."

"Nora. We"—she waggled her finger between them—"are not the same. I've never seen you feel *anything* deeply. Even when the video came out. You just . . . shut down. You used to run victory laps and blow kisses, but now you sit in quiet rooms and watch ASMR videos and have panic attacks if anyone mentions your past."

Nora blinked. "I didn't shut down. I was *upset*. Did I burn the whole school down? No."

"But you should have. You took the fall for everything. While Nathan has a degree and a new life in Arizona, you lost everything, and you were too afraid to be pissed!" Yanne's voice bounced around the hospital room.

Nora neatly folded Yanne's clothes into the day bag, and Yanne snatched it away and ripped the clothes out.

"I don't need you to make things neat. I need you to recognize that Jon and I are in love. It's not a distraction. It's not me taking my eyes off the prize, it was the universe knocking me upside the head."

Nora put a candy bar wrapper into the bin. "You said this about Moxcy just two weeks ago."

"God." Yanne shook her head. "You're so cynical, sis. It's sad."

"*I'm* fine, Yanne. *You're* the one in love every other day. And each time, you fight to convince me it's never-ending." Nora packed the bag again, this time with more force. She punched everything into the day bag and zipped it. Yanne wanted Nora to burn high and bright about every slight and injustice. Yanne felt the same level of exultant passions at the taste of a fresh blueberry muffin and during a moving poetry session. She had no gradients.

"Let's go, Yanne."

"Jon is taking me home." Yanne's chin tilted up.

"What?"

"He wants to show me something, and I don't want to rush back to that gross inn just to be bossed around by you and Ennis."

"Fine, Yanne. I'm going to go and single-handedly make sure we don't fall on our ass. You go be in love for the weekend."

"Are you mad, Nora?" Yanne stuck her neck out. "Slap me. Scream. Shake my shoulders! Anything but your holier-than-thou routine."

Jon opened the door holding two small pizza boxes and wearing a bright smile.

Nora snatched one and pushed past him without a word.

CARTOON BEAR

SAME DAY, EVENING

YANNE HAD ALREADY DUMPED HER.

But now she had an even bigger problem. *How am I getting back home?*

Her phone was dead, otherwise she would have called a Lyft for herself.

She sat in the waiting room for twenty minutes.

Should I ask Jon? That was the logical thing to do. He was here, and he had a car. He didn't seem like he would be put out by anything Yanne related. Yet an hour later when she saw him wheel Yanne out down the hallway with a goofy triumphant grin on his face, she couldn't ask. She hid behind a potted plant like a damn spy in a kids' movie.

In hour three, just as she wondered what it might be like to live at the hospital, she saw Ennis in some old Timberlands, worn Wranglers, and a thick skullcap, his chestnut hair spilling over the shoulders of his rust-colored Carhartt jacket.

Ennis scanned the waiting room and stopped when he saw her.

The feeling in the pit of her stomach was relief.

"Nora, there you are." His low voice carried across the room.

Nora pressed her hands to her chest. "Me?"

Ennis pursed his lips like he was trying to hold back a smile. "Of course, you."

The words rolled over her a bit differently. No big deal, just—different. Nora walked over to Ennis, her shoulders nearly touching her ears.

"You okay? You look tense, yeah?"

"No, I'm perfect. I'm perfect." In fact, she felt so brittle she could crack. Which was pretty standard for her lately.

"Your sister texted me asking me to come get you. She said to look behind the tall plants?"

He had a soft way of speaking that made everything seem like a request. He shouldn't be dragged into this disaster. He would regret getting into business with them. If she messed this up, both their business would tumble to the ground. "She should have come herself. I'm sorry she bothered you."

Ennis shoved his hands in his pockets. Swirled something invisible with the toe of his boot. "No, not at all. Not a bother."

They stepped outside, and she looked up at the clouds. They looked heavy and gray. Nora didn't want to spend the weekend trapped in the motel with TV dinners if it stormed here. She didn't even want to be *here*.

She wanted to go home.

Without Yanne, it washed over her just how impossible this was. Just how wrong and prideful she had been to accept it. That damned Balenciaga had possessed her. Her chin wobbled.

"Hey, hey, is everything okay?"

Nora swallowed back a sob as they made their way to his car. "It just seems like we're never going to pull this off in time."

"What you're trying to do is . . . ambitious." Ennis strapped himself in and turned to Nora. "But if anyone can do it, you can."

It was a while before he spoke again. "What are you reading?"

Oh shit.

"Oh it's, um . . . it's nothing. I—"

"You're being pretty sus right now, yeah? What is that, an Andrew Jackson devotional?"

Nora pushed the book deeper into her coat pocket, but then the flash cards she'd made slipped out of her hands.

"*And* notes!" Ennis smiled. "With a cartoon bear?" He looked closer and frowned. "That's my tattoo."

Nora pulled out the book and sighed. "I'm so sorry. We were just bombarding you with information last week, and I was reading this book . . ."

Ennis pulled over on the side of the road, looking genuinely troubled. Oh god, she'd embarrassed him. That was the last thing she wanted to do.

"I'm sorry. I just . . . I wanted to know more, and the book says that memorization and singing can help in speech confidence, so I'm making notes to the rhythm of a song."

The words fell out of her mouth like Ennis had been pulling them with a string.

Silence.

"What song?" was all he finally said.

"Uh, you have that Def Leppard bumper sticker, so I was using 'Pour Some Sugar on Me.'"

He made an impressed nod. "I'd love to hear it so far."

"Really?"

"Really." He rested his head on the steering wheel and turned his face toward her. The smile was easy, reaching his soulful brown eyes in slow motion.

Her jacket felt tight, and beads of sweat trickled down between her breasts. She cleared her throat.

"Step inside. Walk this way—"

"Oh god, this is going to be terrible," he said. Those big smooth shoulders shook with laughter even as he lifted his forehead from the steering wheel.

But now she was into it. Excited to show off her own cleverness. "You haven't heard the hook yet."

"Drop-offs are in the lob-bey." Nora strummed an imaginary guitar and kept going with what she had.

Ennis watched her entire performance with a straight face before he spoke. "This is probably the most thoughtful thing anyone has ever done for me."

"No, it's silly. I just have too much time on my hands."

"May I take these?" He took the index cards out of her hands. The cool pads of his fingers slipped over her knuckles. "Did you draw my tattoo yourself? This looks great."

Nora could slide between the cracks in the seat and die. He flipped through the cards, and she tried to reach for them, but he held them just out of reach. He fingered the drawing with his thumbs and slid them into his jacket pocket.

"I don't stutter all the time, you know. Just when I'm flustered."

"Oh, of course," Nora rushed to agree.

"Anyway, great idea," he said and sniffed. "You'd be a tight fit, though."

Nora's breath caught in her throat at his words and at the low register of his voice.

"It. It would be a tight fit." He squeezed the steering wheel until his knuckles were yellowish white. "My tour is already jam-packed. I'd have to make room."

After a moment, the car lurched into drive. And too soon, they were in front of her drab, dingy motel.

"We're here," Ennis coughed out. The temperature difference between the inside of the car and the growing cold outside fogged up the windows like they were hot-blooded teenagers. Nora twisted to her left to unfasten her seat belt just as Ennis reached over on his right to push open the door.

They collided so softly it felt like a hug. Nora's lips pressed into his warm neck as his nose nuzzled into the hollow of her collar. Something wild and irrational in her wanted him to wrap his arms around her. Complete the circle. She heard a tight whiff of air.

Does he have a cold? Wait . . . did he just smell me?

He drew back a millisecond before Nora did, but they both could feel that they had lingered a moment too long to feign innocence.

"Well, we're here," Nora repeated unnecessarily. *Get your shit and get out of this car, girl.*

"Yep." Ennis looked forward.

Nora grabbed her keys and exited the car. The cold snap of wind instantly made her teeth chatter. She slammed the door and waved. But Ennis made no move to go.

Was he one of those watch-you-enter guys? She was fighting with the key in the lock when she heard the car door slam and saw him approaching. His smooth stride made him look like he was moving slower than he was.

"Is it jammed?" he asked.

"I think it's sticking."

"Should I try?" He maneuvered her out of the way and shook the key into the lock until it gave up its futile fight. The door pushed open.

"There you are."

Nora reached for the handle mostly to give her hands something to do.

Ask him inside.

Don't you want to see where his tattoos end?

Show him a tight fit, Nora.

He eyed the doorknob too. Nora stepped inside with indecisive feet. Before she closed the door, she reached out for a handshake while he raised his hand for fist bump. It ended in a slow, limp, paper-covers-rock gesture.

Oh god. I am too awkward for words. Save yourself, Ennis. Nora nodded and made to close the door.

"Hey!" She startled at the volume. "Um, sorry, that was loud." He scuffed his foot on the ground. "Nora, do you still r-run?"

"Yeah. But I haven't scoped out a place here yet."

"I can show you some awesome trails. It's a great way to learn your land, and I'd be here—t-there with you. We could run together."

Together.

"I'm not practiced on this natural tread in the winter. I'll slow you up."

That blush crept up his neck again. "I'll, er, go as slow as you need me to."

"I want that . . . I mean, I want to." *Shenora Elizabeth Dash, get a fucking grip.* "That is, I'll be there."

"My next week is open or the week after," he shouted, sliding back into the car. "Get some gear!"

Nora closed the door so hard, it shook the interior walls. She stood against the cold metal of the hotel door wondering why Ennis smelled like cinnamon all the time.

JUST RUNNING

LMOST TWO WEEKS LATER, BEAR BLEW HIS WHISTLE and dismissed the exhausted students.

"Saturday morning. I'll be here. Eight a.m. I better see all of you, yeah?"

Pulling his gloves on, Bear was surprised to see the ardent stride of Brandon Kern approaching him as the kids dispersed.

"The lunch lady said you were out here," Brandon said.

"Betty's a security risk," Bear muttered. "Did you come here for a sprint?" Bear did two quick high knees.

"Ha! You're an old man now. I can't smoke you anymore without feeling guilty."

"You. Have. Never."

Brandon's laugh came out rusty. He looked nervous himself. "So I never told you the *whole* Nora story from a few weeks back."

"What more is there to tell?" Bear asked.

He's totally going to go for Nora. Moxcy's voice clattered around his head.

This is where Brandon told him that they had a date planned later in the week.

Good for them. Good.

"What's wrong with you?" Brandon squinted.

"What?" Bear looked around.

"You look like you're bracing for impact."

"Brandon, I'm in peak physical condition. Of course you think I'm flexing." Bear took a deep breath out to slow the jackrabbit pace of his heart. "Do you think you can help her?"

"Save money? Absolutely." Brandon kicked at the weeds poking up through the track.

"Then why is your face doing that thing?"

"What thing?"

"This little sad sigh thing," Bear said.

Brandon sighed again. "Well, I was surprised. She was a little, I don't know cold with me? Is she like that? Cold?"

Bear thought of sugar cookies, index cards, plump lips on his neck. But out of kindness to his friend, he only shrugged.

"Met her sister, though. Maryanne. She's like the total opposite. Soft and curvy, intelligent and lively." Brandon's voice went an octave lower.

Uh-oh.

"Good luck. Yeah?" Bear hid his smirk as he rubbed the bottom of his chin.

"No, I'm aware how ridiculous this sounds, but that woman looks like a damned *after* picture on those acne infomercials—"

"What?" Bear was going to start back up laughing again.

"You know what I mean. The after girls. They're all smooth skinned, they have their life back, big white smiles. She's *after* Proactiv."

Brandon, his severely rational friend, had lost his marbles. Yanne was MIA with a rich white man on most days. If his friend has set his sights on her, the poor bastard would need all the help he could get.

Bear breathed out, releasing the tightness in his chest. "Well, I'm glad you agreed to help them, Brandon."

Bear unlocked his car. "We're going to start running."

"You and I?"

"Nora and I." He didn't know why he was telling Brandon, but it felt like some kind of confession.

"Together?"

"Yeah, I went to check out her gear last week. She needs a few more layers for the cold but she's ready."

"Bear." Brandon pressed the button on his ridiculously expensive car. Probably pre-warming the seats or something bougie like that.

"Brandon?" Bear copied his tone.

"Um, that's dangerous, Bear." Brandon put his hand on the top of his car.

"What's dangerous? She needs to survey her own land. I need to run. Where's the danger?" Bear asked.

Brandon rested his hands on his hips. "Two reasons. One, we're getting into cuffing season. When the weather turns cold like this, you're gonna go looking for someplace warm to lay your head."

"I have a place to lay my head." Bear rolled his eyes.

"Do you, my brother? Because I've been thinking, it's about damned time that you got on with—"

"My life?" Bear finished. "Yes, I know what you think. But I *am* on with my life. This *is* my life."

"I read an article in the doctor's office about nonverbal

mimicry—makes people feel emotionally attuned with each other. You two, every day, pacing each other, breathing together—"

"It's just running."

"Running?" It was Brandon's turn to laugh. "Brother, I seriously don't think you saw the woman I saw in that house. *She's a five-alarm fire.* You'd be a goner by the post-run stretches."

"I'm *so* happy to be the recipient of *all* the knowledge you gather from magazines at the doctor's office or checkout line. But it's just a run."

Brandon squinted at Bear.

"What?" Bear turned up his collar, rubbing his hands until they were warm again. Brandon had a look that made him feel exposed, like he saw lies where Bear saw logic.

"It's not a crime to run with someone." Brandon eased into his car and rolled down the window. "But she's a nice woman, and you can't"—Brandon huffed—"until you fix your little mess. Let's leave it at that."

Another snap of anger. "We're business partners."

"I know. I'm not accusing you of anything. It's just the type of situation that can get dicey—fast."

NORA WAS UP AT FIVE THIRTY A.M. SHE LOOKED AT THE clock and decided that she couldn't go back to sleep. Little jolts of excitement kept popping her eyes open. It felt a little like the night before a track meet. It was just as well she couldn't sleep, because Yanne came stumbling into the motel room squealing with delight. Frantic kissing and smacking sounds bounced off the walls as a cloud of hands and elbows tumbled to the twin bed on the other side of the room. If Yanne thought she was going to screw in the bed next to her like a rude-ass college roommate, she had another thing coming.

Nora pulled the light switch. "Yanne, cut it out. I'm trying to sleep."

"Oh, sister mine!" Jon said between loud smacks. "Five thirty a.m. is the time to commune! Nora, you should really—"

"If you say the word 'radical' or 'acceptance,' five thirty in the morning is going to be your time of death," Nora said.

"I apologize, I really do." Yanne giggled underneath Jon. "But who can sleep amidst so much beauty?"

"Yanne." Nora directed her warning tone to her sister. They hadn't spoken much in two weeks. Yanne could fuck completely off for leaving her at the hospital. And for disappearing nearly every day with this large, unhinged cartoon character.

"Oh, Jon." Yanne read the trouble in her sister's tone. "I think you'd better go so I can get some rest." She pushed him off, eyeing Nora.

"I'll go, but I'll be back in four hours, and even then I'm pushing the limits of how long I can be away from you." Jon left the cramped hotel room with a grand flourish. "I shall return, milady."

Nora pushed the covers off her body, and Yanne was already mounting a defense.

"Nora, I know you're still pissed about the hospital, but I called Bear to come get you. It's not like I left you."

"You did, Yanne." Nora threw her feet over the edge of the bed and shoved them into her slippers.

Yanne pressed her palms together as if in prayer. "I made sure you had a way home."

"You. Left. And for a man you hadn't known for forty-eight hours. And you've been MIA for most of the time here." Nora stalked to the bathroom.

Nora pulled her hair up in a high ponytail so tight she had to retry three times to not give herself a headache.

"Wait, where are you going?" Yanne sat up.

"On a run." Nora slammed the bobby pins into the container.

"Gosh, you will find any excuse to punish yourself." Pulling the covers over her head, Yanne yawned. "Good night, Nora."

"Good morning, Yanne."

Yanne popped back up. "Wait. By yourself?"

Nora exhaled. Yanne would make too much of this. "Ennis is guiding me through the property."

The smirk came fast. "That big ol' Bear wants to guide something else through." Yanne punched her pillow.

"Yanne, we're just running."

"I'm not judging. I'm delighted. You've been too focused on the inn, and it's been hashtag BummerTown to hang out with you."

"I have one goal, which is making sure we don't lose our inheritance."

Yanne turned and yawned into her pillow. "'We may outrun with violent swiftness that which we run at, and lose by overrunning.'"

"You and Shakespeare are not off the hook. You need to step up, Yanne. Tell this Jon guy . . ." Yanne was already dozing.

Maybe it was for the better Yanne was asleep so she didn't see the pains Nora took getting ready. Finding a sports bra that didn't give her uniboob, finding a rose ChapStick, applying tinted BB cream and lemon-and-vanilla hand lotion. She curled the ends of her high ponytail and put the faintest coat of mascara on her lashes. Intellectually, she knew she was doing quite a bit of work to look effortless. But she told herself that she had to start to look the part of a business owner, even out for a run.

She was pacing in the dark when she heard the hum of a vehicle outside of the motel room.

Why her heart tumbled around in her chest was the greatest mystery. She snatched a look over at Yanne, then peeked out the door to see Ennis's ten-year-old sedan idling—one of those dependable models that never gave any trouble. Too bad she could never say that about any of the men she'd ever dated. That's all Nora wanted, a Honda Civic of a man.

The cold was biting, but Nora knew that she would heat up as she ran. So she only held her coat in her arms.

The car was so warm when she slid inside that Nora wanted to curl up and take another rest. Spicy cheap cologne curled around her.

"Good morning." His voice was still filled with the morning crackle.

Ennis wore a hoodie with jogger sweats—thankfully not those deadly grays that she and Yanne had dubbed Plantain Pants—and his big hands cradled a green smoothie. That seemed like a much better post-run snack than the microwavable mac and cheese she was planning when she got home. "Morning. I realize I never thanked you. First for the hospital and now—you've been running to get me quite a bit."

Ennis turned the engine. "It's no problem."

"No. You're not our personal chauffeur, and Yanne shouldn't have called you."

"Nora." Ennis pulled out of the driveway. "Are you aware that you are going to need a lot more help to get Barton Cove operational? If you are getting twisted up in knots for someone giving you a ride home, you're going to be a wreck by summer."

"I just don't want to—"

"You don't want to owe anyone. Only people who always pay their debts think like that."

"Yeah. I mean, doing what you said you were going to do is important to me," Nora said. "My father—" The crack in her voice betrayed the dull ache still grinding at her. If she tried to finish the sentence now, she would bawl all over his faded vinyl dash. She was nine again waiting in the church basement with her bright yellow dress on for the Valentine's Day father-daughter dance. She sat in that hot itchy dress for three hours waiting on that man. She ended up being forced into a pity slow dance with a senile deacon. Those were the memories of her father. Nora wished she had more, or that her few were better.

Ennis sucked in a breath slowly like he was taking a drag on a cigarette.

Does he do breathing exercises like me?

When the panic attacks started, her therapist had suggested a breathing series that was not unlike the slow breaths Ennis now took. What on earth would he have to be anxious about?

"Yanne told me you lost him recently," he finally said.

"What *hasn't* Yanne told you at this point?" Nora looked at him from under her lashes. "My dad, he just . . . broke so many promises. Including Barton Cove. It's another promise he didn't keep."

"That you're going to keep for him? I've made so many foolish promises, I have no room to take on anybody else's."

Nora wondered whom he had made promises to but checked her curiosity. "My dad was just living these splintered lives, lying to everyone, promising the moon and stars. It makes me wonder if he ever really loved us. Like, was it all a lie?"

Something sad flickered in his eyes. "Aren't you sometimes different things to different people?" His gaze on her was so piercing, like he needed her to know this. "It doesn't have to be a lie, who you are with someone else."

"No, I guess not." She didn't know why those quiet words made her feel better. But they rolled over her. A memory bubbled to the surface. Later that night after the dance, the smell of her father's cologne as she curled into him. Had he come that night? Memory was a tricky thing. But he had this smile. Toothpaste-commercial bright. And in her memory, that smile was for her. Maybe his cozy cologne and his smile didn't have to be a lie just because he had another family. But telling his daughter to pick out the prettiest dress because he was going to take her out and then never showing up, that was the offense. "It's the promises you make or break," she finally said.

"I think we can agree on that."

He looked away, then out toward the window. He didn't speak again until they reached Barton Cove.

ROOMFUL OF PASTRIES

I N THE PURPLISH, BITTER COLD MORNING, AFTER BRIEF
stretches, Nora and Bear eased wordlessly into a jog. She'd purchased three base layers and now she was starting to wish she
had worn all three. Nora kept pace with him where there was
room on the path, but as the path narrowed deeper into the
woods, she fell behind.

Ennis pointed to the ground. "This path is over a thousand
years old. My people and the Penobscot have been walking these
trails forever, and we've been guiding people through these
woods since before recorded history. You can see how excessive
fencing can cut these trails off." His breath puffed out in front of
him like steam off fresh bread.

Nora remembered how he and Moxcy had reacted when she
mentioned putting up fences. It seemed silly to do that now. Who
would she be keeping out, throwing up miles of fence? What
good would it do her or the environment to carve up the land?
Ennis seemed to know it like his own hand. He stepped over
roots that tripped her up and dipped just in time before low-
slung branches could smack him in the face. His way of knowing

seemed bottomless to her. Not just the land, but her furnace and the contractors. He was a library, the internet. She bet if she asked him something, anything, he'd know it.

She pointed to a briny patch. "What's that?"

"You have a real bad spot of poison ivy there. Even in the winter, if you touch the stems, you'll break out."

God, it was like a magic trick.

"What happens to lava when a volcano erupts underwater?"

"What?" He squinted. "Uh, well, it's actually kind of cool. They make pillow-shaped rocks—"

Nora slowly nodded like she gave a damn.

With the cover of tall trees, the winter wood grew darker. It occurred to Nora that she hadn't known Ennis that long either. Just two weeks before Yanne met Jon.

But she and her sister were different. Yanne didn't vet people. Old folks and aunties would always scold her, *Act like you got some sense.* Their own mother used to say Yanne was all heart, no sense. It wasn't a compliment. Sense was a way of understanding the implicit unwritten rules. To the people in that generation, acting like you didn't have sense could cost you your life.

Nora couldn't describe why she felt safe—more than safe, at ease—with Ennis, but she trusted her sense. The only gift she got from the aunties and grannies of the world.

They were in Nora's favorite part of a run, that instinctual meditative flow. Their footsteps hit the soft ground in unison; their breath plumed out in rhythm. It was as if there were some conductor twirling a baton behind one of these ancient oaks. They moved like music, an operatic concert with as many spectators as performers. She hardly felt the cold. She saw Ennis's strong back, noticed his excellent breathing and sure feet. His body was made to cut through the air.

He reversed course, and Nora followed suit. He was getting faster. Soon she would be in an all-out sprint, and her body was anticipating it. She had no idea how much she'd needed to give her body over to something more than worry and self-doubt.

She only heard twigs snapping and their rhythmic exhalations of breath. What a symphony of movement they were. The shoreline appeared in front of them, and she saw him power on. They were in full sprint now, arms pumping, legs hurtling toward the sunrise. Her breath came out in soft white puffs in front of her.

Nora's heart rate was drumming, and her muscles trembled. At the rocky shore now, they slowed. Then Ennis turned around, running backward to face her. He flexed his bicep in a showy flash of confidence. The thing about a run was that it never lied to you. You knew when you were running well. No one could fake that zone. Ennis slowed up.

Holy . . .

Strings, percussion. Music swell.

Nora's stomach dropped. The sunrise seemed to sit on his shoulder like a boom box he'd brought just for the run. His hair whipped in the wind, alternately painting streaks and tendrils across the sun.

Ennis Freeman was magnificent in the coral pinks and apricot oranges of the sunrise.

Magnificent was the only word that leapt into her mind. While her lungs expanded to their fullest and the sun rose over them and her head buzzed like fizzy water, she let his glittering eyes and dark ribbons of hair be magnificent.

Nora sighed and slowed down to do a forward bend. She was glad she'd agreed to this. A peaceful morning run won over arguing with Yanne.

"You kept up well. Maybe next time I won't hold back."

Nora shot him a glare just in time to see him pulling up the hem of his shirt to wipe his brow. Nora's lips separated long enough to let out a soft whoosh of air.

Damn, boy.

Sinewy muscles flexed and moved under his tan skin. He had a body like carved granite. She took strange pleasure in the solidity of him.

His earbuds fell out of his front shirt pocket as he readjusted his shirt.

Nora caught one, and the other one dropped to the rocky sand. "If you wanted to listen to music, you could have."

"I normally do, but I wanted to hear you."

"Hear me run?" She tilted her head.

"Hear your pace, your breathing. It helps me know if I'm going too fast or too slow." He fished for the other tiny bud in the sand.

She wanted to say she didn't need headphones because she heard a real live orchestra when he turned to face her. Movie-score violins. But the gesture was so quietly attentive that the words kept running over her. *I wanted to hear you.* She turned the earbud over in her fingers. Would he be that considerate at dinner—pulling out chairs and opening doors? Would he save her the last spoonful of creamy dessert in a candlelit restaurant? Would he be a thoughtful lover, sinking himself inside her, listening to her moans and taking cues from her gasps? She realized she was squeezing the earbud, then shoved it back into his hand before she cracked it with the sheer force of her Lisa Frank–Technicolor desperation. *Can this man do anything without you taking it sideways?*

"That was really considerate" was all she said. When Nora ran, she did it with the express purpose of not caring for anyone else. It would be hard for her to give up the reprieve of peace for a person she barely knew.

She fumbled for a new line of questioning.

"What do you normally like to listen to?" she asked.

"Movie soundtracks, lots of metal, R and B for cooldown."

Nora's eyes bounced from his mouth to his hands. "I like a lot of really brash hip-hop for running and slow jams for cooldown. I used to listen to this local DJ in DC who did a ton of really cool international mixes, but she got kind of famous so . . ."

Stop. Talking.

"Why don't you let me make you a playlist?"

Nora's face twisted. "I can't just trust my flow to *anybody*."

"Try me."

"Okay, I need to ask a couple of qualifying questions."

Ennis put his hand out and splayed his fingers over the sunlight beams. Like they were tangible things—shoelaces to tighten.

"Shoot," he said.

"Best sports film ever?"

"*Space Jam.*"

"Oh, sorry, the judges were looking for *Mighty Ducks One, Two,* and *Three.*"

Ennis slapped his chest. "Hit me again."

"What was the last thing that made you cry?"

"Rewatching *Smoke Signals.* That damn Jesuit basketball scene." She noticed how he made time for himself to speak using deliberate pauses and filler words.

"Partial credit."

"For which part?"

"We can't share our scoring rubric."

"What's my score?"

"Meh."

"'Meh' is not a score."

"But it's a vibe," Nora asserted. "You did well."

"But was it enough?"

"Yes. You passed, but barely. You *may* make me a running playlist."

Ennis folded his arms over his wide chest. "I *also* have extremely high standards for running . . ." He broke his cadence searching for the word. "Partners."

"No, you don't," Nora shot back.

"Okay. I don't." He gave up with an adorable shrug. "It just *seems* like I should?" Bear kicked a twisted curl of driftwood.

"Why don't you start now?"

"I only have one question. Jordan or LeBron?"

Nora sucked her teeth. "I can tell this is going to get ugly, due to your *Space Jam* reference, but LeBron."

Bear stopped in his tracks. "Wow. Wrong and loud about it. I really can't overstate how wrong you got that answer. This isn't looking good for you."

"How bad is it, doc?" Nora asked.

"Well, you're not allowed to touch my playlist for one. I am Spotify Lord, you are Spotify Serf." Nora smiled up at him, and he winked.

Winked. Like an old grandpa.

Nora—maybe drunk from the endorphins of the run—pinched his cheeks like a great-auntie. Between his old-man wink and her cheek pinching, they were Metamucilic.

Still laughing, Ennis pulled her into him in a surprisingly tender embrace. How did they get here? From *Mighty Ducks* to the first time she had been held so fondly by a man in a year and a half.

Did he feel this good because she was lonely?

He pulled away only slightly and walked to the car with his arm around her. "Can I tell you why you're wrong about Michael Jordan?"

"Nope. I said what I said."

Ennis fought valiantly for *Space Jam* the whole ride home. When they made it to the front of the motel, Ennis turned the car off and huffed. "In a way, *Space Jam* is a metaphor for life."

Nora rolled her eyes. "This is so fake deep."

"You're fake deep." Ennis wordlessly passed the green smoothie to her, and she took it.

Had he brought it for me all along? She didn't know why this did it, this tiny offering, but she slid down into the seat. It made her think she was capable of feeling something fierce and powerful for him.

At least for the smoothie.

"Thank you," Nora said. She tasted wheatgrass, cinnamon, avocado, and banana whipped up with a touch of rich yogurt.

Ennis watched her drink with a dumb smirk. "It's my special recipe. Marvin the Martian, I call it." His huge hand clamped down and shook her shoulder. He was an affectionate man. Touching her in ways that felt warm and friendly, not suggestive or slimy. Her stomach still flipped traitorously. No matter how friendly the touch, Nora didn't have a "friendly" response.

How did I fuck around and catch a vibe?

"Will we never escape *Space Jam* references?" Nora laughed.

"I am made up of hair conditioners, Icy Hot, and sports movie quotes. Take me or leave me."

Nora gripped the cup. "I'll take you, as long as you come with the Martian." She slurped ungraciously.

"Then, I-I'll make you one tomorrow."

Tomorrow. He would come again. It was the same line

Brandon had used, but while Brandon's suggestions slid right over her, Ennis's hint at tomorrow had her wiggling her toes in her sneakers. She was looking forward to something for the first time in . . . a while. Why did it feel like she just slid into Ennis like a silk sheet?

Record time, Nora. Four weeks and you're hearing symphonies. A snake of panic slithered around her stomach.

Here's what's bound to happen when you start acting like a Basic Bitch for a boy with bedroom eyes:

1. You start baking too much shit—pies and cakes and cookies—for him.
2. You try to stuff him like the witch at the end of "Hansel and Gretel" with your love (read: pies).
3. Then he realizes where he's seen your face before.
4. You're stuck in a hot house with a roomful of pastries (read: love) that nobody wants.

TL;DR: fix your face.

Sure, he was kinda dope right *now,* but all of that would fly out the window once he googled her and discovered he could see her ass for free without the pleasant conversation.

Come on, Nora, you know how this shit ends.

She did.

She pinched the side of her thigh to give herself the resting bitch face that had become her comfort.

She forced her smile down. He'd seen too much of her teeth in the past hour. She should have spent this morning hustling contractors or finding a landscaper. With Yanne's inconsistent attention, Nora didn't have time for symphonies and sunrises. Nodding in a way that she hoped meant business, she pulled on her coat and left the warmth of the car. "Thanks for the run, Ennis."

"Call me Bear," she heard him shout out the window. She shrugged her shoulders and waved goodbye.

Inside the hotel room, Nora cleaned nervously, stopping to hug herself and pin green smoothie recipes to her Pinterest board.

Her phone pinged and Nora clicked open the text.

> FYI the dry-cleaning bill for the estate's Balenciaga is $393

> Pay whenever you can.

Felicia must be fully delusional if she thought Nora would respond to this. Maybe she wasn't expecting a reply at all; maybe she just wanted to remind Nora that she was watching and waiting for her to fall on her face.

SEXUAL CLEANSING

A T BARTON COVE, YANNE AND JON RAN THROUGH THE upstairs room following a Reiki energist with sage as she *balanced the energies in the home.* Bear unwrapped a fried bologna and potato chip sandwich and tried not to SOS text Nora.

"I call in positivity and peace. I release the spirit of sexual rapaciousness that has pervaded this place." The tiny woman whisked past him, touching doorknobs and filling every room with smoke. She tripped over extension cords for Christmas lights and crushed candy canes as she marched through the house with the singular purpose of a general. Bear knew a medicine man that could smudge this house for fifty bucks and a pack of cigarettes, but Yanne had paid this woman a thousand dollars already, and this was only the first installment. *An intention-setting session*, the woman had called it. Now Brandon was on his way, perhaps smelling money wasting.

Bear had a to-do list a mile long, but in his head, he was already in tomorrow and the morning after that, running with Nora. He practiced the note cards she had given him and rewarded himself with the sketch of his tattoo she'd done. How long had she been looking at his tattoo? At him? Committing lines of his body to memory?

A dark brown hand slapped the crumbling countertop.

"Bear!"

Bear's head shot up.

"Bro, I've been calling you for two minutes," Brandon said.

"Oh damn, I didn't even hear you come in."

"Do you see this ridiculousness? What the hell is Reiki, and why is it three thousand dollars? She can patch up the floor upstairs for that cost."

Jon slipped into the room again and nodded to them both. Bear didn't like his face. Never had. Couldn't shake their debtor–creditor relationship out of his head. When he saw Jon, he only thought of what he owed, or where he was not allowed. That was white man's magic, he supposed—you look at them, and you see the boundaries of your power.

"Jon, how could you encourage this wasteful expense? You know they have to conserve," Brandon asked.

Jon slapped Brandon on the back, and Brandon ground his teeth.

"Oh, Brandon, if the energy isn't right, the whole endeavor won't work. This is essential."

Walking in with the Reiki mistress, Yanne wore a multicolored crochet dress with a wide brown belt. She seemed to dress like she was on her way to a folk music concert all the time. Brandon bowed to the woman and took the smudge.

"Thank you for your amazing work so far. We won't be needing any more cleansing." He nearly pushed the small woman out the door.

"What do you think you're doing?" Yanne took the sage from Brandon's hand.

"I'm saving you two grand." He yanked the sage again. "Does Nora know about this?"

"Uh-oh, he's going to tell your mom," Jon said. Was Bear overthinking, or was Jon instigating an altercation?

"Nora is not my mother." She turned to Brandon. "We are supposed to be partners, and you all are treating me like I report to her."

"She *has* made most of the financial decisions," Brandon pointed out.

"And she is stifling Yanne's personhood, her creativity. She says no to all of her creative ideas. Yanne just wants the home to feel like hers too," Jon said.

"Can she do that for less than three large?" Bear asked. Yanne narrowed her eyes to little green lasers.

Brandon seemed to think a minute, then relented. "I think you can." But his tone was softer.

"And all you do is agree with her, hoping she'll feel grateful." She pointed to Bear's sweats. "You can put your raging boner for Nora Dash away. She's never going to say yes to either one of you. 'No' was her first word, and it will probably be her last." She glared at Bear again, and Bear looked around in confusion.

"What did I do?" he protested.

"You're worse than him. 'Yes, Nora.' 'I agree, Nora.' 'She's so difficult, Nora.' 'Come run with me so I can see your titties bounce in that shirt, Nora.' Like, seriously, you've been so obvious from day one."

"Y-you don't know anything about running if you think it's about titties." Bear crunched into his sandwich. If anything, the ass and thighs were really the stars of the show.

"What conversation am I coming into?" Nora laughed, dragging heavy bags inside the house. Bear was at the door in an instant, taking the full bags from her reddened fingers and placing them on the counter.

"It was silly," Brandon said.

At the same time, Jon belted "Bouncing titties" in his booming operatic voice. When everyone turned to look at him, he shrugged. "Radical honesty."

"Nora, did you know there was a Reiki specialist coming to the home? A grand per session, of which your sister booked three?" Brandon said.

"Yanne." Nora looked so tired. "We talked about this. You can't be in charge of the 'vibe.' It doesn't mean anything, and it leaves me doing all of the real work. Get a refund."

She spoke with such a clang of finality that Bear felt bad for Yanne. Maybe he would find that medicine man and ask him for a favor.

But damn, Nora was stressed on all sides. The whole endeavor seemed to truly rest on her shoulders. He followed her into the front room, watching her unload the bag. She smelled like trees and mint. He followed her into a second room.

"I think this is going to be my bedroom," Nora said, stepping around the room in a lazy circle. He needed to ask before she got too preoccupied.

"Nora, I can see you still have a lot of the fundamentals of running down, and—"

"*Excuse* me?" Nora turned around to completely face him. He knew that would rile her up. He softened his voice with a smile.

"Okay," Bear said, dropping the bags and placing his hands up in surrender. "You know you're a mean machine, and I think it would be really cool if you came to talk to my team. We qualified for state, but we're not doing well on hurdles."

"I'd love to come."

"Oh, good." He let out a nervous chuckle. "I can help you come—er, no, I love that you want to come. I can help you. As in, driving you." The Reiki specialist missed some sexual energy over here.

Bear thought he heard groans in the kitchen. Was his voice carrying?

Nora, bless her laser focus on the house, had already shifted her attention. Bear feared she didn't need these morning sprints the way he did.

These runs with Nora were an essential part of his morning now. He spent sixteen hours a day, working six, sometimes seven, days a week, just to break even on the business. It was humbling and sometimes thankless. Plus, all the things he did in the community. Driving this uncle to the methadone clinic, changing that tire, taking one sick auntie a tray of fry bread. His time didn't belong to him.

But his mornings were his.

And he chose to greet the sun with Nora, who gave more than she took, hadn't tired yet of his stutter, and had googled terms the contractors used when she thought no one was looking.

His favorite part of the morning was after the run.

Sometimes the windows in the car would fog up so much while they talked that they couldn't see outside. He loved that feeling, like they had closed off the world. It was cold and hard and sharp out there in the real world, but in his old car, they were warm and soft and safe. He touched her more freely with the windows fogged up. Playful pulls at her high ponytail, gentle taps on her soft upper arm. Like he was trying to reassure himself that she was really there and with him. He'd followed her in a complete circle as she put things away from her giant hardware store bag. Somehow, they were back in the kitchen with everyone.

"Is that true, Bear?" Brandon was looking for backup.

"What?"

"Forget it, I know what he is gonna say anyway," Yanne dismissed him. "Jon is the only one who sees me like a woman." To Bear's surprise, she looked like she was close to tears. Brandon slowly dropped the smudge and looked to Bear like he might interject.

What the hell did I miss? He looked over at Nora, but she was bent over on her knees with a Hannaford's saver card scraping off the wax that the Reiki healer had dropped on the new floors.

The ass and thighs are the real stars of the show.

Punishment.

Yanne hurried out of the room. And once again Bear's attention snapped back into the current conversation.

When he looked up, every pair of eyes in the room was on him, quietly calling him on his bullshit.

SITUATIONSHIP

B EAR AND NORA SAT IN COMPANIONABLE SILENCE, soaking in the warmth of the car. As warm as it already was, Nora cranked it up to the max. No one is ever really prepared for a Maine winter, and Nora's frustration with her stiff limbs turned her onto incorporating yoga and meditation with their runs. The yoga *did* help with flexibility, but the meditation was just a bunch of heavy breathing. He handed her a Marvin the Martian smoothie, and she smiled that commercial smile. They had been running for a solid month together and she was hell on wheels.

"So, *friend*." He said the word with too much emphasis. Nothing to see here. "How is the roof coming along?"

"Great. Your guy is good. I think we're gonna come out under budget." Nora sipped the smoothie and made a face.

"Too much cinnamon," they both said in unison. He wished he could bottle this feeling right now. He had polished off the last of the birthday cupcakes she's made him this morning, and it made for a terrible run.

"I can't tell you how good it feels to run again," Nora said as she washed the taste of the smoothie out of her mouth with water.

"I need this" was all he said in response. It was awkward, but it was true. He needed to be here. It had become an essential part of his morning. Making Nora's shake, listening to a shared play-list, greeting the dawn with her—these were no longer choices for him. She was a blessed second wind in a race he had been flagging in.

He pulled open the glove compartment for mints or gum, but instead a slew of bills slipped out.

His stomach churned. Reality insisted on pushing in on his cozy perfect moments. Bear awkwardly reached for the bills, but Nora saw them.

"Whoa, that's a lot of paperwork," she said. "Is this your or-ganization system?" She reached for the envelopes splayed on her lap, and Bear pulled them out of her hands.

"These are very important, sorry," he rushed out. His body tightened up with tension.

"Lot of hospital stuff. Are you—"

"I'm fine, Nora." He flexed a bicep, hoping a show of silliness would make her roll her eyes or smile and forget what she saw.

"But those are addressed to you," she pressed.

"I-I'm the financially responsible party, so . . ." He was start-ing to get that viscous, churning, burning sensation.

"That's . . . a lot. On top of all the things you're trying to do with Sunshine Trails and your coaching?"

He shrugged and swallowed down sour bile. "I'm responsible for it, so I do it. But sometimes I need to breathe, which is why we should press play on this expensive-ass meditation app."

She pressed play and closed her eyes.

I'm responsible.

He gathered the bills, but they just kept slipping out of his hands. There were too many of them. This was too much.

"Breathe," the app demanded.

The more he gathered, the more envelopes slipped between his fingers. He remembered the woman's hair wrapped around his fist. Hair slipping through his fingers. In some recollections he was in his back seat, in others he was getting head in the bathroom of a bar. But they all ended the same. Absolute upheaval of his life and hers.

Three years ago, Lucinda Seal Neptune had lost everything because of him—because of his incredibly selfish acts. He had no right to sit and bask in the glow of running with another woman.

Nora wiggled her feet in the seat. She wasn't doing too well staying focused, and neither was he. The cabin of the car smelled like shea butter and Downy. They were gossamer light, these expanding threads between them, but he wouldn't deny their existence anymore.

"How long have you had this business? Is it . . . is it doing okay?" Great. Now Nora was getting nervous about their partnership. Nothing like a pile of bills to induce confidence in his business choices.

"Nora, the business is fine. Much better now, in fact. It did start off a little rough. I was playing catch-up for a while. I was young when I started to run it."

He flicked through the bills: hospitals, vendors, more hospitals, insurance. He had to admit it was a scary pile. He had taken them from Lu's apartment so that she didn't feel overwhelmed, but in truth he'd stashed them in the glove compartment because they overwhelmed *him*.

"Breathe and hold for four counts," the app gently reminded them.

Bear pressed his palm to the center of his chest. Heartburn roiled at his insides. His lies were physically painful to remember, drawing up acid and bile.

Three years ago, Bear had stayed with Lu as she breathed artificial breaths for weeks. Each breath she took felt stolen back then. He and Lu Neptune had been together since she was thirty-one and he was twenty-nine. Their relationship had been fun until it wasn't. When it ran its course, and it did *fast*, Bear had his breakup talking points written out on sticky notes, praying Lu would see which way the wind was blowing. And he wouldn't have to go through with his painful speech.

The breakup never came.

She'd applied for a position as a flight attendant on an airline based in California, and she got the job. It was a perfect moment to say, *Hey, it's been fun. Enjoy your life.* He was supposed to drop her off at the airport and have a mature talk, about how to repay her money—and how to end their flagging relationship. Instead, he had been chickenshit, or what Brandon called "avoidant."

So he ghosted her. In fact, he was at a bar fixated on the bubblegum-pink tongue of a tourist who liked his tattoos. He'd blown Lu off, and she'd had to take a cab for a red-eye flight at two in the morning.

That cab came, but it was too late. She was robbed and pushed into a curb by some meth-addled teenagers. She said she didn't remember her head hitting the concrete, but it must have. She seemed unharmed at first, but the next day she didn't wake up and couldn't be roused. For three weeks, she didn't. And Bear still remembered the terror of those nights, hoping she would wake up. When they finally caught the assholes, the public defenders claimed that she had fallen and had not been pushed.

When he finally saw the CCTV footage, Lu had fallen a full thirty-seven seconds after the boys sped off, sensible heel twisted in a storm grate. So her attackers got off scot-free.

She was alone and didn't even get the comfort of justice.

None of this would have happened if he had just been there. The guilt was inconceivable, combined with the fact that she had floated him money—two grand here, a thousand there, for business expenses. He was happy to take her money only to blow her off when she needed him. Her faith in him had cost her everything. Even now when he thought of himself sending her calls to voicemail three times while he encouraged a woman whose name and face he couldn't remember to "take it deeper down her throat." He burned with shame. The acid bubbled up in his gut.

"You can't breathe yesterday's breaths," the soothing voice of the app reminded him. "As you breathe in, try to focus on right now."

Right now?

Nora unrolled a bar of antacids from her fanny pack. She had taken to calling it an Ennis Emergency Kit since he ran so freely on the trail with her. Band-Aids, ointments, alcohol pads, sewing kit. She had everything in that neon fanny pack. Despite Nora's complaints about Maine being akin to Antarctica, the season had been mercifully mild so far, no nor'easters or twelve-inch snow dumps that forced them inside for weeks. Not that he would mind being trapped at Barton Cove with *this* woman to warm him.

"You may have GERD. Did you think of that?" She pressed his sternum. He held her hand over his chest and kept it there. Now, he breathed deeply.

Touch me, he begged silently. *Don't ever stop touching me.* He was doing absolutely everything to not drag her onto his lap, to pull her into a kiss that would melt these curled, peeling leather seats. She freed her hand and hastily closed her eyes, skittish as a colt.

He couldn't remember Nora not being here. How was it possible that he had just met her? Her knee bounced. The gold *S* on her necklace shimmered in the dim light. He reached out to touch her knee. When he was touching her, only the light came in. She kept saving him from his dark train of thought.

"You're shaking the car," he said.

"Sorry, I . . . I'm just thinking that, barring anything crazy happening, we just might pull this off, Bear. We just might get back to Maryland. We could buy our old house, have a place for my mom. We could show everyone that the 'other Dashes' can make it too."

Nora wanted to go so badly.

"I wouldn't depend on anything *not* crazy happening," Bear said. Something was always happening to change the trajectory. It was better to not fight the currents. He felt the cold curling around him. Nora wouldn't be here forever. What could he promise to make her stay, though? He had promised himself to exhaustion.

Lu had pulled through the robbery—nothing miraculous, just slow and steady healing, thank the Creator. He promised her he would stay with her until she was better. He said he would pay her medical bills. And pay her back all the money she had given him. He must have made a hundred wild promises, as racked with guilt as he was.

He had nursed her back to health and spoon-fed her in the hospital. Months flew by, then years. She never got truly better. By the time she began to gain mobility and independence, a landmark she hit nine months ago, it had started to feel like his life forever. Paying one bill this month. Paying Lu back little by little the next month. It would take him ten years to get solvent at this rate. Ten years to do right by Lu.

If he married her, he could pay Lu back in one fell swoop with the money from Thunderbear's trust.

All I have to do is give up on collegiate coaching and give up on Nora.

Or he could say yes to the river dam proposal.

He could take the forty pieces of silver from Maine Power and run. He could pay Lu back *and* have Nora.

All I have to do is sell the community out. Let them destroy the delicate ecosystem with a dam that would choke the Penobscot. All I have to do is give up.

BEST, BEAR

HAVE TO RUN A FEW ERRANDS BEFORE WE GET TO school. Do you mind?" Bear asked. Nora smoothed a curl in her ponytail, sudden anxiety about being in his home whipped up to a froth in her head. She kept thinking about how her life and his had crashed into each other without so much as a hiccup. Didn't it mean something? Was this a casual trip to his school or would his mom and dad be inside? What if his parents googled her? What if this was a huge community intervention to convince Bear to leave her the hell alone for his own good?

When he pulled up to a home, Nora tried to put on a casual, unaffected air.

"Is this . . . your house?" Nora asked. It was so . . . beige, and the size and shape of a cargo storage container. She'd never actually been inside of a trailer home.

"Yes," he said, already out of the car and turning the key. "I need to get some dinners that some aunties dropped off. Come in."

The front yard was strewn with river rock and no less than three Bigfoot statues. In place of a driveway, he had a towering canoe stand with the same Abenaki double curve carved into the wood that he had tattooed on his pecs.

When he pulled the door open, the house smelled like stale beer and garlic and tomatoes, and sure enough there were ten foil-covered plates piled on a nearby table. Bear's home was compact, a little musty, but organized. The furniture was mismatched, all from different decades ranging from the seventies to the nineties. The only thing from the twenty-first century in the house was a sixty-inch television taking up the entire wall. Underneath it, piles of VHS tapes and CDs littered the floor, each one meticulously labeled by date, meet name, and race length. She bet if she rummaged, she could find video of herself. Video she was proud of.

"Welcome to chez Bear." He whipped his arms around in a nonchalant welcome. The peeling linoleum he stood on creaked under his weight.

He popped into the bathroom, and Nora heard him pee. It was such a surprising thing to find intimacy in, but here it was. She imagined it could become one of the things women knew about their partner, one of those things like wet towels in the bathroom that wives and girlfriends roll their eyes about.

A pile of notes shoved underneath the plates caught Nora's attention.

Keep at it, Bear. We know it gets hard.

Proud of you!

What a man should be!

Geez, did this man save a busload of nuns? What was the deal?

After a quick hand wash, he scooped up as many plates as he could and Nora took the rest.

"Are these all for you?"

"Uh, yeah, but I give them away."

"Why?"

"I can't eat them." Bear looked away. "They give me terrible heartburn."

"No, I mean why are they sending you food?"

He looked impatient to leave. "Just some old stories about me people still believe."

If anyone here had embarrassing stories about Bear, she was all ears. She wiggled her eyebrows. "So, you're a legend and a saint?"

"No," he answered simply, sucking the humor out of the room. "I'm just a man." He said it with so much gravity that Nora was waiting for a flag to unfurl behind him.

They made two relatively straightforward visits to elders, but the third one went to hell fast.

A woman Bear called Elder Wilkes opened the door, then immediately slammed it in Bear's face.

Nora's brow creased. "Are we selling life insurance or something?"

"My grandfather's work," he told Nora. "He told me to watch out for Elder Wilkes. Every week I try, and every week it's the same fight."

"Why did your grandfather—"

He was silent for a moment. "P-people are complicated," he finally said. He said this a lot. Like she was too simple to understand nuance and complicated love. *My grandfather had a mistress* was not that hard to comprehend.

He knocked again.

"Bear, I said no, and you should respect what I say for once." The woman struggled at the door, but Bear had managed to wedge a foot inside.

"Auntie, I wanted you to meet my friend. And you're not being very hospitable."

"I don't believe you." But she loosened her grip on the door.

Ennis nudged Nora's side.

"Oh. Hi, nice to meet you, Ms. Wilkes," Nora said, smiling so big her cheeks touched her ears.

"Oh, this is the girl, huh?" she asked.

"What girl?" Bear said. Her eyes flitted to his. *Was he blushing?* Shit, her stomach tumbled around like shoes in the dryer.

"Well, you can come in. I've been needing someone to gossip with."

"Thank you." Nora nodded and handed the woman the plates.

"So you're the one Bear's running around quiet side with." The woman started in on Nora as soon as she stepped inside. "They say he's acting out of character." She looked at Bear. "Or maybe he's just now being himself," she mumbled. "Either way, you're gonna have a fight on your hands if you're expecting him to leave."

Nora held out the plates in confusion. "Leave where?"

"Here, girl. He's been talking big shit about being a coach. Talking like he talked ten years ago. When men get like this—restless—you know they're leaving."

Nora bit her lip and set the other trays down. She glanced at Bear, who was trying to fix a leak underneath the woman's sink.

Nora swallowed. So the whole town thought she was here to swoop up their golden boy? "Ennis is an amazing coach. I'm proud of him for following his dream. But that has nothing to do with me."

"He's going to let that power company dam up the river. Everybody suspects it. But what about the kids? What about Lu, poor girl? What about Basil?" The woman began to rattle off names and people and endless responsibilities. Wow.

How could he leave if any of these coaching positions called him back? There was no way this was healthy. His chronic indigestion was probably stress related. Nora wanted to breathe into a paper bag listening to that litany of work, and it wasn't even her responsibility.

"Whoa, whoa." Bear waved his hand. "Auntie, no one is dumping the community. You don't have to list my responsibilities. I am well aware of them."

"Is she?" Elder Wilkes tilted her chin at Nora. "And then you drive all around the rez with her on your arm to rub it in everyone's faces? You're just like Thunderbear."

"Here we go." Bear put the wrench away and pulled his jacket on.

"How?" Nora asked. She couldn't help it. Every bit of information about him felt like a step closer in a direction she didn't know she wanted to go.

"For one, Thunderbear used to walk around here proud as a peacock when he had a pretty woman on his arm. He'll be knocking on every door on the island here to show you off."

"I'm not showing off," Bear protested. "And I think we'll head out." Bear cut the woman off before she said something else. "We have to make it to practice so—"

"So half the island can see you?" She snorted with laughter. "If you want to end it, just be a man about it."

Okay, we are wading into to some real mess now. Nora was riveted. "If he wanted what to end?" All of his responsibilities to the community?

"Auntie, please." He cautioned a look at Nora.

"Yeah, Auntie, please." Nora pushed at Bear's shoulders as he tried to usher her out of the house. She wanted to hear everything this woman had to say. He said yes too often, and this sweet little woman was proving her point for her.

Elder Wilkes's eyes narrowed on Bear's shoulders, her hands on him. Bear looked like he was torn between wanting to pull Nora into him and wanting to yeet her into the Penobscot River.

"Has Bear always been there for everyone?" Nora sat down, and Bear immediately lifted her back up. The physical intimacy of the movement—hands on either side of her breasts under her armpits—made Elder Wilkes's eyes bounce between them. Nora wrestled to stay seated and hear more, and Bear gave a harder jerk that nearly launched Nora's wiggling body to the ceiling.

"We should get going," Bear said.

"If you want to talk to me about *any* Bear-related anything, please send it by Jennings." Nora smiled. But the woman's face was grave.

"Just know the truth has a way of popping up at the worst time, pretty girl."

BEAR GRIPPED THE STEERING WHEEL. THAT WAS A DIS-aster. Why *did* he bring her all around the rez? Was he soft-launching Nora subconsciously? Why couldn't he just tell everyone that he wasn't with Lu? That the perfect story he had let them believe about him was false?

Sure, the constant responsibility was exhausting, but only just now he could admit he was also *benefiting* from this narrative of perfection. Every auntie that patted his cheek, heaped praise on him, made him dinner—that feeling of acceptance and security was like a drug. He knew what it looked like to be on the outside of that. His father and his cousin Basil were both desperate for it. But telling the rez he and Lu weren't really together, that their relationship had warped into this strange transactional financial promise, would make him real. Make him his father. Could he fall that far? Did he even deserve his own happiness after what he'd done?

"Can I ask a really dumb question?" Nora interrupted his dark thoughts. "Are we in America? Is a reservation like its own country or—"

He covered his eyes. "Don't finish. Yes, a reservation is land held in trust by the federal government for Native Americans."

Nora hopped out of the car as soon as he stopped it, face flushed. "Oh god, Bear, I thought reservations were like the embassies we have in DC, like their own nations within."

"Don't feel stupid. In fact, we have a little time before the kids show up, so let's just ask each other stupid questions. Let me start with the basics. I *do* pay taxes. I *don't* have casino money. My Native percentage is *none* of your business. The reservation is my home, not a museum."

Nora lifted her chin, teeth chattering a bit from the bite of winter. She looked proud, like she got through that list unscathed. "I would never ask any of those."

"And traditional clothes are not a costume."

"Damn, I almost made it." Nora put her hands on her hips. "I'm sorry about that. I didn't know."

Bear waved her apology away.

"So, let me clear the air." Nora cleared her throat. "*I'm* good at sports. Me, Nora. *Not* Black people. I can't dance. I'm not *urban*. I'm from Montgomery County, Maryland. No, I *don't* know that other Black person you know, and you may not start sentences with 'girlfriend.'"

"Got it. Okay, start your questions." He clapped like a . . . well, like a coach.

"What do I call you?"

"Bear. I like it when—"

"No. Like, what do you call yourself? Do you call yourself Native American?"

"No."

"First Nations?"

"Ew." Bear wrinkled his nose.

"Tribesman?"

"Gross."

"Indigenous?" she offered.

"Sounds like a kind of fungus."

"Bear." Nora stomped her foot. "What can I call you?"

"Call me Abenaki," he said, holding her gaze.

She nodded.

It was his turn to ask questions. "Why do you take ten whole minutes before we run to lotion?"

"Did you just ask an African. American. About lotion?" She clapped between the words. "You don't have the time, sir."

"Should I call you African American?" Bear asked.

"Kind of a mouthful."

"Sista?"

"Don't."

"Girlfriend?" he teased.

Her eyes widened. "No" was all she said.

"Black?"

"Say it loud." Nora held up her fist.

"Do people really ask to touch your hair?" Bear asked.

"Yep, you?"

"Do *I* want to touch your hair? Yes." Bear winced at how thirsty that came out.

Nora looked down at her feet. "I meant, do people ask to touch your hair?"

"Oh. Always."

"But your hair is . . ." Nora paused. "Different. I . . . you can barely look away."

Bear smiled at her admission. "Do *you* want to touch my hair, Nora?"

Nora punched his arm, then took a tentative tug.

"You should let me braid this up," she suggested.

Bear froze. He *knew* she didn't, couldn't know. What it meant to braid a man's hair. But her words went off like a firework inside his chest. He looked at her then and just said it.

"Nora Dash, I would love for you to braid my hair one day." A flush of warmth under his clothes made him know it was the truth.

He had to be careful. He had to be much more careful than this. He thought of the old woman's eyes knocking between them. What were they doing that others seemed to pick up on so quickly? Whatever it was, they had to stop.

Something slow and soft was expanding between them like a marshmallow in the microwave. The harder he tried to bat it down, the stickier he got.

Damn that old woman. She was ruining a perfectly functioning work partnership.

FOLK.LORE

I T SEEMED LIKE A GOOD IDEA AT THE TIME WHEN BEAR had asked Nora to talk to his team. She was well trained, had perfect form, and a gentle approach. How often would his team get to learn from track superstars here in Maine? But now, all Bear could think of was what everyone would say. He had never seen so many eyes on him as he cruised down the main street. People twisted around like owls to peer at Nora in the passenger side.

His cousin Jennings was not helping Bear's reputation either. Every time he told a story from Barton Cove, he managed to make the whole thing sound like a letter to *Playboy*. But save a few perfectly explainable sleepless nights, what he and Nora had was entirely wholesome.

He had practically been living at Barton Cove these past few months. He wanted her to see the river and paths that made him. He wanted to see her run her hand across fenceposts and Bigfoot porch statues. Maybe she would come to understand him better in this place, learn him through osmosis—the way he had learned her at Barton.

Now on this blustery February day, he ushered bouncy teens into the heated indoor track on the other side of Oldtown. The walls were layered in peeling paint, some spots revealing patches of bare concrete beneath. He brought his team here every winter but suddenly, with Nora in tow, he was hyperaware of the spiderwebs stretching across the corners, their delicate threads swaying slightly when the heat noisily kicked on.

Can she relate to my kids?

That enormous cotton candy ponytail was pulled through the slot at the back of her hat. She wore a puffy jacket and three-hundred-dollar running shoes. Whether she meant to or not, she signaled comfort with money, a kind of natural ease with luxury that marked her as a visitor from another world. The kids were going to either think she was fake or only care about the sea of name brands in front of them. Indecision roiled within him.

This all suddenly seemed like a bad idea.

"Okay, here come the kids." She bounced excitedly, and Bear felt it necessary to give her fair warning.

"Now, they may be standoffish, but when they warm up, they are really great."

Nora started with introductions and drills. The kids only half listened, lazily running through cones. Then they all started to talk over her.

"Hey, I need your attention," she tried to speak over them. A few of them laughed, but they mostly ignored her.

Bear was going to have to step in here. He tried, but this may not have been a good idea for a lot of reasons. He was about to blow the whistle when James, his strongest runner, stepped out of the circle.

"Coach, why do you have us talking to your freaking cheerleader about track?" The kids started to laugh.

Your cheerleader. So this was the gossip.

Mari agreed. "She looks like a *commercial* for track." More laughter.

"This expensive-ass shit don't even look used."

"Hey!" Bear started.

"No." Nora put her hand to his chest, and eyes widened around them. Why had he never noticed how much they touched each other?

She pulled up her socks. "The kid is right." She popped her neck on either side.

"Kid?" James scoffed.

"Kid," Nora repeated, moving her hands to her pockets. "Why should you listen to me?" She pulled her ankles toward her butt in a quad stretch. "You like this gear? Anyone who beats me can have it."

The entire group laughed. "What if we all beat you?"

Nora looked down at the jacket, then her shoes. "Then you can have it all."

"Yo, this is about one G worth of clothes you have on."

"Split between you is about a hundred bucks each." Nora pointed out.

"Nora, you don't—" Bear started.

"Mr. Freeman." Nora angled her head toward the curve of the track. "Could you mark the finish?"

Her face was closed and predatory. While the kids laughed and took pictures of her outfit, Nora's eyes never left the marked finish.

"Yes, ma'am."

"Do you need me to start a stopwatch?" the equipment manager offered.

"That won't be necessary." Nora's gaze was far away. "Shall

we?" The kids were out of their minds with excitement. They were already making plans for their one hundred dollars. James offered to take the whole team out for Pat's Pizza. They walked toward the lanes laughing and high-fiving each other. None of them stretching, none of them taking it seriously.

He saw them lazily lining up along the lanes. Nora had taken the inside. He'd taught these dopes better than this. He *knew* he had.

"Oh god." Bear folded his arms and stood on his tiptoes.

"Why is she racing them?" the equipment manager asked.

"So they can shut up and learn from her."

He heard someone shout, "Go," and geez, those idiots tried. God help them; they tried. One tripped on his own laces, taking three other racers down; another one sputtered out after a few paces and pulled out an asthma inhaler. The rest were so far behind they couldn't read the Swoosh on the back of Nora's jacket.

When she was done, she turned around, running backward and blowing kisses. She even added his bicep flex to her victory lap.

It's my move!

She was in her zone. Power, playfulness, grace. She made it look so effortless. All hell broke loose inside of Bear's head. His stomach turned over like an engine.

Lord help me. I'm on fire for Nora Dash.

He elbowed the equipment manager. "That's my move!"

The assistant looked at him with raised eyebrows and patted his back. "Sure is, Mr. F." She sounded like she was placating a senile uncle.

Nora made her way back to the crowd of boys and girls to a rush of high fives. He heard her laughter booming across the field. To his surprise, the defeated kids weren't churlish. They crowded around Nora as well to laugh at the humiliation of

James, who clutched at his chest, and Mari, who pocketed her inhaler.

Bear broke into the crowd of kids, heroically tamping down the impulse to lift her up and hug her.

"I think this means you can come anytime you want to, Nora."

"Ohmygod, Ms. Dash, can you?"

"I would love to." She smiled. She said goodbye to the kids, who all dispersed at the end of practice.

"Do you mind signing a few forms?" Bear asked her. "Just some conduct stuff. I work with young people, so we have to be extra careful about who we bring here."

"What do I have to do?" She was radiating, and she looked so damned excited. He walked her back to his car, his body humming like he'd just run instead of her.

"It's literally no big deal. Don't talk to the kids about drugs or porn."

But she looked unsure, like that was exactly what she meant to talk to the kids about.

"Nora, it's no big deal. If you want to continue to come, we'll do a quick background check. . . ."

"I . . . actually, it's okay. I don't need to."

"Nora."

"Just today," she said with a sharp finality.

"Okay . . . whatever you want." Skittish about a background check? She didn't look like she'd killed a man in Reno just to watch him die.

Strange.

THAT NIGHT HE LAY IN BED STARING UP AT THE CEILING. That run would be a story told and retold. With Nora getting faster, the kids betting bigger until it was told at gatherings with the same combination of truth and exaggeration to bring the point home. She was already becoming folklore for him too. A story he kept telling himself over and over. He was a star player in desperate need of a trade to a new team, but the entire franchise's hopes rested on him to win the championship. The same kind of pressure LeBron felt when he moved to Miami. The difference between him and LeBron was that LeBron had the balls to go.

Why wouldn't she come every day? At first, she seemed excited, but it just fizzled suddenly. Did she have some crazy police record? He googled her name again, looking for an arrest history. Instead he found a link to a video entitled "Nasty Nora." From the GIFs, he knew this was something she wouldn't want him to see, something she didn't want him to know.

Damn.

This was enough to make someone skittish about background checks. How had she been living her life with this looming over her? How must people approach her? She must be surrounded by the long shadow of this.

When she wanted to talk about it, he would be here.

He would have a hell of a time getting that GIF out of his head. After a few quiet minutes, he realized after a decade-long feud and bad blood that ran deep, he knew only one person who could possibly help. His pain-in-the-ass cousin Basil had a very particular skill set that Nora needed desperately right now.

SAINT ENNIS

T WAS SOMEHOW *STILL* JANUARY IN MAINE. NORA AND
Yanne shivered in the back seat of the Lyft on the way to the
Chamber of Commerce Expo. The towering pine trees wore a
dusting of fluffy snow, their branches laden with delicate icicles
that shimmered in the moonlight as she rushed past them in the
car. When they stepped out on the harbor, the icy waters glis-
tened under the pale moon, while fishing boats and ice bumped
and groaned lazily. The lodge's roof was pitched and covered in
a thick layer of snow, with icicles hanging delicately along the
eaves. The sprawling lodge was lit in a warm glow and valets
buzzed around frantically at the entrance. The sound of laughter
and muffled conversation drifted through the crisp winter air
outside.

Damn, Nora wanted to be in someone's arms tonight.

Yanne had done that magic thing that she did. She picked out
a dress Nora would never pick up. It was tight, pocketless, and
uncomfortable, but Yanne had lost her mind when Nora put it on,
and no one—*no one*—was immune to that much flattery.

The dress was navy blue and mermaid cut, with long sleeves

and a high collar. To the naked eye it looked conservative. But the cutout at her left rib was a surprising show of skin, and it hugged her figure like it had been airbrushed on.

She wore her hair flat ironed in a soft-waved shaggy bob that danced on her shoulders.

"Fuck it up, sis!" Yanne snapped photos, and Nora snatched at the camera.

"Do *not* post those."

"I know the rules. But what a waste of a body. Lord, girl. You and Bear running and drinking grass every day is paying off."

Nora smoothed the front of her dress. When Yanne was right, the girl was right. Their runs had become as necessary to her as food and sleep. If he knew the depth of sadness he had dragged her from, if he knew how desperate she felt if he were one minute later than he was the day before, he would run in the opposite direction.

"Bear is going to absolutely eat you with a spoon tonight, Nora."

"Bear has his own work to do tonight and may not even notice me." She wished he would open up to her about what kept him so troubled and distracted. Whatever duty he was upholding was essential to him. And none of her business.

"Have you considered the possibility that Bear's codpiece may have a sprain? That Ogun's machete isn't working?" Yanne wiggled her index finger suggestively.

"Yanne, what are you talking about? He sees me every morning at six in sweats and a ponytail. Real people don't walk around with erections all day."

She folded her arms. "Well, this dress should change that."

"I'm not here to give anyone an erection. And believe it or not, neither are you."

"An erection sought is good, but given unsought is better!" Yanne nudged her.

Nora had no idea if Shakespeare had actually said that. Only Yanne could get her so sidetracked that they were talking about accidental erections. Nora rolled her eyes heavenward. "Okay, we need to get in this summer book before it's printed next month. And we should look nice doing it. That's all we're here to do."

Before Yanne walked away, Nora pulled her close. "You look lovely."

Yanne's long locs were down her back, and she wore a white dress with a dropped waist and handkerchief hem along with ostentatious blue paisley Doc Martens. Her skin looked radiant, her figure lush and inviting. Nora had to finally admit to herself that Yanne looked happier than she'd ever been. No matter how Nora felt about Jon, he was lighting a fire under Yanne to make her want to stay. It didn't hurt that he was well-connected and knowledgeable about the resort community. Maybe Nora could take it easy on him.

The expo was a strange combination of local vendors and state and regional government representatives in a sprawling complex housed on over seventy acres. It was the central hub of the region, where weddings, conferences, and all manner of events were held. Maybe she'd watched too much *Downton Abbey* or *Roots*, but in places this old and stately, Nora couldn't help but think of the servants that must have come and gone.

"Just what Bar Harbor needs, another inn," Jon said, introducing Yanne. Saying *Baaa Haa-baa* like that, he sounded like a braying sheep.

Yanne countered, "Oh hush, we're no competition for you. We're on the quiet side with no tourists!"

"Do *you* have a quiet side, sweet pea?" Cue laughter, rinse and repeat.

They were naturals. Yanne had been seriously underperforming as far as the renovations, but if she could make it up in terms of charm and access to the summer book, Nora would take it.

Everyone continued to swirl around Yanne and Jon as they rode on a wave of sexual innuendo. It was as if they were the hosts of the event rather than the Northern Maine Chamber of Commerce and Department of Recreation. Nora was all too happy to give this part of the work to Yanne.

The man who they had come here to charm chatted with Nora. "It can't be too much trouble to make a late edition. Your sister already emailed me the proof. I want to ask you about your food vendor." Yanne had made actual connections! Wheeled and dealt like a businesswoman. Yanne was a businesswoman!

Nora sat at a table with her nth glass of the pomegranate champagne. She felt a little outclassed by her sister. In truth, she was the one who hadn't been very much help tonight. Yanne had pulled it off for them, and they still had two hours left in the expo. And then, she saw him.

Ennis Freeman without his gray hoodie was a sight to behold. His hair was parted down the middle, and the blunt tips kissed at his gray lapels. He wore an actual suit, no tie, and a shirt unbuttoned so low he had to be trying to make a point. The pants fit his form like they had been tailored to his body. On his feet, of course, a pair of vintage gray Air Jordan 11s. It was funny how much she knew his body, could spot his smooth glide from the length of a football field. He moved through the world so effortlessly, like one of those long-legged pond skaters that walked over water. Even now he slipped through the crowd without breaking the surface tension. She saw Moxcy trailing behind him, also in a suit, dark red with a black shirt and tie. Her hair was shaved on the sides, which Nora only noticed because the rest of her hair was in a topknot. She wore dark sunglasses even though it was evening and they were inside. Moxcy saw her first.

She looked at Nora the way she always did, with a sly kind of suspicion. She let out a low whistle. "Damn, Nora, I didn't know you had clothes without three stripes down the leg."

"Very cute, Moxcy."

"How'd you get a ticket to this anyway? We had to suck a mile of dicks for one ticket that I had to palm and pass to Bear." She finger rolled her hands like a showy magician. Bear was taking his sweet time getting to them. He passed out flyers and shook hands, then finally strolled toward Nora.

Nora lifted a shoulder. "Are these tickets hard to get?"

At the sound of her voice, Bear's head snapped up like it was attached to a marionette string. From the tiny burst of shock in his eyes, Nora guessed he hadn't recognized her standing right next to him. His gaze slid from her eyes and moved down her frame slowly, stopping at the peek of brown skin at her ribs. His gaze slipped down her body like a heavy hand. He had few expressions and even fewer words. If he'd ever liked anything she'd worn before, she'd never known. But right now, his appreciation was unmistakable.

"Nora." Bear finally spoke and inclined his head in greeting. But words felt perfunctory. He had already said what he meant to say to her. The atmosphere was strange in the lodge. Thick with expectation. Like they were all waiting to scream *surprise* when the right person gave the signal. Every tight look Bear gave her, eating her alive in that dress, sent her the same signal.

All bets were off.

"Ennis." Moxcy pulled at her cousin's sleeve. "Do you hear me? I said they have those lobster tails you like."

Yanne snapped her fingers in and out of Nora's periphery. "We have to pass these pamphlets out." She pointed at the bags of Barton Cove leaflets they had printed.

"Yanne, why don't you and Jon do that?" Bear cocked his head. It was amazing how quickly Yanne and Bear's relationship had settled into sibling ribbing.

When Yanne pouted and pretended to scratch her eye with her middle finger, Bear added, "It would be the first finger you and Jon lifted for the inn."

"You think I buy your little Saint Ennis act?" She looked his outfit up and down. "You've got your nips out tonight. Button shortage in the Freeman residence, Bear?"

"Oh." Bear held his hands to his chest pretending to be shot, then nudged Yanne into Jon's arms. If Nora told him Yanne had already clinched the spot in the summer rec book, Bear would fall over.

When she turned back around, Moxcy was tasting food from three teetering sample plates. She looked like a squirrel storing up for the winter. Moxcy shoved a wineglass into Bear's hands, and he drank it like a frat boy taking shots.

"Are you all actually looking for a food vendor, Moxcy?" Nora asked.

Moxcy, cheeks filled with puff pastries, rolled her eyes. "Were you actually looking for meatballs at the Costco last week? Don't sample-shame me."

Moxcy went to offload her plates and returned with two more champagne glasses in her hand. "They're giving it away, dude." Moxcy was being very attentive to Bear's wine needs.

"Thank you, Moxcy." Bear pulled them both out of her hand and handed one to Nora.

He looked at her like he had a secret. Or like perhaps *she* had one and he knew it.

"Let me show you around the lodge, Nora. If you've never been here, there are quite a few beautiful rooms here."

She nodded, not speaking for fear that she would break whatever spell she was casting to keep his eyes so intent on her.

Moxcy returned with even more wine, this time blueberry.

"Drink up before they start to recognize me at the tables."

"Moxcy, this is quite enough." Bear's words were slower than usual.

Moxcy slapped her cousin's shoulder when she caught him looking at the smooth skin of Nora's rib cage. "Messy, yeah?" She looked at Bear now, and some knowledge passed between them.

Bear's telltale blush rushed up his chest, turning his umber skin purple in splotches. Nora's lips turned up at one corner. She liked this little open-book moment and how powerful she felt right now. She let the little currents of desire flare up into lightning.

Done sowing chaos like the little demigod of mischief that she was, Moxcy made her way back to the vendors' table, taking samples from every display until she was out of sight.

"I'd love for you to show me around here." It was half-question, half-command.

For a split second, he looked at her. His hands fidgeted until he wrapped his arm around her waist. Nora, god help her, liquefied at the center of her belly. She knew to an outsider it looked harmless—a man guiding a woman out of the ballroom and down the hall. But with his hand pressed over the cutout of her dress, the pads of his fingers brushing her rib cage, she felt a tremendous anticipation roll over her. The inevitability and palpability of their attraction rushed toward her like a truck—she saw the high beams but walked toward the danger anyway.

ADVANCED TRIGONOMETRY

SAME EVENING

ENNIS'S ARM AROUND HER WAIST WAS UNMOVING. IT was monumental, an ocean wave of a gesture, but few people even looked up from their glasses.

"Bear?" someone shouted with a question in their eye. She'd seen this man with Jon and Yanne. President of the chamber of commerce and leader of the Maine Power Dam Initiative. Michael Conners.

"Ennis, it's a pleasure to see you here." Michael slurred his words and shook Bear's hand in a limp wet tissue of a handshake. "So glad you could meet the new owners of Barton Cove. Jon tells us you are special girls." He nodded at Nora—eyes never lifting above her breasts.

Nora tilted her head down to find his eyes. *I'm up here, ass-hole.*

"We're special *women* and excited to be here." She smiled too wide. Trying to hide her own slight tipsiness.

Bear was *not* smiling. "You've gotten quite a few folks to vote yes with your dirty tactics, Conners. But some of us can't be bribed," Bear snapped.

Connors's neck popped up, and he met Nora's eyes. "Bear

here has some old-fashioned ideas about the dam project. Thinks we're going to use the Penobscot as a toilet, for goodness' sake."

"Just holding on to the last scraps of tribal sovereignty," Bear said.

Conners laughed awkwardly as Bear's true meaning flew over his head. "Just be smart, son. You don't want to get in over your skis." He reached out to touch Nora's shoulder, but Bear maneuvered her around him.

Bear slipped past the man without a benediction, holding so tightly to Nora that she had to take short breaths. It seemed like everyone wanted to use every waking second to remind him of the dam project and the money. She was starting to understand the extent of the pressure he must be operating under every day. Doing the right thing when the bribes, the money, and the easy road were right before him.

He finally spoke once they'd moved past the din of people. "How did you manage two tickets to this event? It was sold out before you all even moved here."

"Moxcy asked the same thing. Jon just gave them to us."

"He just gave . . ." Bear shook his head. "Nora, do you not know who Jon is?" He turned down a darkened hallway. It should have concerned Nora that they were going from brilliant, fluorescent light to smoky rooms and heavy shadows.

Nora's heels sank into the high-pile carpet. "My sister's idiot boyfriend?"

Ennis shook his head. "He's a Bradley—oldest money in Maine. He wants this dam project to go through, so just be careful with him."

"He's a huge environmentalist. Why would he want to cause so much damage? The pollution, the rotting plants, the flooding, the poor fish?"

"He's a capitalist before he's an environmentalist. I'm just telling you to watch out for him," Bear said.

Nora held his gaze. "He said the same thing about you."

Bear nodded as if confirming the warning. It *should* have concerned Nora that the din of people in the expo room began to fade away, and if she couldn't hear them, then maybe they wouldn't be able to hear her scream or moan.

He should stay away from me right now. She was feeling reckless and rootless, and that was a dangerous combination.

"But he's not just loaded, he's *connected.* Three years ago, he didn't even have an inn. But he got his cousin to agree to have his wedding here, and it put the Willow Bee on the map." Bear flashed her the photo from his phone. "It was the biggest thing to happen in the region for a while."

Nora's eyes widened. "Wait, I know her."

Ennis turned to look at the photo. "The bride?" He pushed open the heavy wooden double doors into a ballroom the size of a Walmart. It *should* have concerned Nora that he so carefully and quietly closed the doors behind him.

"That's Liza Bennett's sister. Janae the beauty queen."

Ennis tried every switch on the light panel until it was just about as dim as the hallway. Too dim to take in the detail of the room. The very thing he said he wanted to show her. He looked at the photo again. "You know *her?*"

Why'd he have to say it like that? Nora straightened her shoulders. "Well, I know their mom."

Ennis cocked his eyebrow.

"Really." Nora snatched the phone. "We used to buy homemade dresses from them. They could all sew."

Bear walked to the middle of the ballroom and hooked his

index finger with her own and gently tugged her along with him. "That's adorable that you wore homemade dresses," he said.

"No, we were the worst kids. We hated those things. My mom bought them because the Bennetts had it pretty rough. She called it 'charity with dignity.' We thought we were so damned wealthy. Now Janae Bennett-Bradley could buy and sell my ass."

"You should text her." Bear shrugged

"Are you insane?" Nora's head was buzzing with possibility— or maybe just buzzing.

"No, really, you should text her, tell her about your business, and ask her to come down."

"She's going to ignore me," Nora said.

"She's i-ignoring you now."

Nora pulled out her phone and scrolled down to the Instagram image of Janae's perfect face and her perfect life. She clicked on the message icon and typed.

"Bear! I can't believe I'm doing this!"

He gave her the thumbs-up.

Dear Janae ur soo beautiful like soo pretty.

I'm in Maine!!! let's be black together up here amiright?

Also come live at my place!

"Nora, wait, let me check it." Bear touched her elbow. "You're going to wish you spell-checked that."

"Done." Nora clicked send. "Now she can ignore me with purpose."

"You're kind of hard to ignore," Bear said.

Nora's mouth twisted in disbelief. "Okay, your check's in the mail." She had to keep talking. Right now, silence was deadly. If she kept babbling, she wouldn't notice the soft romance and old-world elegance of the space and how her shoes made dramatic clicks across the starburst-patterned wood floor.

The room was dim with spherical ballroom sconces creating a warm glow. Bear looked down at her, and his hair spread like a privacy curtain on either side of them. "I mean it, poor little rich girl."

Nora looked down. He was so close. If she tilted her head up, she would meet his mouth. It was strange. She was alone with Bear all the time. But this felt wholly different, and her heart could tell the difference, too, drumming out of her chest like it wanted out. In this light with only them, it didn't feel so impossible that they could be together. The video and all of that ugliness felt so small compared to her growing sense of safety and affection toward him. Maybe she could tell him and he wouldn't run.

"Well, we're running through the last of our inheritance money," she said. "When our dad died, things . . . changed."

Ennis nodded. "My dad won the lottery."

"What?" Nora couldn't help the laugh that came out with the question.

"Yes, my dad found the most ridiculous way to get rich I've ever heard of. By being one of sixty-seven people to win a small jackpot. It was enough to buy a big ugly house and an inflated sense of his business acumen."

His fingers grazed her belly as he pulled at her lanyard and pointed at the printed words:

Shenora Dash
Proprietor, Barton Cove Inn

"How does it feel to be a successful business owner?" Bear asked.

"You tell me. People of the Dawn Sunshine Trails has a ton of five-star reviews. Everyone in this town trusts you. You're well-connected."

He still hadn't let go of the lanyard and playfully tugged at it. Bringing her, in a way that could *not* be denied, too close.

Another swig.

"You seem to be even better connected." Bear shook his phone. He seemed satisfied with their proximity because he finally let the lanyard drop. "If you could get that beauty queen to stay at Barton Cove, you would be the *it* destination in Maine."

She noted the way his shirt gaped open when he placed his phone in his jacket pocket. His smooth expanse of skin, perfect with peeks of a jet-black tattoo crawling across his pecs.

She shook her head. "No way." Janae Bennett-Bradley would never set foot in their place. She was all glamour. Their vibe was rustic. It would be a miracle. Nora laughed again, and the sound echoed in the vast ballroom. Reminding her once again that they were alone in the dark.

This was Bear's power: endless silence and ruthless, merciless patience. Create the environment—a grand old ballroom, lighting so dim it could have been candles, the hint of tattoos peeking out of a crisp white shirt, that defined mouth always holding back a grin—and watch Nora crumble.

And she *was* crumbling. As evidence, she took another drink of champagne and with shaking fingers almost missed her mouth.

Ennis threw back his head and downed his wine in one gulp and grimaced at the bitter taste.

"This wine is terrible. I hate events like this. I hate dressing like this. This jacket is my younger cousin's, so at least it was free, but it's so damned tight. I feel like I'm hulking out."

"Take it off. You can still wear it over your forearm and look like a gentleman."

Nora gestured down her body. "This dress cost money *and* it's terrible."

"Whoa, whoa. What's wrong with *this* dress?" Bear looked genuinely concerned.

"Look." She smoothed the sides of her hips.

He looked too. Following the trail of her hands with his eyes, squinting a little in concentration. Nora patted her hips. "No pockets. Also, it doesn't give me a full range of motion."

"No range of motion, no pockets. Take it off. Just wear it over your forearm." He said this without any sly flirtatious winks or wry smiles. But the way he whispered *Take it off* made it sound like a pleading request.

Nora was suddenly overly aware of the scar that interrupted the perfect lines of his mouth at the corner. His lips parted, then closed.

What are you trying to say, Bear?

He reached for Nora's hand and put it to his chest.

Her universe narrowed down to the feel of her hot palm against his body, the cool cotton of his shirt, the hardened pebble of his nipple, and a wildly beating heart. Once again, his body spoke when he couldn't.

"I'm nervous," he whispered, chuckling a bit. "I'm out of my league, fucking out of my mind with . . ." He trailed off. Bear was so close his breath tickled her lashes and made the hair on her neck rise. He took deep breaths in and out. "This is how I keep myself from stuttering."

Nora's throat was dry. *Out of his mind with what?* "So, breathing helps with it."

"And touch." His eyes fluttered open.

Those deep, dark eyes were pulling her in. It could have been the pomegranate champagne, but she felt light-headed and soft. She tilted her head slightly, unconsciously giving him access to her neck. It surprised her how much she wanted to submit to something. To be overcome with something. Could she let Yanne be right? Yanne's passionate way of rolling over the world felt so good. But the results always cost more than she could afford. But right now, with Bear's chest rising and falling beneath her palm and his mouth so close, she wanted to see the world like Yanne did. So she tilted her chin and rose on her tiptoes. Bear sighed as his hand rose to cradle the back of her head.

God, how can hands that rough be so soft against my neck? Yesterday morning he was ripping bark off the trees with his bare hands for canoe siding, and tonight he held her tiny face with the delicate appreciation of a fine jeweler.

"I feel funny," Bear said. "Do you feel that?"

She did. A freight train motoring through her belly. He traced a tender kiss up her neck. One, then two. Her body arched under his mouth, and she let out a soft whimper. Oh, she felt that. Hot ribbons of desire unfurled from her belly.

He pulled back then, and for a second Nora thought she'd done something wrong. He looked her in the eyes again.

"Is this too much?" he asked.

The question was absolutely absurd, and she shook her head. "Not enough."

His eyes creased like he couldn't believe what he'd heard. he looked so pained.

Why?

Kiss me.

Touch me, Bear.

Fuck my mouth and pull my hair.

Do something . . .

"If I kiss you, I'm afraid I won't know how to stop," he said softly.

"Then don't," Nora said, half-delirious, but it felt true. What was he warring against? What was he fighting? If he waited long enough she, too, would think of all the reasons this was incredibly stupid. She pulled away slightly, then he snatched her back. "Fuck it."

His mouth caught hers, and Nora's knees buckled. She felt like one of those fish, swept up by a bald eagle right out of the river, gasping in surprise, unaware of their fate, and rising to dizzying heights. Her neck bowed back at the intensity of his body's crush. His mouth opened over hers, and he tasted her murmurings and sighs. His hot, slick tongue met hers, and she moaned again with the contact. The kiss was so deep and so fast that Nora didn't have time to do anything but respond. His body demanded the truth from her right now, and she wanted to give it to him. His kiss was as impatient as Nora felt. Restraint had been choking her, or her dress was too damn tight. What could she ask of him now? Could he rip away everything that constrained her?

His hands cupped either side of her face, and he pulled away from the kiss just to whisper, "You're so soft." The reverence and rasp in his voice made her heart split. "I bet you're soft everywhere."

And then his mouth was on hers again. His hands slid down her body and up again, lingering on that exposed swath of skin, then lower, moving over the plump curve of her ass and pushing her into him so she could feel his huge erection. He let out a low-decibel groan that vibrated in her chest.

His hair fanned through her fingers as she ran them across his head.

Finally.

It slipped through her hands like heavy silk. Then she pulled it, just enough to get his attention.

It was his turn to gasp in pleasure, and Nora devoured his mouth. She felt Bear everywhere. His tongue, his hair sliding between her fingers, his lips, his teeth, his hands, his smoky cologne, his dick against her belly harder than advanced trigonometry.

He pulled away one more time from the kiss and eyed the doors and exits. She knew that desperate darting—he was looking for a closet, an alcove, a dark enough corner so they could soothe this burning ache. How would he feel pushing inside of her? Would he tell her to put her hands on the wall while he pulled her dress up to her hips? Would he reach for her neck as he pummeled her from behind? She could find out tonight. She spread her hands over his chest and was rewarded with another thunderous kiss. There was a moment in the kiss in which shit got real, when the kiss shifted from exploratory and tentative to a clinging and grasping prelude to sex. The way he crushed her to his body, squeezing her ass and thighs. The way his tongue slid over hers, the way she kept gasping with the newfound pleasure of his hands on her. Nora had the scandalizing thrill of a thought that if they didn't find a closet, they would fuck on this polished ballroom floor. He searched the back of her dress for a zipper. She had never wanted out of a dress so much in her life.

"Take it off me," she begged.

"Yes, ma'am," he whispered hoarsely into her shoulder.

He peeled one side off her shoulders, and she groped the front of his trousers, massaging his thickness with a feverish purpose. She had finally got her hands around this fucking fire hose. She would suck the soul out of this man if he let her.

When the lights came on, Nora was in such a state that it didn't register. When the haughty voice of a tour guide rolled over her, they each jerked apart like the other was made of acid. Their breathing was still elevated, but they stared at each other in shared disbelief and slowly cooling desire.

What in the hell is wrong with me?

"Nora? Bear?" She heard Moxcy exclaim and Yanne laugh.

"As you can see, the grand ballroom, long a hot destination for weddings, attracts lovers from everywhere." The party's muffled laughter made Nora's stomach turn. She hated being on display. She hated the looks in their eyes, like they had seen her naked. Like they knew about the video. As much as she tried to run from her, Nora *was* that woman in the video. An easy lay that would have let a man fuck her on the floor of a public building because it felt good temporarily.

This is what "thinking like Yanne" got her. Every. Damned. Time. Her throat tightened, and the room was spinning. Where was her breath? There was no air. She clawed at her throat. The room full of eyes was too much, and Nora pushed herself fully out of Bear's grasp and ran toward the exit.

LOVE WITHOUT DUTY

SAME EVENING

BEAR FOLLOWED HER, YANNE AND MOXCY TRAILING behind him. Nora collected her breath in the stairwell.

He knelt down and reached for her hand, but she moved it out of his reach. She looked scared. Terrified.

Yanne brushed passed him with the Willow Bee owner attached at the hip.

"I knew it. I knew your dick wasn't broken!" Yanne's shoulders shook. She looked either drunk or high, and so did Jon. "I hope you know, Saint Ennis, the whole assembly saw you getting milked by my—" She was all laughs until she saw her sister.

"Nora? Whoa. Okay, okay. It's happening. You're okay."

Nora reached for her sister. Bear inched farther away. She looked like she was in the grips of a panic attack.

Moxcy grabbed a bottle of water. "Bear, what the hell happened? Were you kissing her or sucking her soul out? You seriously looked like a vampire."

"I—we . . ."

"Never mind." Moxcy threw him the bottle of water, and he caught Nora's eyes.

God, she looked frightened.

He had come on *way* too strong.

It's all too much. You need too much.

He just needed too much from people. It was safer to not expect people to meet your needs, especially when they were excessive. The rate that he thought about Nora—how much he had wanted to taste her—it was too much. And this was a wake-up call.

"Moxcy, let's head out."

"Holy shit, Bear." Brandon pulled the stairwell door open and made the exploding head symbol with his hands.

When had Brandon gotten here?

"Bear, Nora, what the hell?" Brandon sounded like he didn't know whom to scold. Bear turned his friend and his cousin back toward the door. "We're going to give them some privacy. Are we ready to go?"

"Wait. We didn't even go to all of the exhibits. It took a lot to get in here."

When Bear shook his head, she pouted. "There's a cake section!"

"Okay, let's have cake." Bear pushed Moxcy back into the grand ballroom, where lingering partygoers looked up and smiled knowingly at him.

Brandon's posture was rigid. *Shit.* Was he interested in Nora? Was he hoping to be with her?

"Look, Brandon, I thought you and Nora didn't really hit it off romantically—"

Brandon rounded on him. "Bear, I told you to fix your shit before you made a mess."

"Oh."

"Oh," Brandon repeated sardonically. "I pegged Nora for you on day one. You have been lying to me since November, Bear—"

Moxcy cut him off and patted her cousin on the back and exhaled. "Give him a break, Brandon. That blue dress was a winning hand."

Bear had lost all of his joviality for the night. His head was pounding, and his balls were so tight he could sing soprano. He was also irrationally pissed at Brandon.

"Brandon, we—I . . ." Bear's shoulders sagged. "I'm just as surprised as you are, I swear. We weren't sneaking around. This was the first t-t-time I've ever touched—"

Moxcy and Brandon laughed. "So, you're doubling down," Brandon said.

Moxcy folded her arms. "Bear, you can fool a lot of people. But *I* know what it looks like when someone's taken a few rides in the rental. You knew where all the knobs and buttons were."

"How can you be this loud and this wrong at the same time?" Bear had been an absolute Boy Scout where Nora was concerned. But even *he* had to marvel at how well he knew her body. How he'd unconsciously anticipated her next moves. Even she, tugging at his hair like that and giving him tiny little demands— she knew, or was making damned good guesses about what he liked. Damn, they were moving like one.

"Get your cake. I'll be waiting in the car."

MOXCY SLAMMED THE DOOR OF THE CAR, JOSTLING HER tower of pastries.

"Did you need to walk out with all of that?"

"You can stop with the holier-than-thou bit, cuz. I just walked in on some next-level nasty shit. Did you ask if *I'm* okay?"

"It was a kiss, not the sinking of the *Titanic*, Moxcy."

"A kiss? What I saw in there? She needs a full-blown pregnancy test."

"Moxcy. You have made your point."

"No, I haven't. You're going to hurt people, including yourself, if you keep on like this. These three months have been hard to watch."

"Don't you think you're being a bit dramatic?"

"You put on cologne at five a.m. to run." She held up her index finger. "You're lost in thought all the time. I have to call your name three times to get your attention. If you think you're hiding it, you're not."

"Don't think I didn't notice you and Yanne feeding us all of that wine, Moxcy. Don't turn this into something it's not."

"It wasn't just me that saw you. The entire party saw you. This could be on social media. Lu could be looking at it right now."

Bear had to get out of this car. Maybe he would take an extra run tonight. He had so much nervous energy buzzing out of his fingers, and Moxcy's lecture was not helping. He had sacrificed everything so everyone around him was happy, and the moment he tried to snatch a tiny bit of joy for himself, the entire world came down.

It was exhausting holding up everyone's world.

As the quiet boy with a stammer, Bear learned fast to keep his thoughts and desires to himself. But hearing Moxcy peg him made him realize he was doing a terrible job at hiding it. If Moxcy saw it, did Nora? Did she pity his long looks? Did she know how long he idled outside her door, long after she closed the door and showered?

But she kissed me back.

He held his chest. Lord, did she kiss him back. Nora felt good. She simply sank right into him, filling his hollows with her fullness. He smelled her skin on his hands, tasted her on his lips, felt her hands searching for his hardness and finding it throbbing and ready for her. She would have taken him inside her, given him her tight little body. He didn't need Yanne's tarot cards to see where they were headed. Whatever was happening, he and Nora were feeling it together.

"See what I mean? You're a space cadet, Bear."

"Moxcy, I can't . . . I'm not perfect."

"I'm not asking for perfection, Bear, just the truth. Go to Bangor. Sort this mess out with her, once and for all."

The phone buzzed over the car Bluetooth, and Bear made startled eye contact with Moxcy. It was Lu.

Shit.

"Bear?" Lu's voice was weak.

"And Moxcy," his cousin piped up. "We're in the car."

"She's seen it," Moxcy mouthed.

The first thought Bear had was a dark rush of relief. Then guilt rolled in for daring to feel relief.

"Lu, is everything okay?"

"It's fine, I just want to talk to you about something."

Someone had posted it. He hadn't meant for it to end like this. "Lu, about that—"

"Just wanted to tell you they put a hold on my account."

"For school?"

She didn't answer. Of course for school.

"How much do you need to pay? What's the minimum?"

"Bear, paying the minimum got me into this mess. I want to pay for this last semester. And take the exams."

He couldn't fault her that. Ten thousand dollars was enough to finish her degree. She'd wanted this for so long.

"I can't pay that amount right now." He wished he could pay her back sooner. Half of his guilt was the fact that he was paying her back so slowly. Ten thousand seemed a fine amount to pay back over three years. It was a nice round number, but between the business expenses and the exorbitant medical bills and living expenses, he hadn't made much progress on that number at all.

"Let's get on the phone—" Bear started.

Lu cut him off. "It's late now, so we can't even pay the minimum. My account is locked."

"Damn." Bear sighed, covering his face with his hand. "I'm sorry." All he had for Lu were sorries. She deserved so much better than this. The dream of becoming a nurse got her up on the hard days.

The silence on the phone was so chilly and uncomfortable that Bear squirmed in his seat. His stomach gurgled in agitation.

"It was due on the eleventh." Her voice strained. "What were you doing on the eleventh?"

"Ah, that was my um . . . birthday, so it must have slipped my mind."

Another brittle silence.

"So I guess that's it." False enthusiasm dripped from her voice. "I'm out of school because it was your birthday."

He saw Moxcy roll her eyes dramatically.

"We'll get this sorted out," Bear said.

"Bear, it's—" Her voice cracked. "It's the only thing I have," Lu said.

"I know. I'm sorry. I'm going to fix it." His voice took on the hushed tones of a man trying to settle a horse. When she hung up, Bear and Moxcy exhaled.

"Bear, what was that?"

"What?"

"You all sounded like you were reading from Vulcan cue cards."

Ennis shrugged. "We're just not that emotional."

"Were we listening to the same conversation? You heard all that silence as *unemotional*? She was livid, Bear, just in the coldest way I've ever heard." Moxcy said. "And she didn't even know your birthday."

"She knows. She's just really disappointed right now. You know I don't need that birthday nonsense."

What was I doing on my birthday? Last week, Yanne had written him a poem about dead leaves and mortality as a gift. And Nora had made twelve cupcakes from a viral social media recipe. He was surprised by that. It was sweet, but he didn't *need* it. When he resisted the cupcake, Nora pulled off a piece and commanded him, "You made another revolution around the sun. That's good enough to stop and celebrate. Eat your cake."

Yanne warned him, "You don't want that smoke, son. Eat your cake."

Nora shoved the cupcake piece in his mouth, and he involuntarily closed his eyes, allowing himself a soft suck of the frosting off the warm pad of her thumb. After his tours, he stroked himself into a stupor calling Nora's name. He watched some highlight reels and ate three more cupcakes. Depressing actually.

That was how Bear turned thirty-two.

"No way y'all are together," Moxcy said with a touch of finality. "You bastard." Her voice rose like she was piecing together a mystery. "You're pretending for the clout. Did you even help her these three years, or is she somewhere in a facility?"

"Moxcy, that's not—"

"Saint Ennis is a dog, holy shit!" Moxcy was practically humming in her seat. "Is *any* of it true? Did you really fight off five meth heads? Did you work with her legal team to find the attackers?"

"I *never* said that." Bear stared at the road. "Where does this stuff come from?"

"Did you carry her to the hospital in your arms or not?"

"No," he said softly.

Moxcy pulled at either side of her face. "You have to understand this is legend, Bear. Legend. The women say that you carry her around the house every day because her legs are all unstable."

"She's completely mobile! She came to the bingo hall reopening last year." Bear shook his head in disbelief.

"Why does she stay away from the rez then?"

"She wanted to be close to the hospital. She's trying to be a nurse, but her head injury was making it hard to remember things early on. She's getting her stride, though."

"So it's all a lie. Why would Lu go along with it?"

"I think she's hoping I would use my trust to pay her back," Bear admitted.

"Bear! Just marry her. Your cousin married that widow. They did the six-month cohabitation, then went their separate ways. So easy."

"I kind of wanted to use the trust to start *my* family. I always dreamed of building a house for my wife. I dreamed of getting my kids all of that expensive baby shit, not hand-me-downs from aunties. I want to build a usable track on the rez and start a scholarship program. I just wasn't ready to give up on that."

Moxcy nodded in understanding. "You don't want to use your life raft to bail out the business and pay Lu off."

"Because once that trust is gone, I really am stuck."

Moxcy covered her hand in his. "People get hurt, Bear. Like, really hurt. I know you feel like shit. But you can't eat guilt. You can't get warm under a guilt blanket."

"I should have been there, though. I was . . . I was ignoring her."

I was getting my dick sucked. I was sending her frantic calls to voicemail. I came a whole day later.

"Bear, no. So you missed a few calls, but this . . . doesn't feel healthy. I mean, I actually think your dad is right here. Take the damned bribe from Maine Power. Give Lu her money and go."

It was the exact wrong thing to say.

"My dad may know everything about taking bribes, but he doesn't know shit about duty. Dad loved *me*, didn't he? But he had no sense of duty. He and Mom left me whenever the mood suited them. Love is a childish notion without duty, Mox." By the time he finished his sentence, he was shaking with fury.

Moxcy's eyes shifted to the floor. "You're still *so* mad, Bear. Shit. You're ruining your life to prove you're not like your dad. But tonight proves you don't have anything under control. You gotta choose your reputation or your soul."

"There's nothing to choose. You're overreacting." It was a lie. The second one he told himself today, the first one being *I can appreciate Nora's dress and keep my hands to myself.*

"Ennis, just . . . be careful." His voice softened. "Lu is your duty, and I get it. But there is a chance she doesn't know the extent of her debt and your pressure. In the meantime, a woman you love—"

"I never said I loved Nora," Bear shot out. Too fast. The

admission had the opposite effect. It hung there for a while like a confession.

"Jennings said you called Basil for her," Moxcy said. "You refused to call Basil when his sister had her baby last year! Like, what in the hell kind of natural disaster could make you call him?"

"I'm *not* calling Basil. Jennings is asking his brother to come down to help with some internet stuff."

"Some internet stuff for *Nora*, who you *definitely* don't love and who has no plans of staying past Labor Day."

That landed like a bucket of ice water. Nora was going to sell. She planned to leave. She told everyone that would listen that her only goal was getting back to her perfect life in Maryland. Were eight more months of those hot, wet kisses enough to throw his carefully cultivated life away?

He knew the answer. He just hated that he knew.

"And god help you if Basil finds out you're faking with Lu."

Bear recoiled. "Why the hell would I care if he found out?"

"Bear, you are such a blockhead. Basil has had a thing for Lu his whole life. The entire rez knows about it," Moxcy said.

"Are you kidding me?" Bear asked. Remembering the night he met Lu—it was Basil who had pointed her out. Basil who bought her a beer.

"Not kidding. Why do you think he hates you?"

"Because I'm athletically superior, because I have Grand-father's name, because it's Friday. He doesn't *need* a reason. It's Basil." Bear's frustration with the day strained through his sentences. He was disappointed, embarrassed, horny enough to fuck a knothole in a tree, and exhausted on top of it all.

"I gotta run." Bear parked the car hastily in front of Moxcy's mom's house. When Moxcy opened the door, he nearly pushed her out. He needed to think. He needed pace and meditation and rhythm. He was breaking everything, and there was no choice he could make that would actually make him happy. He pulled his gym bag from the back seat and pulled it forward. There were at least fifty places he could run. It was eleven p.m. and dark as pitch, but there was only one place he could run in the dark. He headed to Barton Cove.

GAME SIX

NORA HAD TO CLEAR HER HEAD.

For the third day in a row since the expo, she pounded the ground. Anger, fear, and exhaustion consumed her, and to add insult to injury, Yanne and Jon had run off to an "explore polyamory" retreat in Taos.

Nora could see Yanne returning with Jon and two more wives, not even thinking about the foreclosure. Her sister could potentially inherit three million dollars, and she was probably in a candle ceremony marrying a woman named Stardust.

But she had had her share of irresponsible behavior too. The expo kiss was disorienting. No. That kiss was stunning. There was no other word. He stunned her down to the soles of her shoes. And where the hell had her desperate, clinging kiss come from? The way she had kissed him back was a definitive answer to his bold statement.

If I kiss you, I'm afraid I won't know how to stop.

They couldn't turn back from a kiss like that. A kiss like that could only end one way—hot and hurried thrusting in a coat closet. Nora didn't even know how she would face him without her face burning. God, she had practically milked the man.

She was sprinting now. She hadn't waited for Bear because she was just too embarrassed. She came off so thirsty at that expo, and she couldn't unring that bell.

Get out of my head. Get that kiss out of my head.

In the shower, she prayed harder than she'd ever prayed. This feeling, whatever powerful ache was making her burn for Bear, she prayed away. Three and a half months was record time for her to sabotage the only thing that could save her and her family right now.

Nora had so much to do. The days were shorter than the task lists, and she was drowning under it. There was a two-digit number of contractors coming in the next two days. She would break if she stayed at this pace. In fact, she was sure she was breaking already. And Yanne was nowhere to be found.

The cabinets were being installed today so they could finally finish the kitchen. Her new bed was en route, so she would at least be able to throw away the rollaway cot she'd been sleeping on, and the landscapers were going to try to do something about the felled trees on the beach. If everything went remotely as planned for the next few days, they would still be on schedule and under budget.

The first knock at the door, hard and fast, was Brandon. He wore an unnecessary hard hat and a neon-yellow reflective vest.

"Morning, Nora." Brandon looked down at the floor. Bear rolled up on his heels, compounding Nora's embarrassment.

"Nora, did you run already?" Bear asked.

Did I run? Boy, I've been beating back the memory of your hands on my body for four nights in a row. "Oh, um, yeah. I felt itchy this morning, and I—"

"Nora, I was coming—I just . . . can we talk?"

Nora looked over her shoulder to Brandon, who was clicking his pen and shaking his head.

Nora led Bear into the nearest room, and he turned those dark eyes on her. The directness of his gaze made her want to sprint away. She took a deep breath. This didn't have to be awkward. She should tell him that the kiss was an accident. No, he wouldn't buy that. Not with the way she'd kissed him back.

Ennis must have noticed her hesitance. "Nora, please don't . . ." he started, then shook his head. "You remember LeBron's first championship? Game six, NBA finals?"

"Of course," Nora said, like the question was silly.

"It was the first time LeBron had made it to the finals. It was him and some rando collection of players going up against *the* Gregg Popovich and the San Antonio Spurs," Bear said.

"It was murder," Nora cut in.

"A bloodbath," Bear said. "LeBron had *just* enough magic to get to the finals, but the pressure got to him and his team collapsed."

"And this is game six," Nora finished, letting it sink in. *He can't do a relationship right now. His eye is on the ball, and yours should be too.*

"Exactly, so right when they—when we," he corrected, "need to be clearheaded."

"I agree," Nora rushed out, wanting this embarrassing conversation to end. "The championship ring should be the goal. There's too much on the line to fall apart in game six."

"Exactly. And I—for my part, I won't do that," he breathed, "touch you like that again. Despite what you saw that night, I'm not an out-of-control person."

"Agreed. I think the fruit wine was flowing," Nora said.

"Right, and then the lighting and that terrible dress," Bear continued.

"Leave my poor dress out of this. She was just doing her job."

"Now she's a 'poor dress'? You were talking shit before."

Before you told me to take it off, Nora wanted to say. Instead, she blinked hard against the black dots that began to swirl in her vision.

Okay, note to self, don't close the door in a freshly painted room.

"I think we need to get out of here." Bear pulled open the door.

A company of contractors pushed past her and stood in front of Bear. "There you are, Mr. Dash. We have a problem."

Nora moved to stand in front of Bear. "Hello, *I'm* Mr. Dash. Er, Ms. Dash. What is the problem?"

"We can't place these countertops until the cabinets are in." The contractor was *still* looking at Bear.

"Okay, the cabinet guy should be here by"—she flicked her wrist to check her watch—"an hour ago."

Nora whipped out her phone and dialed the saved number. "Cozy Cabinets, how may I help you?"

"Yes, we have an appointment at nine a.m., and it is ten a.m., and I don't see any cozy cabinets."

"Yes, are you Norm Dash?"

Nora groaned. "I guess."

"Yeah, we tried to call you about an hour ago. Dan's not coming today. Seems the next time he is able to come all the way out there is in"—she heard the receptionist click on the keyboard—"three weeks. Will that work for you?"

"No, that absolutely will not work for me. The countertop people are here right now."

"Well, I think your cabinet guys and your countertop guys

should be the same. For future reference, we were running a hell of a deal on granite."

"Can you get anyone out here sooner?" Nora asked.

"I'm sorry. We gave you a tentative date before, but three weeks is a firm date. We'll see you then."

So dismissive.

"No, you won't see me. I want my deposit back," Nora said into the phone.

A short, dark-haired man waved at her frantically from the window.

"Oh god, what now?" She walked to the window with Bear so close behind her she could feel his body heat on her back. The landscaper dusted his hat against his hip.

"You got tree root infiltration of your septic tank." He said this like he was delivering a death sentence.

"Okay, you're a landscaper. Can't you take the roots out?"

"I'm not a plumber, ma'am. When a tree root penetrates the septic tank, it could break open the sides and cause a severe spill of septic fluid."

"What is septic fluid?" Nora felt so stupid all the time here.

He looked over at Bear and shook his head as if to say, *Women.* "Sewage, ma'am. It's cracked up pretty bad." He pointed to a particularly lush patch of grass. She hadn't thought to wonder why it was pale green in February.

"Is this an emergency?"

"A sewage spill of this type will trigger patches of green growth that are denser than usual for your lawn. But once you go over there, you'll start to smell the pretty potent smell of sewage."

"Nora, this is bad," Bear said. "Very bad. Sick animals. Sick trees. Sick people. Health-inspector-shutdown bad."

Nora blinked her eyes against the onslaught of everything going wrong.

Brandon patted her shoulder. "Let me follow up on that vendor cancellation. Where is your sister?"

Nora didn't answer because she didn't want to say, *I don't know.* She could feel her throat constricting and her stomach churning, and the world going dark.

This is going to be a failure. Who the hell do you think you are, taking on this type of project?

Bear grabbed the keys. "You need to call a septic tank specialist ASAP. I'll drive to Lowe's and see if we can drum up some cabinets." He squeezed her shoulder. The firm sensation slowed down her heartbeat and grounded her in the here and now.

She opened her eyes and nodded. "Okay, I'm calling a specialist."

Bear was out the door fast, and Brandon was immediately on the phone haggling with the cabinet folks. Even with Yanne MIA, Brandon and Bear made her feel like a competent little family. They made this all seem just a touch more possible than it felt yesterday.

Nora took a series of centering breaths, then texted Yanne. **911.**

The phone rang instantly.

"Nora!"

"Yanne! The house is blowing up right now."

"Nora, is it on fire? Are you okay!?"

"Me? I'm fine, no fire."

"So, the house is in trouble?"

"Yes, it's imploding, Yanne. The contractor didn't show up and—"

"Ugh, don't misuse 911. I thought you were unsafe," she said, cutting Nora off.

"How is this a misuse—" Nora gave up. "Yanne, where are you?"

"Oh, we're on our way. We'll be home in a few." Nora ended the call and furiously began googling emergency plumbers.

An hour later, Yanne breezed through the door, a hand full of duty-free airport bags, locs tumbling over her shoulder with wide square sunglasses that looked more like a Mack truck windshield than sun protection.

"Maryanne Dash, I will—" Nora reached for her, and Yanne instinctively swerved out of the way of her sister and twirled inelegantly toward the kitchen.

Moxcy had just finished a tour and sat with her feet on a crocheted doily, drinking her third Pepsi of the morning. When she saw Yanne racing past her, she stood to block Nora from chasing.

"Chill, Flo-Jo. We have a new batch of tourists on their way." Moxcy rummaged through Yanne's bags until she found cookies suitable enough to place out for her tour, allowing Yanne to escape back toward the kitchen.

"Nora, I got you those giant Toblerones you like! Wait, listen!" Nora and Yanne held on to either side of the kitchen island, each watching the other's movements. "Nora—"

"No. You don't *do* that. You don't just *leave* in the middle of a big project."

"What would you have said if I asked?" Yanne countered.

Her phone buzzed. It was Bear FaceTiming. "Saved your life!" Nora hissed at her sister as she pressed answer.

"Hey, turns out they have a lot of cabinets here. Do you see any that you like?" He flipped the phone camera to the array of cabinets. Nora shook her head, letting the adrenaline come down from wanting to murder her sister. Honestly, she could not possibly care less what cabinets they chose right now. The ones that would get the most customers in here, she supposed. Remodeling a house was just decision after ridiculous decision.

"Nora, can I?" Yanne held the phone, sensing the fraying edges of her sister's nerves. "Oh, I like those. That cherrywood is gorgeous! That one."

Yanne yelped when Brandon slid up close behind her and snatched the phone out of her hand. "Ignore her. Get a cheap paint-grade wood, and we'll paint it."

"Excuse you?" Yanne blustered, her cheeks burning pink.

"Excuse me indeed," Brandon said.

"Those cherry cabinets were divine. What is wrong with you?"

"Divinely expensive. Is your goal to pay off this foreclosure or have divine cherry cabinets?"

"The first one," Nora interjected.

On the phone, Bear moved through the aisles. "So a maple or birch?"

"Please, Bear, can you get something we can stand to look at for the next year?" Nora asked.

"Why do you beg for me to be here if you're just going to ignore what I say, Nora? I don't have a voice in any of this. Why does this guy get a vote?" Yanne flicked her wrist in Brandon's direction.

Brandon quirked his eyebrow and pushed her reflective sunglasses to the top of her head. To her credit, Yanne didn't flinch. "I'm the accountant. I'm just trying to make sure you all can receive your EIF by being economical."

"Why is the *accountant* telling us how we should spend our money?" Yanne's glance lingered on his shoulders.

His voice was dry, but his tone was meaningful. "That's precisely my job."

"Forcing us to live in a brutalist dystopia for the capitalist agenda?" Yanne accused.

Brandon cleared his throat. "You *are* the agenda. You *are* the capitalists."

Yanne reached for her neck. "How dare you! You clearly don't have a true appreciation for any kind of aesthetic vision."

Nora didn't know if it was her sister's bodacious body, her face, or her antics, but Yanne had Brandon's full attention.

"Brandon Kern"—he held Yanne's gaze and continued—"admires beautiful things all the time." He paused long enough for Yanne's breath to catch. *She caught that freaking fast one, didn't she?* "It's just, your sister has impressed upon me how important it is that you all turn a profit."

Nora and Moxcy exchanged looks while Moxcy ate more cookies than she set out on the plate. "Let me help you with that," Nora offered.

"Help me by telling Bear to bring his ass home. I'm not taking this next tour. I have to study."

"Did you hear that?" Nora held up the phone, remembering Bear waiting on the other end. "Bring your ass home."

There was a quick flash of something impish in his eyes, but he only nodded and said, "Yes, ma'am."

Nora ignored the light-headed feeling that the tiny smile caused. Probably still high off paint fumes. When Nora hung up the phone, the entire room's eyes were on her.

CONCEAL, DON'T FEEL

WINTER PASSED IN MAINE LIKE A LOVESICK EX, OVER-staying its welcome and DMing at weird times of the night. February was excruciating. Moxcy and Bear kept telling her to somehow expect it to get even colder. Nora did *not* understand how it could. Her brain just stopped working under zero degrees. All she wanted to do was make soups and hibernate, but Barton Cove kept demanding attention—which was why she liked to hide in the kitchen. Nora had fought Yanne all the way on the ridiculous abundance of plants on the first floor. But sitting in the sunny kitchen with fresh herbs and budding flowers at the buffet-style heavy wood tables was cozy. The floral loops and swirls felt romantic and naturally connected with their rundown cottage-chic decor of chipped vintage teacups, yellowed antique lace, and washed-out blues and turquoise ceramic pots and pans hanging from a rack.

Outside, the gray winter ocean now largely free of litter rocked and roiled. Standing near the sea made her feel small and anonymous. Not an *unpleasant* sensation for a person like her. Yanne had tried to write about the beach in their brochures in a fun-in-the-sun kind of way. But that was an outright lie. Barton Cove's rocky shore was *not* a swimsuit shore, it was a "chunky sweater, hair whipping in the wind, moody white people"–type shore. You could only listen to Bon Iver and Boyz II Men on that beach.

But watching that stony, moody shoreline from this spot was one of Nora's new favorite pastimes. Putting on a small cup of tea, lo-fi hip-hop floating in the background, surrounded by knit doilies and huge leather volumes on mushrooms—Nora felt at home. Now she found the kitchen to be her favorite room in the inn. Maybe Yanne *was* the VP of vibes.

She flipped another page of *Conceal, Don't Feel: Hack Your Emotions Like a Disney Princess*.

Some forms of physical touch are associated with erotic arousal. Try to keep your touch in neutral zones or in spaced-out increments.

Time was passing in increments of touch for Nora. Since the night at the expo, she noticed how intentional Bear had been about *not* touching her. In the short time she'd known him, he had always been naturally affectionate. She thought of the tender embrace he had pulled her into after their first euphoric run. The easy way he had walked with his arm around her.

There would be no more of that. True to his word, he hadn't touched her like that again, and damned if she didn't feel the hollow absence of his touch down to her bones.

It's safer this way.

But it was those accidental moments, so few that Nora could count them on her hands, that kept replaying in her head like a GIF on a loop.

IN EARLY MARCH, IN THE TOOLSHED, AN UNSTABLE SHELF came tumbling down, and Bear swept her to the other side of the small outbuilding and pressed himself so tightly against her she could barely breathe. Her breasts pressed into his belly. After the debris settled, Bear stared down hard at her mouth until her stomach did flips inside her body. He finally pushed free and stormed out of the shed, leaving her gasping, dusty, and wet.

Nora let the days rush together in a flurry of plumbing disasters and contractor arguments. March was the first of the random and unwelcomed visits from Felicia.

She twisted the door handle and walked into Barton cove without so much as a *How are you?*

"Nora, this place looks a mess. Maybe you've been spending more time running than running a business?" Nora didn't think to ask how Felicia knew about her mornings as she watched the other woman step over a loose canvas tarp striped in spattered paint. The house, which Nora was growing quite proud of, seemed to crumble underneath Felicia's cold scrutiny.

The floor-to-ceiling windows were smudged with fingerprints and dust, and the minimal window dressing seemed too bare and simple for the neutral loops of jute and creams she had planned as the base. "I received some paperwork about your permits."

"Oh, to pave the driveway! They've been waiting for weeks to start." Nora reached for the envelope, and Felicia pulled it just out of her grasp.

"It was addressed to my stepfather, so naturally, I opened it. Seemed as though you have a rare species of"—she peeled open the paper—"prototype quillwort? Globally endangered."

"What does that mean?"

"It means I saved you the headache and called the EPA. They should be out here to do a full environmental impact report on all of this building you are doing." She looked at Nora's face with something like pity. "It means you won't be getting your driveway or anything done anytime soon." She finally handed Nora the paper. "This is the moment where you realize you're not on HGTV."

"YOU KNOW I DON'T MAKE PROMISES I CAN'T KEEP." MOXCY drilled holes into the basement walls. Bear hammered nails with too much force, and Moxcy winced at every pound. Nora had said they could use this basement space and any excess material for whatever they wanted, and Bear wanted to make a little office space.

"You said you would cover me this weekend."

"I don't frivolously promise away my time or money." She looked at him pointedly. "You misheard me."

"I covered you yesterday," he reminded her.

"Yeah. Those Maine Power assholes came to see me yesterday."

Bear stopped pounding. "Did you tell them to get lost?"

"Well, I started to but—"

"Moxcy!"

"They kept reminding me of my law school fees. They knew the *exact* amount, Bear. It was scary. They are done being nice. They mentioned Grandma's bookkeeping—how everybody knows it was a little off."

"That's a threat. If I don't allow the use of the river, they'll hobble the business."

"I mean, would it be that bad? If you took the money? You want to coach full-time. You want to snag the cheerleader with a clear conscience. Why are you holding out?" They worked together to position the roughhewn salvaged wood on top of the steel shelving frames.

"Why am I holding out? Moxcy." He grunted to lift the small

granite countertop. It was a bit of an unconventional desk, but it could work. "You didn't read what they wanted me to sign. Not only am I expected to vote yes for the proposal, they want me to be the voice of the project in commercials and at conventions. They want a fucking mascot."

"They want you to sell out the rez, then sell yourself?" Moxcy groaned, leafing through his mail. She lifted up a red past-due hospital bill. "But you're in way over your head with this Lu shit. You overpromised, and you're too stubborn to walk it back."

He snatched the letter and shuffled it back underneath the pile. "And how do I do that? How do I go to every hospital and make myself not responsible? Even if I don't help with medical bills, I owed her 10K, and that's black-and-white."

"I mean, pay back what you owe. No one is saying skip town on her. I know you don't have ten Gs to throw around. How about you go to the courthouse? Marry her now, give her the money, and tell her she's on her own for the medical stuff. You can't spend your whole trust on her. She has to understand that."

"So I give her ten grand, then saddle her with seventy thousand dollars in debt?" Bear said. The thought of it made his stomach ache.

"Isn't that enough for her to finish nursing school?"

"And how do I explain to"—he paused—"everyone that I'm a little bit married?"

"You mean Nora, right? How do you tell the woman you want to bag that for at least six months, you're technically married."

"More than that, how do I tell everyone on the rez that all of it was never real? Even if they see Lu and me getting married, how do I walk back all of those Bear fables? How do I tell them it's strictly business? How do I tell the aunties who're making us a hand-stitched blanket that this was all for show? What about the folks weaving baskets for Lu and me right now? Do I say this is just for funsies?"

"This is why you don't tell a soul. Marry Lu, give her *only* the money you owe and nothing more. Disappear the next day with your brown runaround. Your dad is an absolute genius at this. Tell everyone you died in a fire and move to Maryland. Learn to love crab instead of lobster." She clapped triumphantly. "Bear is finally happy."

"Foolproof." Bear smirked and rubbed the smooth surface of the polished granite.

"You're still too afraid of rejection." Moxcy put the drill bit down.

"You make rejection sound like a trip to Disneyland. Humans are pack animals. Everyone is afraid of rejection." He rummaged for a hammer.

"You gotta let yourself be the asshole sometimes."

"Oh, is it just fine to be hated here? The butt of every joke? My dad would beg to differ."

"Francis owns his mistakes, Bear." She handed him a rubber mallet. "You hide them."

MARCH ON

BEFORE NORA KNEW IT, IT WAS LATE MARCH AND STILL freezing in Maine. By now, in DC, Yanne and their mother would drive down to the Tidal Basin to see the cherry blossoms just about to burst to life and turn the entire world pink. In this bitter-cold March, Nora would have loved to see the hope of a budding cherry blossom.

Because of the EPA investigation that had not even fully begun, they were never able to pave the driveway. So instead, Nora strung outdoor patio lights along knobby wooden posts about every eight feet all the way up the drive until they met the sprawling blue steps spilling out from the porch like river rapids.

Brandon had championed Yanne's rock landscaping idea because it was cheaper and more climate friendly. Nora had been skeptical at first. But the boulders and the smaller pebbles, plus the large balanced rock cairns out in front, invited a kind of peacefulness she'd always wanted in a home. Barton Cove was finally letting her have her way. Who knew all she had to do was let Bear stand in the back of the room when the contractors spoke? Suddenly they could find the part or talk to a guy about permits. Sometimes the whole work of being a woman was simply fooling men into taking action.

The white columns and trim framing the grayish-blue exterior were crisp and clean. You would never know Nora and Brandon had been the ones to finish off the trim when the budget ran out for the painters. They had even managed to save that damned gambrel roof after Nora had gotten so frustrated with the roofers she had threatened to flatten the whole thing and hammer a tin roof herself.

By March, Bear's post-run green smoothie habit had spilled over into breakfast invitations and long, elaborate brunches. *Nobody* ate like Bear. Every bite was a thank-you, a close-lipped, closed-eyed reverent prayer to whoever prepared it. She was gathering all kinds of data about a man she could never be with.

Here was a list of useless information she now knew about Bear:

1. He pees with the door open.
2. You can't mention the Olympics without him going on a ten-minute Jim Thorpe history lesson.
3. ~~He likes to suck her tongue when he's kissing, and rock her against him.~~
4. He puts salt on everything before he even tastes it.
5. And he liked to use the exact same dishware every time. So much so that Yanne had started to call the green earthenware bowl Bear's bowl.

TL;DR: she really knew this man.

Nora was doing it. Maintaining a healthy friendship with Bear and keeping her attraction out of sight, no more of that grabbing-for-his-dick nonsense she did at the expo. No more vibrating with desire when he touched her. She had the reins now. And if she really thought about it, wasn't she getting everything she actually wanted out of a relationship? She was getting his companionship on their runs. His strength to open those damned artisanal jam jars and his bravery to trap racoons and set them free without losing his shit. His business acumen. His centuries-old knowledge of the land. And most important, she wasn't getting hurt. There was nothing to reject. She closed her latest self-help book with a wild sense of accomplishment.

Against her will, she was starting to bond with this moody home and its neighbors. It was starting to feel like something she wanted to keep.

BEAR DIDN'T STEP INTO THE BAIT-AND-TACKLE STORE ONE cold March morning expecting to be shouted down.

He needed a better lightweight freshwater spinning rod, but chances were high he would get some of these cool-looking glittery spoon lures that flashed in the sun. Fishing always cleared his head, and after the few months he'd had, he needed to be on a boat for the rest of the year. But even fishing wouldn't clear his head, because John Michael Neptune rolled around the corner and glowered at him.

He'd seen John Michael only once, but it was enough to make an impression. He'd thought John Michael seemed massive because he had been a child. But no, John Michael was a linebacker with no quarterback to defend.

"How's my baby cousin?" he asked, the wooden toothpick in his mouth wobbling with his words.

"Lu's doing great." Bear mentally calculated the space to the exits.

"Really? That's not what I hear." He stepped closer and flicked a glittery lure on the wall.

"You should ask *her* then." Bear tried to move past him. But his deer-sausage fingers pressed into Bear's chest.

"What kind of game are you playing, Freeman?" he asked, throwing the toothpick to the floor.

Bear slid John Michael's hand away from his chest. "No games." He thought of Thunderbear's dull knife under his jacket.

"I asked her when's the wedding, and she said you haven't asked her." He looked aggressively perplexed. "She also told me she's got a freeze on her account at school because she loaned you money. Is that true?"

"Not technically. But the spirit of the complaint is true."

"Don't be a smartass, Bear. You're not half as charming as Francis and not near as scary as your grandfather. It won't work."

"Just answering your question to the best of my knowledge."

"'Best of my knowledge'—listen to the college boy! When your shit-ass dad left you at home for three days without food, who told your grandmother Francis was gone again?"

"You," Bear confirmed.

"And have you ever wanted for *anything*, Bearcub, since your grandmother took you in?"

"Nope."

"Didn't your community have your back *all* the way to college?"

"Yes."

"So why the hell am I hearing that my baby cousin can't finish school because you're holding your precious trust over her head? You need to find a way, to the best of your knowledge, to pay what you owe."

"Are you here to break my kneecaps, John Michael?" Bear

asked, making eye contact with the store attendant, who looked away as if to proclaim that this was none of his business. "I'm not holding anything over Lu's head. There are medical bills, fees, credit cards. There is more I'm paying for than the money I owe her."

"Yeah, I took a look at what else you're paying for." He made an hourglass figure with his hands. "That kitty's a little too expensive for *you*, ain't it?"

"John Michael, my money is going for the business and keeping up with Lu's medical bills. But since we always look out for each other, I-I would love for you and her uncle to help with payments."

John Michael's mouth fell down to his belly. "Bearcub, you're out of your mind if you think we're going to shoulder what you owe. In this place, on this land, if we say it, we do it. Did you say it?" John Michael challenged.

Bear looked down.

"I can't hear you, Bearcub. Did you promise out of your mouth to pay for all the things you are paying for? And did Lu ask you for anything other than the money you owe her?"

"She was in a coma! She couldn't ask for anything. And you and her uncle were *nowhere* to be found. Which I find a little *too* convenient. You didn't start crawling out of the woodwork until you heard *I* was paying. You never visited her until she could see you. You never made one meal, and you never took one shift. *Someone* had to step up." Bear stood his ground against the huge man. If he was getting his teeth kicked in today, he would earn it.

"Oh, *for Bear so loved the world, he gave his only begotten fuck*. Yeah, right, you're blowing all of your money trying to stay between that other woman's legs. I haven't told my baby cousin what you're doing, but I will if you keep up this dirty business."

Bear tamped down his rising anger. "I am not doing anything dirty. Lu and I aren't even t-t—"

"Aren't even what t-t?" The big man mimicked Bear's stammer and pushed himself into his personal space, and Bear, smaller and faster, dipped just out of punching reach. "Are you trying to *deny* her? *Now* she ain't your girl? Now you don't recognize her?"

He shook his head in open disgust. "There won't be a place you can hide where you're not Abenaki, boy. You opened your mouth, and you made an oath to her, or have you been hanging with off-island folks so long that you forgot that your word is a sacred commitment?"

"I haven't forgotten anything about who I am." Bear put the fishing rod back on the wall display and left the store.

QUATRO DE MAYO

WHITE PEOPLE LOST THEIR MINDS ON CINCO DE MAYO. Cultural appropriation reached peak levels as college fraternities donned mustaches and sombreros and hired mariachi bands to play as they guzzled cheap tequila. This was how Bear met Brandon Kern the day before a track meet in Portland. His team was at a nameless bar decorated with taco pinatas and Mexican flags. He saw Brandon—new transfer army brat and future uptight accountant—with a multicolored poncho on, poring over books. Their eyes met, Bear sat down next to him, and they'd aggressively declared war on bullshit holidays ever since. For April Fools' Day, they'd have March 32nd, a very serious holiday where they talked about philosophy; and on February 15th, Palentine's Day, where they talked about love; and, tonight, Quatro de Mayo, a non-silly answer to Cinco De Mayo where they talk about the direction of their lives.

This Quatro de Mayo festivity would be small. Bear had too much on his mind.

They met up on the Penobscot River, Bear's first love and his only true home. The full moon cast a silver light on the still freezing river that flowed silently beneath the canoe. Water lapped softly against the sides of the boat, and the occasional splash of a fish jumping startled Brandon into another sip of warm brandy.

Bear, wrapped in a thick woolen coat and a woolen hat pulled over his ears, sat hunched over in the canoe, his fishing line trailing in the water. He loved being out on the river at night, when everything was quiet and still. A faint mist rose from the water's surface, adding to the eerie beauty of this spot.

"*Almanac* says record heat is coming," Brandon warned.

"The *Almanac* is bullshit. I swear you're turning into a homesteader."

"I am thinking about buying a bit of land—"

"Brandon, please. This sounds like your I-want-to-start-a-podcast phase . . . just don't."

Bear occasionally looked up to check the canoe's position. He knew the river like the back of his hand and could tell when the current was starting to pull them too far downstream. To keep the canoe in place, Bear gently paddled against the current, barely making a sound.

Brandon looked up at the night sky. "I wouldn't want to do it alone. I just think men in their thirties are lonely, you know? We don't do that BFF stuff that women do." He passed the flask of warm brandy, and Bear sniffed and sipped. Brandon continued, "I mean, count your moments of genuine connection. It's hard."

After a long while, Bear finally spoke. "I think you can't just rely on connection to find meaning. You have to also add your duties and your honor. It's a braid, you know? *All* of those things make a man." He passed the flask back to Brandon.

His friend nodded his head. "I think my duties and honor as an accountant brought me into my connection with Yanne."

Bear laughed but sputtered to a stop when he saw his friend's face. "*What* connection with Yanne?"

Brandon was unfazed by Bear's five-minute laughing break. "No, brother, there is a *thread*, and I'm determined to pull it. I can't get her out of my head—those big green eyes and her soft skin."

"Brandon, she's practically sworn herself to that chin of a man, Jon Bradley."

"There is a thread," Brandon repeated, slower this time.

"You're delusional."

"I'm passionate! Look at me being passionate about something! Someone. It's hard to let go of once you've felt it!"

Bear twisted his mouth in disbelief.

"You wouldn't know passion, Bear, if it grabbed you by the pubes," Brandon said.

That was rich coming from an accountant. "Brandon, just be careful. Yanne doesn't seem like she does forever."

"You and Nora treat her like a child, but she's a grown woman who wants to live life on her own terms. You and Nora live on everyone else's terms."

When Bear shot him a glance, Brandon offered, "But we need that. We need people to fall on their swords for the greater good. To consider the needs of many. You and Nora make good leaders. But Yanne and I are different."

Ennis checked the contents of Brandon's drink.

"You and Yanne have literally nothing in common except for the same boring books."

"Look, I started my own firm because I hated working under people. My entire career has been about distinguishing myself. You were always trying to prove you *belonged* in the crowd. And it stops you from doing what needs to be done."

Bear didn't like his friend's characterization of him. He did what needed to be done all the time. It was, in fact, exhausting. He looked around to try to ground his swirling emotion. The river was surrounded by tall trees, their branches stretched toward the sky like a mother's arms.

Comfort and affection felt so far away from him right now.

"There are some serious things in your life that need doing. You need to leave this dead-ass Lu situation in the past. You need to tell those assholes at Maine Power you won't be intimidated; you need to drive to Barton Cove and shake Nora awake. Tell her y'all got thangs to do."

"Thangs?" Bear repeated.

"Grown-up thangs."

Encouraged, Brandon piled on. "You are neck-deep in love with Nora. Don't"—he held up a hand to fend off Bear's automatic reaction—"try to deny it. And I love you, Bear, but you and Nora are *never* going to be a thing."

Ouch. The smile slid off his face like spaghetti down the wall. "Because I have obligations." He sounded strained.

The only time he had had a reprieve from the crushing duties and responsibilities of his life was last month, when Bear drove his students to Barton Cove so Nora could run another workshop for the track team. Bear was less concerned her background would be the problem, though she still obviously thought it was. But coming to her house was a workaround that the kids enjoyed. Bear made spaghetti and built makeshift hurdles out of scrap wood. Nora painted them all white and encouraged the kids to graffiti them. This time, the team hung on her every word. She was so damn happy. Bear would work until his fingers cracked and bled to make her that happy again.

His team must have told Nora about not being able to afford

the competition, because two weeks later, they received an *anonymous* donation totaling the registration fees for the underdog team to go to state.

After saying yes all of his life and being a caretaker for others, Nora's quiet understated care for him was a balm he had no idea he had been desperate for.

It wasn't that he resented being a caretaker. There was just such a stark line between duty and fulfillment. Taking care of someone wasn't one-sided. It wasn't all thankless nights and tired mornings. There was joy in seeing the person you were taking care of doing well. The problem was, he could never seem to fulfill any of Lu's needs, especially her mounting financial ones. And that fear of not doing enough put him on a hamster wheel of exhaustion and duty, but never joy. Like love, joy was another thing he told himself he didn't need. Even if everyone on the rez thought that they were a couple, he and Lu knew the truth. That they were forced together by a tenuous promise. He could sense her angst sometimes, how badly she wanted to cut and run. He did too—but to where and how? This was why Nora had been a revelation in his life. Her love was a relief, a weight off him when the weights just kept piling on.

It was damn dangerous to start to depend on the kind of feelings Nora gave him.

"Those aren't obligations, those are old patterns. Lu is healed, Bear. You did the savior thing. Everybody knows you're good."

Anger, hot and tight, flashed through Bear. "That's *not* why I stayed," he said. His fishing line shook, and Bear didn't even yank it.

"The hell it isn't. All of those folks patting you on the back for staying." Too drunk to notice the change in his friend's mood, Brandon drained the flask. "Admit it felt good. You want everyone to see the miles of separation between you and your dad, and you're killing your spirit to prove it."

"I live by the rules of a community, not just myself. Do you understand what it would mean to leave Lu? Do I just pack up and leave with Nora back to Maryland? Do I leave my family business? Do I let go of the river dispute? I can't just . . . The rules, Brandon."

"There you go. King Bear rules over his fragile fiefdom." Brandon held a new beer to his chest. "And you would never break the glass in case of emergency, and neither would Queen Nora. Y'all are trapped in prisons of your own making." Fully drunk now, Brandon started in an impromptu bout of "Return of the Mack."

SWEET, SMALL LIFE

SAME DAY, LATE NIGHT

BEAR KNEW THIS QUATRO DE MAYO CELEBRATION HAD gone off the rails. But he argued with Brandon anyway. "You use the exact same lines to try to get me to blow up my life. Remember when you wanted me to try out for varsity? You said, 'You're trapped on JV.'"

"I was right then, and I'm right now." Swinging his head to a completely imaginary beat, Brandon pointed at his own face.

Bear's jaw flexed. "I'm not trapped."

This man was past drunk. "You lied to meeee." He had been singing "Return of the Mack" for half an hour. "Prove it."

"What?"

"Call her. Call Lu right now and tell her you're in love with someone else."

He squeezed the phone in his front pocket.

You could do this. But still his stomach twisted. The consistent avalanche of what-ifs and whatabouts tumbled down to his feet. Besides, why would he blow up his life when he knew Nora was on the next plane out after Labor Day? There were fleeting things that felt good in the moment, and there were real solid, heavy things that grounded him in the day-to-day. His duties and the promises he had made were the only *real* things in his life right now. And he intended to keep them.

"No."

"Trapped."

"No, you don't understand."

"You won't punch your cousin in the face, and you won't fight for the woman you want," Brandon said. Suddenly he seemed stone-cold sober.

"There's *always* something, Brandon. This will end up being a three-hour conversation."

"Call her and see," Brandon demanded.

Could it be as easy as this? A phone call to Lu, and he could be off like a gunshot to Nora? Him still smelling like the river, her sleepily taking him into her arms. She could make him that pull-apart bread, and he could build her a pagoda with a little bench. Over the years, it would get heavy with bougainvillea and would sag a bit in the middle. They would have hushed, stealthy sex before wild-haired children woke up. He would promise to fix a creaky step, and she would remember his doctors' appointments. They would finish puzzles on cold evenings and not leave the house for days. Creator save him, he could hear his heart in his ears. He would do anything for a sweet, small life with Nora Dash.

Even blow up his current one.

Bear pulled out his phone. All kinds of thoughts ran across his mind. She could not pick up. She could pick up, he would say the phrase that crystallized and dissolved on his tongue every morning. *This isn't working. We never really worked.* He could be free this time tomorrow. And then wild horses couldn't keep him from Nora.

She picked up on the first ring.

It was a small tug, but the current shifted, pushing them faster than he wanted to go downstream.

"Lu, I n-n-n-need—" His stutter popped in like an uninvited guest, twisting the impact of his words. The silence on the line was thick but real. He heard her breath and movement, so he knew the phone hadn't disconnected.

Brandon began paddling rapidly then, moving them in a frenzied loop. Water sloshed over the sides, and Bear signaled for Brandon to slow down.

"Lu, is everything okay?"

The line crackled.

"The electricity, Bear." Half whisper, half command.

"What's wrong?"

"You forgot to pay the electricity." A cold spray of water cascaded down his shoulder.

"Oh, Lu, I'm so sorry. W-when was that due? Shit. I was—" He looked at Brandon. "Distracted."

"All of the food's spoiled," she said softly.

Bear ran his hand down his face. Guilt cramped his stomach. The beer tasted sour on his tongue.

"I'm heading over."

The cold river current fought against his paddle as he powered to shore.

ON THE DRIVE TO BANGOR, BEAR COULDN'T SETTLE ON one emotion. Guilt, then fear, then shame fought for primacy in his mind. He had let that bill slip, and now Lu was in the dark, hungry and alone while he was waxing poetic about another woman.

When he turned the key to her Bangor apartment, he saw Lu

sitting in the living room with a candle, still as a statue. Soggy TV dinners were spread out on the coffee table like playing cards.

"Lu, what are you doing with all of these?"

"I was trying to remember what each of them cost and if I got them on sale or not."

Lu kept an internal tally sheet a mile long. Bear stacked the trays on top of one another and threw them in the trash.

"Lu, I'm so sorry. I . . . don't know how I let this bill slip my mind—"

"I think it's ninety-seven dollars and seventy-three cents." Lu spoke quietly. Her eyes were sharp as jagged glass.

"What?"

Lu cleared her throat. "It's ninety-seven seventy-three for you to add to, um . . ." She trailed off and nodded to the calculator at her side. "That brings us to nine thousand seven hundred sixty-four dollars and twenty-nine cents. Total."

"You've added the lost food to the whole amount. I don't think—"

"I think it's fair because you forgot to pay the electricity. You've been quite forgetful lately."

This was Lu's language. It was her way of expressing frustration. Everything had a price on it.

Forgot to pay electricity, forgot about me . . . that'll be ninety-seven dollars.

"Lu, I'm sorry about this."

"Those are new shoes," she said. "You've been running again."

"I just started." Why was his heart hammering? Six months wasn't exactly just starting. The answer was simple. He was a liar, and had gotten too comfortable easing away from the truth. "That's not true. I've been running for a few months."

She pulled out her phone, googling the brand. "If you're within your ninety-day window, you can return those, pay the ninety-seven, and still have fifty-three dollars left, assuming you got them at this price at the shoe store." She showed him her phone screen.

"Lu——" Bear dragged his hands through his hair. He didn't want to say what was at the tip of his tongue: *I don't want to return my shoes. This is my first new pair in three years. I don't want all our conversations to be about money.* But he didn't say any of that. He never did. "Let's get your lights on." Bear flicked the switches like an idiot with nothing to say.

"In three years, the electricity has *never* slipped your mind, Bear. I just, I think——" She faltered, and Bear let words rush out of him before he lost all of his nerve.

"I think we should end all of this."

SUPERPOWER

MAY 5
15 WEEKS UNTIL FORECLOSURE

NORA MIXED CAKE BATTER IN A LARGE BOWL AT HER hip. They were making cupcakes for Bear's track team and filling them with toothpaste, mayo, mustard, ketchup, all kinds of gross fillings to prank—and celebrate—the new team captain. She and Yanne were so excited about it, but when she told Bear about the plan, he only rolled his eyes. Nora placed the bowl on the counter, watching intently as Yanne talked to their mother.

"Nora is fine, Mom. She definitely didn't crank a man like a Model T at a party," Yanne said and swerved out of the way of a projectile stick of butter.

"Nothing. Nothing, it was a dumb joke. Yeah, you just missed her. I'll tell her to call you." Yanne made big expressive eyes at Nora.

She was avoiding her mother. It was helping Nora to compartmentalize her anxieties, and she'd put her and her mother's drama underneath a pile of Barton Cove worries. At this rate she'd never get to it.

"Why haven't you told her about Gangsta Boo?"

"What is there to tell about Bear, Yanne?"

Yanne shrugged. "It's not just that. You don't talk to her as much anymore. She notices."

"What else is there to talk about? She lied for years. She signed her name Dash. Her legal name is Watson! Watson, Yanne. That whole generation just thinks they can lie with no consequences. We're her children. We're Watsons!"

"I've been thinking of asking her to come stay with us."

"No."

"You think fixing this house is going to heal you and Daddy? He's gone, Nora. What are you doing to heal you and Mom? She's still here with us, and she's *been* with us."

"What is *she* doing, Yanne?" Nora hissed. "*She* lied. *She* fucked up."

Yanne took the bowl out of her sister's shaking hands and nodded. "You just don't want to have to explain about Gangsta Boo," Yanne said. She had a growing theory that Bear was a gangster based on absolutely zero units of evidence.

Nora rolled her eyes. "Yanne, stop this."

"He always has to run to Bangor abruptly, he's always taking calls in another room talking about payment plans. Dude's moving drugs."

"In a Honda Civic?" Nora laughed, but the truth of her words jolted her. He was taking care of so many people. She remembered the cascading bills in his glove compartment, second notices and final notices for a family member. She'd followed him around running endless errands for friends and family. He was spread thin. Too thin. He didn't have anything to give anyone else. Especially her.

She had spared herself. She was *not* getting hurt. She'd done it right.

"That's how the big ones trick you."

Nora, feeling a little smug, shrugged her shoulders. "He's not tricking me. Bear and I have mastered the art of platonic friendship. I know he has a lot on his plate, and he takes his responsibilities seriously. It's neat. We're neat. No messy emotions."

Yanne's hands popped to her hips, getting her overalls dusty with flour. "So, you *have* emotions?"

Nora straightened her shoulders. "Platonic emotions."

Yanne's side-eye could have wilted flowers. "Heffa. This brotha is out here making you Jodeci playlists. There ain't nothing platonic about 'Freek'n You.'"

Nora slid down in her chair. "Yanne, those are for our runs. That song has a perfect BPM for cooldown."

"It's a perfect BPM for going balls deep too. But it's not just Bear. You're throwing out every recipe Dad ever taught you. It's like you're personally preparing him for hibernation."

"I am guilty of that. But you have to admit he's such a good eater."

Yanne stretched across the countertop. "Oh god, Mom would love him. When I made pancakes the other day, I genuinely waited around for y'all to get back just so I could see him take that orgasm bite he does."

Nora raised her hands pretending to be in church. "Yes, lord, I know that bite."

"Shit made me feel like I won *The Great British Bake Off*." Yanne picked up the mixing bowl and swirled the whisk around. "Do you think he knows? About the video?"

"Oh, definitely not." Nora shook her head.

"Why? If he even moderately checked you out, he would see it. When he asked you to volunteer at the school, you freaked out and felt terrible about it. So he brought a van load of kids *here* so you can teach them and feel comfortable. He fucking knows, Nora."

"Yanne, I know how men act when they've seen that video. I've been living this life for eight years." Nora faltered. There *was* a moment when he'd made a pointed comment about *not* caring about her past. But afterward, he'd been so . . . regular. *Nothing* had changed. Those videos always spoiled how men saw her because she stopped being a person. They turned her into an object—a pair of breasts, a mouth. She could always clock the change.

"What if Bear is different? I think he loves you." Yanne's voice tapped around inside her head.

"You said the same thing about Daddy right before I told him, and he never spoke to me again."

That was the first time she had said it out loud. Except for the hefty checks he deposited and the communications through her mother, her dad hadn't spoken to her in seven years. A man with a whole second family shamed *her* sexual misconduct.

"Just give him a chance, Nora. He's not like Daddy." Yanne clanged the spoon on the side of the bowl, flinging the batter onto the counter. "Have you ever *seen* the video?"

"What do you mean, have I seen it? I'm *in* it."

"I mean, I don't think you get the joke."

"What joke?"

"Why it was such a long-standing meme." Yanne pushed the bowl aside. "Sis, you did everything. You gave *everything*. You did *all* the work, and you didn't even come."

"What's funny about that?" Nora blinked away wetness from her eyes.

"It's not about the sex, Nora. Oh my god, no, it's about the lack of returned effort. It resonated with women everywhere. It's a meme because we've all been there. Faking for the sake of a partner's ego and getting nothing back for ourselves."

Nora's index finger swirled around on the counter. "Have *you* seen the video?" she asked.

"I mean, yes, and you should watch it too. I think if you saw that video again, it would make you reconnect with your desire. Make you fight for something for once. It's always been your superpower, how hard you work for the things you want."

Nora tapped her sister's hip. "What's your superpower?"

"Oh, knowing exactly what people need. Like Brandon, for example, craves order." Yanne bit her lip, stirring absently. "This is how he eats: ham and cheese sandwich with chips on the inside. Grapes. Cut carrots. Fizzy water. Every damned Tuesday. And he saves the cookies I make until the very end."

Nora looked around. *And who exactly had asked about Brandon?* Her sister offered up this tidbit of information with no prompting. Did Yanne really understand all of her emotions? "I didn't know you made cookies for him."

"Not *for* him, just every Tuesday," Yanne said. Defensiveness crept into her voice.

"He comes every Tuesday," Nora pressed.

Yanne stopped stirring. "Coincidence."

"Okay . . . and how does Brandon eat your cookies?" Nora asked.

"Ugh, like an accountant. A robot accountant. All measured and slow and neat. I think he would use a knife and fork if he could." Yanne stabbed the batter.

Nora laughed. "And does that make you angry?"

Yanne finally looked up. "Actually, yes. He bothers me. Something about him."

Nora waited.

"He's a pompous know-it-all who thinks being a CPA makes him all-knowing about how to run a business."

"Sure, but that doesn't seem like *it*. You seek him out to irritate him. You shout outrageous things you don't even believe just to hear him contradict you." Nora stopped short of saying that her behavior was extremely attention seeking. Not to mention that she had the best pair of boobs in this entire state, and her shirts had gotten tinier and tinier in the past few months, and it was already May in Maine and still cold. By the summer, Yanne would be naked.

"I may be pushing his buttons, but he deserves it. He's paternalistic—opens the doors, drapes a jacket on your shoulders like a nineteen fifties very good boy." She tapped her fingers as she made her points. "He has the sensible Prince George's County fade every mother loves. He said Jill Scott is auntie music. He plays the acoustic guitar like a damned youth pastor. He thinks weed is a gateway drug. He thinks khaki is a style of pants and not just a color. I could go on."

Nora was shocked at just how much Yanne knew about this man she was so steadfastly claiming not to like. She put her hands to her face, not even trying to sell her fake disbelief. "That sounds terrifying, Yanne."

Yanne squirmed. "He looks at me . . . and it bothers me."

"A lot of men look at you." Nora pulled out the cupcake tray and started placing paper liners in the rings.

Yanne grabbed a ladle and started scooping up batter. "No . . . Brandon *look* looks at me."

Nora sat back in her seat and pulled the self-help book back to her. "You do understand that didn't make *more* more sense?"

"He looks at me with that dimple and the skeptical eyebrow,

and it makes me . . . I don't know, want to run back to find a mirror, you know? To see what he's seeing. I know me. But he makes me unsure of the me that I know." Yanne slid the pan into the oven and set the timer.

Nora shook her head and opened the book to chapter fourteen with the smug confidence of a woman who had figured her shit out. She pointed to the title. "Beauty and the Beast: Handling Conflicting Emotions."

Yanne made a disdainful sniff but dog-eared the page before slamming the book shut.

That night, in the quiet of her own room, Nora did something she'd never done before.

She watched her own video.

By the end of the night, she had watched it four times, each instance pulling out a new experience.

Here's what's bound to happen when you watch your own sex tape:

1. You'll begrudgingly admit that your sister was right—you *are* doing all of the work.
2. You'll laugh at Nathan, who thought he was really *putting it down.*
3. You'll cringe. It's still so embarrassing to see yourself like this. Would it ever not be?
4. But lastly, and most interestingly, you'll accidentally turn yourself on wishing it were Bear.

Would the world really turn upside down if she told Bear about the video?

THE COLD

GOD, BEAR FELT SICK. THE WORDS KICKED OUT OF HIM with so much speed and no tact or emotional understanding. *I think we should end things. You could do better than that, Bear.*

"I . . ." Lu blinked. "Where is this coming from?"

Bear rummaged through the bills until he found the electric bill. It was so cold in here. How had she stayed here this long?

Because she has nowhere else to go.

"Look, I'm right in the middle of my nursing degree! What the actual fuck, Bear. I know we're not—" She stopped herself. No word seemed right. Lovers? Romantic? In love? "But you do *owe* me."

"Lu, I'll help you with anything you need. I just can't continue like this."

"Why now? Did you take the money from Maine Power?" She looked shocked. "I didn't think you would do that. But if you have my portion—" She reached for her purse and opened it slightly as if ready to receive her big payout.

That her first thought went to the money wasn't surprising. He didn't know how he had expected her to react.

"No, I did not take a bribe. I don't have all of the money I need yet. But we're having a great year—"

"You're having a great year but not so great that you can afford to pay me back? I'm stuck with my account on hold at my nursing program, and now you would like to cut ties?" Her utter surprise mingled with a confusing cold fury. Bear wasn't shocked that a woman would be furious at the suggestion of a breakup, but that *Lu* would be furious truly astounded him.

"You're pulling a fast one." She pushed at his chest.

What do I say? "Sorry, Lu, I'm in love with someone else?" What good would it do? What peace would she get from it?

"No. It's time, Lu." He held off her flying hands. "I'm going to get the lights on. That's my first concern."

"Your bank statements stopped coming here. Normally we would go over the finances and see what money we could move from one account to the other. Or we would talk about payment plans." She looked at him with folded arms. "But now you don't want me to know how much money you have. You're buying one-hundred-and-fifty-dollar shoes. You're trying to pull a Francis!"

"Lu, listen to me. I'm not skipping out on you or what I owe you." Shit. He had done this so poorly. This was just too much for her.

"Then stay. Stay until you pay me back. Bear, a nurse is all I've ever wanted to be." She rubbed her shoulders. "You know that."

"I can pay you back whether I'm with you or not. Our relationship isn't insurance, Lu." He'd said it. What had been churning in him for years. That they had both been treating their relationship more like a loan guarantee than a source of connection. And it turned out he actually needed connection.

She looked up at him, her smooth, pale face a little hurt, even a little bewildered. "Why would you never just marry me? If you wanted to be rid of me and the debt so much, why not do the obvious thing? I waited so long, Bear. Why didn't you just ask me?"

I want to mean it when I ask. I want to build a house for my family, build generational wealth for my daughter's daughters. I can't do that with you.

When he didn't respond, she nodded, like that was all the answer she needed. "I knew you were going to do this. But I told myself, 'Bear's not like that. He wouldn't.'"

"Lu, I'm not."

"Tell me why I saw an application from some college down in North Carolina and some other rejection letters sent here. Admit it, Saint Ennis. You're trying to revive that old coaching itch, right? You're getting the fuck out of here."

"Look, I meant to tell you about applying to colleges again."

"Why do you get to run off into the sunset with your dreams? I was in nursing school when you met me! I have finally crawled back into some sense of normalcy. We're right back to where we were before the accident, and you're snatching the rug from underneath me, again. I never met a man so spoiled rotten."

Bear blinked. *What in the actual hell.* He had broken his back for everyone, asking for nothing in return. Saying yes when he should have said no. Working sixteen-hour days. All of this to be told he was spoiled?

"Lu, I think you've known me long enough to trust me."

Lu pushed her thin hair behind her ear. "Make me trust you. Don't leave me until you can produce a cashier's check for nine thousand seven hundred and sixty-four dollars."

"Why would you want me to stay? This is not a relationship, Lu."

"So don't call it a relationship. Call it a loan grace period.

Call it what you need to call it. But you're not going to discard me or treat me like I don't know which way the wind is blowing. I *will* be a nurse. I *will* leave this shitty apartment. I'm not going to let you Francis me. I know you have it in you."

His father was a verb. The way he used and discarded people—they would say, *You got Francised.* Could he live like his dad? On the outskirts of respectability? The cold terror of being held in the same contempt his father was felt like a slow death. He thought of walking into a room and having all conversation cease. He thought about his dad, sick and walking for miles to the methadone clinic because no one would give him a ride. When elders talked about people bringing vice back into the rez, they were talking about Francis Freeman.

"I'll get the money to you in a month," he said.

She nodded her agreement. Their breakup, like their relationship, had been about transactions, bills, and appointments, and insurance coverage, leases, and deposits. Lu was in the last stages of being approved for disability, and Bear had tried to help her focus on the financial independence it would offer. Since she was applying retroactively, the back payment, along with the money he was going to pay her, could be enough for her to be independent.

By the time the lights blinked back on, Lu was closed up in her room for the night, and Bear was in the front room watching sports documentaries and *The Bachelor.* The thick, cold rolling fog of silence, coupled with the dramatic music and horny humping of the reality TV dating show, seemed to double down on Bear's sense of crippling loneliness.

He slept on Lu's couch, woke, and called the university, begged a poor office assistant to return Lu back to good standing—he couldn't. Bear tried to undo the mess he made—that he continued to make. He shopped for new groceries and refilled prescriptions. At night, he curled in on himself, eating ramen and boiled eggs. The loneliness felt like a frozen brick tied to his feet. No matter how many blankets he pulled over his chin, he shivered with the violence of it. In the middle of the night, he turned up the heat on the thermostat, and on the last morning, he saw a Post-it with $33.17 written on it. Lu had calculated the cost of the heat. A bill *he* was paying. Bear crumpled up the note and threw it fruitlessly at the television. He could never go back to feeling this lonely again. How had he been living on scraps like this?

Lu only came out of her room to eat, so Bear jolted when she stopped in front of the couch. She dropped her college course schedule on the counter, and circled a date roughly one month from now. She didn't speak to him or make eye contact. He grabbed the papers and placed them in his backpack.

"I will pay you back and get you back in good standing. Before the end of the month," Bear said.

Lu slapped her palm on the counter. "Enough with the promises, Bear. The only thing I want to see is my money in a month."

GO FAST

NORA HAD TO REMEMBER BARTON COVE WAS *WORK* for Bear. Everyone was entitled to a vacation. He should be on a very well-deserved break in Tahiti. There was Cinco de Mayo, maybe even his own cultural holidays. Moxcy and Jennings were running tours. It's not like he was a missing person. Everyone still spoke of Bear in the present tense.

He deserves a vacation, she kept reminding herself.

Yet, she was poised to take a two-hour Lyft to Old Town and walk around the city center screaming his name, but she pulled open the front door and found him just outside on her porch.

"Bear? Oh, my goodness. I was about to file a missing person report."

He embraced her briefly in a hello hug, and Nora nearly climbed out of her skin.

A hug?

"I want to run—" He spoke like it hadn't been eight whole days since they talked. Since they ran.

"Me too," Nora said, cutting him off.

"I want to go fast," he said. "I . . . I, er . . . I don't want to hold back, Nora."

Her stomach flipped. "You know, I've been thinking about game six, and LeBron's focus," she said softly. Her heart was racing like she was running for her life.

"Go on" was all he said, placing his Carhartt coat on the hook.

"After a few more really bad games with the Cavaliers, Le-Bron made the super-controversial decision to move to Miami," Nora started. The slight tremble in her voice betrayed her nervousness.

Bear caught on to her meaning immediately. "People hated him for it. But he had to go in a different direction to get that championship ring."

Her heart sped up. "Yeah, he was the villain, but he needed game six with a bad team to help him realize . . ." She trailed off. When LeBron moved to Miami, he had better infrastructure, a stronger team, and he dominated the championships. Sometimes you win by stepping outside of fears of people's expectations. "He didn't need to beat his head against the wall to get the Cavaliers to work—he just needed to get to Miami. He needed to win his own way," she finished.

She could see understanding shining in his eyes, and all of a sudden, he looked lighter. "Nora." He took her hand, looking her in the eye. "Fast today." The way his eyebrow rose gave Nora's heart a little start. "Let's take our talents to South Beach. Fast."

AFTER THE RUN, BEAR SEEMED HAPPIER AND MORE ENER-gized than he had been before. Remarkably, miraculously, he pulled her close, wrapping his big arm around her shoulders like the first run. Nora's belly flipped.

He's back to touching.

What in the world had happened in Bangor? Whatever it was, there was a cloudiness lifted from his expression. His big, broad mouth looked like it was seconds from breaking out in a smile for the whole run. He talked incessantly about his plans at the college and a smoothie he wanted to patent.

He yelled, "Feed me, woman!"

Nora rolled her eyes but let her arm curl around his middle.

"If Yanne hasn't cooked, we're both out of luck."

"I have a huge appetite right now. I swear I could eat a horse. I want to eat and drink and fuck and run, in that order and on a loop."

"Goodness. What happened?"

"I just finally t-took my foot off the brakes in my life. I finally had a hard conversation. I see the light at the end of the tunnel, you know?"

Ennis opened the car door for Nora. "This day is big, Nora. We should go through the whole set of Sunshine Trails offerings for the inn—crafts, beading, canoeing, the wigwam, all of it."

"We don't have to cram it all in in one day."

"I *want* to cram it all in, though. I'm going to push this month to increase profits considerably, and I'm going to need you to be receptive to some big, intrusive changes." *Is everything this man says a sexual innuendo, or am I just extra pressed?* Her skin burned. She'd be receptive, all right.

When they got back to the inn, Bear rummaged through the pantry while Nora stepped in the shower. She turned the heat all the way up. They *had* run fast this morning, and she would feel it tomorrow. But she loved the way her body felt when it was pushed to the limit, and loved the aching feeling of her limbs crying out. She let the hot water run over her body, beating at her skin until it reddened. She wished she'd thought to bring her toy in the shower. Then she could think about Bear *cramming it all in* with purpose.

Once out of the shower, Nora rummaged through all of her clothes. She pulled out the dress Yanne had insisted on bringing for her, a short, flouncy, off-the-shoulder yellow floral sundress.

She'd been thinking about her no-distraction rule, and honestly she was more clearheaded and driven with him by her side. When he left to do whatever he did in Bangor, she was distracted, slow, scattered. Bear turned her thousand points of light into a laser beam.

When she stepped into the kitchen, Bear fumbled the box of Raisin Bran, and it hit the floor in an explosion of crunchy flakes.

"Oh god, I'm sorry. I can get you a new box." He reached down and grabbed the flakes with his huge hands and tried to shove them back in the box. "I-I-I have a day planned."

Nora reached over and took the box away before he crushed it. "A day?"

"I want to show you the full breadth of the Sunshine Trails package now that the weather's good, and why it's such a value-add. I want you to be able to upsell it at sign-in. I want to start with some arts and crafts, then we can get to the wigwam experience."

Nora squirmed. "What is that again?"

He was looking at the ruffle at the hem of her dress, then his eyes slid up her bare neck and shoulders. "It's outside camping in a wigwam."

"You and I?"

Bran cereal fell from Bear's shirt. "Yeah. Moxcy is taking finals so . . ."

"So overnight camping?" Nora rubbed her hands together. "Are there sleeping bags?"

"Nope."

"Blankets?"

"Moose skin."

"Ugh." Nora shuddered. "Is there at least food?

"I make venison stew."

"And venison is?"

"Deer."

Nora made a face. "What if you just *told* me about all of these activities?"

"Not the same. You'll learn how to light a fire, how to fish, how to skin a rabbit . . ."

"I swear I do not want to learn any of this."

Bear sat down on the barstool, and his long legs fell over the edges of the seat. "Are you afraid? Of us being alone?"

When she was in a room full of people, it was easier to keep a lid on her attraction to him, but here, with no one looking, she felt it swell and knock over vases and pots in the next room.

"No!" she blurted out. "In fact, I, um, wanted you to know that at the expo that night when . . ."

Bear played with the ruffle at her sleeve. "We kissed." He said it so sleepily, so lazily, like he'd just rolled out of bed.

"I was having a panic attack. I have those. I'm sorry for making you feel . . . like I didn't want you," she pushed out. His knuckles grazed the tops of her breasts. Nora almost reached for his hand and held it there. She didn't realize how touch-starved she was until his hands were on her. Bear's touches made her feel fizzy and powerful, like she'd been dropped in a vat of McDonald's Sprite. He pulled a wildflower from the pile she left on the island, and slid it into her ponytail.

"I never felt that way."

Then he took another flower and slid it behind her ear.

When his eyes rested—no, lingered—at the fabric stretched across her breasts, Nora knew she was bound go to jail tonight for various sexual crimes:

1. Forcible Fellatio, Class 2 Misdemeanor
2. Aggressive Face-sitting, Felony
3. Titty-smothering, Class 1 Misdemeanor
4. Nipple-biting, Citation

TL;DR: she would do the time.

"Bear." Nora swatted his hands away when he reached for another flower. "I want to talk about my house."

Bear gasped. "Did you hear that? You called Barton Cove your house. You love this house now?"

"Bear," Nora began.

"Do you love it enough to stay?" he asked. Nora looked down at the newspaper, where she had circled the sales on furniture. Nothing says *I'm in this for the long haul* like purchasing a new bed. A king bed.

"So, there's a position coming up at my high school—assistant coach position. The pay is shit, but the kids love you, and you're damned good at it—"

"Bear," Nora warned. Here he was, asking her to stay. Building a space for her in his community. But she would let him down. She knew she would.

"What if you applied?" he said.

Nora clenched her fists and zipped and unzipped her purse. "What if I couldn't?"

"What do you mean?" Bear pulled a broom and dustpan from the pantry.

"I mean, what if I couldn't apply?" She bent down to hold the dustpan while Bear swept bran flakes into it. "What if there was something in my past that would make it difficult to work with minors?"

He leaned on the broom. "Nora. Talk to me."

If you lose him because of this, you never had him, Nora.

It's now or never.

LOW EXPECTATIONS

SAME DAY, AFTERNOON

I MADE A SEX TAPE WITH MY BOYFRIEND IN COLLEGE."
Nora took at least seven breaths. "I lost my track scholarship,
and this video follows me everywhere I go. I know you work
with a lot of young kids, so I understand if you need to process
this or if—"

"Nora." He closed the distance between them, letting the
broom clang to the floor. "I know you had a sexual history before
me. I'm an adult. And I knew about the video."

It took a few moments for what he said to sink in. For a
minute, she only blinked at him. "You knew?" Nora stepped back.
Heat rose in her cheeks. Damn, she didn't expect that. "Have
you . . . um, did you watch it?" Nora searched his eyes for disgust
or ridicule, even lust. Instead, he bent his head down and whispered so damned softly in her ear.

"I didn't watch it. I figured if there was anything you wanted
me to see"—he paused, pulling back to look her in the eye—"you
would show me." The look he gave her sent heat all the way
down to the soles of her feet. She shook her head. *He saw the link
and passed it up.* It was actually confounding.

"You didn't even want to?" Nora asked, now following him around the room as he put away the broom.

"I didn't say that."

Nora had a million more questions. But they all choked in her throat. *Do you still want me? Why?* Maybe he was pretending to be okay with it because she was standing here.

She found herself in the insane position of arguing that the video was actually a big deal. Because if Bear had just shrugged those links off, that would make *her* the one who had put too much weight on her past. It would make her the ridiculous one for not just telling him months ago.

Am I the drama?

No, he had to understand how bad the video was.

"I don't think you're taking it seriously."

"I am. I'm not pretending. I know this could be tricky for someone working with minors."

"Not tricky. A nonstarter," Nora corrected.

"But this is the future, and I happen to know there are ways to delete those."

"If you're talking about reputation services, I've already tried. They don't delete everything, and they are hella expensive. Well, more than my dad was willing to pay, at least."

He didn't say anything at first. He only grabbed the heavy backpacks and slapped them onto the counter. "Next month, we're throwing one of the biggest business events in Old Town. News outlets, other media, everyone is gonna be there. We're gonna be talking about tribal sovereignty and partnerships with other businesses. I'm telling you this because one, you're my business partner, and two, there's going to be someone there I think you should meet."

"Who?"

Again, no answer. He pulled a small saucepan out of the pantry and placed it inside the bag. "Will you come? I'm giving a speech."

Nora knew what that meant. It took Bear an extremely long time to plan for speeches. To memorize words and pauses, to sound natural. And if he was giving the speech, it was a big fucking deal. "I want to be there," she finally said.

He threw a pack of gum into the bag. "Cool, I want to introduce you to some other people too." He must have seen her face fall slightly. "Nora, what?"

"I, um, I just keep thinking about the video. I think you should watch it."

"What?"

"I think you're being this cool because you haven't *actually* seen it. Maybe when you see it—"

"I'll change my mind?" Bear's eyebrow rose.

"I mean, maybe. I want you to know this about me. I want you to see it all, and if you still want me after seeing it—"

"Then I pass some test?" Bear shook his head. "Put me to the test in a way that matters, woman."

"Bear, the video is me. It's who I am."

"Wholly disagree. Did you even make that video?" He bit into an apple, then added a few to the bag.

Of all the emotions she expected to feel telling Bear about the video, she was surprised to feel anger. His whole who-gives-a-fuck attitude was infuriating. She'd been the object of disdain and ridicule for nearly *eight* years. In the early days, she didn't even leave the house. "No, my ex made it," she said through gritted teeth.

"Then it was being filmed for him. If you want *me* to know about it, you should tell me about it from your perspective. It's the only one I care about."

"Bear, you *should* care about it. People are going to judge you. They are going to speculate about you if you're seen with me." This was what it was like to always be the apple of everyone's eye. He didn't understand rejection. "You could lose your job. I know you've never had *one* day where you haven't been adored, but could you take this seriously?" It was almost like she wanted him to run. He needed to hear this. He couldn't be nonchalant.

He paused mid-bite. "Adored? All my life?"

"From what I see." Nora folded her arms.

He sat the half-eaten apple down. "No, no, I was a chubby kid with a debilitating stutter who lived with his grandparents. I learned to run so I could be faster than my bullies. But as much as I loved the sport, I wasn't like you. My running wasn't enough to go pro. I also wasn't particularly smart like my cousins. Do you know why my gma gave me this business? I wasn't anointed or special like everyone seems to think. She told me, 'You're too ordinary to ever get out of here.' She left it to someone she knew would *never* leave." He pressed down into the countertop with his index finger. "Low expectations were the *only* thing ever set for me, Nora. So when I tell you you're going to have to do a whole hell of a lot more than fuck a terrible guy eight years ago for me to let go of the highest, brightest star I've ever touched, I mean it."

Nora swallowed a hard lump in her throat.

"Bear, I—"

He cut her off. "I don't want to watch *him* telling me a story of his conquest. That's what videos like that are. Trophies. I think you and I know that it matters *who* tells the story." He held both her shoulders the way he did when he was pretending to shake some sense into her. "I want you to tell me everything about that video until it doesn't hurt to talk about it anymore. I want us to be able to talk about that video over eggs and pancakes and bacon."

Nora let out an incredulous laugh. She could never get there. Her nostrils flared like tears might be coming, but she staved them off.

Highest, brightest star? Me?

"I don't think it's fair for you to be the subject of gossip because of me," she said softly.

"Everybody's got shit, Nora. The only difference is that they can google yours. What you see as being adored, I see as actively cultivating a life of duty so that no one could reject me. I didn't have any thunder in my mouth, so I had to make lightning in my hand. I had to do exactly what I said I was going to do. Turns out that alone was *so* powerful for people."

Lightning in my hand.

That's what she had now. She couldn't bury it any longer. She would talk with him about anything. She wouldn't hide herself anymore. Let him keep his lightning. She would have thunder enough for both of them.

"Maybe we could talk about the video." She held his gaze. "On . . . on my terms."

Bear flipped his hair to the side and turned to rummage through the fridge. He popped open a Tupperware container and sniffed it before dramatically throwing it into the trash. "Do you remember the day after we met? When we watched the qualifier races? We saw our old colleague J. Mail coaching those Olympic hopefuls?"

Bear took the phone, iPad, and Nintendo Switch out of Nora's bag. "The thing we both remember about him was how slow he was. He loved track and field. But he wasn't a runner. Now he's absolutely at the top of his game as a coach."

Nora surreptitiously slid her phone back into the side pocket of her bag.

"You should stop thinking about that video as something that DQs you. And start to think of it as something that *qualifies* you for something else."

Nora touched her hand to her mouth. Leave it to Bear to use a rusty track metaphor to reframe her deepest insecurity. *What do I know now because of this experience? A hell of a lot, actually.* There was no point denying that her heart was fully in this. She was two feet in, and she hoped to God he was too.

"I, um . . ." *Why is my voice shaking?* "I'm glad you're back, Bear."

Bear cleared his throat and straightened. Ah, mercy, she wasn't going to get to the end of this day without touching herself or touching him. Gooseflesh sprang up and spread across her skin. He watched it with smug fascination.

He *knew* what he did to her. He knew it.

She *would* tell him every detail of the video. She would tell him until he was squirming and aching and desperate for her. That should help restore some damn balance to the universe. When she looked up at him, his face was heavy, more somber than the occasion called for.

"Nora, you were honest with me. Now I want to be honest with you. I have—"

"Goats!" Yanne burst through the kitchen mudroom holding at least four cloth bags in each hand. She wore an orange crochet halter top that was doing all it could just to cover her nipples, and a long skirt that dragged against the floor, sweeping branches and dirt into the house.

"Jon got me goats!" Yanne pulled a sack of goat food out of the bag.

Bear's hands curled over her left shoulder, and his thumb whispered over her collarbone. The tenderness of the gesture made her force her eyes closed and count to five.

Nora eased out of his grasp mostly because Yanne's eyes bounced from his hand to Nora's face. "Yanne, what now?"

Yanne put her ridiculous groceries on the island, crushing the wildflowers Nora had cut. "For that nasty patch of poison ivy you pointed out to Nora, Bear. He read that goats are a really natural sustainable way to get rid of it."

"Why did Jon have to get you goats? Why not just send you a link to an article?" Nora plucked a petal off one of the flowers.

He loves me.

"Jon—aah, bless him, he listens. He's a man that listens. He got me these goats!"

Brandon eased in the door, looking like the day had already taken a lot out of him.

"Yanne." Nora pulled the flower from behind her ear. "How are we going to *keep* goats? Did you ever think of that?"

"Nora, once you see them, you will fall in love."

Bear shook his head. "Goats are going to steal my thunder. Do you know how hard it is to keep people's attention? Now *goats* will be roaming the area?"

Yanne led her outside, where two goats stood tethered to the beach shower. She pulled out a sheet of paper, and Nora nearly stumbled backward. "I made a little chart to track their feeding schedule." Yanne was unfolding a *spreadsheet.*

"Okay, so one had a little dark patch over his eye like my high school English teacher, so I named him Mr. Middleton, and this is his wife, Mrs. Middleton."

"Terrible names," Bear said. "The first one has an eye patch, but it looks like a basketball. You should name her Michaela Jordan because he's the GOAT." Nora rolled her eyes, and opened her mouth to speak, but Bear cut her off. "Not a debate, woman." Bear kept going. "And the second one has that smooth beard and he's a billy goat. He should definitely be—"

"Billy D. Williams." Nora, Brandon, and Yanne said the name together, nodding at the obviousness.

"Okay, that's not at all what I was going to say," Bear said.

"So can we keep them?" Yanne batted her eyelashes, and made a note on her spreadsheet. Bear squeezed Nora's shoulder.

I know, I see it, she said with her eyes. *This heffa has a spreadsheet?*

"I mean, how do we even feed goats?" Nora waved at Billy D. His rectangular pupils unnerved her. .

"Feed them anything!" Jon walked in as he usually did, like the handsome hero in a stage play. "Goats eat everything, my love."

"No, you actually can't," Brandon cut in. He always began conversations with the long-suffering exasperation of Severus Snape. "We should invest in alfalfa, hay, and oats. Yanne and I have already built a sheet."

"Brandon, we can't all live by the books." Jon laughed. He cut his eyes to Brandon, and Nora could see a touch of annoyance play in his eyes. She looked over to Bear, who raised an eyebrow.

Drama.

Brandon continued, "These are milking goats, so you could also work up a profitable cheese, milk, and soap products addendum to the inn. It would double as advertisement if you took your goods to the farmers' market."

Yanne nodded. "Brandon, it's genius." They returned to the

kitchen island, gesturing wildly about goat milk by-products while Jon stood still in the doorway, unused to not being the center of attention.

"He's just an accountant," Jon countered.

Bear walked back into the kitchen. "And he works for them. Why are *you* investing so much time and money into a rival inn?"

Jon smirked. "No offense, Nora and Yanne, but by no stretch of the imagination is this a rival inn."

Yanne looked away into the beachfront windows.

"Okay, Nora and I have to go." Bear touched Nora's wrist. All he had to do was keep touching her, and she would follow him off a cliff.

Yanne shot Nora a playful glance. "Where y'all going?"

"Adventuring?" Nora said.

Yanne looked suspicious. "In that?"

Nora looked down, suddenly self-conscious. "Should I change?"

Bear looked panicked. "God, no. We're crafting and beading, not heavy lifting."

Nora pressed the point. "Just so you know, I'm not eating deer or skinning bunnies."

"You're going to do what I tell you to do, Ms. Dash," Bear grumbled as he closed the door. The bran flakes falling from the crease in his shirt took the sting out of his false threats. She was so happy that it completely slipped her mind that he had meant to tell her something.

WIGWAM EXPERIENCE

SAME DAY, EVENING

BEAR SMOTHERED THE FIRE AND BAGGED THE REmains of the venison stew. He walked a few yards away to hang the food up in a tree. In this part of the woods, bear bags were essential.

He was surprised to see his cousin's name flash on the buzzing phone screen.

"Basil." Bear kept his tone flat. "Thank you for getting back to me, a week later."

"I was just surprised to hear from you. Business must be in real trouble if you're calling me." Basil chuckled.

God, his cousin was insufferable.

"No, cousin, actually we're thriving. So much so that we only need to be open during high season to make the same amount of money for this year." Damn, it felt so good to say that.

"I guess you picked up a couple of business books since we last chatted."

"Looks that way. Basil, I wanted to know if you could help my friend."

"Yeah, your friend with some bad links out? You're not trying to use your cousin to delete bad reviews, are you?"

"Sunshine Trails doesn't get bad reviews, Basil."

"Boy, you don't sound like you need help at all. Sounds like you got everything all squared away."

Bear sucked his teeth. "Okay, I do need your help. I just need you to be discreet about it."

"Then am I invited to the memorial this year?" So this was his bargain.

Bear rolled his eyes. His grandmother's memorial was going to be big this year. The city was highlighting the importance of private business and tribal relations by honoring Sunshine Trails. It was less a memorial and more a photo op for the state of Maine to show they made good with the Indigenous community. He would get a spot on the local news. He would make his big speech. His big stance against the power company. It would be his personal triumph, and he didn't want any part of Basil's particular brand of chaos. He just sucked up the oxygen in the room with his money and his flashy gifts.

He wanted the memorial to be a slap in the face for faceless moneyed bigwigs. How would it look if his moneyed bigwig cousin showed up? But he wanted Nora to be free from her concerns about the video, and he would do anything to help her. Despite his feelings about his cousin, Bear knew Basil was whip-smart and could do what Nora needed.

"You're welcome to come, Basil."

He hung up the phone and put it on silent. After closing everything down for the night, Bear crawled into the warm wigwam.

IT SMELLED LIKE A WET FOREST INSIDE AND NOW LEMONS. He and his father constructed the dome with tree saplings, bark, buckskin, and some cloth. He'd painted pitch over it for weather-proofing. It wasn't the most beautiful thing to happen upon in the summer wood, but it kept out the rain and the bugs. The solar light hung on the crossbeam and cast its flickering light across Nora's face and shoulders like those criminals getting questioned by the cops in old movies. The moose-skin rug added padding and softness to the floor.

"I put the food away for breakfast. You're not wasting this stew."

"Oh, I am." Nora fidgeted with her dress. There was no elegant way to sit in that tiny thing. "People pay five hundred bucks a night for this?"

"They are paying for an experience, for the magical 'Wise Indian' helping them feel connected to something other than their corporate jobs and ungrateful children." Bear pulled at a splinter in the bark.

Nora nodded. "You're like a Native American Bagger Vance."

Bear's laugh bounced off the domed walls. "Exactly, or that big dude from *Green Mile*, but less magical and more mystical and wise." He crossed his legs and held out his palms in a yogi pose.

Nora finally settled in, folding herself and modestly placing her hands over her legs. "I don't think people think you're wise because you're Abenaki. I think you're wise because you're slow and thoughtful and full of restraint."

He glanced at the hem of her dress riding up her thigh. "Not that restrained."

She caught the movement of his eyes and pulled fruitlessly at the fabric. "Oh wise one, I, um, want to tell you a story."

He folded his arms. "Tell Bear a story then."

She faltered for a moment, then smiled. "I made this video."

"What, a dance challenge?" Bear teased, watching her hands.

"No, it was kind of sexy."

Bear's eyebrows rose up his forehead in mock surprise.

"It's probably not as sexy as you think," Bear countered. "I've been around the block with those videos."

Nora tapped her thighs with her robin's-egg-blue nail polish. "Oh, it's sexy."

His eyes lapped up the image of blue nails on long elegant hands, florid swirls of soft fabric kissing at supple, hazelnut-brown thighs. How could she be *right here* with him like this?

It was all he'd thought about since he'd crashed into her at Barton Cove. "Tell me everything, and I'll decide if it's dirty." Bear licked his lips and sat up with his forearms on his knees.

Nora sat up and folded her legs underneath her. Her soft summer dress and ballet flats had seemed so appropriate during the day. Crafting and beading in an innocent, fluttery, breezy dress seemed like a great idea. Now in the swinging light of the cramped wigwam, the tiny dress was a weapon. One pull downward, and she would be bare breasted. One misplaced leg, and other parts would be laid bare.

Nora crossed her arms over her plump breasts, pushing them close together against the cotton fabric. Bear wiped his brow. It wasn't a warm night but the portable heaters on either side of them were definitely doing their job. Sweat beaded on his forehead and upper lip. Nora's eyes bounced all over him.

I want to touch you.

Nora pulled back and forth at the collar of her dress. She was getting warm too. A trickle of sweat disappeared between her breasts. Finally, her eyes met his and held him pinned against the bark walls of the structure. If he were an animal in a dark wood and had happened upon that look, he would have known to back away.

Nora wanted him. *Him.*

Slow, shy, stuttering Ennis Bear Freeman.

The knowledge seemed to fill up the room until both of them were high on it. Nora broke the silence first. "I, uh, made a video with my boyfriend."

If he had blinked, he would have missed her flick a taut nipple. *Sweetgrass, this woman!*

"You weren't alone, Nora?" Bear pulled at an imaginary wrinkle in his jeans to check if his growing hard-on was noticeable.

"No, but he only helped a little."

Bear's shoulders shook with laughter.

Nora laughed and shifted again, folding her knees to the other side. Bear registered a flash of white lace panties as she shifted her leg. The way she caught his eyes again made him know she meant for him to see. She liked to watch him watch her. Bear gripped the moose-skin rug.

Touch her.

"Did your boyfriend post it without your permission?"

"Not exactly. At the time I thought it would be . . . I don't know, hot."

"The video?"

"To be watched." Her eyes flashed to his like flint on steel.

"Pretty respectable kink." He held her gaze. "Right now, I'm bored. These videos can be pretty basic. Everyone knows how to line up the parts." He found himself flexing his fingers, almost reaching out. "How does it start? Make sure you leave nothing out." He hoped he sounded measured and restrained, not desperate for another flash of lace.

Nora looked at him, then down at his pants. Oh, he could cut a fucking diamond with this hard-on.

See what you do to me, Nora?

She dragged her eyes away from his middle. "Well, it starts off with me in the bed. I'm facedown—"

"Ass up?" Bear finished, a little hopefully.

"You're familiar with the position then?" Nora asked in her most professional tone.

"Quite," he bit out. Her nipples poked through the fabric, and she bit the corner of her bottom lip.

Touch her.

"Good. So the guy comes in, naked, dick out, and he wants . . . he wants me to suck it."

The pressure on Bear's jeans felt like a button was going to pop out and shoot right through the bark roof. For the first time in years, he felt that his desire had a home. That he wasn't greedy or gross or desperate.

Fucking touch her.

Instead, he ran his hand over his cock, then pantomimed a yawn. "Whoa, we got a badass over here. So what? You're sucking a dick? That's the video?"

Nora moved her legs from underneath her and sat with her knees up. There was a competitive flash in her eye. "Not just that."

Bear's heart hammered in his chest. With her knees up like this he could see . . . oh god. "N-Nora . . . what else?" Was it a question? A plea?

Nora let one leg fall open slowly, and he saw her swollen lips on either side of a thin strip of white lace. "It gets pretty nasty from here," she said. She traced the scalloped edges of her lace underwear.

"Show me." His voice was thick. "And I'll show you."

His zipper sliding undone sounded as if he'd attached it to a microphone. His pants had never been so tight. He held the base of his throbbing cock and moved over it to soothe it, the pre-cum moistening his hands as he massaged it in his palm.

Nora's eyes widened at the sight of it. Was he hallucinating, or did she just lick her lips?

She watched him work his cock, and she bit her lip as her own slim fingers worked over her clit in circles.

"Let me see all of it, Nora," he rasped out.

She slid the lace to the side and moved her fingers around her clit. She was beautiful everywhere, all the way down to the core of her, gorgeous like a pulsing daylily.

Bear's voice was barely audible. "Did you suck it?"

"I did. Deepthroating until I gagged," Nora said. Bear could hear her staccato breath, the slick sounds of wet skin and her soft mewing. She was so hot and she knew it. She knew what she was doing to him, and she wasn't afraid.

Oh god, I'm going to feed this woman my cock inch by inch. If they went this far tonight, there would be no return. He couldn't let her go. How could he have gone three years without ever feeling wanted like this? He had no idea.

Bear slowed down. He'd be done any minute at this rate. "Did he taste you?"

"No." Nora sighed.

"No? Fucking ingrate."

"He grabbed my . . . my hips." Nora's eyes were closed. A mist of sweat gave her skin a dewy look. He hoped she was remembering him in the basement and how he had been so desperate to touch her.

"And does he go slowly, little by little?" Bear asked, following the circular movement of her hips.

"Nope again. He just drives right in."

"Oh, fuck this guy. Show me w-where he drives his cock."

She bucked her hips toward him, slipping two fingers inside herself. "Right here." She gasped. Her eyes flew open like she'd surprised herself. And he was doing everything in his power to stay on his side of the wigwam.

"Were you wet enough?" Bear asked.

She was looking him in the eye, hands traveling in tight loops. "I'm sopping wet."

Their little story time had tipped into the present. The slip somehow made him harder. Watching her two fingers slide into her pussy was undoing him. He was seeing white spots.

His balls tightened. Staying tentatively in the present, Bear hummed. "Do you like it, Nora?" His breath was hot and erratic.

Nora was close, fingering herself and pulling down the top of her dress to play with her soft, tight nipples. She moaned his name.

"Bear . . ."

"That's it, baby, call me by my name." The unbearable tightness started to move up his shaft. He was going to come so hard they were both going to have to canoe out of this wigwam. His dick pulsed in his hand. God, the way she watched him. She was hungry too. "Oh god, I bet it's so hot and tight. Do you like it, Nora?"

"I love it. I love it when you watch me."

That was it. Her toes clenched and her hips bucked. She popped like a champagne bottle.

He froze, and a low-decibel rumble came from his throat. He was coming. He wanted to race across this wigwam and sit her down right over his cock, to fill her up until it all came sliding back out. He spilled himself over the moose-skin rug and let out a roar of satisfaction and contentment.

"If you liked it, fuck everyone else, Nora," he rasped out, chest heaving. "That's the only perspective I care about."

THE NIGHT SHOULD HAVE BEEN AWKWARD. THEY SHOULD have looked over at each other and laughed. Instead Bear crawled over the moose skin rug and closed the length between them. Like a big brown panther, Bear lapped at her slick hands, and then his mouth closed over her breast. He drew hard on her nipple, and Nora whimpered at the feel of his rough tongue against her. She held his head in her hands and kissed him deeply, and suddenly he was falling all over her. Lips together, they rolled down to the floor. Her panties were off, and his pants were stuck around his boots.

"Fuck!" Bear kicked at his pants.

"Bear. Ennis. Bear." Nora tapped his shoulder. "I don't have any protection. Do you?"

"Mmm," he hummed over her nipple. "My protection is from the Creator."

"Bear, I—" She moaned. *God, this man's mouth.*

Bear reluctantly detached from her nipple. His eyes were droopy with shining purplish lids. He looked like he might just drift off if she didn't hold him down.

"I want to." She pushed her hips against him.

He kissed her lips. Nora felt wavy, liquid. His mouth on hers felt like home.

"We are."

"Do you have anything?"

She let her hands smooth over his back. She felt his shoulders sag.

"No. I . . . I . . . I can go."

"Bear, it's forty minutes, driving there and back."

He kissed her shoulder.

"We could . . . I haven't been with anyone in three years."

"I haven't had sex in an embarrassingly long time either."

She was in love. Was she rawdog in love? While she went back and forth in her head, Bear pulled back and watched her face.

"I want to make love with you, Nora. I want to do it right now, and I never want to stop. But I can't be trusted. Are you on the pill?"

"No, it gives me terrible migraines." She said. "But you can pull—"

"Oh . . . No, we're not testing the Creator. You can look at me and tell I'm potent as hell." He kissed a bicep. Nora rolled her eyes but she secretly loved when he did that. "I will fucking impregnate you." He kissed the hollow of her neck. His rough chin tickled her collarbone. God, but she loved this man.

He laughed into her neck. "Oh no, you mean coming inside you over and over makes a baby?" he said in a dry voice.

"You can't make me pregnant on sheer will alone."

"The hell I can't." He laughed. "We don't have to do anything right now. It's like that song you put on the cooldown. 'These are the times we all wish for,'" he crooned.

"'A moment when less means so much more,'" she finished. Then they were screaming Dru Hill to the smattering of stars visible through the hole in the wigwam roof.

He held her shoulders. "We can lie right here, Nora, and talk until our throats get dry and our eyes get heavy."

"I want to hold you, Bear."

Bear bowed like Nora was laying a crown over his head. When he looked up again, his eyes were wet.

"Hold me then, Nora."

They lay facing each other, fingers interlaced, saying nothing. Saying everything.

Nora committed to memory the flicker of lashes against his cheek, the inky depth of his eyes, the pacing of his breath. He rested his head on her chest and whispered softly in a language she couldn't make out. It occurred to Nora as she pressed Bear into her that this big man who looked like he could protect an entire apartment complex needed her to hold him. She didn't have to be a vamp or a nun. In him, she found a place for her anxious fussiness *and* her wild, reckless desire. She felt safe to go as slow or as fast as she needed to. If they didn't make love tonight, Bear would be here tomorrow. And the next day. And maybe forever.

Here's what was bound to happen re: falling completely in love with Bear:

1. Eh . . .

Shit.

First he would . . .

She couldn't think of *any* scenarios. For the first time in a long time, she didn't anticipate disaster. She had really fucked up and fallen completely in love.

She would relive this night a thousand times. As long as she lived, she would remember his dark eyes on her as he stroked himself, forcing details out of her, making her face him as she said it. Nora felt the weight of all that shame falling away as she lay there with him, whole and happy. And foolishly, she thought she would stay that way.

SOMETHING SERIOUS

NORA WOKE WITH THE SOUND OF BEAR RUMMAGING around the wigwam. Her neck was stiff and her hair was probably full of twigs, but she felt incredible. Not just cozy, but light and fluttery, like if the blanket weren't holding her down, she'd tilt up to the thatched ceiling of this place.

"Finally up?" Bear's eyes were alight with fire behind them.

Was it joy? Or was it her own joy reflected in his eyes? Nora didn't know and didn't know if it mattered.

"Bear." Her voice was croaky and raw. "I had an amazing time."

When he met her eyes with that slow, deadly smile, her chest warmed like a hot plate. He never had to say much. She'd laid down her heart last night. She'd told him everything, and miraculously he wanted her even more. The fact that he already knew about the video turned everything upside down in her head. Bear *was* different. He was *her* person.

"Oh, you're not done having an amazing time," Bear cooed. They cleaned up and walked the half hour to Barton Cove. Brandon and Yanne were already in the kitchen when Nora and Bear walked in.

"I'm trying these fluffy Japanese pancakes, and y'all are going to be my taste testers." Yanne paused. "I bet you two are starved."

"Well, Nora should be because she refused to eat my venison stew." Bear pulled the barstool back and sent another call to voicemail. The fourth one this morning. Nora smiled. He was finally letting the world wait, letting requests go unanswered for more time with her.

"So, Nora." Yanne licked her lips. "How was the tepee?"

"Wigwam," Nora corrected her. "Completely different structures for different purposes and different regions."

"Wow, you actually went out there in the woods and came back with actual knowledge about actual Native American structures." Yanne rolled her eyes. "Glacially boring."

"Yanne, what exactly were you expecting to happen?" Bear lifted the fork to his mouth, then paused as Nora and Yanne leaned in to watch him bite. "What?" He ate the pancake slowly, licking his lips to catch the syrup and closing his eyes.

Yanne leaned in with her elbows on the counter and her chin in her palms. "I was expecting *that*, but to my sister."

The pancake bits came flying back out as Bear coughed and laughed at the same time.

Brandon glared at Yanne. "I think it's noble, man. I think you're a noble dude, and you're a noble lady, Nora Dash."

"Oh gosh, you are so pent-up," Yanne sneered at Brandon.

It was surprising what types of action had started to feel like a rhythm. Bear politely choking in embarrassment at the breakfast bar while Yanne and Brandon picked fights with each other. It was the way she wanted every morning to feel.

She wanted this feeling forever.

"All that's missing is Jon screaming 'radical acceptance' at the top of his lungs," Nora said.

"Oh weird, where is he?" Yanne looked puzzled. "I haven't heard from him since yesterday morning. It's a little unlike him to not text." She scrolled through her phone, then shot Brandon another rueful look. "I wouldn't have taken so long if Brandon hadn't argued with me about everything I picked up."

Brandon closed his newspaper. "She went goat crazy. Tell this woman goats don't need sweaters."

"My goats will have whatever I want them to have because you're not in charge of them. Jon and I were supposed to hang out last night, and I bet he's a little miffed." Her eyes were back on her phone.

Brandon slammed the newspaper down. "Why don't you get Jon to take you all over creation? I'm through being your chauffeur."

It was his third proclamation in as many weeks, and they all knew he would take her anywhere and do anything.

While Yanne and Brandon invented another argument that trailed off into the parlor, Nora and Bear simply buttered pancakes, passed juice and bacon, and smiled shyly at each other. To Nora they looked like synchronized swimmers. She gave him the last lonely strip of bacon, and he cut her pancakes into symmetrical eighths. When he reached for the salt to douse Yanne's perfect eggs, she'd cupped her hands under the shaker. When she stood to scrape the food into the composter, he was running water to rinse the plates.

"I'm sorry. Just let me——" Bear pointed between them. "Do you want to try . . . us?"

"Yeah, I——" she started.

Put yourself out there, Nora.

"Bear, I want to try——"

He shook her shoulders. "Something serious," he said, finishing her sentence.

"I do," was all Nora could choke out. It wasn't what she was about to say. She had planned to soft-pedal it a bit, but he seemed *all in*.

"I have a plan." He pulled away from her, a grin broadening across his face. "But right now, I have to go. There is something I've been meaning to do for three years." He patted his hips for keys. There was something frantic about his search for his phone. "You don't go *anywhere*. Do not fucking move today." He slammed the door, then hurried back in. "Okay, you can go buy some condoms, but otherwise stay right there."

"I won't move." She smiled.

But she did.

As soon as he closed the door, she rushed to Hannaford to purchase more condoms than were legally allowable in the state.

She was rustling the bags when Yanne rushed downstairs, made up like a high school prom queen. "Why did Bear run out of here? Did you guys fight?"

"No, no, the opposite. I—" Nora lifted the bags (plural) of condoms.

"Wait, Nora." Yanne's voice was thick with emotion. "I pulled a card, so the universe could guide me to Jon—"

"As one does," Nora said.

"I got the Moon card." Yanne rushed on heavy earrings with shaking fingers.

"What's wrong, Yanne? That sounds beautiful."

Yanne rolled her eyes. "It's illusion, deceit. I have to find him. I think maybe he got the wrong idea about Brandon and me."

Nora folded her arms. "Now how would he have gotten that idea?"

"I should have asked him to take me to the pet store. Why did I ask Brandon? It was so disrespectful. I can't believe I did that to him. Now he thinks I'm a cheat."

There was a wildness in her eyes that Nora recognized. She was afraid of losing something precious. Nora had felt that terrifying fear herself. But it was too soon for this level of panic.

"Yanne, come on. Jon is not in contact for fifteen minutes, and you think you've lost him? How deep could this relationship be?" Nora regretted the words as soon as they fell out of her mouth.

Yanne's neck jerked back. "Well, we've been in constant contact for six months. According to us, our rhythm and chemistry, this is off."

Yanne was escalating. She really was scared.

"I get it. I really do." Nora knew she sounded like a hostage negotiator.

"Don't use that talk-her-off-the-ledge tone. I hate when you do that. You don't agree with me. You don't get it."

Nora's teeth set on edge. Here she was being Yanne's punching bag when things went wrong. "All I'm saying is give it time."

"Somewhere in there is the woman who stripped at a funeral to *fight* for what was rightfully hers. You don't have any fight left in you, Nora." Yanne jammed her feet into sandy Crocs. "I want to go to the Willow Bee. And I'm going to fight for what I want."

Nora dropped the bags. "Yanne, this is what fighting looks like!" Nora's elbow clicked with the sharpness of her pointing. "What we're doing now! Trying to make sure we can pay the foreclosure payment, *that* is the fight. And I'm the only one still throwing punches. Our season opens tomorrow. And you are running to chase a man down. You're overreacting."

"Compared to you, I'm always overreacting. Well, sorry I'm not a robot. I can't be like you and Bear in this fuckless homeostasis while my life is falling apart." Yanne massaged her temples, and Nora raised her eyebrow, always on the lookout for the early symptoms of a sickle cell pain crisis.

"You need to relax. Get a heat pack. It's been a little under twenty-four hours since you heard from a grown man, and you're going to make yourself sick over it."

"Oh, come off your bullshit, Nora." Yanne stomped over to the kitchen and snatched a cloth rice bag and popped it in the microwave. "You are so smug. You're like radiating joy. I see this little gleam in your eye like you're dying to gloat."

"I might have a gleam, but it has nothing to do with you or Jon. Bear and I—"

"Ugh, if this is going to be another platonic feelings masturbatory sermon, I'm gonna pass." Yanne wrapped the warm pack around her forehead and stormed out.

In a sudden turn of events surprising no one, Yanne was confused about her feelings and overreacting, ditching Nora a day before they opened for the summer.

Yanne was all mixed-up, but Nora wasn't. She saw with startling clarity. She and Bear were solid as a boulder, and they were ready for the championship ring. She touched her fingers to her lips. His kisses burned right through her and made her bold.

I told him.

It just flew out of her, and she was right to do it. They had decided to try something, and that was what she would focus on. Now, more than ever, she and Yanne needed to focus on profiting this summer so that maybe . . . they could stay. Nora was preparing to shower, dress, and wait all made-up in the bed like Carmen Electra did for Prince when she heard stirring in the front.

The front door creaked open, and Nora thought it was Yanne storming back in to yell some point she had forgotten. Soft shoes brushed against the wooden floor. It wasn't Yanne.

Long was the first word that came to mind when Nora saw the woman. She had long legs with the skittish side steps of a colt. Her dark hair, parted in the middle, lapped at her waist. Her hands looked like she could palm a basketball. She was whip-thin and six feet tall if she was an inch.

"You have to be Nora." It came out sounding like an accusation. The woman's voice was high and reedy.

"How may I help you?" Nora had to remember that this would be an inn by tomorrow, and folks could just walk in.

The long woman let out a dry chuckle. "Someone really bought this old place." She stretched her long arm out, and Nora wondered if she was expected to help her walk. The woman examined her clothes and hair. "That jacket is three hundred forty-eight dollars. I circled it in *Shape* magazine." She laughed a wet, phlegmy laugh.

"It was a gift. This is . . ." Nora's smile tightened. "I'm sorry, who are you?"

The woman plopped down on the sofa as if the trip from the door to the parlor had exhausted her. She twisted the ends of her long hair and twirled it under her nose like a mustache. "We're having a bit of a family emergency, and I can't ever seem to get in touch with Bear, so I thought I'd come to the place where he's spending *all* of his time." Their eyes met.

Nora's heart tumbled down some secret flight of stairs she didn't know existed inside her.

"Is everything okay? Does Moxcy know? Are you a member of his family?"

"It's private, if that's okay. Could you just grab him?"

Nora's lips tightened. This woman had a lot of nerve. "He's out. He said he'll be home in a few hours. You can wait here, if you like."

"Home?" The woman squinted at her. "This is home?" She tilted her head. "Oh my god." Her hand flew to her face. "You poor thing." She looked Nora over again, slowing down at the swell of her hips, then raking up to her face. "You have the look, you know." She laughed, a big incredulous guffaw that split Nora's aching head.

"What look?"

"Of a woman dickmatized by Bear."

"Excuse me?" Why was it taking her so long to process these words?

"Did he give you the greatest hits reel? Rescued me from meth heads, took care of me for three years? All the aunties tell you he's perfect? Sweetheart, when a guy seems too good to be true, he usually is."

"Who are you?" Nora's voice trembled.

"I knew it." She folded her arms, ignoring Nora's question. "I knew he was acting different, trying to get out of it." Her eyes went to Nora's coat again, then she looked around to case the house. "How much has that son of a bitch promised you?"

"You need to tell me who you are right now, or I'm going to have to ask you to leave."

She pulled her long black strands away from her face and sat up. "Oh, I'm sorry." She held out her hand. "I'm Lucy Neptune, and looks like I beat you to the punch. *I'm* about to be Bear's wife."

AN AUDIBLE

EAR MADE IT TO BANGOR IN RECORD TIME. HE WAS IN flight. He'd driven here, but he could have run. He felt like a new man. Nora wanted him. Their situations were tricky, but they could work it out. He'd never loved anyone this fiercely, with his whole soul.

And she loved him back.

This wasn't the deal. He knew that. He had promised Lu a month. He was supposed to write up a contract, and they were only halfway through, but she would understand. She had to. He had to stop this now.

He fumbled with the key to Lu's apartment. She never went anywhere, so it was surprising to see that she'd stepped out. He flipped the switch and gasped.

It was a complete mess. Food and beer were everywhere. The television was still on and buzzed on about home décor trends. The kitchen counter overrun with paperwork looked like one of those arcade machines with coins just over the edge.

Second notices, angry red final notices. The bills had no order, new bills piled in with final notices. What was surprising was the sheer amount of them. Had Lu found all of the bills he'd been hiding? He picked up a bill from a company he didn't recognize. A personal loan with a payday lender, with nearly fifty percent interest. No, these weren't his bills.

Oh no, Lu.

She'd been trying to pay these hospital bills off on her own without him, but she'd only made it worse.

She wanted her freedom that badly. God, he was trying like hell to stay on top of every bill. But it was like every single person who had ever touched her in that hospital had a separate bill. It was like playing Whac-A-Mole.

He'd abandoned her again. If he'd come up here more often, he would have seen her spiraling. Pill bottles open near butter knives—she was cutting her prescriptions in half again trying to make them stretch between refills. His eyes flitted across more paperwork. Scary attorney letters telling her they would pursue legal action against her. She was terrified. He had no idea her situation was this bad. That's when he saw it. The envelope from the Social Security Administration. He pulled the letter out.

They denied her disability.

Those fuckers denied her.

The disability back payments were her way out of this grinding wheel of debt and poverty they were both in. And it was gone.

Bear's eyes darted around the room. He raced to the closed door of the bedroom and pushed it open. He didn't know what he would see, terrified of every possibility that darted across his mind right now. He pushed open the bathroom door with so much force the knob loosened in his hand. He ripped open the shower curtain with one heave. Cheap plastic clips rained down over his arms and shoulders. He had lost too many cousins to hopelessness. Death by the bottle or their own hands. Reeling, he ran back into the bedroom.

There were clothes everywhere and drawers pulled out. Her suitcase was gone from the closet. She'd packed up. But where?

He tried her number again. Nothing.

It was time to panic.

He would call her once more before he told the island she was missing.

The slow trill sounded, and his heart jumped when she picked up.

"Hi!" The gaiety in her voice was so emotionally jarring, Bear had to sit down. "Bear. I can't believe you." Her words didn't register.

"Lu, I'm in Bangor at your apartment. Where are you? Are you okay?"

"I'm at Barton Cove." Her voice was shrill enough to shatter glass. "I met your running buddy slash business partner."

The blood drained from his upper body, and his stomach plummeted to his pelvic floor. "Lu, why are you there?"

"There's an emergency, and we couldn't reach you. So I came here. Everyone said you spend all your time here now." A wave of nausea washed over him.

"Lu." His voice was pleading. "Please, you need to leave that place."

"Excuse me, can I use the little girls' room?" He heard Nora mutter something in response.

Oh god, Nora. Bear sank to his knees in the apartment.

No.

Creator save him. He was here to make it right. Why did everything have to turn to shit?

"Bear, are you there? Your father called me. Told me there was some big emergency. Do you know yet?"

He scratched out, "What emergency?"

"You don't know? You should have been the first to know. Look, I think it's obvious why you wanted to leave and who you wanted to use the trust on. But this is the only way, so I told Nora we're getting married."

Bear was quiet for a long time on the phone. White-hot rage cracked through him, jostling with the guilt, fear, and worry. It didn't mix well with his roiling stomach. He couldn't trust his responses, so he said nothing.

After three full minutes, he spoke, "Why?"

"Why, Bear?" She was quiet on the phone, logical to the point of pain. "You have no idea the deep shit you're in. While you were trying to skip out on me, someone told on your grandma and that illegal accounting system she had."

Acid rose in his throat. He couldn't bring himself to speak.

"Bear? Look, I'm sorry for what I said about Gma. Are you there?"

"I'm here." But he wasn't. He was in his childhood home, begging his father to stay—punching his belly with childish force. He was ashamed of the enormity of his need and the force of his anger. "You need to tell Nora you were mistaken."

"I don't have to clean up your mess. You lied to her *and* me. I'm trying to help us."

"This isn't help, Lu. I know they denied you; now my trust is all you have."

"All *we* have. This isn't about what we *want*, Bear. This is about what we need. If you think rationally for a second, you'll see that I'm right."

He did not want to think rationally. "I know it was a shock. A disappointing shock to lose your disability case." His voice shook with the effort of trying not to scream.

"No, Bear. It wasn't *just* that. You need to talk to your father. He was the one to call me." Her voice was trembling. "And I . . . I wish you would acknowledge that you lied to her *and* me."

"So you raced down to the inn and lied to Nora some more?" The anger was coming from everywhere, a noxious gas he was choking on.

"No. You can't do this. How was I supposed to know you were sleeping around? This is your big fat mess and . . ." She seemed to run out of steam. "You'd better come down."

That stopped him short. It really was *his* mess. Something really was wrong.

"They called a meeting yesterday?"

"Yes, and I called an audible because you couldn't be reached."

"Lu, you have to tell Nora that I . . ."

"Bear, why are you still trying to protect her? *We* are in crisis right now. Me and you. She has a three-hundred-dollar jacket on right now. She's going to be just fine. Get down here so we can save your business."

His mind split in seven different directions.

"I will come to this emergency meeting, but, Lu, you need to leave the inn." He hung up on her and dialed Nora, palms sweating and breath ragged.

"Hello."

"Nora, p-p-please let me explain. I'm on my way back home."

"To where? To Barton Cove? Is *here* home?" Each word felt like a heavy clanging bell. The kind rung when something has died.

"Nora, just let me talk to you. I can explain—"

"Stop talking. There is nothing to explain. Absolutely nothing between us. We're business partners. And I will be long gone before you explain all the lies you told me." Her voice was clinical, but not completely untethered to a simmering anger.

"Nora, you are so much more than my business partner. I lo—"

"Don't. You. Use. That. Word. Don't you dare use it." Her voice was a quiet hiss, but it still knocked the wind out of him.

"Nora, I'm c-c-c—"

She hung up.

"I'm coming," he said flatly.

Fuck.

His stomach took a final lurch, and he raced to the bathroom to empty his belly, his whole soul of whatever childish, foolish notions he had held just an hour before. When he was done, he felt empty and drained.

He had almost been happy.

DEATH AND TAXES

SAME DAY, EVENING

THAT EVENING BEAR BLEW THROUGH HIS FATHER'S front door like thunder. When he shouted for Lu, everyone in the room snapped like lightning had struck.

Bear's anger was new and unwelcomed in the Freeman home. It expanded in the living room, filling the corners and dark spaces. He could feel the rage rolling off him like radiation. Moxcy ventured toward him first. His cousin looked like she was feeding a tiger with her last good hand. "Bear. She's in the room, and before you go in there"—she held him back with her fingertips—"calm down. She thought . . . She was trying to help."

"Is that the line she fed you?" Bear swiped his closest friend's finger away. One minute she pushed Nora on him, and the next she defended Lu. "I thought you wanted something different for me too?" He hated how his voice cracked. How hurt he sounded.

Moxcy blinked hard, willing tears away. "I do, Bear, or I did." She let a tear fall down one side of her face. "I am so sorry, but Lu may have known something you don't yet . . ."

Francis's wide face was easy to read—unmitigated glee. He was like a bridge troll, excelling at thwarting anyone trying to get to a new place. The toothpick wobbled in his mouth. "I may have told her about these." He handed Bear a ruffled pile of papers. The top letterhead had the terrifyingly official seal of the IRS. "Back taxes," Francis said. "Told Lu to come. Look, no one here can say you didn't fight for it. Just marry the girl."

Bear's pounding heart drowned out the sounds in the room. The paper was full of numbers and years and fines. He was being dragged underwater, everything in his hands floating away from him, weightless trinkets moving toward the light as he sank into icy darkness and the crushing depths of his life. His anger, hot and righteous, seeped out of his body, and was replaced with bitter, cold resignation. The weight of it sat him down.

Moxcy clasped her hands together. Worry was a new look for her, casting her face in unfamiliar shadows. "We're broke, Bear. This wipes us out. We barely even have enough liquid cash to pull off Gma's memorial. I tried to get him to pay for it." She jerked a thumb at Francis. "She was your mother."

Francis's shoulders raised to his ears. "He was the only person she treated like a child. Me, she treated like a dog. You ever stop to think about why we're doing this memorial? We had our remembrance two days ago. This party you're having is for the Anglos."

Moxcy searched Bear's eyes, maybe afraid they had finally struck him dumb. Her voice was tenuous. "I just wanted you to know that your dad told her about all this. And we had a meeting."

"We? Where was *I*, Moxcy?!" Bear demanded. "I was the subject, verb, and predicate of the damned meeting"

Moxcy looked from Bear to his father. "In the wigwam."

Francis whistled. "Hope it was worth it."

"Ennis, please say something," Moxcy pleaded. She never called him Ennis unless she needed reassurance.

"I'm calm. I just want to talk to her."

Francis shook his head and put his hand to his heart. "I hate to see you like this, kid. I really do. But you could have guessed the folks at the Dam Project were going to use Uncle Sam. Death and taxes and all of that? Before you give her the ring, I want you to consider something."

Francis shuffled with newfound speed to a leather briefcase. For a second, Bear thought the case would be full of cash, but he pulled out a checkbook. He flashed Bear a scribbled check. It was, Bear knew without doing the calculations, the exact amount he needed to get out of tax debt.

Francis's voice softened. He edged toward his son like he was holding a live grenade. "Let the power company help you, Bear. You've borne this weight for too long."

Silence.

Francis stepped even closer. "This also frees you up from Lu and all of that debt. You're a good man, Bear, no one would ever deny that." His voice—the soft tones you would use to settle a startled animal—were hypnotic.

Bear wanted to take the bribe. He wanted this to all be someone else's problem.

Moxcy's eyes were as big as plates. "I think you should listen to him, Bear. Considering recent events."

"What recent events?" Bear snapped. His voice made them jump. Why? He was calm. *Was* he calm? He wasn't sure what he was.

"Oh, son, it's a scandal. The whole rez is talking about you and that girl running all over creation making wolf eyes at each other. Just this morning I heard she was at the Hannafords purchasing all manner of sexual items—whips, chains, rope."

"They don't sell BDSM gear at the grocery, Uncle." Moxcy sighed. "Trust me, I looked."

"That's not how a good man behaves. You're more like Thunderbear than I thought. Being led around by the dick by some off-island—"

"You need to choose your words carefully," Bear clipped out. This was a fight older than Bear. Francis and Thunderbear's discord began and ended with warped perceptions of duty. A man to his wife, a man to his community, a man to his children.

Francis took a wobbly step back. "I'm just saying I know what you actually want. The whole rez knows what you want. This"—he waved the check—"is an out, Ennis. A simple way to get it, to get her."

"The dam," he said.

"I'm sure we can work out fishing rights without getting the tribal council involved. We'll work it out, Bear. I know you've been fighting for that river a long time."

It was so tempting. His arm twitched with the desire to snatch the check and run back to Nora.

See, we can be together! I fixed it. I only sold my birthright and broke every promise I hold dear.

But nothing was ever simple.

"Let it go, Bear," Francis entreated. Bear wanted the check. He wanted to cut free and run from all of this. He flexed his fingers, about to relent, but Francis lost his patience.

"Damn stubborn fool you are, boy. A damn fool," his father spat out.

Bear dropped his hands and pushed past Francis.

"Don't repeat his mistakes, Bear!" his father shouted down the hallway. Nothing he hadn't heard all of his life. Nothing new.

He was the proxy for his father and grandfather's animosity toward each other.

When he opened the door, Lu jumped at the sound. He slammed the door so hard the walls shook and pictures flew off the wall. He wanted to shut his father out of his head.

"Why." He asked the question like a statement.

"Bear . . ."

"Why," he said again.

"I had to. You didn't leave me much choice," Lu said. Bear's eyes rocketed to her.

"Everyone has a choice." Images of the check blinked in and out of his vision.

"Oh, come on, Bear, you think I didn't see where this was going? You were going to fuck me right over." It was a dagger of a statement. "Are you going to take the bribe?" She cut right to the quick. Efficient in everything. "I heard Francis. I know you can walk away right now. Take the bribe, pay the taxes, and leave to coach in nowheresville, America."

"I'm not taking it, Lu." He slammed his hand so hard on the dresser three track trophies toppled. "Why did you tell Nora we were engaged?"

"Wow, you're about to be inmate number 1749B and you're worried about what now? I told her that because it was the fastest and the simplest. The most obvious lie to tell, Bear." She said this with the weary exasperation of a person talking to an idiot. "Unlike you, I take action when a canoe is sinking. You were going to sweep me and our *whole* relationship into the river and give her the trust money *I've* been waiting on for three years. I know what needs to be done. It doesn't have to be romantic. But it has to be *done*."

"Lu, you went too far—"

"I didn't go far enough, Bear. Perfect Bear. God's-gift-to-the-rez Bear. You don't think I hear what people say about you and me, the mountain of lies they bought into?"

"I never started any of those tall tales," Bear said. Of course, she had it all wrong, everyone did.

"Bear. You *never* stopped them." Lu stood up slowly and walked toward him. When she reached out, he instinctively shifted out of her way. It wasn't a cruel move, just muscle memory. When had she ever reached for him? But Lu chuckled—taking it as yet another slight. "We can't even touch each other." She righted the toppled trophies. "You know, I was supposed to be *so* damned happy that you stayed." Her voice dug like gravel. She was reddening with unspent emotion. "I was on my deathbed, and when I woke up and read my notes from well-wishers, they were all about you. *Bear stayed. Bear got a second job. Bear organized a fundraiser. Oh, by the way, get well soon.*" Her eyes burned into his. "My illness has just been a story of Bear's greatness."

He didn't know people had been so callous. He'd also felt the incredible pressure to be a *good* man. The more people came to pat him on the back for being nothing like his father, the more he wanted to believe it.

"Lu, I gave you my word—"

Lu's voice was soft and vicious. "Your *word* may be law over at Barton Cove, but I know who your daddy is. Your business is in legit crisis, and we couldn't even *find* you because you were drunk off champagne pussy in the fucking woods. That's not Thunderbear, that's Francis." She shook her head. "Your *word* is not going to do it for me, Bear. We're going to marry and do the cohabitation thing for six months, and I'll start a new life at the beginning of the year. So if your girlfriend's waiting on a commitment from you, she's going to have to get in line."

Something bubbled up in him, and Bear was smart enough in the moment to recognize it as fear. The rejection he'd always been so terrified of was seeping through the tops of his carefully plastered walls. *That's not Thunderbear, that's Francis.* A premonition perhaps of the flood to come.

THE OTHER DAMNED SHOE

THREE DAYS SINCE LONG LUCY WALKED INTO NORA'S inn—matter-of-fact, devastatingly, ruthlessly unemotional—and told her that she was marrying Bear. For the first time in months, the sun came up without Nora and Bear meeting it. She stared at the muddy shoes in the corner of her room. It was like this whole place belonged to him now. The inn was drafty and cavernous. The Maine woods were becoming thick and impenetrable in the spring. The paths hid from her and slipped into shadow without Bear here. It was like the entire world had suddenly scaled to him, or maybe she had gotten smaller. Nora gnawed at her bottom lip and sat up to kick the covers off her feet. She drank well into the night, and when she stood, the world seemed to tilt sideways like a Stanley Kubrick film. She was squeezing her phone so tightly the virtual assistant chimed in. "How may I help you?" It was the smartphone equivalent of *Damn, you aight, sis?*

She let the water run over her in the shower from hot to cold, but Nora didn't register the temperature changes. So even as gooseflesh peppered her skin and her teeth chattered, she stood under the shower not washing, just being rinsed.

This was one long con. Bear . . . no, Ennis fucking Freeman had showed her how big a fool she was. He led her on. She thought she felt something real and solid blossoming between them for a second. She'd felt . . . well, she was ashamed of what she felt. Did he double over laughing, remembering how she had touched herself for him? Did he tsk over how desperate she was for him to touch her? She must be hilarious to him.

There it was. The other damn shoe.

She'd hoped that maybe this time would be different. She really had. Something gnawed at her belly, and Nora realized it was hunger. She hadn't really eaten since closing the door on Bear's fiancée that night.

Fiancée.

Lucy Neptune was a mystery. She asked relentless questions, all in the name of polite interest. Nora gave away as little as possible. So Lucy flipped through her phone and showed Nora tepid photos of her and Bear:

Lucy and Bear outside the hospital.

Bear with his arm in his shirt like the photographer was taking an engraving instead of a photo. It wasn't an intimate photo. It was more like a postcard: *Wish you were here, xoxo from Maine.*

Lucy and Bear in an ER, Lucy tilting her head toward the light, Bear looking off camera.

It looked like their entire relationship had taken place in an inpatient facility. Nora detected a sad weariness in Bear's poses in all the photos. In every smile that didn't reach his eyes and every distracted half-hearted pose, Nora saw a new Bear, one who could simply go through the motions.

If Nora had photos like this of her fiancé, she would never let them see the light of day, much less whip them out for people she barely knew.

"Nice," Nora had finally said just to get Lucy to stop showing her that sad-ass parade of blurry selfies. When she had finally left, Nora sat against the broad door and let go a torrent of wrenching sobs.

I already knew about it. Bear had said it so nonchalantly. He didn't care because it didn't matter to him. He had no plans of becoming serious with her. He withheld who he was from her, but Nora had cut open her veins, spread her legs, and showed him everything. She had cried on his damn shoulder about her dad leading his double life and leaving his daughters with nothing. Bear had patted her back and murmured in her ear like he would never.

But he would.

They all would.

How had she traveled to the baldhead top of the country and found a man *exactly* like her father? Unfortunately, these would forever be the only types of men who would want her—liars, cheats, and freaks.

She wrapped a bathrobe around herself and shuffled to the kitchen. Her eyes were puffy, her nose ran, and her cheeks flushed a reddish purple. The view of her face in the polished pan bottom made her want to cry out.

Lucy's sad photos crept back into her head. Bear's vacant eyes and listless poses. Lucy looked at those photos and felt like it was proof of something. She shared them all, flipping quickly through her distant-looking selfies. Nora didn't think Lucy looked that in love either. Was this what happened to all women when the scales came off? They went back and looked through photos and realized they weren't happy?

Was Nora that blind too? She opened her phone to look through the few photos she and Bear had taken together.

But shit. She shouldn't have done that.

One photo was of Bear running his students through drills, his face alight and eyes soft. Another picture she'd taken for an Instagram green smoothie sweepstakes where he was mixing his Marvin the Martian drink with the diligence of a chemist. There was another where he pulled her along and turned over his shoulder just as Nora took the shot. She loved this photo not just because of what everyone could see: the juvenile backward cap, the beckoning smile, those sharp dark eyes. Nora loved this photo because of what only she could see—that he was looking at *her*. No one would ever look at her that way again. No one would kiss her that intensely again. No one would stroke himself off looking into her soul like he did. So much wasted energy for them to end up like this.

There was still so much to do. Being used by a man didn't stop the runaway train of the summer season or the finishing touches she needed to put on the house.

She would run errands today, trying to avoid everyone in the town while she did it.

Should be easy.

RIBBED FOR HER PLEASURE

SAME DAY, AFTERNOON

TWO HOURS LATER, NORA SLID ON HER RAY-BANS IN-side of Hannaford's grocery department. She fit her puff around a baseball cap and pulled a heavy jacket over her shoulders despite the spring mildness. Bear told her that a lot of folks from his community transition here for the summer and Nora was taking no chances. Looking around her over the dark glasses, Nora tapped the customer service Plexiglas.

"Can I help you, ma'am?"

In and out, Nora.

"Yes, I need to return these." Nora disguised her voice the way actors who played Batman did, a dry half rasp that scraped her throat.

Nora dropped the seven—yes, seven—boxes of condoms on the counter. They didn't feel heavy until they smacked against the counter. The sound made the bored cashiers turn in her direction. She didn't remember the packages looking this skate-party neon bright when she bought them.

What was I thinking?

The clerk opened his mouth mid-gum smack. "All of these?"

"Yes, all of them." Nora gave the clerk the wrap-it-up sign with her hands.

"Wait, I remember you. What kind of game are you playing?"

In a town of five hundred people, *Wait, I remember you* felt hostile. Of course he remembered her; he just wanted to make her suffer.

"I waited on you for half an hour finding those condoms."

"How are you the only employee?"

Three days ago she was a different Nora; she was full of vim and vigor. The sight of Bear's cock had turned her blood. And she was one hundred percent sure she was going to be dicked down for most of the month. So when the attendant told her they were out of the "ribbed for her pleasure" variety, she had marched right up to the manager and asked them to check The Back, that mythical retail space where all the blue tops in your size were hiding. He rummaged around for twenty minutes and came back empty-handed.

When he insisted that there were only flavored ones remaining, Nora bought them all in an unnecessary show of her purchasing power, all while promising to write a letter to the higher-ups. Yes, seeing Bear's dick had turned her into a Karen.

Now Nora stood, shoulders slumped a little too short for the humiliating customer service counter, asking for her precious money back.

"I don't want any trouble. Just please give me a refund."

"I'm going to have to talk to my manager," he said pointedly. *My, how the tables turn . . .*

She wasn't prepared for the loudspeaker announcement. "Manager to customer service, manager to customer service. We have condom scam attempt."

Nora reached for the handheld. "Hey! Wait, there's no need for that."

In two blinks, a small, green-eyed woman appeared. Her name tag said Beth.

"Beth," Nora started, "this is all a misunderstanding."

Beth looked like Dolores Umbridge in khakis. "Oh, I'm sure."

Before she could begin, the clerk told Beth, "She's trying to return all those condoms."

A few onlookers slowed down and pretended to shop as they listened. She noticed a few administrators from the school and other town members she'd met over six months here. This would be everywhere fast.

"Are they used?" Beth asked, tone still syrup-sweet.

"No."

"See? Why is this box open?" The clerk cut her off, still rummaging through the bag.

"Oh, the, um, the Magnum box I did open. I wanted to make sure it would cover the whole—that it would do the job. But that's the only one I opened. I can take that box back." Nora snatched the box out of the clerk's hand. But she used too much force, and the clerk held fast to the box. The condom box ripped, and the contents flew up and splayed around them like spring break confetti. The packets hitting the floor sounded like fat raindrops on a raincoat.

Nora dropped to the ground. "I'll just take these, no problem."

On her knees, she heard the voices around her.

Homewrecker.

Is that her?

Oh yeah, poor thing.

This proves it.

I was so embarrassed for Lu. Three years!

She seemed so nice.

Nice? She tried her damnedest to get that man's trust.

With every whisper, her back straightened. It was what she was most afraid of being whispered about—everyone dismissing her and making her feel small because of who she was and what she wanted. This was her worst fear, so why hadn't she disintegrated? Why hadn't the earth opened up to swallow her whole?

It didn't, and it wouldn't.

Nora stood up and pulled off the hot-ass jacket and baseball cap. She shoved the fistful of condoms in her purse and eyed the small crowd. Finally, she yanked the intercom from the store clerk and cleared her throat.

"Yes, I bought over one hundred condoms in anticipation of having intercourse with everyone's beloved Bear. But you will all be happy to know that I'm returning them." She shoved the bag into the clerk's stomach. "Once this cashier gives me my money back, your Bear will be safe from the outsider and you all can be safe to fuck off." Nora's hands shook as she dropped the handheld, and the clerk counted out bills in her fist. So this was the woman who had stripped at her father's funeral.

If only Yanne could see me now.

Just before the automatic doors flew open in front of her, she heard a soft clap behind her. An old woman, eighty if she was a day, patted her shoulder.

Nora recognized her from the senior citizen food runs Bear did. Elder Wilkes. The woman put her arms out for a hug. When aunties' arms went out for a hug, Nora knew better than to ignore them. Inexplicably in the foyer of Hannafords, Nora was hugging a strange senior citizen. "I want to make you some tea," the old woman whispered.

"We're in a grocery store."

"I have a little clam cottage nearby."

"I, um . . ." How was she going to get out of this?

"You came by once to deliver meals. Lied to me about needing help."

"I remember." Nora was not getting out of this.

THEY SETTLED IN THE WOMAN'S TINY HOME. SHE'D HAVE some tea, then move on with her day.

The older woman stirred the cup of tea and looked at Nora with curiosity.

"Before he was married, I used to fuck Thunderbear. Bear's grandfather."

Holy shit, old lady, zero to one hundred. "Wow, um, okay."

Her bird chest expanded. "I was a real dish back then."

"Oh, I believe you." Nora sipped the tea.

Elder Wilkes sat quietly for a long time, so long Nora was afraid the woman had forgotten about her.

"But no one wanted anything to do with me. All because of Tommy Wilkes." She paused for a long time again. Nora opened her mouth to prompt her, but the old woman continued. "Tommy Wilkes was an Indian with yellow eyes and yellow hair. He didn't live on the island, though. He had a wealthy father, and when he came back to the island, all the girls went crazy. He'd just gotten a Polaroid camera. Those were expensive back then, like you kids and your iPhones."

Nora flipped her phone on its face, hiding the notifications.

"I was a real dish back then," the woman repeated, "and I was proud of it. So when Tommy asked to take some pictures of my tits . . . I was more flattered than anything."

Nora nodded. She knew this all too well.

"You know the rest. He showed those pictures to anyone with eyes, and I became the whore of the island."

Another long pause. Nora was getting used to the cadence of her speech. "I'm saying all this because I saw those people whispering about you, and I just wanted you to know that people whispered about me my whole life. It gave me the backbone to make choices without needing everyone to like me. There was freedom for me in that. I'm not saying it will be the same for you. But sometimes making sure you don't offend anyone holds you back."

"Did you ever get back at Tommy Wilkes?"

She cackled. "Yeah, I got back at him, all right. I married him."

Nora placed the cup back onto the saucer and sat up in her chair. She had so many questions. "How'd you meet Thunderbear?"

"Oh, he was the chief's son. He was untouchable. The chief's son made a big show of sitting next to me, said he hated the way people treated me. By the end of the summer, I was in love with him. When he laid me down, it was with so much tenderness. Nothing like Tommy Wilkes."

"But you chose Tommy," Nora said.

"I was already pregnant by that fool Wilkes, and I had a choice to make. I knew if I told Thunderbear it was his he would take care of it, even if the child came out with those yellow eyes. But I couldn't start our life with a lie. So I told Tommy. And his father made us marry. I had a good and kind man, but I married a cruel one to protect me from gossip."

Her words landed like a cannonball.

"It was Thunderbear whose death I mourned. It was Francis's birth that I cried over like it was my first son. I hoped he would take after his father, but he was . . ." She trailed off. "When Bear was born, I beamed like a proud grandma. It felt like Thunderbear had come back to us in a small way."

"So this is why everyone is so gossipy about us?"

"The island loves him. They are afraid of you, though."

"Why?" Nora didn't want to ask, but she said it. "Because I'm Black?"

"You're an outsider. And he loves you. And he loves like Thunderbear, so he won't stop."

Nora lifted her eyes to the stained ceiling. Anything to keep from crying.

"You'll take him off-island. And your children's blood . . . that's how the Government determines our rights to the land, you know. Blood quantum. It's fucking barbaric. But you have to have a certain percentage to own land or do anything on the island."

"Sounds like a fucked up one-drop rule," Nora said. There it was. She *was* too Black. "So, give it up? I'm two steps ahead of you." Nora snorted.

"No, don't give it up, stupid girl. How did you miss this point? I told you I fucked Thunderbear." She said this like it explained something. "Sometimes a man like that is worth the ruckus."

"I don't do ruckus." Nora sipped the last of the tea.

"I don't suppose *you* do. You walk around like somebody stole your pearls and white gloves and dropped you off at the Greyhound stop."

Nora smoothed her ponytail. She couldn't help how she was perceived. But it still surprised her how many people read her reserve as priss.

"I want you to have this." The lady walked to the back room and came back with a picture. "I'm terrified of my children finding it when I go to meet the Creator."

Nora fingered the photo; it was a nude, smiling woman holding up her fantastic breasts.

"Wow, you weren't kidding, were you? A dish and a half. Tommy took these photos?" Nora squinted.

"No, I took them." Nora noticed the tick of pride in her voice. "For Thunderbear. When he died, his wife sent them to me. She said, 'I could never get him to get rid of these.'"

Nora laughed all the way back to the Hannaford, holding the photo like a talisman.

She thought she'd be humiliated. She thought all the whispers and the stares would slice through her, but instead she was laughing in the front seat of an old van holding a sixty-year-old nude pic in her hand like a prized possession. And just like that, Nora had an idea.

MERCURY IN RETROGRADE

JUNE 4
10 WEEKS UNTIL FORECLOSURE

NORA CLICKED HER PEN RAPIDLY IN HER EAR. AN-other morning without a good run. Another without a big breakfast. With her anti-anxiety meds kicking in she could slow down and focus on this miles-long PDF Brandon sent her. He was adamant about a meeting this morning, but she had no idea why he couldn't just send an email explaining this huge document. It was likely a flimsy excuse to see Yanne. She didn't want to engage with him. She didn't want to pull her hair into a ponytail. She didn't want to force a brittle smile today. Bear didn't run the tours three times a day anymore, and Nora saw more of Jennings, Moxcy, and even Francis leading folks around.

Three weeks! She remembered when she thought she would die when he disappeared for a week on her.

As if conjuring him up from her thoughts, Bear stomped the dust off his boots and ushered four people toward the warm cookies. A light crowd. He tried to find her eyes, but Nora pretended a keen interest in Brandon's paperwork.

"Nora," Bear whispered. She could smell him near her but she didn't look up. She saw his hand reach then stop out of the corner of her eye. "Nora, I got the first interview at U Maine. Right in Orono—"

He was doing it! This was his first call back in months. For a second she forgot that he was complete bullshit.

"OMG, Bear! That's perfect!" Nora slapped her hand on the counter. When he reached for her, the reality of their current situation suddenly slammed back into her.

How could I have forgotten for even one minute? Bear had always been a mirage, and she needed to look past his shimmering visage to her real goal.

Yanne swooped in looking like a lavender cloud and pinched Bear's stomach. "Looking thin. Are you too cool for breakfast now?"

"Busiest time of the year," Bear said, shifting from one foot to the other, turning his body away from Yanne's inspection. Yanne only looked at the four lonely travelers milling about.

"Yeah, it's a madhouse," she said, then mouthed to Nora, *Gangsta Boo.*

"We have to head back." Bear nodded his head and left the kitchen.

"That was chilly. He must know I'm onto him," Yanne said and checked her phone. "Maybe Jon's the one moving drugs. I never asked him how he made his money."

"Have you heard from him yet?"

"Not yet, but I will. I know it. I'm fasting for guidance."

"The only thing you're going to find is a flat ass," Nora warned.

Brandon announced his arrival by dropping his bags in the foyer. "White dudes love flat asses. I say go for it," he said.

"Did anyone ask you? What do *you* know about what men like?"

Brandon slapped his briefcase down on the counter and held

Yanne's gaze for a beat longer than decency allowed. Nora looked between them. Despite their bickering, they were hot and electric together.

"You two, let's just talk about what we need to do to stay on track," Nora said. She stopped clicking her pen at Brandon's annoyed glare.

Brandon sat at the bar and pulled a neat stack of papers from his accordion folder. The deep breath he took did nothing to reassure Nora that what they were about to hear was good news. "So do you want the good news or the bad news?"

"Bad news," Nora said simultaneously as Yanne said, "Good news."

"Bad news," Nora repeated.

Brandon slid the paper across the kitchen bar. "Current projections have us about fifty thousand short of meeting the foreclosure date by Labor Day."

"No!" Yanne squeezed her neck. "Is Mercury in retrograde?"

Brandon shook his head. "'The fault, dear Brutus, is not in our stars'—"

"'But in ourselves,'" Yanne finished. "I—I wasn't as helpful as I could have been, Nora." She looked from Nora to Brandon. "I'm just so sorry."

Nora still couldn't find the words to express herself. She suffered wave after brutal wave of disappointment. It was like some sort of reverse Midas touch.

"Nora?" Brandon reached over the counter to touch her hand. She pulled her hand back, surprised at her anger. It had crystallized in her belly like a hard lump of coal.

When Yanne went to the bathroom, Nora wasted no time. "You knew." Nora said. Her first words to him in weeks. Her voice sounded distant.

To Brandon's credit, he didn't pretend to misunderstand. "I was there when Bear met Lucinda."

Nora folded her arms. "Was this all some joke to you?"

"Nora, I—" he stammered. "Listen, you two 'business partnered' and 'platonic friendshipped' the hell out of everyone for months. I saw it. Yanne saw it. Everyone in town saw it. You and Bear were a unified front of bullshit denial."

"But you knew." She wasn't letting him off the hook.

Brandon dipped his head low. "I knew. But I was focused on making sure you were positioned to leave. Have you told me anything different? You tell me how you can have both Bear *and* Maryland."

Nora shook her head. "I would have figured that out."

"Oh, come on. Bear wanted to close the deal with you months ago, and all you talked about was leaving. You weren't ready for whatever you're claiming to want now—"

Nora saw Yanne coming, and cut him off. "Don't tell me what I'm ready for. You were obviously wrong. That's not even the point now. I don't know why I brought it up."

"Brought what up?" Yanne squeezed her hand and snatched a look at Brandon. Nora didn't know why she was keeping this from her sister. It was part embarrassment, part pride, part shame. She couldn't name all her emotions right now, but she knew what she didn't want—Yanne's overemotional outrage or triumph or sadness. It was exhausting on top of all the other feelings she had to manage.

"Maryland. This means that we should start planning to return to Maryland. Maybe crashing with Aunt Charlene?" Nora said. "In Prince George's County." Nora said the last part with flat distaste.

Yanne stomped her feet. "My life! 'Out, out, brief candle!'"

"What is the good news?" Nora asked. "You said there was good news."

"Well, despite everything, the impossibility of this task, you both came incredibly close. You should be proud of what you've done. I love being here. It always smells like cookies and plants and lemons and cinnamon. Everyone who's been here once wants to stay. You didn't *fail*, is all I wanted to say."

Yanne's face cracked, and silent tears rolled down her face. He looked between Yanne and Nora and sighed. Brandon stood up to pull Nora and Yanne into a hug, and after a brief pat on Nora's back, he turned to fully embrace a sobbing Yanne. He closed his eyes, and they sank into each other. His hands kneaded her shoulders, and she nuzzled his neck.

Should I leave them alone?

A pang of jealousy tugged at her low belly. She thought she had found something like this. But Yanne was too lovesick over Jon to notice the real thing right before her.

"Brandon, I wonder if you might help me with something else. It's not . . . it's not something we could do now, though." While Brandon felt Yanne up under the guise of comfort, Nora pulled out her photo of Elder Wilkes.

"Anything, Nora." He reluctantly disentangled himself from her sister and quickly sat to hide what Nora guessed was his arousal.

Nora pulled the old photo out of her back pocket, her talisman. She couldn't let go of the photograph especially after the whole Bear debacle. So she handed it to him.

"Holy shit, what am I looking at?" He put the photo down, looking around guiltily.

"You're looking at my pet project. I know it's not the mission right now—"

"An old photo of a naked lady is your pet project?"

"It just kind of came to me. Was also thinking of selling condoms." It was a joke only she would understand.

"Nora, I'm not following at all."

"When we go home . . ." Nora looked to Yanne, who started to protest, then surprisingly closed her mouth. "When we go home, I don't want to leave empty-handed. Felicia may take Barton Cove and profit off our labor, but she can't take what's in here." Nora pointed to her chest.

"You want to divert money now to your project?" Brandon was catching on.

"Just a little to get started." She winced. "I'm not giving up."

"No, it's smart. Let's see what we can do."

This had to work.

WHITE MAN'S MAGIC

NORA WOKE UP IN A GOOD MOOD FOR THE FIRST TIME in weeks. It had been a month since Lu's big bombshell, and Nora had done a great job staying out of Bear's way since then. Barton Cove suddenly seemed so small when she was trying to minimize her interaction with him. When he entered the room with a tour, Nora would slip out, sometimes even hiding in her bedroom, breathing with her head between her legs until she heard him leave. He used to try to get her attention, to pull her into washrooms and kitchens with one of his just-wait-six-months speeches or to plead with those devastating eyes, but Nora could barely look at him. All she had to do was get through nine more weeks of this. Bear was her past. He wanted her drinking white wine, singing "Saving All My Love for You," while he got his life together. But she was a person, not his damn deer meat that he labeled and froze for future use. She knew how waiting always ended up. Six months would easily turn into two years living off him, with no identity of her own but *Bear's woman*. She would just replace Lu in his Rolodex of people he had to *do right by*.

In two short weeks, she would meet this Basil guy. It could be the beginning of a new life. Nora slipped on her shoes and knocked on Yanne's door.

"I'm running to the store to get ingredients for cookies. Wanna come?" Nora opened the door to a cloud of smoke and sitar music. "Yanne, what are you doing?"

"I'm casting a spell to make Jon fall back in love with me or tell me what I did."

"You didn't *do* anything. He ghosted you because he's an asshole. There is nothing for you to understand."

"You're casting a spell too. Why are you making cookies? For Bear? I don't know what you two are fighting about, but it's one hundred percent *your* fault. You've been Frosty the Snow Bitch, and all this man wants to do is talk. I've seen you run out of the room when he comes in."

"You don't know what you're talking about."

"I do. You've been avoiding him for a month at least. Did he find out about the links and say something stupid? Heterosexual men are possessive chimpanzees. Give him time to feel some kind of way about it. It'll pass. He's too crazy about you. It's as real as this chair I'm sitting on."

"You're sitting on a stool," Nora grumbled as she closed the door. She would go to the store by herself. Nora wanted to grab a thoughtful card as well. No matter what Jennings said, a memorial was still a memorial.

At the store, Nora tried to decide between refilling her fanny pack with antacids or not. Bear's acid reflux wasn't her damned problem. It never was. She hated even reflexively reaching for them. She was *always* thinking of him, of what *he* needed.

Her ears perked up at the sound of frustrated screams. Nora

knew the shrill entitlement of customer service screams anywhere. Some poor cashier was getting an earful.

"You're not even trying!" Wait. Nora knew that high voice.
That long silhouette.

Lu.

Nora held her bottles to her stomach. She would have to dash
past the pharmacy without Lu noticing the only Black woman
for another hundred miles. She grabbed a family-size bag of pop-
corn to try to hide her face.

She was three steps past the pharmacy when she heard Lu.

"I see your puff, Nora."

Lu didn't lift her head as her palms pressed into the customer
service counter in the pharmacy. She looked pale and tired.
When Lu finally looked up, her eyes were red, her nose was running, and her hair was stuck to her face by the tears she'd cried.
Whatever was happening here was none of Nora's business.

Bear certainly had a type, didn't he? Lu was slight but strong
with a delicate long face that could be beautiful once fullness returned. Nora could tell she was an athlete just by how she wore
her socks mid-calf with Velcro-snapped slide sandals under her
jean skirt and how her knee popped when she straightened it.
She'd given her body over to some sport.

"Are you okay, Lu? What are you doing here?" Nora heard
herself asking.

You simple heffa. Why can't you just nod and get out of here?

"I come up here all the time in the summer to drop fancy
baskets off to sell at the Abbe Museum."

"Cool, well—"

"This 'pharmacy technician' here"—she cut Nora off and air-
quoted the words—"is telling me that the cost of this medicine is

a hundred and thirty-five dollars. Last month it was seventy-five. I've been trying to tell him he's made a mistake." Her voice trembled.

Nora exchanged a glance with the pharmacy technician. She had been in this position before, with a customer flabbergasted at the changes in insurance coverage, taking it out on employees.

Lu fisted the crumbled bills in her hand. "This is . . . this is all I have."

Nora placed her items into a nearby basket and approached the pharmacy counter. "They typically can't do much about what your insurance will cover," she said. "But there are a few ways to get this down to a reasonable number." Nora tapped the counter to get the attention of the pharmacy technician. "Did you look for a manufacturer coupon?"

"I tried that first," he said.

"Okay, let's take her insurance out altogether."

Lu squeezed the bills in her hand. "If I can't afford this medicine with insurance, without it is going to be astronomical."

Nora flicked through her phone. "This is an insurance discount card. BeneRx." She held her screen to the plexiglass window, showing the pharmacy technician the information in her phone. "Input these numbers for the Rx bin."

The pharmacy tech looked at Lu, who nodded quietly.

After a few minutes of waiting, Lu half smiled at Nora. The pharmacy technician clattered loudly on his keyboard. Nora tapped the top of a bottle of antacids—the berry-flavored ones that Bear liked.

Finally the pharmacy tech looked up and nodded. "That'll be sixteen dollars and seventy-nine cents."

Lu looked at the technician and then at Nora like she was waiting for someone to pull the rug out from underneath her.

"Sixteen *dollars?*" Lu repeated.

"Yup," the attendant said.

Lu tilted her head to the side. "How did you do that?"

"I used to do this." Nora gestured generally. Who knew, she might be doing it again sooner rather than later.

Lu slapped down a twenty like she feared the technician would change his mind. "You don't look like you used to *do* anything."

Nora took that as an opportunity to go.

"Nora!" Lu reached for her, spilling coins out of her hand. "Nora, wait."

It was the shouting that made Nora turn around. The last thing they needed was an audience.

Lu looked at Nora with a curious interest, like she had both brown and blue eyes in one face. Lu had not really seen her as a person, Nora realized. When she came to the inn, it was to find Bear, not to see or even antagonize her. Lu tapped her feet. "*Why* did you do that?"

"Oh, a lot of people don't know to ask for help with those types of things." Nora turned around again, trying to get away.

"Please, wait. I just—" Her tone was pleading.

Nora didn't want to wait. Everything around being here with this woman reminded her of Bear. She would never heal if she had to interact like this constantly. "Lu, I didn't know about—"

Lu waved a hand. "I know. Bear's shit about telling people what they can't have. I—" She faltered and rummaged through her prescription bag. Something had shifted between them. To Lu, Nora was suddenly worthy of straight shooting. "We don't have to claw each other's eyes out."

Nora looked directly in Lu's eyes. She realized she didn't know how to do this—small talk with the fiancée of the man she loved. She didn't have the tools. "Bear's not who I thought he was. It's unfortunate, but not surprising."

"Oh, don't be dramatic." Lu tapped the price tags on the shelves like she was doing some kind of inventory. "Bear and I have a financial agreement. *He* was the one that let all of these love stories the old aunties were telling get out of hand because he has an incurable praise kink. So don't turn it into anything epic." Lu rolled her eyes.

Nora's eyes darted around. She was more than a little startled to hear Lu speak so openly about her fiancé with the woman he was presumably cheating with.

"This was pretty epic to me. I know you and Bear have such big important lives that how I feel shouldn't matter. But this was epic to me."

Lu peered at her. "How old are you? Do you even know what's on the line here? All the money he owes me, yes, but his business, his seat on the council, the entire Penobscot River? No disrespect to your ass or your ponytail, which are"—Lu made an okay symbol with her hand and clicked her teeth—"but did you really think he was going to live in your cottage and hold the yarn for your knitting while his entire community and legacy burns? If you *think* he would, you're not in love with the man you think you are."

Nora recoiled. This woman knew the truth of him. Lu knew the inner happenings, while Nora stood outside the house with her hands on the glass. She mustered all her pride and threw it away to ask the next question. "What is happening with Bear's business?"

"Those assholes at Maine Power called the IRS on Bear. He's hundreds of thousands of dollars in the hole for back taxes. If they can get him off that seat and put someone they want in, there's no more opposition to damming the river."

She thought about the cop who came by periodically to ask

about permits and licenses and all of those bills spilling into her lap. Bear was under siege and underwater.

"He must feel hopeless," Nora said almost to herself.

"No, don't do that." Lu swatted her hand in the air like Nora was a disobedient cat. "He made this bed for himself. He could have married me years ago and gotten money from Thunderbear's trust. I would be long gone to California by now, a traveling nurse. But he nickel-and-dimed me. Saving for a family that's never coming. I've been very patient. I've been very *nice* too. Terrified of what people would call me if I told everyone the truth."

Suddenly so many conversation details and throwaway remarks clicked into place—the bills sliding into his lap.

I'm responsible, he'd said.

"He's paying all of your medical and utility bills? And paying you back?"

"Of course he's not paying my medical bills . . . my family is paying for that." Her voice wavered, and Nora knew she wasn't so sure herself now. Had Bear never told her the massive extent of the hospital debt?

She read Nora's expression and shrugged, not unkindly.

"Maybe he is. I wish I felt bad, Nora, but I don't. If I have to jerk Bear's chain to remind him of his promises to me, I'll do it."

"Well, Lu, he knows his promises to you. It's all he truly cares about," Nora said. The truth of it made her start to shake. He would do it. Lu's sense of entitlement to Bear and his money was only challenged by Bear's own sense of ownership of this entire mess. Both of them were stuck in a prison of delusions of grandeur. Both of them thought they could sit her on the shelf while they got on with their life in front of her. She was the second string, one of those players you bring in when the stars have run the score up and need rest.

Just wait six months, Bear had pleaded.

It's not epic, Lu said.

As if waiting here homeless for six months were something she could do even if she wanted to. Nora's nostrils flared, and she feared she might give way right here in the Hannaford.

Lu looked down at her pharmacy bag, then glanced at Nora's shaking hands. "Look, Bear loves you. I can tell by the way he almost snapped me in two for coming to the inn." She said this like she was reading an email.

"But you need more than *love* to make a relationship real. The things you love about a person can sour and turn to ash without money. You think you'll never get tired of his touch. The way he fucks like you're the last woman on earth?" Lu was looking for agreement where there could be none.

Nora looked up at the fluorescent light, willing the tears to stay in her eyes. She hadn't thought of that, that Lu would know how Bear made love, and she wouldn't.

Jealousy wasn't a sharp and angry emotion, just longing in another form.

I will never know.

"But live one year eating fried bologna sandwiches while he pours everything into his sinkhole business, and you'll barely be able to look at him with anything other than disgust." Lu was clear-eyed and rosy-cheeked. She spoke with a touch of wonder— as if it were her first time saying this aloud.

Lu buried her hands in her purse to look for her keys.

"*I* know what it takes to be happy, Nora, and it ain't love. That's white man's magic. *You* and I know better. So does Bear, and he has to take his medicine." She held up her pharmacy bag, proud of her pun.

She looked at Nora's face and tsked. "You want my advice?"

She eyed the exits. "Don't become one of Bear's community service projects." When Lu slipped between the glass doors, Nora
hesitated, then reached for the antacids.

JULY 1
7 WEEKS UNTIL FORECLOSURE

> **You still coming?**

Jennings texted Nora for the fourth time today. He and the
track team wanted her at this memorial today. She'd only agreed
because she'd come to love those little assholes. But Jennings
was also really keen on introducing her to his big brother. Some
tech genius from Cali. Whom he described as "Like Bear if he
would have made the right choices."

> **Yes.**

> **My chariot will be there promptly at
> 4pm.**

> **And we'll drop you off home
> whenever ur ready 🙏🙏🙏 !!**

> **No pressure to stay. 🤠**

Why did he keep mentioning she could leave whenever she
wanted? Nora was starting to think she shouldn't come. He was
acting a little cagey about this whole party.

> **I'll pay my respects to your
> grandmother**

> Will it be somber, should I wear black?

Nah

It was sad like the first year.

This is year five and we just cook out and share memories.

> Cool

But you could be on TV this time!

> Not for me i'll just meet with your brother Basil and go.

He might

. . .

NVM

> KK see you then.

Jennings was turning this into a much bigger deal than it needed to be.

"Promptly at four p.m." came to mean four thirty-seven. Nora and Yanne were in the foyer when the truck honked outside.

"You Nora and party?" A lean, dark man with a thin, graying

ponytail slapped the side of a faded pickup. Two bright orange kayaks shot out over the top like skis.

"Yep." Yanne hopped up and slipped into the back of the truck. Amazing how easily this woman could be kidnapped.

"And you are?" Nora asked.

"James. Cousin told me to come grab you," he mumbled.

"I'm Nora."

"Oh." He chuckled. "I know." He looked Nora up and down, then let out an appreciative grunt.

She wore a figure-hugging soft cream dress with eyelet patterns on the sleeves. She threw on brown ankle boots and a long silver necklace and a wide-brimmed straw hat with a white bow that flitted in the breeze. She blew out her hair into a layered bob and put concealer under her tired eyes.

No one could say she wasn't trying.

Yanne wore a sundress so low-cut one jumping jack would set free her impressive chest. If Jon was attending today, he couldn't miss her. Nora got in the truck's cab and slammed the door, kicking up sand and dust as they powered over the one-way bridge to the reservation.

Yanne was shaking with anticipation on the ride over. "I feel it, Nora. He's going to be here. Don't you feel that zip in the air?" Nora *did* feel it. The possibility of cleaning up her digital history filled her with optimistic anticipation.

She had barely stepped out of the truck when she saw Moxcy rolling toward her like a bowling ball. *What is she doing here?*

Yanne shot out of the car without so much as a *How do you do* to Moxcy. And Nora was left holding a tray full of cookies and absolutely no explanation for what was happening.

"Bear's gonna lose his shit. What are you doing here? Is this one of those race-to-the-airport scenes in a romance?" Moxcy held her head like she needed to hold it together. Her eyes were as wide as paper plates.

"Bear's here?" Nora's heart dropped like a stone.

"Of course Bear's here. This is *his* event. It's *his* gma!"

Nora glared at Jennings, who had come to greet her but was already backing away. "Why didn't you tell me your grandma was Bear's grandmother too?"

"I call him cousin *all* the time!" Jennings pleaded.

"Everyone calls *everyone* cousin," Nora said with a hint of desperation. She hadn't told Yanne about any of this mess yet, and now everything would come crashing down on top of her. This was the same occasion Bear had invited her to last month, and he was giving a speech! Why did Jennings call it a memorial and Bear call it a damned media event? Oh god, how could she get out of this?

"Oh no, you're in it now, Nora." Moxcy sucked her teeth, looking from Nora to Jennings. "If you wanted a train wreck, you're gonna get one."

LET ME

EAR WAS HOLDING HIS COUSIN IN A HEADLOCK. ALL he had to do was tap out. Basil had been needling him the entire morning, busting his chops about the late-model Honda, about Bear being a high school teacher on the rez, about his slow speech. It wasn't a headlock, really; it was more a *gentle* lesson in how not to treat your elders. Bear rarely used his size and strength to win arguments, but Basil was asking for it.

When Basil finally wrestled himself free, his face was red with fury. He was always like this, starting fights he could never finish in his wildest dreams.

"A-a-all you had to do was tap out, cousin." Bear readjusted his shirt.

"I don't tap out, Bear. That's why I'm where I am, and you're still here." *Oohs* rippled over the extended family gathered around them.

"Oh, it must be five p.m. because here's the hourly reminder of how much money you make."

"Maybe it feels like every hour because it's in your head, yeah?"

"Enough, you two!" an auntie called out. "You're going to have to talk this out."

"Nothing to talk out. He's jealous that I made a nice life for myself off the rez, so he wants to block me at every step."

"I've never wanted anything you have." It was only the tiniest lie. Basil's money would be nice.

"You're saying no to the payoff, but you're holding down the rez with your no vote."

"What makes you think the power company has the reservation's best interest at heart?"

"At heart? Maybe they don't, but have you thought of this? Maybe not *everyone* wants to live on the reservation. Maybe if everyone had the money, they would leave."

"And you've come down for the first time in years to deliver everyone from the rez, is that right? Exactly how *much* is your cut, Basil?"

Basil looked around. "Bear, we could split the money."

"They don't have enough money to make me choke the river."

He heard gentle agreement. "Hear, hear."

Just like that, Nora walked into the bingo hall like he had called her from the clouds himself. And good god, he lost all sense when this woman wore a tiny dress. The sun shone through the soft material like a stage filter, turning all the light a soft blue. Her thighs and hips formed a shadowy silhouette through the material. He swallowed against the sudden hoarseness in his throat. The crowd had quieted down to a preternatural silence. He could see their necks craning and ears turning to hear their interactions. She looked like a soft-focus glamour shot of some wistful country girl. All cotton, ribbons, and lace.

She looked thunderstruck when her eyes met his.

"Damn." Basil sucked his teeth. "Is this whose ass you're

trying to keep off the internet?" Basil spoke softly to Bear, and his tone was almost a threat. "Google's gonna be *so* sad to see it go."

Bear's eyes widened with preemptive outrage. "Basil, I swear to you, if you so much as—"

"Relax, Bear. I'm *your* asshole, not everybody else's. I'll take care of your little river stone because I said I would"—he began counting off with his fingers—"because it's an interesting challenge, and because I'm a fucking saint." He added two more fingers. "And who knows, maybe she'll be really, really grateful." That had Bear lunging for his neck again, and Basil ducked behind his mother, who folded her arms in exasperation.

Nora's eyes kept crashing into him, even as little cousins raced to her, showing her their running form. They scooped the tray from her hands and peeled open the foil.

Bear stayed frozen. He wasn't sure whether someone had picked up the drum again or if his heart was drowning out all sounds. After six arduous weeks of avoiding him or not even making eye contact, of slipping out of the same room whenever he was near, she was right there.

She couldn't avoid him.

He would try again to explain, and she would understand. He would start again with an apology, and then he and Nora could be something. He had ways to grovel that she wouldn't want to say no to. They had already proven that they could be an excellent team. This was just one little blip.

The last person Bear wanted near Nora was the person approaching her. "Nora, we finally get to chat instead of passing by each other. The inn's coming along." Francis couldn't keep the flirtatious chuckle out of his voice.

"Thank you. It's doing well. You all should come and take a look."

"Aww, she's inviting *us* to come take a look at our *own* land." Raucous laughter filled the room and bounced off the paneled walls.

"The place looks amazing." Bear's tone, more than the volume, cut through the laughter.

"Yeah, it ought to. You were there every day." He didn't catch who said it, but everyone had a new snide opinion lately.

He lost the thread of conversation as an event planner tapped at his shoulder. Suddenly he was wrapped up in more preparations, and it was half an hour later, after he finalized his remarks, that he looked up again to find Nora.

He saw his chance when she was talking to Basil. He knew *intellectually* that he had set it up. It didn't sit right with his spirit, though. The way Basil looked at her, like he'd be her savior. Like he knew how to protect her. It set Bear's teeth on edge.

She looked deep in conversation, though. What else could they have to talk about? He was sure fixing the video was a thirty-minute problem. *An interesting challenge, my ass.*

Seriously, what could Nora and Basil have to talk about for this long? Aside from his money, Basil was completely uninteresting. Bear kept waiting for a break in their conversation, but it never came.

She's been avoiding me for weeks. How can I get her attention?

She was too far away, first of all. Bear moved toward her with the grace of a bull, shoulder-checking a few uncles on his way toward her.

Fuck it.

He was next to them in an instant, his big hands encircling Nora's upper arm, knuckles flush against the side of her breast. "Nora, could we chat for just a minute?" He looked at Basil, and the asshole gave him the slightest smirk.

"Bear." She twisted out of his grasp. He guided her not completely unnoticed to the dark utility room. The concrete walls, exposed pipes, ductwork, and floors were all graffitied with initials and symbols, the largest scribble proclaiming this room as the best BJ spot on the rez. The overhead bulb that swung above them was harsh and functional, and it cast alternating shadows across their faces. He closed the door and twisted the lock, and it clicked into place with a satisfying finality. He thought of that night at the expo, when he'd closed the door behind him.

Nora moved toward the door. "People will think—"

"Fuck *people*. I'm right here, and I want you to talk to me, Nora. You're driving me crazy. You've been completely ignoring me."

"Is there something to talk about? Do you suddenly have something to tell me? Because I've known you since November. And *now* you're burning with news? What about your business? Why did I have to hear from Lu that they called the IRS on your business?"

"Nora, I would have told you everything if you had let me get near you. If you let me touch you." He slipped his hand around her waist, and she pulled back deeper into the darkness of the room.

"Let me make it up to you. Please don't leave me. I can make you—"

"Make me what? Forget this humiliation? Forget your lies of omission? Forget the lack of trust you had in me?" Nora pushed his seeking hands away.

"No, I . . . I can make you happy," he choked out. "Please, Nora. I wanted to tell you sooner, but you putting an end stamp on your time in Maine made me think you weren't feeling what I was feeling. You were so eager to leave. It was confusing. I started to think it was just me."

"When I came for you in that wigwam, did you still think it was just you?"

"No! No, Nora I raced to Lu's house to—"

"To quietly fix your mess. So you'd *never* have to tell me about it, right? That's why you didn't tell me where you were going that morning, because you *never* planned to tell me. You turned me into a JV runner you couldn't trust with the hard races. And Lu is varsity."

He was moving before she finished her sentence. He walked her back against the graffitied wall. Her eyes flared hot before she gathered her composure.

"What are you talking about, varsity and junior varsity? You're the whole team. Coach, equipment manager, mascot, cheerleader, star runner. You're my whole fucking team. I can't do this, I can't do anything without you." His lip trembled. He wasn't afraid of showing his desperation.

"Bear—"

"You held on to me in that wigwam and told me that it was us." His voice tightened with emotion. "You said you wanted the real thing, so I dropped everything to give that to you. But you were never staying."

"We can't stay. We can't afford—" She licked her lips.

"We could have worked something out. We could have tried. We could have talked about it. But *you* decided *I* wasn't worth the conversation."

"That makes two of us then, doesn't it?" Her foot tapped impatiently. She was so ready to leave everything they were building.

Bear studied his hands, rough and shaking. Defeat was finally sinking in. It burned like a motherfucker. "I'm so sorry. Nora, please." God, he had never begged so long and so hard for anything. His pride was gone.

"Please," he whispered against the shell of her ear. Goose-flesh spread up her arms and across her chest, pressing her nipples into hardened peaks through the thin dress. He let himself look at her body for as long as he wanted, dingy light illuminating her mouth, then her eyes, then back to her mouth.

"Let's only tell each other the truth from now on. Nora, I don't think I can be who I want to be for you right now. But I promise I won't let you wait in vain. I want to make you happy." He wrapped his hand around her thigh. She sucked in a breath like she'd been burned, and that was all it took for his cock to come rocketing to life. "I can give you a down payment on that promise right now." His hand slid higher up her thigh, then curved around until the knuckles of his index finger grazed the swollen fullness of her panties.

"Please," he begged. "Let me."

Muscles softened under his touch. He could feel her resolve fracturing.

"I didn't come for you. I didn't want . . ."

"But you want it now, don't you? Tell me you do," he growled in her ear. With his other hand, he held her palm up and kissed her fingers like he had in the wigwam, when they were sticky sweet with her own wetness. She leaned in to taste him, and he drew back. She was surprised at his tease.

". . . let me." He rocked his other hand below her skirt until it was nestled between her swollen, throbbing lips.

She let out the softest moan. A white flag of a sound that turned Bear on all the way down to his balls. He was hard as granite against her.

All of his emotions, all of his need—and she wasn't running.

THE INFRASTRUCTURE

SAME DAY, AFTERNOON

NORA WANTED HIS MOUTH, AND HE INCHED AWAY.

Bear's eyes were smoky and intent on her. "Wait on me, Nora." His thumb grazed the edge of her lower lip. "It's you that I want." He pulled her to him and crushed his lips to hers.

Finally.

He did everything with such intensity. This was how it would have been with them—hard, powerful, unspeakably passionate. He kissed her so damned deep Nora's stomach bottomed out. Slipping under her dress again, he slid the material of her panties to the side. She didn't want to kiss, did she? She was punching his chest with one hand and pulling him closer with the other. Everyone outside this room probably had cups to the door. She wrenched herself free.

"I don't think I can—"

He slipped his warm fingers between her wet slit, cutting off whatever she had in mind to say.

"Wait on me, baby . . ." This man was an Olympic gold medalist groveler. Nora could see when she was outclassed. Desperately, stupidly, after everything he had done to her, her body responded to his touch like no other. She was already wet when he grabbed her by the arm and dragged her to this room.

He kissed her again and she couldn't think, couldn't even breathe. The kisses just kept coming one after the other.

She had always told herself what she wouldn't do, what she wouldn't stand for in a relationship, especially after the video. And then someone came along and told her exactly who she was. She would take him any way she could have him. This afternoon was proof. He had somehow managed to work her panties down her legs, and she kicked them off.

"I know the inn might not make it. You and Yanne can come and live with me. I'll take care of you, Nora. Give it to Bear." He bent his head to kiss the tops of her breasts, and she arched into him. His slick fingers coaxed her clit. She *wanted* to believe this so much.

Two thick fingers pumped inside her, slipping through her wetness like a hot piston.

Nora gathered the soft fabric at her hips without thinking. Bucking her hips. Begging for it now. No shame. No propriety. The sounds her body made were filling her ears, like someone stirring pasta. So loud and wet. She clenched around his fingers.

"Give it all to me, baby, I'll fix it—"

His hands and mouth felt incredible but *something was . . . off.*

"I don't want you to worry. I'll do everything."

"Bear." Nora shook her head

"I'll do everything." His words pulled her out of her stupor. She thought of Lu and the way she said love can sour when other needs aren't met.

Nora shook her head as if waking up.

Don't become one of Bear's community service projects.

"No, no, Bear, don't you see what you're doing? Don't you see that you're doing it again?"

He pulled at the material of her dress. "I want to do whatever this is again and again," he murmured.

She wouldn't let him near her for a month, not because she was resolute and strong, but because she knew that if he nudged, if he cornered her with those hot dark eyes, she would be here. Once again, Bear had her halfway out of her clothes, slick and wet in semipublic. Someone shook the doorknob, and Bear stiffened.

"Fuck." He groaned.

"Bear." She needed him to listen. He needed to hear why she was saying no. "You're adding me to your list of shit to do. You're promising to support me and my sister, who has a chronic medical condition. You're shackling yourself again." Shaking, Nora wiped lipstick off his soft mouth with her thumbs.

Bear looked up at the ceiling, pulling his hands away from her soft wetness. "I . . . I am. I don't know what's wrong with me. I want you. I love you. Need you to know that. I want to prove that to you."

"I already know it, Bear." The sadness overtook her, and she put her head down on his shoulder, sinking into him. She let a sob slide out of her.

The door handle jiggled again. It sounded like someone went to go get a key.

"It was the shame that kept us quiet." Nora wiped a tear forming at the corner of her eye. "I wish I would have told you about the video as soon as we met. Hi, I'm Nora. I gave a guy head on the internet." She shook in sad laughter.

"Oh, we have *so* much in common. I was *getting* head while my girlfriend was being robbed. Now everyone thinks I'm a hero but I'm really a piece of shit. I'm Bear. Let's fall in love." He nuzzled into her neck.

Who would ever love me like this? Nora thought.

She would have to live with these deep mines and tunnels Bear had dug out of her heart. Fucking up the infrastructure, making it unsafe for anyone else to ever try again.

She knew he felt it, too, how futile and grasping this all seemed in the face of looming waves of duty and doubt.

Someone was trying keys one by one.

"I wish I had day one back. I'm so sorry. This isn't enough. I know you deserve so much more than this," Bear said.

The door swung open soundlessly. Bear's father slid inside the door and closed it behind him. He was holding a silver key like he'd got a golden ticket to the chocolate factory.

"You're so goddamned predictable. Can't find you, can't find the girl. You *have* to be somewhere trying to get under her skirt."

Nora scampered out of Bear's grasp and pulled her dress down, and Bear slid her panties toward her with his foot. But she wasn't brave enough to pick them up.

Francis wrinkled his nose. "Oh, don't worry yourself, girl, I've been young before. I don't begrudge the boy his last hurrah."

"Dad. What did you need?" Bear readjusted his fly. He had no shame about being caught out like this. Nora, for her part, wanted to jump out a window.

"I'll just leave you two—" She needed to find a bathroom to clean herself up before she went back out there.

The older man nodded toward Nora. "Actually, you should stay, sweetheart. Maybe you can settle a dispute we've been having."

Nora grimaced at the sharkiness of his smile.

"My dad was a mean SOB."

"Dad . . ." Bear warned.

"He was Grandpa to you, but he was a bastard to me. He had a longtime girlfriend. Everyone knew about it. He put my mother through hell."

"I'm sure that—" Bear started.

"One day, when Dad was at the girlfriend's house, I packed my mom's clothes. I'd saved up my money and bought us bus tickets to Florida."

By the surprise on Bear's face, this was a story she guessed he hadn't heard.

"My mother told me I had no sense of duty. Can you believe that? She told *me*, the son who was trying to save her face, that I had no sense of duty."

"I don't have to—" Nora looked toward the door, wishing she were anywhere else right now.

Bear moved for the door, but his father blocked it, reaching his hand out to Nora. She didn't like to judge people right off the bat, but there was something off about Francis, like a musty baby or a cheap dentist. *Slick* was the word that came to mind.

"Bear has been keeping you stashed away at Barton Cove," he said.

"Not stashed away," Bear countered hotly.

"His little secret."

"Nora was never a secret."

"Nora, if you'll allow me to finish—"

"I really don't—" Nora started.

Francis spoke over her. "So imagine how I feel when I see my son working himself to death on a dead-end business. In a dead-end relationship for three years, keeping a pretty little thing in Barton Cove. All for the sake of duty. Nora, do you know how my dad died?"

"Dad, this is not—" Bear warned.

"Oh, no one told you how the mighty Thunderbear died? He died of a heart attack, fifty-five years old, exhausted in another woman's bed. My *mother* had to come get his body from that woman's house." He shook his head. "My son is the exact same way. He's living the same way. His cousin is working with a company that can offer him a way out so that he's not fifty and in the ground. And he won't take it."

"Wow." Bear touched his hand to his heart. "That is the most noble thing I've ever heard. You're doing it to help m-me. Not for the enormous paycheck that the utility company is willing to pay you and Basil for Sunshine Trails to drop the dispute over the dam? At least the money I make stays in the community."

"Oh, come off it, son. How many people are you helping with that revenue? Fifteen? That five-thousand-dollar scholarship can't put anyone through clown college, much less a real one. Your cousin's plan is sound. And we'll triple the scholarship," Francis said. "Just drop all of this Lu stuff."

"*You're* the one who called her, Dad. You told her it was an emergency. That's why she came."

"I needed you to stare down the barrel of the gun! To finally make a decision. I gambled that you would hate the idea of marrying Lu more than selling your share to your obnoxious cousin."

"Well, surprise, surprise, you bet wrong. I promised Lu I would help her. She put nearly ten thousand dollars into the business when *you* were only dangling help over my head and Basil was laughing at my failure. She's a semester away from getting her nursing degree. She's been fighting with the disability folks and has no real income." He was looking at Nora now. "I can't just—"

"You are supporting her in every way. Mentally, emotionally, financially. And you're grinding yourself down. You have to hump in secret in a dusty utility closet!"

Nora cocked her head. Francis's points were not *not* true.

"If not me, then who?" Bear asked. It felt like a question for her and his dad.

"Nora, are you keeping count of this? What he calls duty is a generational curse. My parents would have had us working for Anglos until we keeled over. It's not the new way. Duty is what people cling to when they are afraid to change."

"Lu—" Bear started.

"No, Lu was happy to give you that money when you were pounding it in." He looked over to Nora. "Pardon my French, dear, but she was practically forcing money down his throat after her father's settlement. She *never* mentioned payment until after the accident. It's like she blamed you, but how could she? You saved her!"

Bear grimaced at that. "*I didn't,*" he said softly.

"What?"

"I didn't save her. I—"

Frances shifted his feet. "Regardless, any court of law would call that a romantic gift."

Nora tapped her lips with her forefinger, while her heart teetered in a surprising direction. "Why'd you take her money, Bear?"

"I shouldn't have. I was just so eager to prove to everyone that I could handle everything. I didn't tell anyone how bad a shape the business was in and how deep a hole I had to climb out of. Taking her little loans, I don't know. It . . . it—"

"Made it easier for you to pretend to have it all together," Nora finished. So people didn't have to be bothered by his needs. Textbook people pleaser.

The simple truth was if Bear married Lu, he could stabilize himself without the power company circling him like sharks.

"So," Francis continued, "he can let his cousin strike a deal with Maine Power, or he can use his marriage trust, marry that greedy woman, continue to keep a bankrupt business barely afloat, and die on top of *you* at fifty-five."

Nora worked to keep her face from reacting. But she knew the latter option would also let him keep his self-respect, keep fighting for that river. Keep his promises, and stay true to his grandmother's vision.

She thought about the money Felicia offered her and Yanne eight months ago at her father's funeral. It wasn't about help. It was about control.

"So, you seem like you got a good head on your shoulders, Nora. What do you think Bear should do? If you two are in love, and I can *smell* that you are, Maine Power seems like the best choice."

He rested his arms on his belly and waited.

But Nora had been there before—forced into a financial corner, bludgeoned into submission, and she had taken the harder road for her own self-respect. She had torn off her own clothes and flown to Maine on a mission sure to fail, just to maintain the shred of dignity she had left.

Did she regret it?

Not enough to go crawling back to Felica.

"What about collegiate coaching, Bear?" Nora's eyes searched his.

"Whatever money we saved to go seasonal would be eaten up in taxes."

"And you'd have to work year-round again," Nora finished.

Everything he'd been working for. The one thing she'd understood about him within twenty-four hours of knowing him was that collegiate coaching was his dream. And here he was talking about it like it was already dead.

When she spoke, it was with a ringing finality. "I would marry Lu." Nora heard the words coming out of her mouth, sealing her fate and snatching away her own happiness. "I'll be your damned flower girl, Bear, if you promise to go to the final interview at Orono and take the job."

Francis's face fell momentarily. And for a second, naked admiration flashed across his face. The first honest emotion she had seen from him all day.

Bear looked up to keep a tear from falling down his chiseled face.

"Yes, ma'am," he said softly. She didn't know how, but his soft *yes, ma'am*s had become a kind of code word. They had started off churlish and sarcastic but had evolved to become the way she knew he was really listening to her. That he *saw* her. Those two words made her feel more understood, more loved, than *I love you* had.

"Could you wait?" His voice was the softest, saddest plea.

Francis scoffed. "Shit, by six months after he paid the medical bills, Lu, the back taxes, he would be back at square one. Can't ask for a woman with nothing in your hand, son."

Bear turned his cheek to her.

Nora traced his jaw with her soft palm and he kissed the inside of her wrist. "Bear, I can't stay," she whispered hoarsely. "And I won't watch."

His face twisted up in a mask of anguish. "I won't make you watch."

They'd lost. It wasn't like running a race when you knew you never had a chance. It was getting that close to the finish line just to have someone shoot out in front of you.

He really loved her. She could see it like it was stamped on his forehead. They would not be together, but the links to her video had nothing to do with it. The video *hadn't* ruined them, even though she'd spent eight months in her head about it. Eight months keeping him at arm's length, reading books about how to hide her feelings, and running through D batteries. If she ever got a chance to love like this again, Nora promised herself she would do it with both feet.

When he spoke, his voice was gravelly with unshed tears. "I'll do whatever you tell me to do. And go where you want me to go," he said, his voice barely above a whisper. "I'll come find you in Maryland when I'm back on my feet."

Nora nodded, wiping her face with the heels of her hands like a child. Maybe he would never be back on his feet, maybe his promises felt so good to her she didn't care if they were real.

She was assuring her own loneliness, throwing her own case overboard, but shit, did it feel good to see someone choose their own way. She wished she had the money or power to choose her own way against Felicia.

It was strange that in marrying Lu and defying this huge power company, Ennis proved that he *was actually* the man she fell in love with. She reached up on her tiptoes, and instinctively he bent down to her level like he wanted to hear the softest possible words out of her mouth.

God, will he ever stop knowing what I need? Nora kissed Bear softly. A tear rolled down his cheek, meeting her mouth and tracing the outline of her lips.

Her voice was thick. "Congratulations."

PERFORMANCE OF THE YEAR

SAME AFTERNOON

THE BINGO HALL WAS A VIBRANT EXPLOSION OF COL-
ors, flags, and movement. Television vans and black town
cars crowded the small center. Brandon stood sulking against a
doorframe and perked up like a puppy when he saw the soft flut-
ter of Yanne's dress swish by him. He was head over heels. Nora
could see it, and at this point, she felt like Yanne knew it too.

Yanne stopped in her tracks and pointed to the hall doors
every ten minutes, sure that Jon would walk through at any second. Nora had to muster up enough excitement for her sister, but
honestly she was emotionally spent and wasn't sure how much
more of this spectacle she could take. Yanne was desperate to see
Jon, but Nora could feel that they had overstayed their welcome
and it was time to go.

"Nora!" Yanne bounced with excitement. "I was right! Jon is
here."

Before Nora could hold her back, Yanne shot out like a can-
non to greet Jon at the bingo hall doors. Cameras flashed as
Yanne twisted herself around Jon Bradley like a vine. She
smoothed his hair and squeezed his shoulders, but there was

something different about him. He looked around nervously and peeled her arms away from him. He said something roughly. It looked like he was sneezing, his head shook so violently.

What the hell is going on with him?

Yanne was not to be put off. Nora saw her shuffle through her bag and hold up the Moon card.

Oh lord, do I need to get involved in this?

Nora straightened her shoulders and stalked toward them. But she was stopped short by a hallucination.

This couldn't be real.

Her life in Maryland and Maine came crashing down into the sneering, pinched face of Felicia Dash.

YANNE STUMBLED BACK AS FELICIA SIDLED UP TO JON IN A cozy hug.

Here's how you know if two people used to fuck, or the anatomy of a hug:

1. A polite hug where shoulders meet, faces turned in opposite directions, says, *I work with you, but you don't know anything about me.*
2. Church side hug, one shoulder touching, gentle tap on the other shoulder, usually while walking, says, *You know most of my family's gossip, but I wouldn't touch you with a ten-foot pole.*
3. Hug around the waist, face in crook of shoulder, says, *We are fucking / have fucked in the past.* Watch out if your man greets a woman like that.
   #YouInDangerGirl

It was the third type of hug Nora observed with Felicia and Jon. Their waists were completely aligned, and their arms were wrapped around each other's waists. They leaned back and looked into each other's eyes.

That rotten asshole.

Now Nora was stomping toward them, and Felicia's face lit up prettily at the obvious shock her presence had caused.

"Little sisters! It looks like Maine agrees with you."

"Felicia, what are you doing here?" Nora skipped the false greetings.

"I can't check on Barton Cove?" Felicia tsked. "I'm rooting for you girls, but the bookings don't look promising."

"How do you know about our bookings?" Yanne asked, pushing herself into Nora. She was signaling something Nora's big-sister radar heard loud and clear.

This is more than I can handle.

"Oh, you'd be surprised what I know, Maryanne. How's your love life?"

Yanne stumbled back again, tripping over her flowing skirts and falling clumsily on her backside.

She landed with a heavy thud.

Felicia covered her mouth, fake shock in her eyes and a delighted smile behind her hand. The eyes.

Everywhere.

Like knives.

Nora saw Brandon slicing through the crowd like a sword, dropping to his knees at Yanne's feet. Her own heart lurched at the valiant care he had for her sister.

Brandon asked Yanne softly, in all seriousness, "Do you want me to kill him?"

Her sister blinked like she was seeing him for the first time.

"Yanne, they're in on it together," Nora whispered in her sister's ear.

"What? Nora. No. Felicia just wants us to think that because she's a stank bitch! She's been married for ten years. Or should I call your husband to confirm?" Yanne yelled the last part. Their little corner of the center had begun to garner too much attention.

Oh lord, let us get the hell out of Bear's grandmother's memorial before we cause any more ruckus.

"Yanne, we should go. Let's talk about this at home."

Yanne was hot with anger or hurt or humiliation, Nora wasn't sure. But her eyes were dry.

Don't show them shit, Yanne.

Felicia stared back. "Yes, Jon told me he didn't even have to *try* to get information about how Barton Cove was doing. He said it . . . What did you say? '*She* was so easy'?"

Jon fidgeted with his shirt collar, the coward. "*It* was simple, I said. *It*, not you." He finally met Yanne's eyes. "Never you." His eyes traveled to Brandon.

Brandon stepped in front of Yanne. "You might win some, but you just lost one, Jon, and I have a feeling this *one*, you're going to regret."

"Oh, relax, he wasn't spilling trade secrets." Felicia tossed her head back. "I just wanted to confirm what I already knew. Barton Cove is not making enough for you to get even close to profit, and with two months left at your current rate, you're still in the hole."

Of course she's been keeping tabs on us.

"I came to tell you your mother has incurred a significant amount of debt on a credit card we didn't know about until recently."

"Are you seriously adding that to the tab right now? If you

know the financials, then you know it may as well be a million British pounds because we *can't* pay it," Yanne said.

"And," Nora added, "this is my business partner's memorial service for a family member, so this is not the time."

"Ha! That's rich coming from you. I hear you disappeared with that overgrown camp counselor for an hour, and now you have graffiti down the back of your white dress."

Brandon turned to look at her, and she didn't know how she would respond if he offered to do *another* murder. But he didn't. Felicia *always* tried to poke there first. Like this was the first time someone had ever implied Nora was a slut. *Oh, honey, you're gonna have to work a lot harder to hurt my feelings.*

"What else did you tell her, Jon?" Yanne asked, her demeanor so cool it was scary.

"I stopped, Yanne, I—" He reached for her wrist, and Yanne snapped it away like she'd been burned.

"Don't touch her again," Brandon warned.

Yanne's shoulders trembled. She spoke with a gravity and slowness that commanded attention. "'A most notable coward, an infinite and endless liar, an hourly promise breaker, the owner of no one good quality.'" Spittle shot from her mouth as she kept eye contact with Jon.

Jon looked as if he'd been shot. His cartoonishly dimpled chin actually wobbled. Nora bet he was stunned to find Yanne's deadliest Shakespeare lobbed in *his* direction. It had been their love language. Now Yanne stabbed him with it.

"Yanne!" he cried, sounding for the first time like he was in physical pain.

"You don't do this to people, Jon. She loved you." Nora's body shook with recrimination. "Let's go, Yanne. Let's just go."

They had made it to the other side of the hall when Yanne shook loose from Nora and Brandon.

"I want to support Bear. He needs us."

"You don't have to stay," Brandon said. His hand was firm and reassuring on her shoulder.

"I'm going to have a talk with our friend Jon." Brandon's eyes and the set of his jaw did not communicate *talk*.

"Brandon—" Yanne's voice had taken on such a delicate quality. Whether she knew it now or not, she seemed a little bit in love with Brandon too.

"No, not catching a case." He held up his hands. "Just a good old-fashioned talking-to."

They watched Brandon march across the room, but Nora had no interest in seeing that through to the end. They had to leave. This day had to stop. Nora could see the exits blinking at her.

"Brandon's right, Yanne. We don't have to stay."

Almost there.

"What has gotten into you?" Yanne's face twisted up in surprised pain. "Yes, we do. There are *no* good men. Bear is the last. Fucking. One. Nora. Bear's the real deal. You know how long it takes him to practice his speech? And you know he's going to say something sweet about you. And you don't even care." Yanne looked so deathly serious that Nora nodded.

"Love comes so easily to you, so naturally, and look at what you do with it," Yanne said.

Now she was directing her anger at Nora.

"Fine, we can stay for a minute." If staying for Bear would help Yanne maintain faith in humanity, then who was she to rush them out the door?

Bear stood, but Francis shot up faster and grabbed the mic.

"Before we hear from Bear, I'd like to announce that a con-gratulations is in order! Lu, stand up," he boomed.

Lu looked stricken and uncurled slowly.

"A lot of you know Lu's story, and how Bear took care of her for years, never asking for anything in return. He gave his life over for this woman." Nora's eyes volleyed from Lu to Bear. Both winced as if in pain but probably for entirely different reasons.

"My Bear is the reason why Lu here is walking again, and now I'm thrilled to announce, he'll take her as his bride! Despite some unsavory recent events, the wedding of Ennis Bear Free-man and Lucinda Seal Neptune is *on.*"

A few let go some quiet awkward applause. But mostly they turned to look at Nora. She was the shoo-in actor the camera pans to when she *didn't* win the Oscar. They wanted to see her face break. Curious and even sad faces looked at her now. So she did what any actress does.

She smiled so big it hurt her face and clapped hard enough for her silky bob to slide like windshield wipers across the back of her neck. Even as her throat tightened and her vision blurred, she clapped the longest and the loudest. Her ears popped with the sheer force of her thunderous clapping. Her hands burned, but she welcomed the pain. Slowly the crowd joined in, and Yanne snapped her head in utter disbelief from Bear to Nora.

Performance of the year.

HARD NO

SAME DAY, EVENING

B EAR STOOD ON THE DAIS OF THE BINGO HALL WITH his hands clammy and his heart racing. He hadn't known he was going to do it until right now. He looked into Nora's eyes and realized he had already lost everything. Why not go for broke? There was a moment of silence, and Bear could feel everyone's eyes on him like tiny pins. He fought the urge to shrink into himself, to yes everyone to death so they would smile those open-toothed, accepting smiles.

It was the shame that kept us quiet, Nora had said.

He opened his mouth to speak, and he had to take a deep breath to keep from gagging. "Ah, everyone, I have something to say." He watched the door, watched her. He mentally threw away the speech he'd spent weeks perfecting. He looked directly into the Channel 5 camera. He would get his point across to the whole damned state. That, and Gma, was what this day was about.

"I just wanted you all to know I may be taking a job in Orono. But Sunshine Trails is still mine." He looked directly at Stubbs and the executives from the power company. "You all name streets and parks after us like we're always in the past to you. Turn down Abenaki, make a left on Penobscot. But I'm here right now, and I will not relinquish my seat on the council. I'm still a hard no for the Penobscot River dam proposal." The crowd of nearly five hundred erupted into whoops and yelps.

Spontaneous shouts of *Save our salmon! Save our salmon!* rang out like a chant in a football stadium. His cousin Basil sneered at him, while Stubbs and the execs exchanged rueful looks. As long as he had the power to block this, he would.

But he wasn't done saying no.

"I also plan to leave the high school." The crowd's chants died off as fast as they started, and suddenly the room was as quiet as an empty church. Somehow their eyes landed on Nora. The accusation didn't need to be stated. They blamed her.

"I've wanted to do this for years," he said. "It's not new, so don't any of you dare pretend it is." Disappointed eyes shifted back to him. Accusation and mistrust flared again.

He soldiered on. "Lu and I *are* getting married." A light smattering of applause squeaked out from the crowd. It was from his amen corner of aunties and uncles in the front. Holy shit, they weren't going to like this next bit of news. "But there is something you need to know. For three years, you all have believed a lie." The crowd's weak claps whittled down to nothing again. "*I'm* the reason Lu was hurt three years ago. She, uh—" Bear gulped. "Asked me for a favor, to drop her off to the airport. But I didn't want to, and I didn't want to have an uncomfortable conversation. So I left her. She was alone on that street because I left her. We weren't together that night." He turned to look at Lu, who held her head up and nodded.

"But you saved her. Fought off those motherfuckers!" An uncle valiantly came to his defense. But he didn't even deserve that. The story had gotten so overblown, even he had trouble keeping track of the myth.

Bear dipped his head. "I never fought off anyone. I was at a bar. I met her at the hospital nearly a day later."

"But you took care of her single-handedly," another old auntie who had brought him dinner nearly every week for two years said. She sounded like she was coming out of a dream.

"I tried as best I could, but I also hired home help and that maxed out her credit cards." He scanned the audience for Nora's face. He would be relieved if she had left. How could she look him in the face after knowing all of this?

"Don't forget she can't get back into school 'cause you're defaulting on all her bills!" John Michael, Lu's cousin with deer-sausage fingers, shouted. "Now her credit's shit, and she can't afford to move!"

Bear looked back at Lu, who took a napkin out of her purse and patted her face.

She walked to the podium. And Bear stepped aside. "My electricity went out in my apartment. I had no food, and he walked in with new hundred-fifty-dollar shoes."

"Living above his means for that other woman!" someone shouted.

"He special orders fifty-dollar rosewater shampoo now!" Another person whom he recognized from the drugstore. *I've been ordering that for years!* he was about to shout but held his peace.

Lu continued, feeling the crowd's chaotic energy. "He took thousands of dollars." At this, many gasped. The tone of the event was turning dark.

Bear twisted the mic toward his face. "She offered me money when she was well. I wasn't taking money out of her purse at the hospital. I've been paying back her hospital bills, but it all just became too much for me."

"My family paid that!" Lu looked around. "My family came." She searched the eyes of the attendants for anybody to corroborate her story. "My family came to help." She whispered the last part. Even as she whipped up the crowd against him, Bear hadn't wanted her to find out that no one had come for her. Lu swallowed and straightened her shoulders. Dabbing at the driest eyes he'd ever seen, she pulled the mic back in her direction. "Most of the food I have spoiled. At this point, I'm just begging him not to leave me."

"We got your lights back on," Bear corrected. "And I bought new groceries. The lights were out for two hours max," he offered. But he didn't have the mic and it didn't matter anyway because when Bear looked back at the crowd, he felt a palpable, rancorous anger roll all the way to the walls like a dense fog.

Directed.

At.

Him.

"Fucking coward," he heard from the crowd. "You spend a lot of time and money on Barton Cove while Lu is in the dark?" Bear ducked just in time before a chunky-heeled boot hit the wall behind him. "I made you spaghetti for a year!"

"So I will return to nursing school. Once Bear pays me back what he owes me——" She gripped the sides of the podium—— nervous but triumphant. He was definitely the villain in her story. "He says there's no real way he can help me right now, and I believe him." Lu held the napkin to her chest.

Waiting.

"Use your precious trust, you tightwad!" the crowd clamored.

"I am——" Bear tried to speak

"We don't fuck over our women here, you know that." Bear dodged balled-up paper programs and stumbled off the stage. Several members of the community rushed to Lu, who cried softly on an auntie's shoulder. Boos cut him off. So this was it. It was finally here. The thing he had avoided all his life, why he had bent himself over backward, to please everyone.

Apple doesn't fall far from the tree.

More like Francis than Thunderbear.

YANNE DRAGGED NORA OUT OF THE CENTER IN A FURY. "Patho-fucking-logical. You want to go somewhere to relax your plastic face? I hope it freezes like that. Smiling and clapping while the love of your life gets engaged to someone else? Pathological."

"Stop saying that stupid word. What do you need from me, Yanne?" Nora's voice scraped against her throat. "You need me to beat my chest? You want some Shakespeare 'woe is me' shit?"

"First, that's not Shakespeare, and second, you *have* to be devastated right now, and you're just putting on this show."

"*You're* the one who wants a show. You need me to perform sadness so that you can buy that I'm actually hurt. I fell in love hard—so damned hard, Yanne, and he's marrying someone else. How much more evidence do you need that shit is not okay? My face is dry, my voice is clear, and my heart"—her voice cracked—"is broken right now. My chest is tight and my fingertips are numb. I'm furious at everyone. But mostly myself because I . . ." Nora trailed off. "Yanne, I . . ."

After seeing Bear subject himself to this bloodbath, she couldn't shake the certainty that it had been for her. He didn't have to burn it all down, but he lit a match to his reputation to save the river and his own personal integrity. And now she was violently, thunderously more in love with him than she had been when she walked into the bingo hall. This was LeBron's South

Beach press conference. This was fans burning his jerseys in the street. The flood of emotions must have read across Nora's face, because Yanne reached for her, all plush arms and lavender perfume. She wrapped Nora up in her softness and finished the unspoken thing. "You still want him." Yanne let sobs rack her body, tears enough for them both. "He's fully marrying someone else and you still want him," Yanne said. "*Damn* those men did a number on us. How long have you known?"

"About a month now."

"Oh my god, Nora, you've been carrying that around for a month? That's why you've been a stone-cold bitch to Bear! He deserved it."

What did deserve *mean?* That there was some order to the world that good people got good things and bad got bad? Did Yanne deserve to be led on and humiliated by such a callous, self-important man? Felicia was going to get Barton Cove and profit off all of their work. Nobody got what they deserved.

They both watched in cold silence as Jon hopped into the passenger side of a matte black Jeep with windows tinted so dark it was impossible to see the driver. But they both knew who it was. Brandon had gotten them to leave. No scene. No mess. Neat as a pin. That's who Brandon was. Yanne was wrong about Bear being the last good man. The Jeep started up, and Felicia drove off with a slow celebratory circle around them in the driveway. Nora had to applaud her, though. Felicia had played the game to win, while Nora and her sister had only gotten played.

DRANK THE KOOL-AID

SAME EVENING

"U M, NORA?" A DEEP VOICE BEHIND THEM RUMBLED.
Even though her face was dry, she swiped her cheeks expecting wetness.

Basil was small, well-spoken, and bespectacled. If she'd met him in another setting, she would think he was perfectly thoughtful and kind. He was certainly generous for helping her with what he called reputation repair. But he had a nasty streak of competitiveness to him too. When he was out in front playing lacrosse with the children earlier, he taunted them aggressively and checked smaller kids with his shoulders. He liked to win. How must he have felt growing up here? Bear's little cousin?

"I was about to head back to my hotel, and I wanted to make sure you had a way home."

"Thank you, Basil, I would like to go now also."

"Do you need to say your goodbyes?" Basil adjusted his glasses.

"No." Yanne and Nora spoke in one voice.

Nora sat in the passenger seat of the car. She self-consciously pulled her dress over her thighs as the material rode up. She didn't have "lose panties at a bingo hall" on her bucket list, but she was definitely trying new things this year.

"I appreciate everything you're doing, Basil. With the video, I mean."

"No problem." He glanced at her. "It's for you, you know. Not Bear. I should thank *you*. For treating my little brother like a nephew. He says you're teaching him how to bake?"

Yanne nodded. "He's so good."

Nora added, "He makes such a moist hummingbird cake."

"Bear treats him like a nuisance. I wish I could take him back with me. But he's so attached to this damned place, even to Bear."

They drove in silence for a while. Nora guessed that it was that his little brother loved Bear so much that hurt the most.

"Hey, did you leave because of Bear?" Basil asked. "Marrying Lu? I know this may be difficult to hear, but despite it all, I was proud of her. Lu finally said her piece."

Nora turned to look out the window. Opting out of answering. Watching Lu work over that crowd was a master class in leveraging social pressure. She had definitely secured the bag, because Bear would marry her, or they would run him out of town.

Basil continued without motivation from Nora. "He really started it, telling the world all of his dirty laundry." He slapped the steering wheel, doing a terrible job of hiding his glee.

"Maybe he felt like he had to say that to move forward," Nora said.

"I'm just glad people are finally seeing who he really is. They are tearing him a new asshole in there. I hated to have to go. But he needed *all* of that. Coddling just rotted his brain, you know?"

Nora uncurled her fist and blew out a slow breath. *That is not your man.* So why did it raise her hackles so much if Basil trash-talked him? She kept reminding herself that Bear didn't need her protection.

"He still thinks he's falling on some sword for the rez, a place everyone would leave if they could. You listen to hip-hop?"

Where was this going? "Yep." Yanne's head popped up from the back seat.

"Jay-Z talks about the Marcy Projects not as the place he wants to stay, but a place he had to leave. That money from the power company—"

"Bribe," Nora corrected.

Basil did a double take and softened his shoulder. "I swear this man must have a golden tip. Are you defending him right now?"

"No, just saying it wasn't *free* money. It was money to stand down on the dam project."

"Okay, that 'not free' money from the power company would have given folks on the rez enough money to live a better life. Bear wants to keep his fiefdom, and he'll even marry Lu to do it."

"And no one's going to stop him," Yanne chimed in.

Nora glanced down at her lap. She had made her decision. She didn't care if no one understood it.

"Do you think you'd do a better job?" Nora asked.

Basil shrugged. "I would never be in this situation in the first place. If Gma had left me the business, I would have handled that funny bookkeeping first thing. I'd show everyone here that—"

"That you're a leader too," Nora finished.

He did another double take, watching her and the road. "Yeah. Yeah, and, like, I'd share it with the community, not just make everybody feel good about themselves. I would change the business model and start making real profit for scholarships and off-island rent vouchers. I never even got the chance growing up. They all loved him . . ." He trailed off and looked over at her, maybe to say, *Even you.*

Basil had to gauge her reaction to everything he said. Nora knew his type. He needed a lot of external validation. People like that were always on a hamster wheel, trying too much.

Nora tapped the dashboard. "Bear can inspire admiration. That must not have been great, growing up with that."

"*I* should inspire admiration, is what I'm saying. I bought a home in Silicon Valley *and* am working with a silent partner to start my own tech firm. My technology powers the algorithm for *Spinster Island*! And Bear is beloved for what? Just being born first and being named Bear. Do you know how many Native men are named Bear? It's like John."

"I don't think that's why people love him." Yanne's head peeked back up again from the back seat.

"I'm saying he could be building something, but instead he's maintaining the status quo. Do you know why? On the rez, *Bear* is the status quo. It's a power move."

Nora was trying to bite her tongue, but she had to say something. "I think he's taking care of Lu." Nora hated herself for this. So cringy even as she said it. "I think he's doing the right thing."

Yanne looked at her with burning accusation. "If it's not love, it's not the right thing."

"It's a kind of love," Nora countered.

"No kind of love." Basil shook his head. "Do you know how he met Lu?" He shot a quick look at Nora.

"I brought some friends back with me after I graduated. Wanted to show them where I lived." He took a sharp turn. "Decided to invite Bear, who was already out of his depth with the business. We were all at a bar knocking back a few beers. We both saw Lu at the same time. My friends were egging me on, and I tried to make a joke about it, but I was kind of serious. She was a knockout. Bear didn't care either way, mind you. He was never really serious about Lu. But *I* bought her a drink. She came over, took one look at his biceps—which he flexed the entire night—and pulled him into the alley. Do you know how I know he was fucking Lu in an alley?"

Nora winced, and Yanne looked from her to Basil. She couldn't imagine Bear, whose entire personality was restraint, being this reckless. But she supposed he could look at her video and say the same thing about her.

"Because me and my friends sat under the window against the same wall. Awkwardly sipping until they all begged off. Bear did it just because he could. In front of all my friends. Just to prove to me that no matter what I achieved, on the rez, *he* was top of the food chain. Now he's using Lu again to keep himself on top."

Basil looked at her like he wanted some kind of affirmation. When Yanne and Nora only looked at each other, he sucked his teeth.

"Drank the Kool-Aid," he mumbled.

Yanne popped up again and rested her chin on the back of the passenger seat, finally deciding to give Basil the affirmation he needed right now. "Basil, you don't need muscles to be important. You have money and a real Lord Byron way of seeing the world. Any woman would fall for your hacker Clark Kent vibe."

Basil flushed dark red. For some reason, he seemed angry. "Why not Superman?"

Yanne shrugged. "Just the first thing that came to mind."

"Don't you think it's weird for you to say Clark Kent first?"

"Um, no. You just seem . . . I don't know." Nora could sense that Yanne was stepping in it. As a top athlete, she had learned long ago not to accidentally wade into someone's inferiority complex.

"No, like, think about it." His tone was a touch more aggressive than the conversation called for. "My glasses? Because I'm a tech guy, because I'm smaller than Bear?"

"No one mentioned Bear," Nora said. She was glad she could see Barton Cove in the windshield, because the conversation had gotten too tense. The sun had never shone on Basil, and he had no idea why.

He stopped the car in the driveway, and Nora almost had the weird fear that he would child-lock the doors. That was the level of intensity he was giving off.

Basil's jaw twitched. "Clark Kent never got the girl, though, did he?" He tapped the steering wheel.

Odd observation.

"What do you mean? He had Lois," Nora said.

"Common misconception." Basil pulled off his glasses to wipe them with his shirt. "Superman had Lois. Clark Kent never took any action. The whole town just waited for Superman to save them. But Basil takes action. You'll see."

QUIET

NORA TAPPED THE BASE OF THE PLANTER AND JUMPED at the sudden loud clang. Barton Cove loved to be filled with sound. It made Bear's laugh bounce off the ceiling and carried Yanne's humming through the other rooms. The foyer buzzed with the cacophony of Moxcy and Bear's tours. It even gave warning that someone was at the door with a telltale squeak of the porch wood. But now, the cottage had gone nearly soundless. She didn't talk to patrons anymore, even though she left a plate of cookies on the bar every day. She took meticulous pains to avoid Moxcy and Bear. They occupied opposite sides of the house and jumped out of the way to give one another room through narrow hallways. Now the place ran with the hushed busyness of a monastery. Her bright spot in the week came while thinking of a song to add to their shared playlist. This week it was Whitney Houston's power ballad "Didn't We Almost Have It All." It was a little on the nose, but Bear was never one for nuance. Maybe when she was back in Maryland, the playlist would remind her of what it felt like to be loved completely.

Now Nora bent over the lavender plant, confused about its wilting leaves. She'd done everything to nurture this plant. All she wanted was to care for something. She held it to her chest and yelled for Yanne, whom the plants opened their leaves for without her even trying. Maybe she could save the lavender.

"Nora!" Yanne shouted her name in a way that shot alarm bells through her.

Yanne walked in clutching her chest. Her eyes were bloodshot, and her fingers were swollen like sausages. "Nora?"

"Yanne, what's wrong?" Nora pulled her gloves off and rushed to her sister's side.

"My . . . my chest. It's like last time."

Nora shot out of her chair. "I'm calling your physician in Maryland."

"What is she going to do all the way out here?" She sat, breathing deeply and wincing at the pain.

"She can call a sickle cell specialist."

"There are not enough Black people in Maine for there to *be* a sickle cell specialist in this whole state," Yanne cried.

"We'll find out."

"This is the worst timing!" Yanne moaned. "High season. I really want to be here for you."

"Don't worry about the timing." They had never really had what anyone would call a high season. Jon, of course, never delivered on his promise to funnel guests from the Willow Bee. It was just another lie to keep their feet off the gas. Nora raced to the kitchen to grab a bottle of water.

"I can't . . . we can't afford . . ." Yanne thrashed in the chair.

"What's your pain level right now?"

"I woke up out of my sleep at about a six, but I'm at a n-nine right now."

Nora called her mother but had to hang up after Diane broke down into fretful tears.

They were screwed. Royally screwed. Now was the time to panic. Nora's palms were slick against the phone. Everything was being snatched from her. Three months ago, she had a beautiful home she had rebuilt herself, the promise of a new love, and fewer panic episodes. But now she was leaving like she came, with nothing. Only with less hope.

Yanne moaned, and Nora snapped out of her self-indulgent pity. She had to get Yanne help.

"Dad's wife," Yanne rasped.

"Mrs. Dash." Nora clapped the phone between her hands. "Dad's wife said she would pay for your treatment."

Nora called Mrs. Dash without a hint of pride.

"My sister is having a pain crisis," she shot out without a greeting.

"Oh, goodness. Did you get her some water?"

"Yes. She says she's at a nine for pain."

"Get her to—"

"Excuse me? What do you think you're doing?" Felicia's voice cracked like a whip over the phone.

"Yanne is having an episode and your mother said she would help." As much as she hated to need something from this family, she had no ego when it came to her sister.

"What is *wrong* with you? She was grieving. She was in shock! You can't believe that she would pay for her husband's outside children to get a checkup."

"This is not a checkup. My father suffered from this same disease and traveled here often. Mrs. Dash knew about Yanne's disorder. She knew about us before we knew about her. *We* weren't a shock to her." Nora tried to keep her voice down but she heard Yanne hurl herself up.

"Shenora Dash," Yanne moaned. "Don't you dare beg that

woman for shit. I don't care if she knows the goddamned cure." Nora heard Felicia and Mrs. Dash bickering, and when Felicia got back on the phone her tone was flat.

"Mom says go to Mercy in Portland, they have a specialist there."

"Thank—"

"And Nora?"

"Yes."

"Don't ever call my mother again." The phone went dead.

Okay, they knew where to go, now they just needed to find a ride. Nora fumbled the phone and accidentally called Bear. He answered at the half ring.

Shit. "Oh, um, sorry I didn't mean to—"

"Please don't hang up," Bear said quickly.

"Yanne is sick, and I was wondering if Brandon could drive us to Portland."

"Nora, I can—"

"No." She almost screamed it. She wanted him to stop being there. To stop being everywhere. She could probably start to process her pain if he would just stay put. He couldn't be everything to everyone, and he should just as well learn that lesson with her first. But she didn't say that. "Bear. You're booked back-to-back for three days straight, plus I won't be here, so you would really help me out if you can take over some operations."

"I can do that, Nora." He sounded resigned.

BRANDON WAS AT BARTON COVE IN LESS THAN AN HOUR, and by then Yanne was completely lethargic.

"How do we move her? She's in so much pain."

"I had an aunt with this. I'll be careful." They drove with

Yanne moaning in the back seat. Brandon would show up for Yanne in a heartbeat—always there loving Yanne without getting anything back. Nora hoped her sister could learn to appreciate that kind of love—soft and slow and nontheatrical.

While the nurses triaged Yanne, Nora fidgeted with her fanny pack, rolling the travel-sized pack of Tums over her palms like a pregame ritual. Brandon handed her a sandwich from the vending machine.

"Nora, there's never going to be a good time to say this. But just as an FYI, if we calculate the cost of this stay, we may fall even shorter than my projections," Brandon warned. "There is no safety net after this."

Nora shook her head. She knew what that meant. They were going to blow through the financial cushion Brandon had set aside. They wouldn't just fail and start a smaller venture afterward with the oh-shit money. They would fail and be completely destitute.

"Nora." Brandon rolled up his sleeves. "Call Bear. He'll—"

"I am not calling Bear, Brandon. Do not ask again." Bear couldn't handle the inn *and* his tours. And he had his own problems.

"Nora, he is your business partner."

"And I will keep him informed," she snapped. "Can we focus on my sister, please?" She couldn't help the anger that kept slipping out of her voice.

"Nora, I—" Brandon sighed. "Let me stay."

"You don't have to do anything for me." Nora felt her nerves snapping and fraying around the edges.

"I can bring my laptop here. My work is remote. I only came to the inn for—"

"For Yanne," Nora finished.

"And you. You *are* a friend." Brandon's shoulders sagged when her eyes met his.

"Thank you for loving my sister, Brandon."

He startled for a moment, then settled. "I do. Which is why I'm staying." Lord, he was relentless. "Go and run the inn. I will make sure Yanne knows you went kicking and screaming."

"You're stubborn as hell."

He handed her the second suitcase. "No, I'm just . . . I'm in love. I'm in love, and I'm doing something about it." It felt like a dig. But she knew he meant it as a statement for himself.

What if Nora *had* thrown herself into Bear's arms after he handed her that damned Marvin the Martian smoothie and said, *I know this is fast but I think I'm falling in love with you*? What if she had told him after he pulled the stars down into her body with that kiss at the expo, *I want your hands on me forever. I want to be full of you*? How would their story look now, months later?

Brandon threw her his keys. It occurred to Nora that it was high time she bought a car.

"FaceTime me. I'll see you in two days," he said.

Nora sat in the car and breathed in and out. *Remember your breathing, Nora.*

She had done everything the wrong way. Jumping through hoops on someone else's journey. Barton Cove had never wanted to be an inn; it just felt like the right thing. The closest thing to her dad's vision. But she couldn't be his perfect little daughter who had never embarrassed him with a sex scandal. And it was futile for her to try to start after he was dead.

Her father had evaded responsibility and consequences all the way up to the end, but Bear faced them head-on. Bear was *not* her father. And that fact made him *less* likely to burst through the doors at Barton Cove, sweep her up in his arms, and say, *Fuck it all, I love you.*

"Fuck it all, I love you, Bear!" Nora screamed inside the car. Her heart didn't even have the decency to use past tense.

Here's what was bound to happen if you didn't empty all the love you have for someone that hurt you:

1. The love sat on your couch like an unwelcomed houseguest, changing the password on your Netflix account and rolling itself up in your covers at night.
2. You'd have to cry in the shower and to tell everyone you were fine, because you're a #StrongBlackWoman™.
3. You'd impulse buy a body pillow from QVC for four easy payment of $15.99.

TL;DR: the love doesn't go away.

TWO DAYS AFTER YANNE'S EPISODE, JENNINGS HANDED Bear a fistful of warm, wilted carnations.

"Can you tell Yanne I'm sorry when you get there?" Jennings said.

"How did you know I was going to see Yanne?"

"You asked Moxcy for the toll pass. You only use the toll pass to drive to Portland. Yanne is in Portland."

"Jennings, your talents as an investigative reporter are wasted here." Bear nodded to dismiss his cousin, but Jennings stayed, rocking back and forth on his longboard. He had news, and by the pitch of his shoulders, it wasn't good.

"Yes, J?"

"We dropped off your pies."

Yes, Bear himself had made pies—meat pies for Nora's birthday. He'd spent hours on that ridiculous recipe only for the pies to cook unevenly and ooze like a Halloween display. He sent his team to deliver them because being with her made him think *too* long and *too* hard about that power company bribe. About how easy it would be to take her hand and the money and run.

"Did she um . . ."

"Taste them? Yeah, first thing. And, Bear, she almost *gagged* they were so *terrible*. She let me try—" Jennings shook his head at the memory. "Shit tasted like you cooked it in vinegar. But she wouldn't let me take them back *and* she cried into the pies for like ten whole minutes. So, I'm guessing, don't make her any more pies?" Jennings offered.

"Roger that," Bear said, keeping his own face neutral.

"Barton Cove is different now, yeah?" Jennings said.

"Quiet now," Bear said. Quiet as a cave. Barton Cove was big when it wanted to be. The weather had turned gorgeous for running, and the trails were boiling with life, but Nora had taken to running joylessly on a secondhand treadmill in the unfinished basement. By the time July rolled around, they had gotten avoiding each other down to a science. But every week they added a new song to their shared running playlist. Communicating in soft rock and nineties R & B the grief they both knew it would be dangerous to proclaim.

Jennings quietly circled Bear on the longboard and doled out his observations at his glacial pace. He recounted the news of the rez like a bored news anchor. Bear had been removed from the inner circle of the rez, and he'd been giving Nora so much room that now when Jennings blabbed about everything and everyone, but *especially* Nora, Bear was suddenly his number one customer.

"Nora is working herself into the ground," he said.

"I see that, J. I *really* do. Tell everybody I see that. We're trying to—" *Forget*, he wanted to say.

She was overworking, and he was the exact opposite. All of his work seemed to crawl to a stop. He didn't want to get out of bed. He didn't want to do the tours. Moxcy had taken up most of them while Bear did admin work. Jennings was remarkably good at the details of the business, and Bear had already pegged him as his successor if he wanted it.

Bear walked on solid ground now. No one brought him dinner. No one smudged his house for free or watched him walk to his car at night. They were treating him like he already left.

But he hadn't had acid reflux for weeks. He was sleeping like a baby, and he held his head high and spoke with authority now. Telling his truth to the whole town hadn't fixed everything, but it fixed something.

"Me and the track team have been helping where we can, but she goes to Elder Wilkes's home a lot."

"Elder Wilkes doesn't like a lot of people."

"A lot of people don't like Elder Wilkes," Jennings countered.

Bear shrugged. "Nora likes her."

"Why? That lady is weird."

"She's fine, just set in her ways."

"She went there with Basil." Jennings stopped his board with his foot.

Bear's throat bobbed. "I can see why. Basil's kind of an outsider too." Bear tried to sound nonchalant, but it was work. What bond had he and Nora struck up? Did they talk about whatever wealthy people talk about? Was Basil taking her to fancy restaurants Bear could never hope to afford?

Jennings pushed faster on his board. "My brother told Lu that even if you married her, you would dump all the money into the taxes, and she would still be in debt. He told her she has legal resource." Jennings's voice shook.

"Recourse," Bear corrected. "And tell Basil to shut the fuck up."

"I mean, if he can convince her not to marry you. That's it, right?"

"He's not going to convince Lu of anything. She's one semester shy of her degree."

"But Basil was bragging about *accreditations*? Getting to do her classes online—"

"That's accommodations, and none of that matters, J. Lu wants her money and this is the fastest route."

"Then why don't you just do it? Marry Lu, pay everything back. Maybe Nora can get used to the idea. Why are you . . ."

"Stalling?" Bear answered. As soon as he said it, he realized that's exactly what he was doing. Just running the clock out or waiting for a bolt of lightning to change this fucked-up situation.

"We'll do it next week." Bear's voice cracked involuntarily. "But right now, I need to visit Yanne. I'll be back at the end of the day."

Driving down 295 was never pleasant but at least it was fast. He made it to the hospital a full seven minutes before GPS predicted. Always great to have those slight victories over technology.

He pulled up to Mercy Hospital and made a small sign of the cross. He never considered himself a superstitious man until he entered hospitals and funeral homes. So many unsettled spirits here.

The hospital room was decorated in quotes and poems. Brandon closed his laptop and picked up a ball of yarn while Ella Fitzgerald crooned about moonlight in Vermont. Yanne looked tiny in the huge bed, knitting what looked like an endless scarf. The door had barely closed before Yanne spoke.

"You fucked up, Bear." She didn't even look up over her knitting.

Bear sighed. "Glad to see you're doing better, Yanne."

"You need to talk to Nora." She finally looked up.

"Seconded," Brandon said.

"Your sister needs some space from me."

"You just missed her. Your cousin drove her up. Super-nice guy. Not weird and overly curious at all." Brandon shot Bear a look and nodded toward the wall of elegantly arranged wildflowers. "He got Yanne some flowers."

Bear slapped the wilted flowers down on the half-empty food tray. Cheap carnation petals tumbled down to the floor. He didn't need this shit. He drove here for two hours just to be told what he already knew.

"She's killing herself." Bear sighed. "Working sixteen-hour days. Changing permits and hiring notaries."

"She's not going to last long like this," Brandon said.

"This is all my fault," Bear and Yanne said in unison.

She looked at him over her glasses. "We're both right." She laughed, and Bear finally saw what Brandon had always seen. Yanne wasn't a nuisance, but a woman with her own unique way of being in the world.

"Nora doesn't deserve this, and neither do you." Bear picked up the yarn. "What's happening? Why are you here?"

"I have sickle cell anemia, so some of my red blood cells turn into pointy fuckbois when I'm stressed and they can't carry as much oxygen. They get stuck at different places in my body. And it's excruciating for hours or weeks at a time. When I'm under stress or sometimes for no reason at all, really, my body attacks me."

"This is actually a clever adaptation to malaria," Brandon offered. He wasn't knitting, just making terrible knots. "Her blood cells are shaped like sickles so they can't carry malaria up her bloodstream. She's actually superhuman."

"She is superhuman." Bear took her hand. "But what's going on with all of this knitting?"

"Oh, we're going to knit bomb the children's ward! The overnight nurses are helping us."

"That's adorable, Yanne. Nora would love—" He stopped himself.

Yanne squeezed his hand. "Can you give me a reading?" he asked. He just wanted to do something that would make her happy.

"Really?" Her eyes lit up.

"Really." She looked so frail in the weak hospital light.

Shuffling the cards with her typical theatrical flair, Yanne only pantomimed pulling out a card.

"My reading is, don't fucking marry another woman."

"Boom!" Brandon shouted.

Bear stood. "Well, I'm glad you're feeling a little better."

"Oh, c'mon, Bear, don't leave. I'm sorry. I just don't think you and Nora tried hard enough. You didn't fight for her, and it just pisses me off."

"If you both want to call me a piece of shit, you'll need to get in line." Bear scooped up his beanie. "You don't have to put those in water, they're already half-dead."

"Bear, for real, though. Why can't you stop this? My sister is gutted. You're a wreck. You have dark circles under your eyes.

You're thinner. Why can't you see that y'all had something beautiful? Why can't you choose beauty and love?"

"I've never had any use for pretty words and poetry and Shakespeare." Bear flicked his wrist toward Brandon. "All of the beauty you mention, I see it. I see it in being the man I said I was going to be."

"Duty," Brandon said.

"Duty," Bear agreed. "And your sister, she thinks so too."

"Don't speak for her." Yanne's voice broke, and her eyes were suddenly fierce. "My sister's as wretched as she's *ever* been. She's two Zoloft in a trench coat and glasses at this point. She is *broken*. Don't you dare speak for her."

Bear looked down at his hands. "I didn't mean to upset you. I think I should get going."

"Bear." Brandon stopped him at the door. "This is an emergency. Break the glass."

SPREADSHEETS

AUGUST 15
2 WEEKS UNTIL FORECLOSURE

HERE IS A MAN DOWNSTAIRS CLAIMING TO BE FAMILY and wanting to come to the room. Could you come down and confirm?"

Nora stretched out of her window seat in Yanne's cozy hospital room. The inn was languishing. No one had come, and Nora suspected no one would. Jon had never suggested their inn to wait-listed customers, since he had never meant to help them.

"Who is it?" Nora asked.

"He won't say, but he says he's Yanne's immediate family."

If this was Felicia trying to rub their noses in everything, there would be some furniture moving around this lobby.

She pressed the elevator down, verbally ticking off all of the things she wanted to say to Felicia.

When the doors rolled open, it wasn't Felicia's superior grin she saw.

Jon Bradley pulled a hand through his windswept hair. "I just want to see her," he rushed out in response to Nora's shocked face. "After all we've been through, I deserve to see her."

Oh, the caucasity of this man telling me what he deserves.

"Jon, just let this go. Is it this hard? To sit in your own mess? To *not* come out on top on *one* thing?"

"That *one* thing is everything to me."

"Why'd you do it then? Why did you make a deal with the devil?"

"I didn't know you. But I knew Felicia. I was interested in buying the property a while ago. She said I could get it dirt cheap if I kept an eye on you two. Made sure the project never got off the ground."

"So you kept Yanne away days at a time and left me to work on my own."

He looked down at his feet and rubbed his eyes. "How could I have known that she would be the love of my life?" When he looked back up, his face was wet with tears. "I didn't account for my heart. And it was the biggest mistake of my life."

"*Is*," Nora corrected. "It *is* the biggest mistake of your life. It's still happening and won't change. How much did she offer you?"

"Two-point-two mil. It's an absolute steal for that place. Even before your renovations."

And Felicia had offered them $200K like she was doing them a favor.

"I'm sorry, Nora, it's not going to work. It never was. But I should tell you once I become the owner, I would never kick you out. Bear obviously couldn't run his business out of the inn and—"

Nora cut him off with a laugh. "You still think Felicia's going to sell to you? She has no incentive to let Barton Cove go that cheap. How you got into this mess is how you'll leave it. Scheming and scammed."

Jon sniffed. She could see the wheels turning. "What can I do to help Yanne? If Felicia kicks you out, I can give you two a room at the Willow Bee free of charge. I can arrange your tickets. I can help." He held Nora's shoulders. "Use me. I can help."

"I don't want anything from you, Jon. And neither does Yanne."

His pleading face turned to stone. "Oh, you think I don't see Brandon Kern's car here? He's been after her since he saw her naked in the sunlight." Nora turned her back on him and moved toward the elevator. "You never liked me."

"Not my family," Nora told the nurse.

"She'll never be happy with him. Spreadsheets don't spread legs. She'll never love the way we loved again!" he yelled. Then he started to quote Shakespeare just as the elevator doors slid closed.

He was miserable and still in love with Yanne. At least *that* had been real.

In the hospital room, Yanne looked up from her bed. This was a long hospital stay. Her longest yet. But the color was returning to her cheeks. She was getting better.

"Who was it?"

"Jon," Nora said, watching her sister's reaction.

Yanne only smoothed the bedsheet. "Thank you for sending him away."

"Felicia promised to sell him Barton Cove when we fail."

Brandon opened his leather briefcase and pulled out two files. He didn't notice a small flyer slip out.

Simple photocopied paper. Times New Roman font. It could have been a flyer for babysitting services.

YOU'RE INVITED TO THE WEDDING OF ENNIS BEAR FREEMAN AND LUCINDA SEAL NEPTUNE.

Brandon grabbed the paper out of her hand.

"I knew they were getting married, Brandon. When is it?"

"Saturday." He looked at Yanne. Nora guessed they had decided not to tell her.

"Big day on Saturday then," Nora said. "Janae Bennett-Bradley's coming to town."

THE WEDDING

THE RAIN PUMMELED THE WINDOWS IN THE SMALL municipal building, and someone had positioned a rusty bucket near Bear's feet to catch the leak.

Lu's uncle and her cousin John Michael stood at the back of the church in dark glasses like bouncers.

"Why can't you just do this on the rez? The municipal building just makes this all look so—" Francis gestured around the Old Town municipal building.

"Clinical? Loveless? Administrative?" Moxcy offered. "Bear, this is hard to undo once you do it."

"The tie?"

Moxcy squeezed the knot.

"It takes like six months after cohabitation to get a divorce. By the time you're free, Nora will have babies with a dude named Jackson Johnson, and he'll wear LeBrons to the wedding. They'll name their first baby LeBronia."

"You are in *no* way helping." Bear slapped her hands away from the tie. "I got an offer, you know."

Moxcy tugged his hair. "At Orono? You went anyway? Even

with all this?" She gestured around. "If you pay the taxes and help Lu, we probably won't have enough to go seasonal." She said the last part softly.

"I know," he said. "I just promised I would go to the final interview."

"Promised Nora?

Bear only nodded. He would have been a good man to Nora. He would have spent his life deserving her.

"Damn, finally a woman who can get you off your complacent ass and she's . . ." She trailed off.

"Gone." Bear sniffed and lifted his chin.

She'd be on a plane next week if they couldn't get Janae to have pity on them.

She needs support.

My cheerleader needs a cheerleader.

Standing in front of the crowd, he pulled out his phone and texted Nora a single GIF. LeBron James smoking a cigar. In his hand, a championship ring glinted in the light.

Francis slapped his son's back. "Where's the girl?" His father looked tired, even a bit nervous. Could Bear's wedding really be moving him?

"It's pouring out. She's just a little late. She'll be here." Bear looked down at his hands.

"Have you spoken to her, though?" Moxcy asked.

"No point in calling her now, the reception's terrible in here." His text hadn't even gone through. "We've gone longer than this without talking."

"Before your wedding?" Moxcy countered. She was such a pain in the ass.

Moxcy played tunes from a very *on the nose* playlist, including a Motown number called "Shotgun Wedding."

Then Lu bustled through the door, shaking a twisted umbrella out on half of the wedding guests on her right. It looked like she had curled her hair at some point today, but the rain had plastered the strands to her shoulder. She looked profoundly resolved as she pulled a soaking bouquet from her bag. The running mascara, the squelching shoes, and the slow, determined gait made her look like the final girl in a horror film instead of a bride.

Lu and he were alike right now, dragging themselves toward inevitability in the slowest way possible. She didn't want to do this. They'd run out of steam even before the accident. They had wasted so much time like this.

She smiled weakly at Bear, and Bear nodded back. He hadn't thanked her for doing this. He had become absorbed in what he was losing, but the truth was, Lu had offered to marry him on a day's notice to save Sunshine Trails. As much as she complained about it being a money pit, she knew what it meant to their community. She was *his* only hope too. He squeezed her hand. They were saving each other.

"Thank you, Lucinda. For everything."

She blinked at him, then looked down at her dripping bouquet.

The JP made a stale joke about the weather to the silent crowd. After another minute of silence, he started with the ceremony.

"We're all here today to celebrate the relationship of Lucinda Seal Neptune and Ennis Bear Freeman and to be witnesses and supporters of the commitment they share with each other."

He spoke for another few minutes, but Bear kept his gaze fixed on a point on the wall. If he focused out on the onlookers, his cousin, his father, his knees would buckle and he would bolt. If he focused on Lu, he would see how badly she didn't want to do this and he would bolt. Best to focus on the peeling paint alongside a crack in the wall.

"I, Ennis, in the presence of these witnesses, do take you, Lucinda, to be my lawful wedded wife, to h-have and to . . ." *I'm stuck.* "To h-h-h—"

No, no, no.

He couldn't get out of this loop.

YANNE AND BRANDON CAME ROLLING INTO THE HOUSE TO "Crazy in Love" playing on her wireless speaker.

"Today's the day. Get ready to sparkle!" Yanne said.

"Oh. Did you get the lobster?"

Yanne nodded and Nora took the bags from her.

"You shouldn't be lifting," Nora scolded.

"Oh, Nora, I've been out for a week!"

"Yeah, Brandon, you were supposed to give *both* of us a tour of your new place, not just Yanne."

Brandon blushed like a boy. "Let's not focus on *my* house. You get your pitch ready. Yanne and I are making white truffle butter lobster rolls that are going to make Janae say yes to anything."

While they prepared food, Nora struggled to get her head into the task.

Bear was getting married. Nora thought of that scene in *The Color Purple* where Shug is running to the church singing, *God is trying to tell you something.* What if she threw on her running shoes and ran all the way to that damned place and begged him not to do it?

Would he escort me out?

By the time most of the food was prepared, Nora was a nervous wreck.

Brandon was absolutely no help. "Get dressed. Your company will be here any minute," he said.

Nora held her arms out. "I *am* dressed!"

"Do you have anything that *doesn't* make you look like you walked off the set of *Roots*?"

Nora looked down at her billowy romantic cotton dress. Simple, cool, elegant.

"No," she said and he shrugged.

"She's here! She's getting out of the car," Yanne shouted across the foyer. There was a great rustle inside the home, like an autumn wind had swept through the house as everyone rushed to the door.

Yanne and Brandon looked out the panel window, heads stacked like fall pumpkins.

"Janae has landed," Yanne whispered.

Nora gulped. "Holy shit."

"Holy hell." Brandon made the sign of the cross. "Who is this woman?"

"Janae is DC's Cinderella," Nora said.

"No, her sister Liza is god-tier Cinderella. Janae is giving Sleeping Beauty," Yanne corrected. Nora nodded her agreement.

"Okay, and if I did *not* grow up watching Disney princesses, who is Janae?"

Brandon could have been elsewhere, she knew. He could have been standing up in Bear's wedding today. Nora couldn't get the image of Bear leaning over and kissing Lu at the altar out of her head. She imagined the whole town was there, handkerchiefs dotting moist eyes. Their Bear doing the right thing.

But Brandon had declined his invitation, fearing it would be more sad than triumphant.

Nope, now she was getting sad. If she thought about Bear too long she wouldn't get out of bed.

Yanne smiled up at Brandon. Her sister, always in a desperate search for depth, had found her quiet intensity in a surprising place.

Nora peeked out the window. Janae wore a sleek black dress just past her knees, the skirt so narrow, it was a wonder that she didn't hop to the front door. She had on a wide-brimmed black hat and black sunglasses. The only spots of color on her were her bloodred lips, fingernails, and, if Nora was guessing right, the red bottoms of her shoes.

"If you told me right now she was born of a virgin, I would buy it," Yanne said.

Even though she had watched her approach, Nora still jumped at the soft knock on the door. *Just nerves.*

But geez, there was something positively spectral about Janae's beauty. It raised the hairs on the back of Nora's neck.

"Nice to see you again." She hugged Yanne in greeting. "When my mother told me our church friends moved here, I couldn't believe it. I had to come and see you while I was up!"

It was an elegant white lie. More like Nora's awkwardly drunk begging her on IG, or maybe Ms. Bev, her mother, forced her to pop in, and she was doing her due diligence. It was still kind of her.

Nora finally found her voice. "Janae, I'm Nora. You may not remem—"

"Of course I remember you. The fastest thing at the church field day. My little brother had a thing for you."

"Ah, Maurice, he was smart. He, um, talks—"

"A lot," Janae finished with a laugh.

Nora relaxed. She was doing it. It wasn't a big deal. Yanne was disappointed they didn't get the "big guns," e.g., Liza, but

Janae had always been more approachable. In fact, Nora was glad it was Janae and *not* Liza at her door. Liza had always seemed a little *too* ready for a joke or a debate. Nora never felt smart enough to know the difference.

Yanne clapped. "Janae, welcome to our inn!"

"Very quiet for an inn." She walked slowly, one foot in front of the other like the foyer was her own personal catwalk. It was less an observation and more like an indictment. She was already making a decision.

Nora had written Janae's child's name on the inside of her palm, but the damn chicken grease smudged the poor little note, **MUQTHRY**, until it was unrecognizable. She still had her table notes and kitchen notes to anchor the conversation.

"Yes, we're always light on guests." Nora rolled her eyes before she'd even finished the sentence. The most boneheaded thing she could have possibly said. *Invest in our empty-ass inn, savvy businesswoman.*

But Janae only looked past Yanne to Brandon, who must have had *math nerd* tattooed on his neck.

"Are you the CPA?" Janae had a funny look on her face.

"Me?" Brandon coughed. "How do you know that?"

"I don't know, you have a mini sudoku book in your front pocket. And you're counting napkin rings. I took a wild guess."

"Yes, but CPA is very specific."

"Oh, Jon mentioned a, um"—she cleared her throat—"a CPA that—"

"Was lying in wait like an opportunistic scavenger? Yes, he's made his opinion of me clear. But what I have"—he looked at Yanne—"was never really his."

Nora should say something. She knew she should be pithy and breezy like everyone, but she had hammered the facts and figures into her head, and she didn't want to lose them. Once she started to speak, all the information would leak out of her head like a sieve.

Right before the pause became awkward, Janae's eyes ticked over Nora again, no doubt doing some celestial calculation of Nora's worthiness. She was not impressing this woman. There was simply no getting around that.

And yet Nora had to make a case to Janae in the world's clumsiest Hail Mary, or they would be homeless, penniless. They'd used their entire inheritance to renovate and pay down the foreclosure. But Janae already found her dull and uninteresting. With a sister like Liza Bennett, most people would have a far way to climb to seem interesting, Nora supposed. She couldn't sparkle, and right now, she felt her lack of charisma like a weight in her chest. *Don't do this now, Nora. Not with everyone depending on you.*

"So." Nora cleared her throat.

You're on. Sparkle, bitch.

NAILS IN A COFFIN

SAME DAY

LU LOOKED AROUND AT THE CROWD. A PLEADING SORT of embarrassment emanated from her. Her head snapped to the back of the room. The small crowd stirred as his cousin Basil walked in, somehow dry, and took a seat in the back. Bear wasn't a superstitious man, but the hairs on the back of his neck crept up just the same.

Something's not right here.

Basil was holding a folded envelope.

"Till death do us part," Bear managed to grind out. It was an August miracle that he got through those vows.

Lu repeated the vows back to him, faltering a bit on *To love and to cherish*, but she finished. He almost wound his hands in the *wrap it up* gesture to the JP. Before this moment, Bear had always thought these last few bits were throwaway words at the end of a ceremony.

The JP cleared his throat, suddenly louder and clearer than he'd been the entire quiet ceremony. "If anyone can show just cause why this couple cannot lawfully be joined together in matrimony, let them speak now or forever hold their peace."

Bear was fishing for the rings when he heard Basil's voice.

"I object." The words seemed to bounce off the walls and

come back to Bear three times like an echo. The onlookers' eyes were all on Basil, who stood up with a slight smirk. He loved being at the center of something. He was finally getting his wish.

"On what grounds?" Moxcy asked.

"Invalid marriage license." Basil pulled a folded sheet of paper from his pocket and unfolded it. "Lu, you filed for this document in early May, right? You told me Bear was acting strange."

"Basil, so help me God," Bear muttered. So she had filed behind his back, after he told her they were done.

"And from the date of issuance, you have ninety days to perform the ceremony in the state of Maine."

"So what?" Bear said. Different emotions warred inside of him, but white-hot fury at Basil's gall was winning. He should have smashed that fly when he had the chance.

"It's Monday, August twenty-eighth, Bear," Lu squeaked out.

"And your little ceremony's invalid," Basil said.

Surprise flashed on everybody's face. Even Francis stood up. "Now look here, Basil, we tried, but this is a marriage ceremony. Bear won. Let's let it go."

Basil only looked at Lu.

Bear held her wide gaze. "Don't worry. We just apply again. It's a Monday. It's a fifteen-minute application. This is a nonissue."

"Ah, see, that's where you're wrong. I have another half-filled-out application here." Basil rushed to Lu. "Lu, if you sign this, we finish the ceremony. I can help you finish your online classes with a top-of-the-line tutor. We can get you certified in California. I'll take care of you."

Bear shook his head. *This* was his play? Lu was a lot of things, but romantic was not one of them.

"Oh, Basil, please—" The laugh died in Bear's throat when he saw Lu's face.

She was listening.

"I can wipe the hospital debt free in a half hour." Basil snapped his fingers. "Don't be the sacrificial lamb for Bear's failing business. It's a dying model. Something always comes up, and he'll put you on the sidelines again."

Bear could see it. This was what Basil wanted to do all along. He didn't give a damn about helping Lu. He wanted to cripple the business. He wanted to deal a death blow to Sunshine Trails so he could pick it apart. He had played right into Basil's hands.

But Lu had more loyalty than that.

"Lu, you say yes, and we're on a flight to California this week. You can start your nursing residency next month. I looked up some places." Bear watched her whole body tense.

She wanted it.

"You're invisible here. You'll never be more than what you went through—never be more than Bear's story. Don't you want to be the main character for once?" Basil's voice trembled. *Wait . . . Could he love her?* Could his cousin have loved Lu all these years? It would explain *so* much.

When Lu looked at him, there was a touch of pity in her eyes. She was wavering. "Bear, saving your grandmother's trail business was never my passion . . . I want to finish nursing school."

"Lu," Bear whispered. "I—I need. . . ." He let the rest die on his tongue. She knew that he needed her. Everyone knew she was his last hope.

She was shaking her head. "I just want to finish nursing school."

"JANAE, YOU GOT MARRIED AT THE WILLOW BEE, RIGHT?" Nora looked down at the list of facts she'd hidden under the plate.

"Yes, it's a lovely inn. I just dropped in to see Jon before I came here." Janae forked over her lobster roll disinterestedly.

"How is Jon?" Yanne asked hesitantly.

"Honestly, he's totally different. He's just kind of sad now." Her eyes flicked over to Yanne. She knew more than she was saying. "I'm actually worried about him."

"Oh, his money should cheer him up," Yanne snapped and lifted her hand for a high-five from Janae.

Janae didn't lift her hand. "Are we high-fiving depression now?"

Nora swallowed a lump of cold air.

Damn.

Damn.

Damn.

Nora pulled Yanne's hand down. "Of course not. I just—he—"

"Nora, I hear you could use a partnership. I don't know if I'm the right person, but let me hear your pitch."

Nora could see that she was losing. She had crashed into a hurdle somewhere and lost control of the race. Janae would go through the motions and tell her mother and sisters about how low the Dashes had fallen. They'd all crack their perfectly symmetrical faces laughing.

"Tell me what you're doing up here all the way from Montgomery County." There was a steely no-bullshit underside to Janae's well-known kindness that Nora didn't like being on the other side of. It reminded her of the way teachers would look at her when she promised her rich father would show up for career day. It was partly *You know better than this* and partly *We can't wait for you to get your shit together all day.*

"Well, we want to continue our successful inn enterprise." She saw Janae look around at the word *successful*.

"When I was nineteen years old, Dash of Love Seasonings was one of my first pageant sponsors. I am forever grateful to your mother and father for that. However . . ."

Just rip the Band-Aid off.

Janae looked like she was mentally pulling out nails for Nora's pine coffin.

"This is the wrong side of the island for foot traffic."

Thwack.

"We know." Nora was trying not to sound defensive. It wasn't working. They would lose their inheritance.

"And your beach is really rocky, with hundreds of fallen trees and heavy branches. Nearly unusable."

Thwack.

"We know that too—" They would return to Maryland with nowhere to live. She couldn't imagine clocking back into the CVS, ringing up blood pressure medicine and Fleet enemas.

"And the Willow Bee is less than two miles away." Clumps of dirt thunked over Nora's imaginary shallow grave. She would see Felicia's smug, satisfied face for her entire life. She would take so much pleasure in turning them out on their asses. It was what she wanted from the beginning. And now Felicia would get the humiliating show she wanted.

It was done.

ACTION, ANY ACTION

SAME DAY

LU SLIPPED OUT OF BEAR'S GRASP, AND EVERYONE IN the room gasped except Basil. He looked like everything was coming up roses for him. He handed Lu a pen, and she didn't even pause to think before she signed.

"You finally got Sunshine Trails." Bear kept his hands fisted at his sides. The last thing he needed was an assault charge. "But why? You can't run it from California. I won't let you say yes to damming up the river to fill your own pockets. What have you won?"

"Wow. It is simply unfathomable to you that I could love Lu, isn't it? How disconnected are you that someone is in love with your woman and you're obsessed with the fucking river? What have I *won*?" Basil scoffed, and turned to hand the license application to the officiant.

Lu fluffed out her hair and straightened her shoulders. She looked wholly unmoved by Basil's declaration of love. "Bear, look. You gave so much to Sunshine Trails but it just wasn't enough. Basil has proven he's a better businessman. I think if your gma would have lived to see him make it, she would have turned it over to him too." She patted Bear's forearm.

Lu was so casually cruel he almost nodded in agreement. *Yes, my dead grandmother would have found me lacking. Thanks for pointing that out.*

"Lu, I—" What could he say?

Basil scrolled through his phone and a tinny version of a Penobscot wedding song floated through his speakers, drowning Bear out.

Bear's stomach lurched. Queasy saliva filled his mouth, and sick crawled up his throat.

"I need a bucket. I need a bucket," Bear said frantically, racing toward the bathroom. His father followed, closing the bathroom door behind them.

Francis rubbed his back and Bear was embarrassed by how soothing he found it.

"If you're here to say I told you so, you can save it," Bear said, heaving over the bathroom sink.

"I'm here to tell you I know why you're doing this. Why you've been doing this for years."

"Dad."

"No, son. Listen. We left you too long—me and your mama felt the change in you as soon as we came back. You got terrified of people leaving you. It made you like river silt, you'd go any way the river ran."

"So I'm losing Sunshine Trails, and you pick this moment to tell me I'm a pushover?"

"I kept trying to tell you that woman was out for number one."

"What wrong with being out for number one, huh? She took the better deal. Something you wanted me to do. Lu was my *last* chance to keep Sunshine Trails. My last chance to be something more than a high school coach. Look around. Dad, I failed *everybody*. No one even looks at me anymore."

"Did you die, baby boy? When the community realized you're human?" His tones were soft and so soothing that they cut the I-told-you-so frankness of his words. Francis rubbed his son's shoulders. "You needed this, Bear. You needed to see you can't hold the sky and land together. At least not by yourself. Not every ash tree can make a basket. You gotta know what to nurture and what to leave."

The officiant tapped the bathroom door. "Hey, I only have fifteen minutes left here. I'll respect your wishes," he said somberly.

"No, no, marry them," Bear said. His voice was weak with defeat. Through the slit in the door, he could see Basil walking toward him grinning so wide it cracked his face open.

"Look, you don't have to stick around," Basil said, "and despite what you think of me, I'm not going to give the Anglos our river when I take Sunshine Trails. But I will make sure we get something out of a deal."

"You've been gone too long, cousin. The power company doesn't want a *piece* of that river. They want it all. And they know a self-interested bastard when they see one," Bear said.

His goodwill salvo thrown back in his face, Basil shook his head. "I want you to remember this." He was practically vibrating with anger now. "This feeling you have, yeah? In the pit of your stomach? I want you to remember it. This is what I felt when you fucked Lu against the wall that night at the bar. It's what I felt when they forgot my name on Gma's funeral program but listed you twice. It's what I felt when Gma took you in and I went to the group home."

He ran away, was caught, and ended up in a group home for a weekend before they found him. But Bear was not going to argue that point. Basil wanted to see him low, and he got his wish.

"Cousin, take care of Lu, but careful you don't let your mouth start something your fist can't finish." Bear gripped the sink and looked at Basil through the mirror.

The ceremony was fast. Less than five minutes. *Why had it felt like an eternity when I was standing there?* The JP was relieved to leave the building and gave Basil a perfunctory handshake as congratulations.

Basil was married. He could access his trust (though he didn't have to) and buy Bear out of Sunshine Trails. He could say yes to the dam proposal and get even richer. He'd played the game well.

The crowd began to rise and pat Lu and Basil on the back.

We take care of our own.

Good on you, Basil.

When Francis came out of the bathroom, he went immediately to the door. To see if the rain had slacked off.

"Uncle Francis is doing what he does best, looking for the exits," Basil said.

Picking on Francis always got a few cheap chuckles from the crowd. Basil finally looked like he had everything he'd ever wanted.

"Please, please eat, everyone," Basil announced. "No sense in wasting all of this food." Like *he'd* prepared the food. Like they'd all come to see him get married all along.

Lu was already on the phone with the university when he tapped her on the shoulder

"I appreciate what you were almost willing to do for me, Lucinda." He said, using her full name felt like a goodbye.

She put her hand over the bottom of the phone and dropped her chin. "Are you about to get emotional?"

AT BARTON COVE, BRANDON STOOD TO GATHER THE plates, taking action—any action—in the face of Nora's failure.

He scooped up Janae's untouched lobster roll. "Well, we still thank you for coming. It was really kind of you to sit down with us."

Yanne cut in. "If you ever need a tarot reading or crystal cleansing or an actress . . ."

Janae stood. "Could you direct me to the washroom?"

Nora led her to the room, and Yanne shook her head. "Damn" was all she said.

Nora didn't have time to react because Janae was coming back from the bathroom and had returned her wide-brimmed hat to her head. She pressed one button on her phone, and a sleek, tinted black car slid into sight through the kitchen windows. Bloodred lipstick reapplied, skirt wrinkles smoothed to perfection—it was like the past two hours had never happened.

So much work erased. So much time wasted.

She heard Bear's voice.

You should stop thinking about that video as something that DQs you and start to think of it as something that qualifies you for something else.

As if on cue, her phone buzzed. Bear? Texting from his wedding?

Today is wild.

She looked at the GIF of LeBron, and her heart stuttered.

This was the championship. She wouldn't go home without a ring. She had to keep fighting.

She looked at the GIF again, then back at Janae.

"Wait." Nora's hand trembled over the doorknob, halting an impatient Janae in her tracks. "You're right. About the inn."

Yanne gasped. "Nora. What are you doing?"

But Janae only eyed her car outside. Her favor to her mother fulfilled, she looked ready to get back to her real life.

"I actually have another thing I've been doing." Nora's voice shook. "Could I just show you something?" She thought of Bear running, turning around to face her with the sun on his shoulder. A rush of adrenaline flushed under her skin.

He was a bright red ribbon at the end of the line. While everyone shouted from the sidelines, Bear would always be on the other side of the finish line for Nora, something she pressed toward and narrowed her focus down to.

Just get there, Nora.

Nora went to her room and returned with the small, faded Polaroid. "This is Elizabeth Wilkes, a Penobscot elder." She passed the photo to Janae.

She finally looked surprised. "This is a nude photo."

"That's right. Her nude photo is one of her prized possessions. It is a symbol of her choosing who to show her body to."

Janae pulled her hat off. A tacit *go on.*

"I want to build a nonprofit summer camp for victims of cyberbullying, digital abuse, and revenge pornography."

A COMET

YOU'VE ALWAYS BEEN THICK, HAVEN'T YOU, BEAR?"
Francis sighed heavily and sat down on the padded foldout chair. Everyone had eaten their fill and made their excuses. Only Bear and Francis were left. "Now. I know I wasn't the perfect father, but one thing about Francis, he knows when to cut and run. This is just about the only thing I can still teach you, son."

"Dad, you can't brag about leaving when people need you."

"Look around, Bear. No one needs you. Now that you're not spending your whole inheritance taking care of Lu, you can marry *anyone* to take care of those taxes and have a nice pot left over to start a family. I can think of a hundred women in love with you enough to marry you tomorrow."

One second.

Two seconds.

Wait.

Bear smiled. "I can only think of one."

Francis held his belly. "Then why are you still here?"

He covered his face with his hands, and his shoulders shook like mountains.

He was free.

The officiant approached him, thinking that he was bawling his eyes out, but he retracted his hands when he realized that Bear was laughing.

Laughing so hard he could hardly catch his breath. His father, the patron saint of escaping duty, had just blessed him with the best lesson of his life. When a burden gets lifted, don't wait around and question how. Cut loose and run.

JANAE PULLED AT HER CURLS. SHE WAS SEATED AGAIN and excited about Nora's idea.

"With a focus on physical wellness, I plan to show campers ages ten to eighteen how to detach from digital content." Nora pointed to the photo. "Elder Wilkes was ostracized, singled out, and forced into a marriage she didn't want. We don't have a safety net for women like this. I know because I am a woman like this."

Nora's voice thickened, and hot shame still stung her face as she said it.

Will it ever not affect me?

"I made a video with my boyfriend at the time, and it has followed me for eight years. I felt trapped, but the outdoors here restored me, healed me." She relaxed into the pitch, feeling the truth of those words. "And, frankly, erasing the links gave me incredible peace. Those three aspects form the heart of my program: Outdoor connections, community building, and digital rehabilitation. Please consider funding the inaugural year of Digital Dawn, an all-inclusive three-month camp for victims of digital abuse." Nora handed her the slim folder and exhaled.

Janae flipped through the pamphlet. "Can I be honest with you, Nora?"

"Please." Nora swallowed. It looked like a big fat no was coming.

"I had a child. We lost him quite publicly. I got the obligatory posts questioning my decisions as a mother, but the worst were pictures of me drunk with my Ms. DC runner-up crown on. They took the pictures from an entirely different time. I wasn't even in the accident; it was my child's father. But that picture is forever linked with a picture of my perfect little boy. And it kept me in a really dark place for a long time."

"I'm so sorry, Janae." Nora had read about this on one of those posts that followed the Bennetts like the Kardashians.

She held up her hand, absolving them all of guilt like some beautiful pope.

"I'm saying this to say that I couldn't be more behind your cause. I know at least five hedge fund bankers who have social impact funds burning a hole in their pocket nearing the end of their fiscal year. They won't breathe down your throat. They'll come down once a year for photos."

Nora's heart fluttered.

Janae didn't look up from the paperwork. "Do you have your articles of incorporation?"

"I do, I do." Nora hesitated. "But there is another slight hitch."

Janae looked up with the first perfectly pulled-off polite impatience Nora had ever seen.

"We have to pay off the foreclosure loan in the next week."

"Or we lose everything," Yanne added.

"I . . . wow. You have a dynamite proposal. Really tight. You need more stories. You need to find an inaugural cohort for next year. I can get you investors fast, but it can't be as fast as next week. I'm so sorry," Janae said.

The bottom fell out of Nora's stomach. She had shown her everything.

There was nothing left. *Now* she was a complete failure.

She wished she hadn't wasted so much time laboring under her old vision for this place. She had been so sure it was the right thing to do.

Janae tilted her head. "How much do you owe on your bank loan?"

Brandon cleared his throat and reached for a messy pile. "We are ninety-seven thousand five hundred and twenty-three dollars shy of foreclosure payoff." He tapped the paperwork.

Janae frowned. "Oh . . . is that all?"

"That's plenty," Nora said.

Janae stood up. "Of course, but this is at least a four-to-five-million-dollar venue, so I just thought . . . I don't mean to be dismissive, but in the venture capital world, anything under a hundred grand is essentially a rounding error. My husband and I are a little bound up in a new venture, so I'm not very liquid right now, or I could fix this today. But I happen to know a woman who never has that problem. Let me have a little conversation."

Janae walked toward the foyer pressing numbers into the phone, and Nora did a little dance.

Could this happen? It was just like chapter four in *Say Yes to Everything: Unlock Your Life with Radical Acceptance*. It was the only good thing Jon ever recommended.

Yanne flipped through her phone while they waited. They were clinking their nails on their glasses in unison when Janae entered the dining area.

"So, a few questions," she began.

Nora sat up in her chair.

"My sister would like to donate a garden. Is that possible?"

"Um, yes?" Nora said. Would her sister be *that* sister? The one who could purchase Belgium and have money left over?

"She would also like it to be called the Evelyn Bennett Memorial garden. Is that possible?"

"Yes, again." Nora swallowed.

Something was happening.

Janae held the phone out, and a round-faced, fully pregnant Liza Bennett screamed into her phone, "Nora! Congratulations! I'm buying your inn for like a week to pay off your bank loan. I'll hold it as collateral until one of the hedge bros cuts the first check. Is that okay with you?"

"Liza! What! This is incredibly generous of you! I . . . I don't know what to say."

"Say she's our savior!" Yanne squeezed Brandon's hand. The tender way he brought her hands to his mouth and kissed her knuckles took some of the air out of Nora's lungs.

"No, not a savior." Liza's voice turned serious. "I'm buying your debt, and being paid your debt plus seven percent. It works out quite well for me, and I can afford to wait. So, not a savior."

"Liza, how did you even think to do this?" Yanne practically had heart eyes coming out of her face.

"I learned a lot about thoughtful application of wealth from a good man," she said softly, and then blushed so beautifully she almost toppled Janae's most-gorgeous-woman-in-the-room tiara.

Nora swallowed. "Liza Not-Our-Savior Bennett, this is a major flex, and we are so grateful you would do this for us."

Liza bowed her head. The Bennetts really were DC royalty at this point. "You made a hell of an impression on my big sister, and she's notoriously hard to impress. I'll be in touch tomorrow morning. And also, I'd like you to think seriously about incorporating the Indigenous community around you. I was doing some googling, and there is an Abenaki trail business very near you. I think you should partner with them."

Nora opened her mouth. "I—"

"Nora!" Brandon was pointing out the window. He sounded like he was seeing a comet rocket toward them.

"Nora!" Yanne yelled.

They both pushed their index fingers into the window panel and shuffled their feet like Flintstone characters starting a car.

"Bear."

HOME

SAME DAY

WHAT IN ALL HELLS IS GOING ON?

A boom of thunder shook the walls. The glass windows seemed to bow with the strength of the wind.

Brandon twisted the handle, and the front door burst open with gale force. Sheets of rain slicked the porch furniture and beat the lavender and sea thrift plants down to the ground. Through the haze of pouring rain, Nora saw a lone figure walking up the path. She blinked, looking over to Yanne and Janae for direction. They looked back at her with the same hapless look.

The room was silent with anticipation. Yanne rolled around until she found Nora's running shoes hidden under the coatrack. She handed her the shoes wordlessly, and Nora looked back one last time at Janae, who was calling her car.

Brandon whistled at the rain, watching Janae worry her curls. "If you go around the back to the parking lot, your car can pull right up and you won't have to walk down that long path in the rain."

Janae smiled and looked past Nora to the man in the distance. "I think I'll do that."

Brandon closed the door. "Yanne, let's help Janae to her car."

Yanne's neck snapped back. "Are you kidding? Bear's coming! This is—"

"Yanne. Then we'll go somewhere and celebrate after."

"Oh . . . okay. Okay. Let's see you to your car, Janae."

What could Bear need? Why would he be here today? On his wedding day?

Nora slipped her shoes on and pulled open the door again. Head down, she pushed out into the rain. The downpour immediately soaked her cotton summer dress, and one wet strap slipped off her shoulder. By the time she reached him, she was nearly blind, with the driving rain draining the hair-care product out of her curls and into her eye. But she could still make him out. Ennis Bear Freeman wore a Stetson. He was slim-hipped and broad-shouldered in his Wranglers and dress shirt. Married or not, he was the first one she wanted to tell that she had done it. She had found a way to pay off the loan on her own terms.

He closed the distance between them in quick strides.

Married Bear looked the same as almost-married Bear.

His drenched dress shirt clung to his body, and his long hair lay flat and slick against his neck and chest. Sloshing in his cowboy boots and slinging arcs of cool rainwater, Bear reached up to touch Nora's shoulder. Tentatively, he pulled the strap of her dress up her arm.

"Shenora Dash." Bear said her whole name like she was in trouble.

I'm not this strong.

The rain pummeled them, stinging Nora's skin and pressing her ponytail flat.

She couldn't look at him, because his eyes would call her, and her body would obey. She had proven that at the memorial when he touched her, and she had spread open like a diary.

"Janae came," she said—or tried to say, but her voice cracked and the last bit came out in a whisper.

He reached for her, but she pulled back.

"You're married now. You're a married man." She stepped even farther away.

"I'm not married. I—I got dumped." Bear took another wet step toward her.

Her heart seized in her chest. Maybe she was hallucinating. She had so many questions. "Wait, what?" she breathed, her tone pleading.

"I'm not waiting anymore," he said, inching closer to her. He wrapped his arm around her as he walked to the porch.

Nora's head swam with one wild thought. *He's* not *married*.

"Dumped?" Nora said, stepping onto the first step. She pressed the water out of her dress.

"Spectacularly. Lu signed another marriage license right in my face. It's trending locally. 'Hashtag Bearial.'" He air-quoted. "Never had my own hashtag before."

"What would make her do something like that?"

"My cousin offered her the world."

Nora rubbed his hand between hers. "Can you pay those taxes without her?"

"Nope. I imagine I'll have to sell to Basil."

Bear was being *super* chill about pretty devastating news. "How can he vote on council matters from California. Bear, the river!" Nora said

Bear touched her chin, a ghost of a touch that made Nora's lip quiver. "Unless I can find a woman in this town who loves me," Bear whispered, holding Nora's gaze.

Nora wiped the corner of her eye. She could marry this man and literally never look back. But would *he* look back? She would hate to become another one of his duties.

"Bear, you're talking about your business like your fiancée didn't just walk out on you. Are you okay?"

"Oh, that." They were on the porch now. "I'm fine." His delivery was so blasé. Nora didn't know how to respond.

"So you're not—" Her shoulders fell slightly. "Are . . . are you sad?" It was the only thing she could think to ask.

"No." His look was pointed. "I'm not." He actually smirked, then snorted. "I'm sorry, this is not funny. It's not." Now he was holding his stomach.

His ridiculous giggle fit was catching. Because even in the face of all his losses, Nora felt it, too, a strange lightness like that kid hiccupping in that old *Willy Wonka and the Chocolate Factory* movie, a giddy kind of relief. Nora realized that the high-keening sound was Bear laughing like a hyena. "Lu signed those papers so quick, Nora."

Nora gave up trying to hold it in. *"At* the altar?"

Bear doubled over, breaking out into a wheeze. "She would have signed it on my back if I let her." They must've looked like lunatics falling over themselves laughing in the middle of the porch like stoners. When recalling this story, she could never pinpoint what was quite so funny, just that she'd never laughed harder in her life.

She sniffled and straightened her shoulders, letting the last of the laughter ease out. "If you're not sad, how *do* you feel?"

"Right now, I feel like a moose just rose off my chest. And that's the feeling I want to feel now."

Nora reached up on her tiptoes to hug Bear's neck, but he bent down and kissed her square on the lips in the middle of the porch.

"Nora." Bear rubbed her shoulder. "Can I come home?"

CORNROWS

BEAR SWEPT NORA UP IN HIS ARMS ON THE PORCH OF
Barton Cove. He was hot and misting and soaked, little
tributaries of water streaming down his handsome face. His
heart was beating so fast, and his arms were shaking.

He was nervous.

Nora touched his chest with her palm. At the expo, it had
calmed him. Bear's eyes rocketed to hers, then he held her around
her waist.

"The first place I touched you," he said.

Nora's hand rested on his bicep as he turned the doorknob.

"Question. Did you ever find my panties at that bingo hall?"

He pushed open the door, and a smile slid across his face.
"I did."

"What did you do with them?" Nora said, pushing his heavy
hair away from his eyes.

When they stood in the foyer, Bear twisted his hair and
wrung it out on his shirt.

He spoke slowly. "I can show you better than I can tell you."
He closed the door. "Take your panties off and give them to me."

Her eyes flashed with the dare.

Instead, she pushed his shirt over his ribs. His stomach quivered when she fingered the band of his Wranglers.

"Nora, I'm so nervous."

"I'm not," she said. As much anxiety as he had seen her display over the past ten months, he noticed now that she seemed solid as an oak. His warm palm covered her breast. Her heartbeat was slow, her gaze steady.

He pulled off his jeans and stepped out of them. His cock was pulsing between the slit in his boxer briefs like it had its own heartbeat, its own desires. He steadied her hand and raised her wrist up to his mouth. He kissed her so softly there, then down her arms like tiny kitten paws.

Nora had him, heart and soul, but he was going for the trifecta now.

"Your panties." He tilted his chin, looking every inch the high school teacher now. Nora slowly pulled her black lace underwear down her thighs, then past her knees.

Bear watched every movement with a hot intensity.

She likes when I watch.

She stepped out of the underwear and handed them over like a student with contraband.

Bear pulled himself free of the briefs, and he balled the panties up. Still looking at her, he rubbed the soft, damp fabric over his cock.

"I'm sorry, but I defiled your panties."

The palms of his other hand grazed her neck, and he caressed her jaw with his thumbs.

"I'm yours, Nora." He kissed her nose. "Body and soul, I'm yours. If you'll have me."

Nora looked like she might burst, but instead she laughed again. Her shoulders racked with the power of her laughter. She was delirious. That's what it was right now—maddening delirium.

"'If you'll have me'?" She sighed. "I can't be with anyone else."

Bear tilted her chin up again and covered her mouth, filling up his lungs with the last of her laughter. She was wet and salty, sweet and smooth. His tongue tasted her, and he crushed her to him so hard she had to tap his shoulder for breath. When he pulled away, Nora kissed his chest. The soft movement drew gooseflesh across his skin covered in Abenaki swirls and geometric-patterned jet-black tattoos.

"Please" was all he said, unsure what he was pleading for. "Nora, god help me, I can't live without you." He placed a light kiss on her collarbone.

In response, she snaked her hands across his wet chest, hooking her fingers on his low back.

Dropping to her knees in front of him, she fisted his swollen cock. Without preamble or any words of warning, her mouth clamped down over his glistening head, and she sucked so hard his knees buckled. The intensity of the sensation had him steadying himself against the table, knocking over a cup full of ballpoint pens.

Her hot, wet mouth massaged his cock, and she pulled on his constricted balls until a strangled cry escaped from the back of his throat. Bear bucked in her mouth like a bronco.

"Yes." His eyes were rolling to the back of his head. "You're sucking like you love it, woman. Do you love it?"

She stuffed her mouth with all of him and placed his hand on the back of her head.

"Suck," he whimpered. "Oh god, suck me off." He was going to come embarrassingly fast if Nora kept doing that tongue thing.

"Nora! Please." He pulled her off him by her ponytail. Her

mouth released the seal with a loud smacking sound, and that was it. He was nearly there. He pulled her up and kissed her mouth while spreading her strong, plush thighs and clamping them around his dick. He thrust twice between her tight thighs before he throbbed and spilled between her legs.

He rolled his shoulders and moaned her name, knees as shaky as a newborn fawn. Damn, he didn't have thigh-fucking on the list of things he thought he'd get done today.

Nora looked dazed and a little too pleased with herself. She pulled the wet dress over her head like she was done with clothes forever.

Let her take her victory lap.

Bear tilted his head at a weird angle. Lord, she looked like she had tumbled out of a damned clamshell. "You are so perfect," he whispered. "Shit, I'm dizzy. I need water. Let me get you a towel." Bear reached for the nearest surface to steady himself.

Great Creator, they hadn't been inside this house ten minutes.

He returned with his briefs back on, two beach towels, and two water bottles.

Clearing his throat, Bear pulled at his unruly hair. The rain and the sweat and hat had turned it into a knotted mess. The mass of hair clamored around his neck and face.

"Nora, would you, um, would you braid my hair?" He dipped his head toward her.

"Sure." Still naked, she layered the beach towel over a dining room chair, grabbed a brush, sat down, and pointed between her thighs.

Another hard knock of desire kicked through him.

"Sit on the floor." She laughed when he couldn't tear his eyes away from the damp curls at her center. Bear sat between her thighs at the kitchen table.

Humming and brushing, Nora worked out the knots in his still-wet hair. The quick zip of her nails on his scalp sent rivers of pleasure down his neck, tightening his nipples and his balls.

"Perfectly respectable kink," she said in his ear.

He murmured under his breath. Her thighs were on either side of his rib cage, and he felt her heat at the center of his back.

"Too tight?" she asked.

She pulled the brush through his hair again, finally through with the knots, and started at the crown of his head. Her breasts swayed at the nape of his neck, and her tight nipples grazed the shell of his ear and shoulder. His hand snaked up to feel her, and she slapped it away with a laugh.

"A top braid?" he asked, feeling the pressure near his forehead.

"What?" Nora asked.

"I'm going to look like a twelve-year-old girl who's into ponies."

"Bruh, if you ask a Black woman to braid your hair, she *will* cornrow it. I don't make the rules."

"Start from the nape of the neck," he said through a smile.

Nora started over, loosening the single braid and pulling Bear's heavy hair into a single, neat plait.

Bear felt the thick rope of hair and was surprised to feel a tear fall from his face. When she was done, he turned to kiss her. She looked alarmed at his tears.

"I can braid it better, Bear."

"It's perfect, you're perfect. This is so . . ."

"Perfect?" Nora teased.

His mouth moved over hers, and Bear knew he would probably never get used to how passionate her kisses were. How open and receptive she was to his mouth, to the intensity of his love for her.

Nora teased at the elastic of his briefs. He kicked them off in one graceful movement.

"Before I . . . Nora, I, um, want to be clear." He enveloped her with his body. It felt so good to be naked together. He was so warm, his dick so full against her belly. He held her gaze, and his heart sped up. "I want forever with you, starting today. This is the beginning of the rest of our life together. I want to marry you."

GOOD BOY

SAME DAY

NORA SQUEALED WHEN HE HOISTED HER IN HIS ARMS.
Skin on skin was the single most comforting feeling in the world, and Nora slipped against him and fought against his hold just for the sport of it, but she didn't want him to put her down.

She didn't want him to ever stop.

Still holding her like a sack of rice, Bear made a beeline to Nora's bedroom. He bounced her on the bed and watched with something close to awe as she starfished onto the white duvet and sank into the bed's pile of decorative pillows.

He was on top of her before she could lift her head. Bear took her nipple into his mouth and sucked. Hard. A deep drag that had his whole mouth full of her, forcing a low moan out of Nora. She fed her breast to him, pushing herself deeper into his mouth. She wanted him to devour her, and Bear was doing his damned best. She leaned back into the bed, and Bear followed her, mouth never disconnecting from her dark nipple.

He touched her with such hunger, like she was a feast. His fingers ran across the seam of her pussy, already so wet for him.

With a sigh, he pushed a thick finger between her slick folds to find her slippery and swollen.

"You're so hot, Nora. Tell me exactly how you want it."

His fingers pushed deeper and slipped inside of her. Her body arched in surprise. This was all she wanted.

"So tight." His voice was deep and sticky like molasses.

He kissed her again, gliding his thumbs across her nipples. She arched her back even more, pushing his finger deeper inside.

"Let me taste, Nora." He kissed down her belly, and her body jerked.

"Please," she moaned.

He lifted his mouth. "Don't beg. Tell me. Tell me exactly what you want."

She held on to his head as he nuzzled her moist cleft with his nose.

"Lick it, Bear," Nora demanded, bucking her hips.

His tongue ran along the throbbing bud, then his lips closed over it, and he gave it a firm, warm tug and moaned. The vibration of the sound nearly stopped her heart.

Her hips rose in rhythm. His tongue lapped at her clit, and his hand squeezed her breast, rolling the nipple between his thumb and forefinger. He sucked her so greedily and earnestly.

She might as well be tied to the bed for all the power she had in her limbs to move. All Nora could do was buck against his rough tongue. She held his hair gently in her hands.

"Pull it," he demanded. His tongue slipped in and out of her, then dragged over her clit, slow and rhythmic. Her hips rose with every tongue lap.

"Oh, Jesus." Nora's thighs quivered. The edges of her vision blurred, and her toes curled so hard she felt the beginnings of a cramp. "Bear, you feel so good."

He didn't respond, his tongue too busy adoring her. She bucked against his mouth. She was going to cry it felt so good. The waves washed over her, and she didn't know if she was screaming or moaning.

Her eyes were all over him—buttery skin, fat cock glistening and so hard she could hang a winter coat on it—so engorged the tip shone purple. And he was hers. Nora pulled open the drawer and winced when she realized there where at least fifty condoms of various colors and flavors.

Bear's eyebrow rose. "I'm afraid to ask."

"It's a long story."

"Later," he said, sliding the condom over his throbbing dick. He placed the tip at her entrance and her eyes widened.

Shit, that thing isn't gonna go.

He teased her, rubbing the thick head over her clit. "I'll go as slow as you need me to," he said, recalling that first run.

"You told me that before." She licked her lips. "And then you ran me hard."

He pushed, and the thick head disappeared inside of her as she arched her body. God, it was him. He was finally here.

His voice was hoarse, and it ground like gravel in her ear. "You want me to run you hard, Nora?"

She wanted it hard. She wanted Bear to fuck every thought out of her head. She wanted a moving meditation.

He leaned over her, covering her body with his, and growled in her ear. "Can you take that?"

Nora, teeth chattering with need, nodded her head.

He pushed himself in deeper. "Can you take all of this?" he rasped in her ear.

Nora bit her lip and cried out, "Deeper."

"I'm trying. It's so tight. It's so hot around my cock." She took another deep breath, and he pushed himself in all the way to the base. It was a glorious stretch, and she put her hand at the juncture to marvel at their fit.

"Oh, Nora, it's so much better than I thought," he mumbled. She thought he would start to move, but he just froze.

Why was he stopping?

Nora began to move, and Bear held her shoulder. "Nora, I—" He was shaking on top of her. "I don't . . . I can't. It's been such a long time since I've been touched."

She shifted her hips and squeezed the peaks of her nipples. She would go alone if he didn't hurry.

"Nora, please, I swear I'm going to nut right now if you move again. Just let me gather myself. I can't control it like I thought."

"Bear." She squeezed his face between her hands and kissed him. Her Bear, who had spent his whole life thinking of others and taking so little for himself. Bear, who even now was controlling himself and capping his pleasure for her.

"Don't control it then, Bear. Come fast, or come slow. Just"— she lifted her hips, rubbing herself against the base of his dick, and ran her nails up his tight stomach—"just fuck me like you deserve to come."

He bit his lip and pulled himself out halfway and thrust into her.

"Yes, ma'am," he rumbled. He made it sound like a plea.

The pound was a reminder of who she was and what she liked. She was no wilting daisy, and she had a video to prove it.

Ask for what you want, Nora.

"Harder, Bear," she commanded. His face twisted for a second like he was in absolute agony.

"You've been such a good boy," Nora said.

"Nora," he warned and held her hips, laying into her like he was getting paid by the pound. Her breasts jiggled, and he tried to follow a nipple with his mouth.

"Nora," he whispered into her neck. He was a thick plug in a hot socket, and the air seemed alive with his power. The rain had broken, and through the curtain gap, streaks of soft sunlight cut across his sharp jaw and fringed lashes, giving him an angelic hazy glow. "I'm going to give it all to you, Nora."

Her slender fingers gripped the crisp white sheets as her walls rippled to accommodate him. As she looked into his eyes, a perfect silence fell over them. He was gazing into her very soul. He had pierced her entire being. There was no sound. Like the muffled silence of a snow-covered clearing, the quiet rolled over her as their eyes stayed fixed on each other. He drove into her with enough power to knock the heavy headboard into the wall and shake the mountain of unnecessary pillows to the ground. She never heard them plop onto the floor. If he moaned, grunted, cursed, Nora would never be able to recall. The feeling and intensity of him inside her had rendered her blissfully deaf and mute. Nora ground herself into his thrust, and a white starburst of pleasure burst into her field of vision. It was just the two of them moving like they'd always moved—in perfect rhythm.

But she wanted more. "You did well, Bear." Nora broke the silence. Looking deep into his eyes, she said, "Now eat your fucking cake."

He stopped for a millisecond and flipped her over on her belly, still miles deep inside her. Somehow he pushed into her deeper and faster. She felt like someone had shouted *Worldstar!* because Bear had flipped a switch somewhere. She couldn't believe he would feel so good. She was stretched to capacity, so full of him she felt it in her belly.

He was growling in her ear, kneading her neck, and he was

so deep inside her that if he came, she was afraid it would come out of her mouth. Bear fucked with such uninhibited abandon that Nora was recalibrating all of her past sexual encounters. This was the new Good Dick Gold Standard(™). Bear was her tether to everything real and right in the world, and she wanted to be engulfed by him. Even with him so deep inside her, that this was the closest they could be felt unfair to Nora.

"I'm coming," she ground out. "I'm coming, Bear," she screamed louder.

She could hear him whimpering and whispering words behind her ear in an old language mixed with English.

"Nora, I wanted you like this for *so* long. My fucking cake. My prize."

"You have me. I'm yours. I always will be."

"Yeah, you're mine."

Her breath was catching. Her heart was beating in her neck now.

He was wrecking her.

And she was out of her body with pleasure.

"You're mine." He gripped her hips and thrust deep.

Her ears popped like she was rushing up an elevator. She cried out, and the release was earth-shattering, so visceral she wanted to curl up in a fetal position. Her cry was so powerful that a flock of birds exploded out of a nearby tree and shot past her window.

That was it.

Time of death: dick o'clock.

Bear screamed, actually hollered, and dug himself into her. Nora was shuddering with her orgasm, feeling hot and cold at the same time.

He beat his chest. "Shiiiiit, woman."

"Bear, I love you."

"I love you, too, Nora Dash," he whispered against her skin. "And you're going to make an honest man out of me."

She would, but there was one more bit of unfinished business.

BIG COMPANY

LABOR DAY
DAY OF FORECLOSURE

NORA WOKE UP IN BEAR'S ARMS, WARM, RELAXED, and perfect. The pulsing heat of his body pressed into her, and arms curled around her in a protective cocoon like she would fall off a cliff if he didn't hold on. This past week they'd been on a bit of a bender, and Nora's body cried out in protest at every movement.

Yanne burst through the bedroom door and ripped the shades open without looking at the bed.

"Sorry, y'all, but we've got incoming in ten minutes. I tried to give you two some time. And from the looks of the house, it looks like you took that time"—she paused—"everywhere."

"Yanne." Nora and Bear rose up from the bed at the same time and spoke at the same time.

"That is some creepy hive-mind *Star Trek* Borg shit." Yanne shuddered and threw Nora a dress. "Get up. Moxcy's here. Bear, I know you have a stash of clothes here somewhere."

"I do?" Bear asked.

"Yeah, Nora would steal your sweaters and sleep in them. *Not creepy at all.* I think she would wear your skin if she could."

"Okay, Yanne, thank you," Nora said. "Let's *ration out the crazy.*"

"Nora, Felicia's coming to collect. Can you look alive? Brandon and Moxcy are already here."

Felicia! Today.

Nora never sent that email. She'd been preoccupied the past week.

Nora dressed and worked her hair into submission and was finally out of the room, when Brandon appeared in front of the bathroom as if waiting on her.

"Where is Bear?" Brandon asked in greeting, direct as ever. "I want to ask him about last week. Public opinion has totally flipped about the dam project since his video at the bingo hall. He's gotta be proud of that."

"We didn't talk much about the dam project," Nora said, walking toward them, overcorrecting for the soreness in her hips and thighs.

"I guess y'all didn't talk much at all." Moxcy furled her brow and looked around.

Yanne threw a warm pile of clothes into Nora's bedroom and shimmied her shoulders. "So . . ."

Crowding her sister into the kitchen, Yanne looked Nora over carefully.

"Stop," Nora said into the steaming pot of greens on the stove.

"I didn't say anything," Yanne said.

"Stop anyway."

After more intense staring, Yanne finally shook her head. "So, Bear fucks, eh?"

Nora looked at her sister.

"Wait, Bear fucks like *that*?"

Nora looked deeper at her sister.

"No, Bear fucks like *THAT*!" she whisper-shouted and then threw the towel into the sink.

Nora shot a look in the direction of the foyer.

"Hush!" But she was smiling. Yanne slapped her sister's butt with a wet spoon.

"When you took your clothes off at that funeral, I thought you would never be cooler. I thought, 'She's a warrior goddess.' But now, looking around at all you've built, you have to know that I look up to you. I always have."

Nora bent down and hugged her sister.

"But don't think I didn't notice that *you've* been at Brandon's for week. What is happening over there, missy?"

"Oh, we put on a play! I met his other friends. He's . . . not what I expected."

"So, he's your man now?" Nora teased.

Before Yanne could answer, her attention was pulled to Bear ambling out of the bedroom and Brandon whistling. "You look terrible, brother. And when I say that, please hear congratulations."

"Don't they look like hell?" Yanne said wistfully, like she was watching a sunset.

"Nora looks like she rode a cactus home, and, cousin, you look like a fucking raisin. Like you need an IV." Moxcy patted his shoulder.

Nora straightened her walk. It couldn't be that noticeable.

But she looked at Bear, slightly bent over like an old mechanic, and she saw it. They both must look like rescued miners crawling out of a cave into the too-bright light.

"Hetero sex ages you," Moxcy concluded, pulling at her face in the hallway mirror.

They heard a car pull up out front. The only person who would drive up a long walkway was Felicia.

"She's here," Yanne said unnecessarily, looking out the window.

Felicia's arrival wasn't half as terrifying as Janae's had been. Nora was ready for whatever this woman could throw at her. Yanne slapped down a jar of Vaseline in case things "get ignant," and Bear and Moxcy invented ridiculous comebacks to potential insults. They were jovial and excited, because they'd already won.

Yanne pulled the door open with a touch more pageantry than usual. She was in a fun mood.

A resplendent Felicia unfolded in the doorway in pale yellow, like a sunflower with a giant wasp at the center. She stepped through the front door and looked around. It didn't escape Nora that she didn't ask to be let in.

She thinks she already owns the place.

"May I sit?" she asked, entering the home with no greeting.

She sat without Yanne or Nora giving her any indication. Her leather briefcase flapped open, and she pulled out an incredible stack of papers.

"I have your roster for the summer. Your guests never really picked up. It's a pity too. I have you still owing about eighty thousand dollars."

"It's ninety-six." Yanne's arms were folded.

"Excuse me?" Felicia pulled down her glasses.

"It was ninety-six thousand dollars we owed."

"We bought a truck last week," Nora informed her.

"You should have bought three!" Her laugh was incredulous. "In for a penny, in for a pound. I mean, you were never going to make it anyway."

"Let me stop you—" Nora started.

Felicia cut her off. "I appreciate all of the elbow grease, though. You girls must have polished off your entire inheritance rehabbing this thing." Felicia adjusted her papers. "And all for someone to swoop in and buy it for so little."

"Yeah, that was a great plan. It almost worked," Nora said.

"Almost? We're past the deadline, and there is not a soul here." She laughed. "You see, I'm not like my mother, ladies. I'm thorough. Just like I would never have a man surprise me with a whole damned family, I would never let you have this property if I wasn't sure of the result."

"Like I said, you were almost right, but you didn't account for a few things," Nora said.

"Like friends," Yanne said.

Felicia laughed again, so certain of her victory. "You sound like an after-school special. You don't have *any* friends with an extra three hundred grand to spare. Trust me, I looked."

"Wow. I feel like I should applaud the lengths you went to to ensure we failed. I want you to keep that same energy when you pay us our three million dollars," Nora told her.

The laugh died away in Felicia's throat when Nora handed her a manila folder.

"Enclosed, you'll find mine and Yanne's separate accounts to wire the money to."

"I—" Felicia started.

"Please also see the enclosed note from Colson Partners, Dorsey Fitzgerald and Liza Bennett, and David and Janae Bradley-Bennett's property lawyers. They took the liberty to draft up a little document for you to sign." Nora watched as every syllable of those names dropped down on Felicia like a brick.

Yeah, yeah, sex is cool, but have you ever handed someone their own ass?

"Yeah, right." Felicia rolled her eyes. "You have a week to vacate the premises. I've already spoken to the local authorities, and they know the procedure."

"You should open the folder before you make any more plans with the sheriff."

Felicia ripped open the folder and rolled her shoulders like an exhausted boxer. Nora could see the names, the dates, the sums, the finality wash over Felicia in waves. Her face rushed through the five stages of grief. She closed the folder and placed it, hands shaking, on the wooden table. "You—" She paused to take a slow, deep breath. "You managed to find the only other women in the DMV *more* famous for lying on their backs than you. What, are you all in a club or something?"

"Felicia, look, we're just asking for our share, nothing more, and we can close this ugly chapter and move—"

Felicia chopped at Nora's words with the heel of her hand. "People like you have to have everything. Your mother and father broke my mom's heart. She married a man who never loved her. Who embarrassed her all the way up to his death. You took away her dignity. You don't deserve this." Felicia's voice broke.

"My dad wasn't a perfect man," Nora offered. "From my perspective, he gave *you* everything and hid *us* from sight. In that way, we're the same—"

"No, no, *Nasty Nora*." Felicia shook her head so violently Nora was afraid it would roll right down the hallway. That name. It hadn't lost its sting. "*I* own Dash of Love Seasonings. *I* have an MBA from the MIT Sloan School of Management. You deposited your daddy's checks and worked at the CVS. I have a husband with a JD from Harvard. And two boys at Georgetown Prep. Your man is a . . . cosplayer. I was a top forty under forty, and you were the deepthroating queen for two years running. Do I need to go on? We"—she gestured wildly between them—"are not the same."

"Objection!" Moxcy raised her hand before Nora could speak.

Felicia sputtered. "You can't object. It's a conversation."

"As counsel for Her Royal Highness of Deepthroating, we are going to have to request that you sign the papers releasing their funds before we are forced to—hold on one minute, I have guidance from my client." Yanne handed her an index card, and Moxcy slid on small reading glasses and cleared her throat. "'Forced to dog walk your skinny ass back down I-95. Hashtag BitchBetterHaveMyMoney.'" Moxcy shrugged. "Does this mean anything to you?"

Nora tapped the contract. "You were so focused on how *beneath* you we were, you never managed to look up. And here we are—"

"On. Top. Of. Your. Neck!" Yanne finished, punctuating every word with a clap.

Felicia shrugged. "Breach of contract cases take years to decide. I could just wait it out while you twist in the wind."

"Nora was so sure you wouldn't stoop that low, but I told her I know my kind. So here's what this bitch has for you." Moxcy handed Felicia a slim stapled document. "What you're reading is Nora and Yanne's petition to your board for partial ownership of the company. As the last and only blood heirs to the estate, they have a right to do so. You have two or three assholes on the board who would love to see anyone but you on top."

Nora held out a sheet of paper. "Yes, Jeffery Graham, Marcy Jackson, and Thomas Reeves were so pleased to hear from me. I told them I only worked at the CVS and I didn't know anything about big scary companies, and they ate it right up."

Felicia's face flattened. All of her poise and practice were spent. She wanted to keep Dash of Love more than she hated them. Nora could see it. Nora had no interest in running the company, but she would do it to spite Felicia. She'd taken on Barton Cove, hadn't she? Just to wipe the grin off her face.

"They'll take a puppet they think they can control over a well-qualified candidate every time," Nora said.

Felicia was cracking. Nora could see it.

"Fine." Felicia rummaged through her purse for a pen. "Is this what it takes to never hear from you again? To make sure you stay up here in the wilderness with your park ranger boyfriend? I'll sign." She scribbled her signature dramatically and slammed the pen down.

"Right now"—Yanne smiled and took the pen away—"'I do desire we may be better strangers.'"

"*As You Like It*!" Brandon clapped.

"You're getting so good at this, baby!" Yanne kissed Brandon and curled into him.

Felicia looked around and threw up her hands in disgust. "What is wrong with you all?"

THE WEDDING, PART 2

FIRST DAY OF FALL

I HATE TO BE THE BEARER OF BAD NEWS—" MOXCY started.

"No, you don't," Nora and Bear said in unison.

Bear looked over at Nora. Unsurprised to be in sync with her, but overwhelmed by it just the same. She was the pulsing, beating heart of this lovely place.

Soft sunlight filtered through the sheer curtains at Barton Cove, making everyone look like they were starring in one of his gma's soap operas.

Yanne was draped over the side of a plush, green velvet sofa, shifting the soft knitted blankets over her and Brandon. The countertops were a mess with rustic mason jars, filled with dried herbs for Nora's homemade hot pickles. In front of him, the over-filled pots and pans bubbled and sizzled and complemented the pleasant house chatter that always seemed to happen around the kitchen.

"But you're still in a shitload of debt. And Beyoncé and Solange over here look like they are staying, so . . ."

"Moxcy, I'm handling it."

"You need me to do it? I can be romantic." Moxcy turned to

Nora. "Do you want to marry my cousin slash boss to help him beat a tax evasion charge?"

Bear dropped the wooden spoon in the pot, not caring that the stew bubbled over it.

The stew was smelling like he'd gotten all of the steps right. The air at Barton Cove always seemed to carry notes of freshly baked bread, hints of cinnamon, and the earthy bouquet of mushrooms and garlic, so he could just be kidding himself.

"I've already asked her," Bear said smugly. It wasn't a question he wanted to pressure her about. If she said yes, he hoped it would be because she couldn't say no, that her whole soul wanted only him.

"Oh, that? I thought—"

"That I'd say anything to get laid? No, I want to marry you. I want to spend the rest of my life with you. I feel like I've been saying this for months."

Nora flushed. "Bear, I do. Or . . . yes, I will."

Bear was never good with poetry. But now he wished he had Yanne's beautiful words for Nora. She deserved beautiful words right now.

Instead, he was clumsy. "I'm going to make you so happy."

"I know." She kissed his knuckles. "I'm going to make you *so* fat," Nora countered.

"I know." Bear laughed.

"Y'all are going to make me so sick." Moxcy left the kitchen.

"Now, it's not going to be that easy. You'll have to meet a few other requirements," he teased.

Bear fished for the lost spoon with another spoon.

"Hit me," she said, smiling that toothpaste smile and kissing her biceps. God, he loved when she did that.

"I can't have a woman who can't stomach venison."

"Deer is a deal-breaker?" Nora gagged.

He leaned over and kissed her mouth. Nora still closed her eyes in wonder every time he did it.

"Very persuasive argument, Bear. I will try the stew."

"Correction: you will *like* the stew."

"Okay, but you have to like greens."

"No. Gross. It's just boiled grass. Who thought boiling leaves would be delicious?"

"Everyone. This is proof you've never been to a cookout."

"Oh, I am invited to the cookout. I two-step at the cookout and slide those slimy greens right off my plate."

Nora gasped. "I feel like Brandon doesn't know this about you."

"If he ever finds out, I'll know who told him," Bear warned. "You know what snitches get."

"Is that a threat? These negotiations are turning sour." Nora leaned into his bicep.

Bear looked at his watch. "Well, we had a good fifteen minutes. When this all blows up, I'm getting the goats."

A WEEK LATER, THE GOATS STOOD ON EITHER SIDE OF THE wedding party. The Maine morning was crisp and clear. The frothy shore of Sand Beach was encased in rocky cliffs like stone parentheses. The wind whipped her curls around her face and had everyone clutching their shawls and hats. Nora could see out to eternity from the sandy basin. She could see out to eternity in Bear's eyes too.

Bear held her arm as they padded to the shore in the wee hours of the morning.

He wore a simple suit with a Stetson hat, while Yanne had found Nora a silky slip of a white dress that looked gauzy and ethereal in the hazy dawn. Nora had never felt more beautiful. Moxcy wore the red tux she'd worn at the expo. Bear's mother and father found chairs on the opposite sides of the beach while Yanne and Brandon held the goats' leads.

The JP had been bribed with buckets of coffee, and Nora's mother passed out warm corn cakes Bear had taught her how to make. It was still too early for chatter, so everyone went about their jobs quietly. The stillness of the morning felt right. No drums, no organ music, no sobbing mothers-in-law—just Nora, face scrubbed clean with baby's breath entwined in her hair, and Bear, freshly shaved, hair braided, facing the rising sun.

Nora cleared her throat. "Bear, you taught me courage. You taught me that I had something in me that was bigger than my past. In *Space Jam*"—Nora paused for the groans in the audience— "Michael Jordan told a losing team that he had 'Secret Stuff' to give them special abilities. It was the second half, and the monsters were destroying them. Finally, they took the drink and won at the buzzer. But the Secret Stuff that he gave to the team was only water."

Bear nodded, tears streaming down his face. "MJ let the team believe the drink gave them his special abilities, but the Secret Stuff was within them all along."

Nora held his hands together. She was done trying to understand why *Space Jam* was this man's love language. "*You're* my Secret Stuff, Bear. You remind me of my strength and never let me fall. My love for you is so deep, and you'll never hit bottom." She let her tears run down her cheeks and down her chin.

Bear was succinct and solemn. He looked her in the eyes and

said, "Nora, I promise to love you, to put you first, to not overdo it with the cinnamon in my green shakes, and to protect you with my life for the rest of my life." Then he kissed her. And Nora sighed because she knew how this ended. Bear always did what he said he was going to do.

ACKNOWLEDGMENTS

I would like to take a moment to express my heartfelt gratitude and appreciation to the amazing individuals who have made this book a reality. Their unwavering support, expertise, and wit have been invaluable throughout this journey. First, a huge shout-out to my incredible agent, Kim Lionetti. Thank you for your tenacity and unwavering belief in my work.

To my brilliant editor, Cindy Hwang, thank you for your keen eye and endless patience with my just-one-more-version nonsense. Your guidance and feedback have been instrumental in making this project a success. A special mention goes out to Angela Kim, the ever-reliable associate editor and the backbone of the operation. Thank you for always going above and beyond. Dache' and Jessica, you both are true superstars on our team. Your dedication, creativity, and infectious enthusiasm have been a driving force behind this project.

I am deeply indebted to Darrin Ranco, esteemed Anthropologist at UMaine Orono, for generously sharing your knowledge and insights. Your expertise in the field has brought depth and authenticity to the research within this book. It is an honor to have had the opportunity to learn from you. A special mention goes out to James Francis, a native artist, writer, and all-around bomb-ass dude. Thank you for your friendship, inspiration, and for sharing your unique perspective. Your creativity and passion have truly enriched this project.

I would be remiss not to express my gratitude to the numerous Black and Native interviewees who generously shared their time and experiences with me. To the ABBE Museum in Bar Harbor, thank you for your tireless efforts to build community and foster understanding. Your dedication to preserving and showcasing Native culture is unmatched.

A huge thank-you to Skye Washington at Skye Fitness, a Black-owned gym in Bangor. Your willingness to engage in open and honest discussions about the Black experience in Maine has been invaluable. Your commitment to fostering dialogue and creating a safe space is truly commendable.

To each and every one of you who has contributed, supported, and believed in this project, thank you from the bottom of my heart. Your presence and influence have made this book a labor of love, and I am forever grateful.

With heartfelt appreciation,
Nikki

SEX, LIES AND SENSIBILITY

NIKKI PAYNE

READERS GUIDE

DISCUSSION QUESTIONS

On Reputation

It's easy to think in modern times that we are not under enormous pressure to uphold a good reputation. But how many times have we seen people lose their job prospects, education, and even their families over a tweet or a video that shows them at their worst?

1. How does the pressure to maintain his reputation impact Bear?

2. What benefit was Bear getting from the largely untrue rumors of his valor?

3. What is Bear's reputation at the beginning of the novel versus at the end? Was the change worth it?

4. How does the need to move away from her reputation contribute to Nora's personal and romantic struggles?

5. Are there instances where Nora and Bear overemphasize their reputations over genuine love and happiness?

On Identity

Let's discuss how the characters' political, racial, and socioeconomic identities impact their choices in the novel.

1. Bear accused Nora of *Columbasing* Barton Cove. Why was she particularly offended by that? Was it true?

2. Yanne is eager to share her alleged Native ancestry with Bear and his cousin. Why was Moxcy so turned off by Yanne's attempts at connection?

3. Why did Bear see the dam project as particularly egregious?

4. Nora and Bear sit down to ask each other "Stupid Questions." Why did that lead to a turning point in their relationship?

5. Nora thinks she can only cry in the shower or she's not a #StrongBlackWoman. What does she mean by this?

On Economics

Let's dive into the economic factors that influence the characters' romantic choices in the novel.

1. How do considerations of financial stability impact Nora and Bear's decisions when it comes to romantic relationships?

2. How do Nora and Bear navigate their desire for love alongside the need to secure their financial and social standing? Compare that to Yanne and Brandon, Lu and Basil.

3. The class divide in *Sex, Lies and Sensibility* is quite pronounced. How do the differences between the upper-middle class and the working class impact Nora and Bear's interaction and perceptions of each other?

4. Lu seems to think the idea that "love conquers all" is just white man's magic. What does she mean by that?

On Characters

It's interesting to compare the different approaches to romance between the Dash sisters and the dynamics at play for multiple characters.

1. How do Nora's measured practicality and Yanne's romanticism affect their relationships with each other and their eventual partners?

2. Is Bear jealous of Basil? Is Basil jealous of Bear? What is the nature of their relationship?

3. Is Lu a villain? Why or why not?

4. Nora thinks she knows how everything will end. How did this keep her stuck in her romantic rut?

5. Bear and Nora bond over sports, Brandon is obsessed with money, and Yanne feels incredibly left out. How does she deal with that loneliness?

By day, **NIKKI PAYNE** is a curious tech anthropologist who asks the right questions to deliver better digital services. By night, she dreams of ways to subvert canon literature. She's a member of Smut U, a premium feminist writing collective, and is a cat lady with no cats.

VISIT NIKKI PAYNE ONLINE

NikkiPayneBooks.com
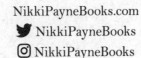 NikkiPayneBooks
NikkiPayneBooks

Ready to find
your next great read?

Let us help.

Visit prh.com/nextread

Penguin
Random
House